The   as
idylli   1931
brou   about her ears
and l   bereft.

Bart   .u always loved her, he said; and
the   .ded a father. Marcia moved to
Blac   with him, where she tried to forget the
past.   .rty, though, sank into bad ways,
tyrar   .ing the family. In particular he would vent
his aggression on Polly, Curt and Marcia's first-
born, blonde as an angel but afflicted since birth
with an ominous shadow over her health.

Even in troubled times, lovely raven-haired Marcia
was a fighter. But news that Curt Ratheter had
reappeared would render her helpless prey to
wildly conflicting emotions.

Set among a close-knit community in pre-war
Lancashire, *Angels Cry Sometimes* brims with
heartbreak and joy, hardship and indomitable
spirit, that will hold the reader enthralled.

ANGELS CRY SOMETIMES

Josephine Cox

WINDSOR
PARAGON

First published 1989
by
Futura Publications
This Large Print edition published 2006
by
BBC Audiobooks Ltd by arrangement with
Headline Book Publishing

ISBN 1 4056 1158 8   (Windsor Hardcover)
ISBN 1 4056 2145 1   (Paragon Softcover)

British Library Cataloguing in Publication Data available

Printed and bound in Great Britain by
Antony Rowe Ltd., Chippenham, Wiltshire

DEDICATION

This story is for every girl or woman who has ever known trouble and heartache. It is a story for you alone—a story to give you joy. It is Marcia's story—though but for the grace of God it could be yours, or mine.

To John, with thanks

AUTHOR'S FOREWORD

At the moment of writing this story, there is an aggressive redevelopment and building programme under way in many areas of old industrial England. Only this week, I myself stood and watched a bulldozer tear into an old Victorian cotton mill, in the northern town of Blackburn where I was born and bred. Many years before, as a small child, I had stood on that same spot waiting for the mill-whistle to go, when my mam would come out of the gates, along with hundreds of other mill-hands.

A cobbled alley I played in as a youngster, and very recently strolled down for a television programme, has also since disappeared. People often wonder why 'Coronation Street' and its down-to-earth characters are so hugely popular. Could it be that the programme reminds many of us of the past, now rapidly being trampled beneath the march of progress? In the North, particularly, it is sadly true that all the Coronation Streets are no longer. And though the streets may be wider, the houses brighter and people more affluent, so much of our history is disappearing.

I hope, for many of you, that my stories will keep alive those down-to-earth characters and that part of our history which will always have a special place in our hearts.

CONTENTS

Part One

1931
Marcia's First Love

CHAPTER ONE

Grandma Fletcher burst into the tiny bedroom in her usual rumbustious way; her short stubby finger wagging a warning to the dark-haired man seated by the bed. 'Come on, Curt Ratheter! Tek yerself off! Ye've been 'ere quite long enough.' She shook her snow-white head and stood before him, hands on hips, her bright blue eyes daring him to disobey. 'This is a confinement! The lass's time is close and 'taint no place for men . . . so be off with yer!'

Taking his life in his hands, Curt brought his dark handsome eyes to bear on the old woman's face, his voice quiet as he ventured to ask, 'Can't I stay?'

'Stay!' Grandma Fletcher couldn't believe her own ears, 'Stay, yer say? Why! I've never 'eard the like in all me life!' At once, she pounced on him, her finger and thumb pinched tight about his earlobe and her expression one of incredulity, 'Ye'll be *off*, I say! This very minute, else yer'll feel the weight o' me foot up yer arse, my lad!'

'All right! All right! I know when I'm beat,' Curt protested as, with a backward smile at Marcia, he allowed himself to be unceremoniously ushered from the room. When the door was promptly slammed behind him, he fell back against the wall and collapsed into a fit of helpless laughter. Oh, that Grandma Fletcher, he thought. Was there ever another like her? She made him feel eight instead of *twenty-eight*! Yet, for all her bossy and cantankerous ways, she was a real darling, with a heart of gold and the ability to take command of a

3

situation when everyone else was set to panic.

Of a sudden, the bedroom door was flung open. Grandma Fletcher fixed him with her bright blue eyes. 'Ey! Don't you be standin' about doing nothing, fella me lad! Get down them stairs an' keep yon fire stoked up an' a fresh pan o' water boiling! There's a child on its way any minute!' That said, Grandma Fletcher disappeared into the room again, firmly closing the door behind her.

'By! that man o' yourn is just like *all* men, lass . . . bloody useless!'

'Now then, Mam, that's not fair.' Marcia was used to her mother's way, and she loved her all the more for it. She would have followed up the argument in defence of the husband she adored. But, at that point she was gripped by a particularly vicious pain which made her cry out.

'Don't push, lass. Not yet.' Grandma Fletcher had the situation well in hand. Fetching babies into the world was one of her favourite occupations. She was accomplished at the job, for hadn't she delivered half the young 'uns down her street, at one time or another? 'I'll tell yer when to push,' she informed Marcia, her concerned gaze falling on her daughter's face, 'Taint real bad yet, is it lass?' she asked, her blue eyes softening as they saw the pain in Marcia's lovely brown eyes and noted the taut set of that extravagantly attractive mouth. The long black hair was pinned back by two mother-of-pearl combs, but all about Marcia's face the stray dark wisps were mingled with the rivulets of sweat, and she looked altogether exceedingly uncomfortable.

'I can't hold back much longer, Mam,' Marcia replied, her knuckles drained white as she gripped

4

the brass bedhead above her. When she began twisting her head from side to side against the brass rails, the combs fell from her hair, loosing it all about her shoulders, as the onset of deeper contractions compelled her body to send the child on its outward journey.

'No! No, lass! Don't push, else yer'll tear yersel'!' Grandma Fletcher could see the dark object forcing its way into the world and her instinct told her that it was too early yet. 'Breathe deeply lass,' she urged, 'sing a song if yer will! But don't push that child on till it's good and ready! D'yer 'ear me?' When Marcia nodded, she hurried to the door, where she shouted, 'Curt Ratheter! Fetch me that pan o' water.' When it was brought to the door and set down on the wooden stand-chair, she promptly wrapped her two capable hands about the big iron handle—lagged by Curt with a cloth to enable it to be held—then, with a grunt of satisfaction, she kicked the door shut and crossed the room, where she put the great steaming pan into the tiny hearth. The fireplace in this room was too small for a pan the likes of that one, but there was just room enough to stand it in the hearth, where it would keep nicely hot.

Marcia's dark eyes followed her mother's every move, thinking if she concentrated harder on that than she did on the impatient child battling to free itself, she might be less likely to give in to it.

After a few minutes, when Grandma Fletcher had got ready a bowl of warm water and all the other necessary paraphernalia, it was plain enough both to Marcia and her mother, that the child would not wait another second.

Downstairs, Curt Ratheter was a desperate man.

He'd lost count of the number of times he had gone up and down those steep narrow stairs, or paced the rug here in front of the fire, or stopped now and then to listen for that wail which, when it did come, he knew would fill every corner of that little house with joy. It had been like that when Polly was born on 4 June 1928, nearly three years ago.

Thinking of Polly brought both a smile to his face and a sense of fear to his heart. A smile because with her bright blue eyes, fair hair and forthright character, she was a little duplicate of Grandma Fletcher—indeed, Grandma Fletcher had often said how, when she looked at young Polly, she could be 'lookin' at mesel' when I were a toddler!' But, if Polly had been blessed with the features of a little angel, she had also been cursed with a problem—which the doctors predicted might grow more serious over the coming years. Above Polly's forehead and just beneath the hairline, there was a prominent swelling. At first, it had gone unnoticed, being no bigger than a pinhead. Yet, by her second birthday, Polly was beginning to find the spot increasingly irritating, always scratching and rubbing at it. Made anxious by its slow but sure growth, Curt and Marcia had time and time again sought reassurance from the doctor, who, after a most thorough examination of Polly, had told them, 'There is no need for alarm, I assure you. Of course it will irritate—as *any* pimple or abrasion might plague a child. But, there is no evidence to tell us it is more serious than before.' Additional tests also revealed that the growth's roots had made no further inroad into deeper tissue, which, the doctor explained, was a blessing,

6

since attempts to remove the tumour would prove more dangerous than leaving it alone. Curt and Marcia had no option but to accept this professional advice and add to it the weight of their own heartfelt prayers. Never a day went by but they didn't thank God that Polly's affliction had not yet interfered with either her general health or her ability to light up even the darkest day with her bright sunny smile. In every sense, she was growing into a lovely, happy child. Only that morning, when Curt had taken Polly to the town of Church, where she could stay with Grandad Fletcher till the new child was born, she had vigorously entreated her daddy, 'Can Polly see her new baby?' Whereupon, Curt had taken her on to his lap and, with her skinny arms flung protectively about his neck, he had promised her, 'As soon as "Polly's" new baby arrives, sweetheart . . . I'll come straight back to fetch you.' Then, only when he had sealed the promise with a kiss, was he allowed to return to nearby Preston and Stoneygate Street, where Marcia lay in the throes of labour.

When, of a sudden, the wail of a child filled the air, Curt sped across the room and into the passage where, being halted by the sight of Grandma Fletcher at the top of the stairs, he asked, 'Marcia?'

'Marcia's fine, me boy.' With a broad satisfied smile on her podgy face, she went on, 'An' so is yer new baby lass.' At this Curt sped up the stairway, clearing the steps three at a time and, in his exuberance, miscalculating the distance between Grandma Fletcher and the wall.

'Watch out, yer silly bugger!' she exclaimed, steadying herself on the banister rail. 'Ye'll 'ave me

7

arse over tip down yon bloody stairs!'

Shouting an apology, Curt flung open the bedroom door, then, having done so, came slowly to the foot of the bed, where he stood awhile looking somewhat sheepish, fondly gazing into Marcia's smiling brown eyes, his love for her painfully obvious in that dark intense gaze which never left her lovely face.

Being the focus of such intense and wonderful emotion, Marcia became surprisingly shy and, of a sudden, she could feel a warm tingling blush spread from her neck all the way up over her face and right down her spine. The feeling was both uncomfortable and delicious. Silly fool, she thought with a little rush of embarrassment, here I am twenty-four years old—a grown woman, and acting like a lovesick schoolgirl!

'Happy, are you darling?' Curt came closer, his gaze shifting to the warm tiny bundle in Marcia's arms.

'Oh, Curt . . . isn't she lovely?' Holding her newborn daughter close to her breast, Marcia's smile was glowing as she met Curt's proud gaze, 'I know you wanted a son,' she murmured, holding out one hand to draw him closer. 'Are you that badly disappointed?'

Curt sat beside her, one hand holding hers, the other tenderly stroking the child's face, 'Disappointed?' he said, leaning forward to kiss her, 'how could I be disappointed, sweetheart? She's so perfect.' Then he went on with a cheeky grin, 'Happen we'll get a boy *next* time.'

Marcia laughed a little. 'Happen!' she said, loosing her hand from his and tousling up his dark hair, 'we shall have to see, eh?' Now, she was serious again. 'Oh, Curt . . . I'm so happy! If all there is to look forward to in this life is our love an' our children—an' growing old together until the children have fled the nest an' we're an old married couple, then I'll never want anything more.' The love she had for this man was deeper now than she could ever remember. Four years they had been married. Four wonderful years, and every day that passed only intensified her love for him. 'You and me—old and grey, and still so much in love,' she laughed out loud, 'and we won't *ever* let anything spoil it, will we darling?' she teased.

Quick to reassure her that no, they would never let anything spoil it, Curt was secretly afraid. He had always been open and honest with Marcia— especially where his love for her was concerned, for he adored her with a passion which frightened him. Yet, even as he agreed with Marcia at that moment, he himself felt uneasy. Honest as he had been with her in these four exquisite years since exchanging their marriage vows, there was a certain period in his life which he had kept hidden from her. To reveal that part of his background would shatter everything they had.

There had been times, in the dead of night when she had been sleeping, or at work at the mill, when there would come upon him such a feeling of guilt that made him sick to his stomach. Lately, he'd had this awful sensation that an avalanche of disaster was careering towards them. No rational explanation for it existed—and he put it down to the fact that his love for Marcia, Polly, and now the new baby, was so greatly important to him that it was only natural to fear it might be threatened.

Into the bedroom now came a determined

9

Grandma Fletcher, demanding, 'Yer can't set there all day, Curt Ratheter! The babby an' its mammy ain't properly washed yet . . . an' yer can surely see as Marcia needs 'er rest?'

'Aw, Mam! Stop fussing,' Marcia protested. 'Another minute, eh?'

'Hmh!' Grandma Fletcher cast a cursory glance at Marcia's lovely pleading face, before shifting a more disapproving glance to the tall handsome man seated on the bed beside her. Try as she might over these past years, somehow she had not been able to allay her suspicions regarding Curt Ratheter. He had always been a kind of enigma to her, for none of them knew too much about his life before his arrival in Preston, only that he'd been such a good worker at the Centenary cotton mill on New Hall Street that he was quickly made up to foreman. It was there that Marcia had met him and, not long after, they had been married. To Grandma Fletcher's way of thinking, it had all been too quick. The dashingly handsome fellow had swept the lass off her feet. Oh, he *loved* her! Any blind man could see that. But, 'twas odd the way he so cleverly shrugged off any questions regarding his past—saying only that both his parents were gone: 'one from tuberculosis, the other of a broken heart'. Beyond that, he would not be drawn. And Marcia was content to leave his past be, considering that to talk on it obviously caused him a deal of pain.

Grandma Fletcher, though, was convinced he had something to hide, even if it was nothing so terrible! Nevertheless he made her feel uneasy and suspicious.

She'd mentioned it to her old fellow, but he

10

would have none of it, remarking, 'Leave the lass an' 'er man be! They love each other, don't they? He's good to 'er, ain't 'e . . . provides well an' lives a decent quiet life, don't 'e?' When in all truth she had to answer yes to all three observations, back came the conclusion, 'Well then! Stop yer bloody moithering, woman—an' give up fancying that 'e's got things ter 'ide. Yer've too fertile an imagination, Florence Fletcher! I've *allus* said it. Aye! Too fertile an imagination fer yer own good!' And, as far as Grandad Fletcher was concerned, that was an end to it. He might have convinced her were it not for that niggling instinct which would insist that Curt Ratheter had not been entirely honest.

Now, when his dark eyes found hers and, with a smile, he promised to stay only a minute before going off to fetch Polly, Grandma Fletcher felt embarrassed and ashamed should he read her thoughts. 'Oh, all right! Five minutes an' no more!', she conceded. Halting at the door, she turned to ask Marcia, 'Are yer settled on a name, lass?'

First giving a little secret smile to Curt, Marcia's dark eyes lit up with pleasure as she told her mother, 'If it had been a boy, we would have called him John—after Dad. But as it's a little lass, we've both agreed, Mam, we want to christen her Florence—if that's all right with you?'

For a moment Grandma Fletcher appeared speechless before a pink and pleasing blush spread over her homely features. Springing forward, she flung her two arms about Marcia, the tears bright in her blue eyes as she cried out, 'Oh, lass! That's grand—that's right grand, bless yer 'eart!' Then,

11

seeming suddenly embarrassed, she looked sheepishly into Curt's smiling face. 'Tek *ten* minutes together. It'll tek that long ter get some fresh water boiled up,' she said, hurrying away down the stairs. Once in the privacy of the little back parlour, she pulled out a stand-chair and threw herself down onto its hard horsehair seat, crying and smiling simultaneously. After a moment she got to her feet, lifted the edge of her long voluminous skin to wipe the tears from her eyes, then told herself sternly, 'Come on yer silly fool. There's no time ter waste spillin' good tears! What! There's the babby an' its mam ter be properly cleaned up, everythin' ter be left spick an' span afore I mek me way 'ome to get the ol' fella's supper. Oh! An' on top o' that, there'll be a christenin' ter start thinkin' on. By! What work an' chaos a child does bring into the world, eh?' As she busied herself, boiling water, collecting together a bar of carbolic soap, fresh towels and a clean nightie for Marcia, Grandma Fletcher paused in the task for just a moment. 'Little Florence, eh? . . . Florence, like its old Gran'ma,' she murmured. 'Oh, won't I be the proud one when the name's read out over the font. I will that! Oh yes, I will that!' She giggled like a two-year-old as she fell to her work once more, humming tunefully.

*　　　*　　　*

'Florence Marcia Ratheter.' Father O'Malley dipped his fingers into the font and, holding them over the infant's forehead, he shook the water gently on to her brow, then after murmuring a prayer for her little soul, he concluded the

12

christening service and gave the child into the arms of the godfather—a pleasant looking fellow aged some twenty-six years old, who, at this moment, looked decidedly awkward with such a small wriggling child in his arms. 'Here, Marcia, you'd best tek her,' he said, holding the shawled bundle out as though afraid he might suddenly drop it.

'Oh, Barty—she won't bite you know!' Marcia laughed. When she took the child into her arms, Barty's heart made a skip and he couldn't help but think how fetching Marcia looked, in that light grey dress which fell in pleats to the hips and there was gathered into a broad hugging band, before falling to just below the knees in a full swinging hem. Her dark stockings flattered her legs and matched her small heeled ankle-strapped shoes. Covering her long black hair, which flowed loosely over her shoulders, was a white felt beret, arranged becomingly to one side.

For as long as he dared, Barty held the child between himself and Marcia, his greenish speckled eyes lingering on her smile and drawing pleasure from it. 'You look lovely, Marcia,' he murmured in a low intimate voice, 'really lovely, lass.'

Marcia recognised that look in Barty Bendall's covetous gaze and, for a moment, was shaken by it. But then she reminded herself that Barty had looked at her that way for too many years for it to bother her now. He and his mother were next-door neighbours to the Fletchers—had been since as far back as Marcia could remember. She and Barty Bendall had played together as youngsters, gone to school together and grown into adults together. Somehow, Marcia had always suspected that Barty loved her like a sweetheart, although, as far as she had been concerned, there was never anything remotely like that in their relationship. Yet he was a nice enough bloke and in her own way Marcia was fond of him. Like Barty, she had no brothers or sisters, and they each seemed to fill a certain need towards the other. In the early days, it had been comforting to have a friend of almost the same age, right next door. She thought by now he should be married or at least courting strong. But, according to her Mam, Barty 'can't keep a lass fer longer na five minutes!'

Marcia supposed he'd just turned out to be a flirt. Certainly, if the look he was giving her this minute was anything to go by, she wouldn't be at all surprised if he led the poor lasses a right merry dance! He wasn't unattractive either, she observed, with those green speckled eyes and fine, wavy brown hair. He wasn't tall or commanding in figure, but had a smart almost military bearing, and at times, he did have a twinkle in his emerald eyes and a lopsided smile which could seem particularly charming. Today, being Easter Sunday and the day of little Florence's christening service, he had on his best dark pin-striped suit and a sparkling white shirt, whose thin collar had been so drastically starched by his doting Mam that it dug deep into his neck like a strangling garrotte.

Choosing to make light of Barty Bendall's forward attentions to her, Marcia eased the child from him, whispering playfully, 'If I were you, Barty . . . I should undo your top button afore you *choke* to death!' Seeing that his heartfelt compliments fell on deaf ears, Barty gave a small grunt of annoyance before turning away in a dark sulk.

14

Later, when the christening party had congregated in the front parlour of the little love-nest at Stoneygate Street, Curt put his arm about Marcia's shoulders. Leaning down to whisper intimately in her ear, he said, 'Whatever did you say to Barty? The poor fellow's been in a dreadful mood ever since!'

'I said *nothing* to hurt his feelings,' Marcia protested, 'it's just that now and again, he has to be gently reminded that I'm a married woman!'

Curt straightened up, his dark eyes fixed on Barty, who, by now, was looking the worse for drink. He watched the little fellow for a minute, imagining what he must be going through and feeling a little compassion for him. Bending again to Marcia's ear, he whispered, 'I can't help but feel sorry for him, you know. The poor chap's totally besotted with you!'

'Nonsense!' Marcia retorted. 'According to Mam, he has more than enough girlfriends to keep his mind off me!' Yet inwardly she acknowledged the truth of Curt's remark, which agitated her strangely.

At that moment, the fellow in question looked up from his glass of tipple. Then, seeing Marcia's dark brown gaze on him, he gave her a most charming smile, flicked the wispy brown hair from his eyes and, raising his glass, declared in a voice properly suited to his brisk authoritative bearing, 'Here's to little Florence! May the powers that be see fit to give her a long and Christian life!' Whereupon, he fell away in a dead stupor—upsetting both chair and table and consequently calling a halt to the proceedings.

That evening, when Polly and Florence were

15

tucked away for the night, Curt pulled Marcia onto the settee beside him—laughing out loud when she squealed that the horsehair seat was pricking her legs.

'Never mind, darling,' he assured her, 'now that the christening is done with, we might soon be able to afford a settee with a softer seat, eh?'

Cuddling up to him, Marcia murmured how wonderful it would be if only they could persuade the landlord to replace all the cumbersome dark furniture with something lighter and more pleasing to look at. 'But he never will!' she concluded. 'Why should he? He can put any old rubbish in here and still get his rent regularly paid!' She had no love for the landlord, who had bought up several houses on Stoneygate Street and was constantly looking for every which way to increase his rent. Also, he was well known for casual treatment of the tenants— thinking nothing of throwing them out on any excuse. There were always plenty of poor souls waiting to move straight in again.

'Let's not spoil a lovely day by talking about "Scrooge"!' Curt pleaded, his dark eyes wide and on his features a most comical imitation of Marley's ghost—the sight of which sent Marcia into a fit of laughter.

A few moments later, when Marcia was quietly content in her husband's arms, the one clasped protectively round her shoulders, the other reaching across her lap to tenderly squeeze her long fingers in his, she thought she would never be happier than she was now. When his lips kissed the top of her head and, after a while, his face stroked her long dark hair, there came into Marcia's heart such an overwhelming sensation of joy that it made

16

her want to cry out. Lifting her head, she brought her dark gaze to bear on him and, for a long exquisite moment, they gazed into each other's eyes—uniquely content in each other's arms.

'I love you, Marcia Ratheter,' Curt whispered against her mouth, 'I'll *always* love you.'

'And I you, darling,' Marcia murmured, before offering herself into that glorious heart-melting kiss, which, for a while afterwards, took her breath away. It had been three months since Florence was born, and longer than that since she and Curt had made love. Now it was time and, oh, how she wanted him!

For now, though, the two of them stayed locked in a loving embrace, content to sit before the fire and reminisce in its comforting glow—Marcia savouring the moment, Curt in more pensive mood, brooding on the past which still threatened his happiness.

After a moment, his thoughts found their way to the christening of his new daughter and from there he was made to dwell on the man whose deep love for Marcia was so painfully evident to him. Of a sudden, he felt obliged to make mention of it. 'Fancy Barty Bendall getting drunk! I didn't know he was a man for the tipple.'

'Oh! He's *not*.' Marcia sprang to Barty's defence. 'I don't think I've ever seen him even *slightly* tipsy afore!' Here, she gave a small fond laugh. 'Barty's an old softie really, you know, Curt. You'll see! He'll be round here tomorrow, full of remorse and thoroughly ashamed of himself.'

'Grovel to a mere woman! The very idea!' said Curt, smiling.

Marcia playfully clipped his ear, warning 'I'm no

17

"mere woman", my man! So, you'd best know your place, if you see what's good for you!'

Catching her to him, Curt told her quietly, 'Oh, I know what's good for me all right,' and Marcia, serious again, reflected on Barty's condition when they'd taken him home. To be driven to drink like that, well—he must have *something* tormenting him. She hoped it wasn't her!

'All in all, the christening did go well, though,' Curt said as he released Marcia from his arms. Going to the fireplace, he poked at the fire and afterwards positioned the wire guard before it

Meantime, Marcia had taken up the local newspaper from the side-table and was glancing at one column in particular. 'You know, Curt, that were a nice gesture for Mam to send details of the christening to the paper. I really can't understand why you kicked up such a fuss when you saw it. It was meant to be a *surprise* for us . . . not a shock! It did upset Mam when you took on so.'

Muttering something about not being too fond of surprises, Curt cleverly skated over the subject. And, putting out his two arms to lift Marcia from the settee, he softly suggested, 'Let's away to bed, eh? Where we might find more exciting things to talk about.' There was no mistaking Curt's intimation as he pulled Marcia to him, at the same time gently propelling her upstairs. All the while, his peace of mind more disturbed by that small, seemingly innocent article, which Grandma Fletcher had brandished under his nose with a triumphant flourish. Oh, he knew she had meant well. But that article could just be the thin end of a cruelly destructive wedge. He hoped not! Dear God above, he hoped not!

18

CHAPTER TWO

Fran Ratheter was by nature and appearance grim and severe. A small slightly-set woman with short-cropped hair and sharp hazel eyes, she was twenty-seven years old but looked some ten years older.

Deeply embittered by the break-up of a recent relationship, her predatory nature had brought her back to Lancaster where, with a deal of cunning, she intended to exploit another old source by which she might be kept fed and clothed. And, if the picking was ripe, perhaps a few odd luxuries here and there.

By her third week in the area, she had almost given up hope of ever finding Curt. Then browsing through the local paper, she had come across a certain article. The report was of a christening, of the second daughter of Marcia and Curt Ratheter from Preston. Fran Ratheter had made discreet contact with both the newspaper and the church mentioned. By presenting herself in a most genial and polite manner, she had elicited enough information to know that the Ratheter family lived in Stoneygate Street. From there she had twice followed Curt Ratheter to his place of work at the Centenary cotton mill, in New Hall Street, the first time to discover his place of work, the second with the intention of accosting him. To her fury her courage had deserted her at the last minute.

Today, however, on this fine April morning, she would suffer *no* such setback, or her name was not Fran Ratheter!

At five a.m. she left behind the seedy bed-sit,

19

caught a tram from the boulevard and settled back against the uncomfortable wooden-slatted seat for the duration of the thirty-minute journey. Some while later she made her way along Puffin Street and, just as the mill whistle was screeching to summon the workers, she spied the tall handsome figure of Curt coming towards the gates.

Positioning herself beneath the lamp where he could not fail to see her, Fran Ratheter ignored the curious looks of other mill-hands who hurried to their work, choosing instead to keep her eyes fixed on that familiar figure which came ever closer. This was a moment she had long waited for. It was a moment she must savour to the full and, she seriously hoped, it would be the time when her fortune took a turn for the better. She was also excited by *another* thought—how shocked and alarmed Curt Ratheter would be to set eyes on her. Yet even she could never have envisaged how utterly devastated was Curt, when, emerging from the hurrying throng, he caught sight of that small upright figure, her eyes searching him out and a look of pure animosity on her pinched features.

At that moment Curt Ratheter saw his whole world turn upside down. As he stood, shocked and transfixed by the sight of his nightmare come true, he might have been persuaded to strangle the life from her for what she could do to him now—and for what she had done to him in the past.

Now that she was satisfied he had seen her, Fran Ratheter came forward, her eyes never once straying from his face, which was now drained to a chalk-white colour. When, in a moment, she stood before him with a leer on her face and an air of arrogance about her stance, Curt could feel himself trembling from head to foot—with fear or rage, he couldn't tell.

'You! What in the name o' God do you want?' he growled.

How he loathed this creature. He had married her some eight years ago when he was a blind hot-headed young man of twenty-one and she was a worldly woman of twenty. Within only months of their marriage, her eye was already beginning to rove, yet, being young and too ready to forgive, he had believed her tales of remorse. When she had miscarried with the child he had eagerly awaited, he sympathised with her—not knowing until much later that he was never the father, and that the child was not lost accidentally, but aborted by some backstreet crony of hers. Later there had been another child, stillborn. The father of that child had been his *own* father. When the whole sorry business erupted like a festering sore, the two of them took to their heels to set up house together and the whole dreadful scandal struck his mother down with a massive heart-attack. A dear, gentle woman he had deeply loved and one who, at the age of thirty-nine, was laid to rest. This foul unrepentant creature standing before him had been responsible! Fran Ratheter! How could he *not* hate her?

'Oho! I can see yer not too pleased to see me, eh?' She swiftly launched into her reasons for being there. She needed money! Money which would buy her silence—without which he would surely be arrested on a serious charge of bigamy. 'An' don't think you'll get off light!' she threatened, 'not when I tell them how I loved and needed you. Not when I tell them how I pleaded with you not to

21

leave me, after I'd just lost our child! And what about the beatings I took? Fair wicked you were! Oh, and don't reckon on your old fella coming to bail you out—'cause he's found himself a floozy, who'd drop him in a minute before getting mixed up in any scandal!' She threw back her head in a gesture of triumph. 'There's nobody else, is there, eh? Not another soul who'd put themselves in the spotlight to 'elp you! Oh, your Mam would 'ave moved heaven an' earth to defend you. But she ain't 'ere, is she? She's gone to the *worms* poor little thing!'

During this avalanche of lies and abuse, Curt had stood tall, his eyes alive with the loathing he felt for her, yet mastering the urge to take her by the neck and squeeze the life out of her. But for all that, when she spat out that last cruel remark, something snapped deep inside him and, springing forward, he grabbed hold of her, shaking her like a rag-doll.

'Help! Help!' she screamed, in fear of her life.

Suddenly Curt was snatched from her by two burly men—one of whom cried out, 'Jesus! He means ter kill 'er!' He never knew afterwards whether without their intervention he might have done just that. The possibility filled him with fear.

'You saw that, didn't you? You saw how he attacked me—meant to strangle me to death? You're *witnesses*, aren't you?' Fran Ratheter feigned a fit of sobbing, while the two men assured her that yes, they surely *were* witnesses.

'But don't yer think yer could both go 'ome an' more *calmly* settle the differences atween yer?' they suggested as they looked at Curt Ratheter's shaking body and the shock on his face. They knew well enough how a woman might drive a man to such extremes.

As the men walked away, Fran Ratheter thrust her face in front of Curt and, in a rasping voice, she asked, 'Well! Will you *pay* to keep me silent?'

'I'll see you in hell first!' he told her. He turned back the way he had come, leaving her to run after the two departing figures—her 'witnesses'. So! He'd see her in hell, would he? Well, if she had *her* way, Curt Ratheter would be there long before *she* was!

The next two hours were the longest in Curt's memory. As darkness gave way to light of day, he wandered the back streets of Preston, lost in tortured thoughts and more afraid than he had ever been in his whole life. He tormented himself with a deluge of guilt. *Why* hadn't he made it his business to press for the divorce he had begged from that woman years ago? *Why* hadn't he fought her tooth and nail? A divorce would have gone right against their Catholic upbringing, but what comfort had that religion been when he needed it the most? Curt was not surprised, for he was not a deeply religious man, only suffering the pattern of it for his mother's sake. He went on punishing himself, even though at that time he *had* done all he could to seek a final way out of that disastrous marriage. But, what with his mother praying that all would come right again, his father wanting to fight him whenever he showed his face, and that creature harassing him unbearably, he had grown weary. Then, when his mother was taken, there seemed no point in anything.

When, just over four years ago, he had simply disappeared to begin a new life and to put the trauma of the past behind him, meeting lovely Marcia had been like a sign from heaven that all would be well. They fell in love so quickly and so completely that he was desperately afraid he might lose her if she knew he already had a wife—a monster who, though she didn't want him, would not let him go. He should have taken that chance and confided everything in her! Once or twice, he nearly did. Even on the eve of their marriage, he had been on the verge of confessing all. But Marcia was so innocent, so trusting and so excited by the white wedding planned in such detail by her doting parents and costing nearly all of their hard-earned savings, that he didn't have the heart. More than that, he now bitterly accused himself, he did not have the *courage*. 'Coward!' Curt's voice rang out in the dark street as he punched his fist into the wall. He ignored the torn and bleeding knuckles for, if it would turn back the clock and put everything right, he would take down every brick in every house along the street. When, finally, he headed wearily towards Stoneygate Street and the family he worshipped, Curt's heart was heavy and in his dark eyes the tears of bitterness glowed fiercely. Whether or not that vindictive woman carried out her threat to go to the authorities, she had left him with no option but to reveal the truth about his background to Marcia. There was no more hiding, no more living day to day in fear of it all. Deep down Curt knew he would lose his lovely Marcia because of it.

Like a man with a broken spirit, Curt Ratheter's every step seemed like a long leaden mile as he dragged himself along the familiar street which would take him home When at last he turned the corner and lifted his bowed head to search out No. 20, his mouth fell open and his eyes grew wide with astonishment. Fran Ratheter had carried out her threat after all!

Because, parked outside the little terraced house, stood an official-looking black car. Stiff and attentive by the door, a grim-faced constable waited—the object of curiosity to the neighbours, who had filed out of their homes and who now stood about in their turbans and pinnies, clustered into busy chattering little groups. All eyes turned in his direction as he came determinedly down the street to the house, where, after quickly exchanging serious looks with the constable, he went on inside. In exchange for the wonderful love she had given him he had brought Marcia such pain and shame. He could not dare believe that she would ever be able to forgive him for it.

Marcia had been at her wits' end since the policeman had arrived some twenty minutes before. She couldn't believe the dreadful things he had told her—that Curt had physically attacked a woman that very morning. And far worse—so shocking that even now the consequences of it had not sunk in—was that the woman claimed to be Curt Ratheter's legal wife!

With her heart feeling like a dead weight inside her and her mind spinning, Marcia had paid little attention to the officer's persistent questions. Did she know where he might have gone? Was there anywhere he could be hiding, a friend's house perhaps? Or did she think it likely that he would find his way home?

'Leave the lass be! Can't yer see she's in a state o' shock?' As on every Monday morning since little

Florence's birth some ten weeks ago, Grandma Fletcher had caught the early tram from Church to Preston. Monday was a washday and, with two small bairns to hamper her, Marcia was always glad of her Mam's help. She was doubly grateful for her presence here this morning, for, without it, she wondered whether she could have coped with these shattering revelations regarding Curt. Even now, with the officer seated at the big square table in the centre of the room, and she with her Mam on the horsehair settee, Marcia felt she was in the middle of some ghastly nightmare from which she prayed she might be delivered at any moment

When Curt came to the doorway of the little parlour, the policeman close behind, what he saw in there tore his heart to shreds. Seated on that very settee where many a time he and his darling Marcia had experienced so many tender and wonderful moments, was that same woman whom he idolised. The child in her arms was gurgling and reaching out its tiny fingers to play on its Mammy's mouth, but she was so engrossed in her thoughts that there was no response. It gave Curt the deepest pain he had ever known when, at that moment, Marcia sensed his presence, for of a sudden she raised her large dark eyes to look on him. Their painfully stricken expression made him ask silently for the Lord's forgiveness.

On seeing him there also, both the officer and Grandma Fletcher got from their seats. He asked whether the fellow's name was Curt Ratheter. She charged forward and angrily demanded of him, 'Is it true what they're saying? 'Ave yer *already* a wife?' Her voice broke in emotion as the desperate look on his face told her the truth. 'Oh! You

26

scoundrel!' She was sobbing loud now and, when Polly struggled to climb from her arms crying out, 'Daddy! Daddy!' she clutched the child tighter, saying, 'Ssh, love! You come with yer ol' Gran'ma into the scullery, eh? I bet there's a fresh bun in there!' She was ashamed at herself for having exposed the little lass to such a scene. But, the promise of a bun appeared to do the trick, as her Grandma swept from the room—momentarily glancing at Marcia in passing, and seeing in her face such devastation that made her want to tear that fellow limb from limb.

In the few moments that followed, Curt Ratheter was duly warned, arrested and unceremoniously bundled into the waiting car. He and Marcia had not exchanged one word, yet in the meeting of their eyes there had been deep and heart-rending expression.

When, some time later, Grandma Fletcher closed the door and the little house grew quiet, Marcia made no move. When, with great emotion in her voice, her Mam asked, 'Are yer all right lass? Is there owt I can do fer yer?' Marcia took a while to answer. Then, keeping the child secure with one arm, she stretched the other out towards the dear old lady.

Seeing the wretchedness in her Mam's kindly face, Marcia realised that she wasn't the only one to be suffering, 'I'm all right, Mam,' she said, forcing herself to smile up at her, 'don't you worry.' Beyond that, she would not be drawn. There were things she must churn over in her mind—things which, for the life of her, she could not understand. When first the officer had outlined the nature of his visit, Marcia had actually *laughed*! She had gone to great pains to explain to the fellow that her husband, Curt Ratheter, could never be the man they sought. Why! She and he had been married these past four years! They were gloriously happy! They had two bonny daughters! *Her* man would never physically assault *anybody*. Let alone a woman! No! They were making a grave mistake, she assured them.

Yet on seeing Curt in that doorway with such a terrible look on his face, Marcia's deeper instincts told her what she had fought against. Curt *was* the fellow the police wanted. When the charges were outlined, there were no protests that he was innocent. He answered but 'yes' to his name—after which he said little. To Marcia, his admission to guilt was written there on his sad handsome face.

*　　　*　　　*

Marcia saw Curt just once before his court case came up and the experience was no less a nightmare than had been the shocking revelation that she was not his wife—that for four years he had deceived her and, in doing so, had bitterly degraded something very precious to her. In the weeks following his arrest, she had performed the everyday routines involved in bringing up two bairns. Little Florence was no real problem. Polly though was, at times, inconsolable—crying for her daddy and fretting over him until Marcia thought the poor little soul would make herself desperately ill. But, as always in times of need, those closest gathered round to do their bit and Marcia could never thank them enough. 'Away with yer lass!' Grandad Fletcher had said when she expressed her

28

gratitude. 'Ain't that what families is for?' When it soon became obvious that, without Curt's wages, the little house on Stoneygate Street would have to go, Marcia's parents at once decided she and the girls must live with them. She was thankful to be blessed with such parents. Grandma Fletcher's oldest friend was also a godsend. Nantie Betts, as she was called, was a delightful woman, who had no children of her own, idolised Marcia and fussed about her at every opportunity. 'God's good, child', she kept saying, 'and I'm sure it will all come right in the end! Oh, but I'll never understand him, lass. Why ever did he do it?'

On that one and only visit to Curt, when they sat one each end of a broad table, with a grill between them and a uniformed officer listening to their every word, Marcia asked him the very same question. 'Why, Curt! Why did you do it?' The tears were bright in her eyes as she gazed on his pale gaunt face.

When, in a quiet voice, he had gone on to explain his fear of losing her, Marcia opened her heart. She listened intently and was filled with compassion for him, for, however much he had turned their lives upside down, she still loved him so much that her whole body ached. Yet she was also angry. Angry that he could stand beside her in God's house, she dressed in the white of purity and he giving the very same marriage vows that he had given to another woman. Angry that he could keep up such deception all the while they were together as man and wife. Angry that he had fathered two delightful little girls—knowing that there must surely come a day when his dark secret would tarnish their lives even more than it did either his

29

or hers, for, to all intents and purposes, Florence and Polly were now branded with the shame of illegitimacy. If Marcia could forgive him the despair he had caused her, she could never easily pardon what he had done to those innocent little darlings.

It seemed that Curt, also, was deeply smitten by how all this would affect their daughters. 'You and I will learn to cope with all of this, Marcia,' he had said, 'but the girls are more vulnerable and must be protected from the cruelty of folks' tongues.' When she made to interrupt him to say he should have thought of that, he put up his hand, saying, 'Hear me out. I've thought long and hard on this and . . .' Here, he bowed his head for a moment before clearing his throat and continuing, 'it isn't easy to say this, Marcia . . . but I must! I love you more than I could ever say, sweetheart. I'll always love you. But after today, I don't want you to see me again. Do you understand?' Without waiting for an answer, he went on. 'Fran will *never* divorce me, I know. She'd rather haunt us . . . even after I've done my time. There's no future for us, don't you see, Marcia? No future for us, and no future for the little ones! They need a father. They need a legitimate name. Oh, Marcia—I don't expect you to forgive me. But I implore you to forget me, and let the children forget me. They're young enough. Put me behind you and start a new life.' He gave a sad whimsical smile, before adding in a softer voice, 'I'm so very sorry, Marcia.' To see her now, so helpless and with the tears flowing down her face at his cruel words, hurt him badly. God only knew how much he adored her! But it was during his prayers that the answer had presented itself.

He must give up Marcia and the children for ever! He had no right to them or to their love.

When Marcia emerged from the drabness of that prison-room, into the brilliant sunshine of a May day, she reflected on Curt's words and her promise that she would comply with his decision. She was deeply tormented by it, and she was in no doubt of the tremendous courage it had taken for him to say what he did. She, also, must have the same strength and courage, for the sake of the children. But, oh, how her heart did ache! And, oh, how she did love him!

Some short time later, Curt Ratheter's case was brought to Lancaster Assizes. It created a deal of public interest. When it was over, there were those who condemned the judge for delivering such an unusually harsh sentence of seven years. But, there were also those who endorsed it, saying in loud voices, 'The fellow deserved every bit of it! Not like that poor innocent lass—left with two small bairns and no name to keep them respectable.'

'Aye,' rejoined another, 'and what of his *legal* wife, eh? Did you see what a poor sorry little thing she was—deserted in *spite* of pleading with him to stay? And as for him calling the woman a downright *liar*! Well! If you ask me, it were *that* scoundrel as was the liar!'

'Beat her up too! Nearly strangled her to death, according to them two witnesses. Oh, I tell you, that Ratheter fellow's a right bad lot and no mistake!' Like the majority who had eagerly followed the case, this observer was of the opinion that Ratheter should consider himself fortunate not to have been charged with attempted murder!

As for Marcia, she cried herself to sleep that

night with Grandma Fletcher sitting up in her bed listening; cursing the day Curt Ratheter had ever come into their lives.

CHAPTER THREE

'Bless me soul!' Grandma Fletcher chased round and round the big old table, her voluminous skirt plucked up into her two chubby fists so as not to become entangled round her ankles as she ran from the giggling child, 'Save me! Save me!' she cried in mock terror, as little Polly, enthused by her Grandma's antics, fell about laughing. Worn out and breathless, the woman eventually collapsed chuckling into a deep flowered armchair, with the child hastily scrambling on to her lap. In a moment she had flung her two thin arms about her Grandma's neck and, in equally breathless fashion, was urging her to 'Come on! *Again* 'Ranma! *Again!*'

'Lord love us, child!' protested Grandma Fletcher, 'me ol' legs couldn't tek me round yon table again! Not if me *life* depended on it!' She squeezed Polly into her and held her fast in a close embrace. Then, hearing Marcia coming down from the bedroom where she had been getting the bairn to sleep, she whispered in Polly's ear, 'Quick! Yer Mam's coming ter get yer off to bed. See if she can find yer, eh? Go on!' In a lower whisper she added, 'Get back o' yer Grandad's chair. It'll tek a while to find yer there!'

When Marcia opened the door from the stairs and came into the back parlour, she knew by her

32

Mam's cheery wink that Polly was playing the game—a game which had started as a desperate means by which she could be tired out enough to get her mind off her daddy. Gradually, the game had become a source of pure enjoyment which both Grandad and Grandma Fletcher eagerly indulged in. And, over the weeks following their move from Stoneygate Street to Henry Street, Church, Polly's nightmares had thankfully diminished.

For some reason, Marcia felt particularly weary tonight. All day long, Curt had been in her thoughts, and the children's futures had preyed hard on her mind. Since the court case and Curt's subsequent imprisonment, Marcia had felt more lonely and vulnerable than she could ever remember. There had to be some sort of plans made, she knew. But what sort of plans? What could she do, with two little bairns to care for? Where could she go and how would they live? In spite of her Mam's reassurance that they could stay here as long as ever was necessary, Marcia knew only too well that it was out of the question. This was a tiny house, big enough for two—but stifling when there were five bodies crammed into it. Also, her parents were not young any more—her Mam being fifty-eight and her Dad sixty-five. It wasn't fair that at their age they should be plagued with youngsters, however much they might protest otherwise.

Sighing inwardly, she pretended to search for Polly, saying in a loud voice which set the child off in helpless giggles, 'Has anybody seen a little girl called Polly?' While she crept about the furniture, it crossed Marcia's mind to wonder whether she should after all accept Barty's proposal of marriage. He had been most persistent—even when Marcia had explained how, though she was very fond of Barty—as appeared to be the children—she did not love him in the way he loved her. Her heart and her thoughts were still with Curt and probably always would be.

Barty's answer had been to assure Marcia that it made no difference. 'I love you enough for both of us. And, I'm sure, in time you'll come to love me, Marcia. Besides which the girls need a father an' I swear I'll do my best by *all* of yer. We can move to Blackburn, where I work for the Corporation. There'll be no problem in gettin' a place to live. You can mek it cosy like—an' I'll do the providing. Oh, go on, Marcia!' he had urged, 'say yes. Say you'll wed me!' It was plain enough to Marcia that Barty did indeed love her. He was certainly affectionate towards the children, although Polly hadn't quite taken to him the way little Florence had. But then, Marcia reminded herself, Polly was only just beginning to get over the trauma of the day her daddy had 'been taken away by the man'. Also Barty had Grandad Fletcher's approval, for, when Marcia confided in him regarding Barty's proposal of marriage, he had lowered the newspaper he'd been reading in which much was written about Gandhi's visit to Blackburn town, tweaked his great bushy moustache with one hand, and with the other had stroked the small terrier ever at his feet. Then, his bright eyes twinkling at Marcia, he had told her, 'Tha could do worse, lass. Yon Barty Bendall's a good worker fro' what I know—an' *anyone* can see 'e's right fond on yer!' Grandma Fletcher, also, fervently echoed these

34

sentiments.

So, it seemed that the only one to have any real doubts was Marcia herself. Time and time again she had sat down with pen and paper. She had written long loving letters to Curt. Afterwards, she had read them over and over, murmuring his name and reliving in her heart the splendid times they had spent together. Then, as always, she would tear up the letters and sob herself to sleep. But Marcia had now decided that she must stop fooling herself. Much as the knowledge weighed heavy in her sorry heart, the plain truth was that Curt had a wife—and that wife was not her! She must put the girls' welfare above all else.

Later, when the children and her parents were fast asleep, Marcia sat downstairs in the parlour, contemplating their future and despising Curt for what he had brought them to. Yet, in the depth of her anger, there was always her love for him, which gave her neither pain nor pleasure. It was just there like the beating of her heart.

'Marcia!' A small urgent cry penetrated Marcia's deep reflections. There it was again, accompanied by a tap on the back window. 'Marcia. It's Barty.' Sure enough, when Marcia went to the window, there in the dark was Barty, asking to be let in. 'I must talk with you!' he insisted.

Once inside, Barty went straight to the fireplace, where the dying embers of a small coal fire burned. With the onset of an unusually chilly evening, Marcia had taken the liberty of lighting it—always acutely conscious, though, of the need to be thrifty.

'By! There's turned a sudden nip in the air!' he exclaimed, rubbing his hands together and wriggling his backside against the welcome heat. The way he did it gave Marcia to smile. Even that homely little movement was executed in a stiff upright military fashion, 'I'll get you a hot drink,' she offered, beginning to rise to her feet.

'No! No!' Barty came and sat beside her, his speckled green eyes intense as they roved her features. 'I've come in to ask you summat special...'

'Oh, Barty!' Marcia sensed he was about to propose yet again.

'No. Listen to what I've got to say, Marcia,' he entreated, his short stubby fingers covering hers, 'I've been to see the fellow as deals with Corporation houses.' Of a sudden, he began to grow restless with excitement, 'I've got us one! I've got us a place in Blackburn, Marcia. A good solid place on Regent Street. Oh, will you not wed me? Will you not let me look after you an' give them lasses a proper name?' When he saw her hesitate, he pleaded, 'Think when Polly comes of an age to go to school. How's the poor thing going to feel when it's found that she's... illegitimate? That she has no father to speak of? Oh, an' what about *you*! I can give you all a proper home an' a proper going-on, don't y'see? Marcia... don't y'see that?'

In spite of her deeper misgivings about a life with Barty, Marcia could see the advantages of all he offered—a home of their own, a man to provide for them, and a proper father to the girls, who would be restored to legitimate status. It was all very tempting, but while she and the girls stood to gain from such an arrangement, Barty himself could not even be assured of her love. Marcia had said as much to him many times before. She said it

36

again now.

'Believe me, Marcia. I'll make no demands on you till you're ready. I'm twenty-seven! It's time I was settled with a family,' he answered fervently. He squeezed her hand and laughed. 'An' what better than a ready-made little family, eh? Oh! Please Marcia! Make me the happiest man in Church tonight—say yes!'

Carried along on the crest of Barty's great excitement and persistence, and with her daughters' welfare uppermost in her mind, Marcia gave in, praying that the day would never come when she would bitterly regret it. Yet, even as she accepted Barty's proposal, there *was* a murmuring of regret already making her uneasy. And, when Barty sealed their alliance with a kiss, it was his lips she felt against hers, but Curt's image she kept close in her heart.

Somehow though, Marcia thought he might just approve of Barty Bendall. He had often told Marcia how besotted Barty was with her.

*   *   *

The next day was Saturday. Following the news that Marcia had accepted Barty's offer of marriage, the two families congregated in the Fletchers' front parlour, amidst Grandma's best pieces of hand-down Victorian furniture and highly prized piano. To Marcia's surprise, Grandma Fletcher even attempted a tune on it, but the noise was so offensive to the ear that Grandad Fletcher shouted 'Christ Almighty, woman! Are thi tryin' ter deafen us or what?' She sulkily put down the lid and resumed her place at the table, where everyone raised their glass of home-made elderberry wine and, with much laughing and chattering, finally toasted health to the happy couple. Bullied by her Mam's insistence that 'the occasion won't feel right till Marcia gives us a song in that lovely voice o' 'ers!' Marcia then gave an exquisite rendering of an old Irish lullaby.

'That deserves a kiss!' cried Barty, leaning forward to brush his lips against Marcia's mouth.

At that moment, when Polly was made to witness this intimate gesture, she began screaming and sobbing. Even when Marcia caught the child in her arms, saying, 'I expect the excitement's all been too much for her,' she herself was not fully convinced of it. Some quiet instinct told her that Curt's daughter had still not quite got over him. Like me, Marcia thought, and I never will.

Soon after, the little party broke up. The children went to their naps, Grandad Fletcher to bury his old head in the newspaper and complain of Ramsey Macdonald's poor attitude towards the unemployed. His wife helped Marcia with the clearing away, and Barty disappeared to see about some furniture.

His mother, Connie Bendall—a little dumpling of a soul with iron-grey hair and pretty black eyes—thanked one and all most profusely. 'It's been grand,' she told Grandma Fletcher. To Marcia she said, 'I pray you an' my Barty will be very 'appy.'

Once inside the privacy of her own parlour, where she gazed most fondly on the silver-framed picture of a straight-faced man in soldier's uniform, Barty's doting mother had another prayer to say.

'I pray to God he'll do right by her an' them children. Oh, an' I can't deny that I'll miss him Jack—'cause I will! But, these past few years since Marcia chose another man instead of him, Barty's seemed obsessed at times!' A sad little smile crept over her face as she went on, 'Oh, he gave us some grand moments as a child, you remember? Barty idolised you, didn't he, Jack? But it won't be long now afore I'm joining you, an' I wouldn't want him ter be left all alone. Hey! Let's think o' the *best* that can 'appen, eh, Jack? 'Appen that lovely Marcia can soften his tyrant ways, eh? An' what with a family ter support, he'll have little brass left fer gambling, I'm thinkin'. Oh, it's been a trial Jack, that it has! But let's hope and pray that the two of 'em will be happy enough, for the lad's not *all* bad, is he, eh?'

With that, she went to sit and think in her favourite armchair. Soon after a deep sleep overcame her, because Connie Bendall's old heart had been sorely tried of late, and was not as strong as it used to be.

Part Two

1937
Marcia and the Tyrant

CHAPTER FOUR

Marcia's heart lurched as she caught sight of the tall shadowy figure which lingered by the mouth of the open tram shelter. Something about the strong measure of his wide straight shoulders and the thick mop of black hair set her heart pounding.

Lifting her hand to shield the light from her eyes, she peered through the tram window, desperately trying to focus on his face. But the darkness outside kept it camouflaged.

As the tram shuddered to a halt, Marcia watched the tall dark-haired man step out, his face now bathed in the light from the tram windows. When she saw him clearly, her heart shrank within her and, turning her dark tragic eyes away, she chided herself for being so naive. Of course it wasn't Curt! How could it be? Curt Ratheter was in prison—had been these last five years and more. Years when Marcia had known little happiness, except from her children, whom she adored.

The man whom Marcia had so foolishly mistaken for Curt came up the tram aisle to seat himself directly in front of her, unaware of the turmoil he had caused. Looking up as he relaxed into his seat, Marcia's eyes swept the back of his head, and the unlocked memories flooded vividly through her mind.

Turning her eyes away towards the window, Marcia wondered whether there would ever come a time when she might completely let him go. Now though, pretending to be asleep, she indulged in precious recollections of her time with Curt—all the while her heart aching and her eyes filled with tears. Yet she was not concerned that people might see her so sad and wonder, for half the passengers were themselves fast asleep. It was only five-thirty of a winter's morning and most of the sleeping bodies were hard-pressed mill-hands, employed at various cotton mills atop Cicely Brew.

Blackburn was a textile town, and the folks here, as in many other Lancashire towns, earned their bread and butter in gaunt formidable buildings from the Victorian era, whose grim outlines were ever silhouetted against the sky like so many sentries watching over the towns below. Folks were more than thankful for the work these great mills brought them, because the depression had struck particularly hard in the North of England, with many a man denied the dignity of work. And many a family going hungry! There was deep bitterness in the ranks, with high-running emotions against the Government, who, many claimed, had turned its back on the working class.

The tram rattled along its pre-determined route, the iron wheels grating rhythmically against the channels along which they ran, the comforting noise lulling Marcia's thoughts back into the past, a past which was still very much part of the present, as far as Marcia was concerned.

Because of the conflicting pull of loyalties, Marcia was haunted day and night. She was married to one man, the father of her youngest son; yet still hopelessly, desperately in love with another, the father of her two daughters. The tender memories now filling her mind spread a warm glow across her beautiful dark features, and she indulged in the painful joy of the past.

44

She had been a fresh young woman of twenty when she had pledged her marriage vows to the dark, handsome Curt Ratheter. In the four wonderful years when they had shared each other's love and devotion, Marcia had borne him two daughters, Polly and Florence. The girls had been too young to know or understand the events which had tom their parents' world apart, leaving them as bastards, and Marcia neither single nor widowed.

When Curt Ratheter was taken away, arrested on a charge of bigamy, Marcia had found herself steeped in disbelief, pain, and finally terrible anger which seemed to swallow her deep love for Curt, leaving in its place a sense of horror and desolation, from which she could find no relief.

It was only later, during the trial, when she witnessed the female-monster from his first ill-fated marriage, that Marcia realised how he might have done the terrible thing he did. It had been the saving of Marcia's sanity when finally she had come to admit to herself that whatever he had done, it had undoubtedly been because of the strength and beauty of his feelings for her, and because of the great happiness and deep love they had shared. And, how could Marcia ever forget the decision they had made in the unpleasant confinement of that room, with a policeman standing over their every glance, every word; a decision prompted by their desire to protect their two lovely daughters, who bore no blame for what had taken place. Marcia had diligently stood by that decision, knowing it to be right—but regretting it all the same.

The tram shuddered to a halt, jerking Marcia's wandering thoughts to the long hard day ahead at the spinning frames. The bleary-eyed workers, tired and worn even before they started, tumbled from the tram, all pushing and shoving towards their place of labour. 'Morning Marcia lass . . .' 'Bit parky, eh . . . shouldn't send a dog out this time o' the day!' ' 'Ow do, Marcia love; weekend coming up, eh . . . thank Christ!'

The muffled-up workers shouted their cheery greetings, as they hunched their shoulders against the piercing cold, and set about trudging their way up Cicely to the sprawling cluster of cotton mills there.

Marcia returned their friendly greetings with genuine affection. It had often struck her that desperate need, for all its horrors, had a strange way of binding folks together, increasing their appreciation of one another and, as a result, there had emerged a kinship between the folk hereabout that was strong and comforting. They were a hard-living courageous folk, whose profound strength and faith helped them to live each day as it came, to forge new friendship and to cherish the old. If one suffered, they *all* suffered. And, if there was reason for celebration—perhaps a small win on the horses, or a young 'un making good—then everyone's heart was lighter for it. One big happy family, that's what they were, and Marcia's heart was big enough to love them all.

Marcia pulled the scarf tight under her chin, her black eyes shining strong and resolute as she quickened her pace. Almost thirty now, Marcia was still a beautiful woman. A creature of gentleness and admirable character; the woman all men dream of, and all other women look up to.

But hers was a poor, hard existence, a

day-to-day struggle to make ends meet. Her husband Barty, three years her senior and a dedicated gambler and drunkard, did nothing to ease her burden. Far from being a comfort and provider, he only added to her considerable troubles. But Marcia Bendall belonged to that unique, enviable band of fighters. She was a born survivor, with a heart as big and embracing as the worries that dogged her. Always strong in that heart was a burning resolution to make the most of what the good Lord had sent her . . . never failing to thank Him for the light of her days, her lovely children.

As the hurrying throng of mill-hands swarmed across the top of Cicely Hill to disperse along various paths leading to their respective mills the sounds of their departing voices was effectively silenced beneath the banshee wail of the five-minute hooter.

'Come on Marcia! You shoulda done your dreaming while you were still abed! Or wouldn't the old fella let you, eh?'

Marcia turned at the coarse laughter which cut through her private thoughts. 'Oh, morning Old Fred,' she said as she stopped for the merest second to rub her hands in the intensity of heat radiating from the brazier. Old Fred was the night-watchman, a harmless little man with a mountain of cheek and more than his fair share of smutty humour. 'I should have thought you'd have been away by now,' she went on, the smile on her face stretched into a mischievous grin. 'You know what'll happen if you're caught in the light of day! You'll shrivel up Old Fred . . . just like that there Count Dracula fella!'

Old Fred roared his appreciation; the oversized neb-cap which all but covered his face wobbled dangerously against his ears which appeared to be its only real means of support. Marcia, not meaning to be unkind, had long ago pictured Old Fred as a grotesque gargoyle; harmless, but incredibly ugly! 'Go on Old Fred,' she told him gently, 'get yourself off home to your bed. I expect it's been a long cold night, eh?' She turned away towards Baines' cotton mill. 'An' I'd best get myself clocked in! Can't afford to lose no quarter! See thi' Old Fred.' 'Aye lass. See thi!' he shouted into the darkness.

Marcia had been given a job at Baines' mill three weeks back, ever since young Barty had started school. It wasn't easy. In fact, it was back-breaking work. But she had been glad of the opportunity to earn a few much-needed shillings.

The most crippling discomfort, and the hardest to get used to, was the noise. The constant high-pitched whine from the machines, tempered with a rhythmic thumping, was painfully deafening and nerve-jarring. In the monstrous Victorian building which swallowed Marcia's days, the spinning and weaving machines dominated thought and action. It was physically impossible for the workers to converse in an easy normal manner. Pitching the mere human voice against the brawling of these tireless machines was utterly futile. So, in the deviousness born of necessity, the Lancashire mill-hands had devised a silent but functional language of their own. With their sophisticated sign and lip-reading language they cheated the screaming machines which sought to render them mute.

Marcia's clocking-in card was the last in the

rack. Everyone had punched their cards and placed them in the in-shelves. She slipped the yellow card into the slot over the time-clock, just as the hand swung round to register six a.m. 'Good,' she whispered, tapping the clock gratefully, 'just in time!'

As she pushed against the heavy green doors leading into the cloakroom, she could hear the machines starting up one after the other. Wriggling out of her coat, she slung it hurriedly over one of the pegs on the rack before hastening to her own machine.

'Come on Marcia! Where the 'ell 'ave you been?' Tom Atkinson was the gaffer. A great elephant of a man he was; shaped like one of the cotton-bobbins, swollen to bulging in the middle and tapered off at both ends. His watery red-rimmed eyes were incapable of direct focus because while the left one struggled to hold you tight in its quivering gaze, the right one swivelled about all over the place, until finally out of utter frustration the pair of them gave up the effort. When that happened, there was no telling *who* poor Tom was looking at! And to make it even more nerve-racking, all of this dubious activity took place behind narrow rimless spectacles which sat daintily on the end of his long bulbous nose. 'Hey! I'm not late, Tom Atkinson! It's only just six, you know!' Marcia knew her rights.

'Aye, well . . .' Tom the gaffer waggled a hesitant finger at her. 'Aye, well . . .' he repeated weakly, already making off down the row of spinning-frames, 'think on! Just think on!' he called behind him, his bravado increasing with the space between them.

49

Marcia smiled after his hurriedly-departing figure, 'Poor old Tom . . .' she muttered, 'fancy putting him in charge of a rabble o' lasses!' Without uncovering her long black hair, she skilfully manipulated the scarf about her head, transforming it into a knotted turban which sat tight and snug, concealing and protecting her magnificent hair from the clinging wisps of cotton which would soon fill the air like sticky snowflakes. Reaching into a small wooden locker beneath her bobbin-crate, she exchanged her ankle-clogs for soft slippers. Then she donned the regular green wrap-around overall. Strapping the deep-pocketed pinny around her waist, and checking the bottom tray-run to assure herself that it was filled all the way along with empty bobbins, Marcia threw the machine into gear. Marcia wasn't normally given to nervousness, but the act of triggering the monstrous machine into life was definitely not one in which she took pleasure.

The machines were an awesome sight to behold. The great iron monsters, proud and domineering, reached endlessly upwards and outwards measuring in excess of sixty feet, and seeming as tall again. Almost touching the towering Victorian ceilings, they blotted out both light and human sound. Hundreds of bobbins spanned each machine, swirling and screeching beneath the weight of spinning cotton.

It was incredible to the watching eye that such heinous constructions could belch forth a cotton as fine and pure as the beautiful delicate strands of a cobweb. The cotton poured out in great abundance, winding and wrapping itself around the receptive bobbins which spun and twirled, until swollen pregnantly with their heavy load. When full, the heavy bobbins would be removed by the harassed scurrying women who constantly raced against time and machine as they darted methodically from one end of the heaving row to the other, their coloured turbans making frenzied patterns as they wove up and down, up and down.

The frequent replacement of empty bobbins for full ones was swift and skilful. The empty bobbins were quickly dropped with great accuracy over the fast spinning core-rods. It took only a few minutes for the empty bobbins to fill to bursting again; allowing the constantly mobile women no rest. They were hard pushed to keep up, and many a trainee had surrendered in tears to the devouring machines. The full bobbins were slipped into the hessian bag which the women wore around their waists until the bag reached overflowing. The bobbins were then emptied into large square wicker containers. These, in turn, were emptied into huge mobile trollies, which were frequently transported to another level of the mill by an organised army of 'trundlers'. The fine cotton would then be woven into endless acres of fresh crisp linen, to be shipped all over the world, as well as marketed locally. Even Mahatma Gandhi had been fascinated by the whole procedure, on his visit here some five years previously.

It was undoubtedly a fascinating process to watch, yet an utterly exhausting and thankless task for the labourers . . . but there was no shortage of that indomitable raw Lancashire humour and down-to-earth application to the job in hand.

Marcia Bendall possessed such admirable qualities. Her husband Barty's shortcomings as an ample provider, might have forced her to seek a regular wage-packet in order for them to keep body and soul together; but like so many other mill-hands, she questioned little, and craved for even less.

'All right are you Marcia, lass?'

Big Bertha mouthed the words against the relentless roaring of noise which rent the air.

Marcia cast a quick calculating eye along the stretch of rotating bobbins. She was all right for less than a minute, she ascertained, as the bobbins she had constantly replaced were not quite filled. All the same, she dared not relax her ceaseless watch.

The difficult silent conversation they held was executed on the move, with each having to wait for the other's undivided attention before shaping the words which remained unspoken, unheard, yet understood. ' 'Eard yon Tom Atkinson 'aving a right go at you! Bloody cheek!' Big Bertha laughed vigorously; and the sight of her generous body wobbling and shaking, silent mouth wide open and eyes disappearing beneath the heavy drooping bags about her face, was a curious sight to behold. 'Poor old sod!' she mouthed. 'Gets led a right dance, don't 'e? Nobody teks a blind bit o' notice on 'im!' Her deft and practised fingers moved at speed as they illustrated her words. Marcia liked Big Bertha. By rights, she should have been looking forward to retirement with the 'old darling' with whom she'd spent more than forty years of her life. But the recent loss of their son following a long illness had proved too much of a heartache for the old man. He just never got over it . . . So Big Bertha lost him too, the 'old darling' she'd wanted to end her days with. Now, her feeble faint-hearted daughter-in-law and four grandchildren lived under her roof, looking to Big Bertha for their every need.

Like many a good woman, it wasn't in Big Bertha's nature to waste time fretting and fussing. A monster of a woman with a big heart and great bawling voice which only the machines could silence, she had taken it upon herself to look out for the younger mill-lasses. This dedicated aim had earned her a special place in their hearts. She'd been relieved of a machine of her own, because she had acquired such knowledge of their workings and temperament that it was thought better use could be made of her as a sort of Welfare-Officer Mechanic. Both men and women valued her judgement on issues involving machine and labourer alike. During a hectic working day, when some overworked fitter or constantly thrashed machine might try and give up the ghost, Big Bertha's skill and patience would coax them back to life.

'He's all right is Tom Atkinson . . .' Marcia moved towards the far end of her spinning frame, with Big Bertha following, '. . . never bothers you if you're doing your work.' Her quick watchful eye caught sight of a spew of cotton which had erupted from an over-filled bobbin.

Reaching with automatic reflex, and hoping no one in authority had seen the waste, she yanked it skilfully from its spindle, the spurting cotton strands vomiting out into thin air.

With swift deft movements Marcia slipped an empty bobbin on the fast-rotating spindle, feeding the flailing line of cotton round its body, where it

53

proceeded to wind vigorously.

'Best leave you to it, lass . . .' Big Bertha knew too well the chaos that could result from a handful of overflowing bobbins.

Marcia nodded appreciatively. There was no time for social exchanges here! By the time she'd pulled the excess cotton from the retrieved bobbin, the whole line had neared bursting-point again.

During the course of the long hard day, when Marcia found a solitary minute here and there, her thoughts embraced all manner of things. The slight shock she had experienced on the tram that morning somehow never left her, and tender forbidden memories of Curt Ratheter crept insistently into her mind. She thought too on her husband Barty Bendall, and the drastic way he'd changed since their marriage. Then she thought on her three lovely children; two of them Curt's but not knowing it . . . and little Barty, a great measure too quiet and withdrawn for her peace of mind.

Now, as always when feeling low at heart, Marcia sang. The songs remained inaudible amidst the deafening roar of the great machine, but they were beautiful songs which helped the workday to pass more quickly, filling her heart and lifting her soul and altogether seeming to make life worthwhile.

Marcia watched the big bold face of the clock high up on the wall, following the progress of its hand throughout the long drawn-out day; until gradually the minutes ate away at the hours, and the hours consumed the day. 'Half-hour to go, thank the Lord . . .' Marcia's lips moved in a great sigh of relief, at the same time her tired fingers wiped the irritating fluffs of cotton from her brow, where the beads of sweat stood out like crystal dewdrops.

As she inhaled in preparation for a long relaxing sigh her eye caught the frantic arm-waving signals of young Daisy Forester; a slip of a lass who managed the machine in front of Marcia's with surprising capability. Marcia held a great deal of affection for young Daisy. Some time back, her Dad had deserted his responsibility—leaving Daisy's Main to cope. She did her best, but it was never enough to fill the empty bellies left behind. Five of them there were: Daisy, her three younger sisters, and their Mam. Being the eldest child, Daisy Forester had unfortunately inherited a tall duty; but she shouldered it well, and rarely complained.

Marcia focused her full attention on young Daisy's face, following the shape of her mouth in order to distinguish its message. 'What's the time, Marcia?' The huge silent clock was positioned in such a way that the high cross-members of Daisy's machine obstructed her view.

Marcia thought the lass looked tired. Her long thin face was pale and sickly looking, like the fine blonde strands of hair which peeked from her turban; but then, Marcia had often noted that young Daisy Forester *never* had any roses in her cheeks . . . nor in her poor confined life neither, she shouldn't wonder!

Daisy lip-read Marcia's answer, turning away with a grateful smile that it was nearly going-home time. All along the numerous rows of spinning-frames, the turbaned women bobbed about busily, collecting and tidying the unavoidable mess which daily gathered round their machines.

55

The factory hooter blew the final shutdown, instructing the mill-hands that another working day had drawn to a close. The spinning machines were now being allowed to wind down, and the many variously-pitched screams were extinguished one by one, each reluctant to become silent as they whined slowly into submission.

'Come on Marcia! Get your apron emptied!'

The short bow-legged man turned towards Marcia as she ripped off the confining turban to release the dark profusion of hair. 'I'm waiting!' the man insisted. He had a square ruddy face and a shock of blond hair, which was squashed underneath the close fit of his flat cap. His dirty white overalls were now festooned with feathery curls of wispy cotton. George Leatheread was a 'trundler' who took an exuberant pride in his work. Taking a forward pace, he shouted again, a little more urgently, 'Come on Marcia! I'm waiting to go.' His tiny pea-shaped eyes fixed Marcia in their sights, then, as Marcia turned, her incredible beauty pinned him fast, when the thick hair cascaded wildly over her shoulders in blue-black waves reminiscent of a raven's wing.

Her large expressive eyes were liquid dark and hypnotic, and lurking now deep within them lay more than a hint of devilment. Her perfectly-proportioned body leaned forward; the sensuous curves discernible even beneath the ill-fitting work-garment tied loosely about her. She seemed totally out of place in this noisy, dirty mill. But the forthright manner in which she addressed him somehow belied her exquisite appearance as she quickly retaliated, 'Full of your own importance again, aren't you, George?' The accompanying

56

smile lit up her face with a radiant glow, encompassing the homely features of little George Leatheread. She was teasing him, and he knew it. But, keeping his distance, George suddenly felt ambitious, for Marcia Bendall was the fanciful dream of every redblooded man here, and the loveliness of her smile seemed to fire his imagination.

'Right,' he shouted back cheekily, 'If yer don't think I'm a man ter be reckoned with, Marcia Bendall, say when and where, an' I'll be there like a shot!' Deep down though, George Leatheread had no illusions. He had long ago accepted that such a beautiful woman would always be out of his reach. The act he put on now was no more than a game of bluff and bravado. Suddenly surprised by the boldness of his own remark, he turned abruptly on his heel, calling out, 'Never mind, I'll drop 'em in the skip in the morning.' He pushed his wicker trolley away, winking cheekily as he went.

Unfortunately for poor George, some of the young flighty girls, always ready for a bit of fun at the end of a working day, had overheard his brazen remarks. He didn't get very far before they were on him, their pent-up exuberance now released in fits of screaming laughter.

'Right, you sexy beast, George Leatheread! You've asked for it now!' 'Don't get worriting, George . . . we're not going to 'arm you . . . we just want to see what all the fuss is about.' 'Come on George! Get them bloody trousers off!' They came at him from all directions.

Screeching and shouting, with Marcia good-humouredly taking poor George's side, they tugged and grabbed at his overalls, pushing him

57

over in the struggle, and throwing themselves on top of his squirming protesting body.

Shouts of 'Geddoff!' and 'Don't be so bloody daft!' only seemed to encourage them in their insistent merciless attempts to strip poor George of his every stitch. George clung to his trousers like grim death itself, helpless in the grip of their snatching wandering hands. Hopelessly outnumbered, poor George tried every way he could think of to point out the error of their actions; he persuaded, cajoled, threatened, until finally, his breathing erratic and nervous, he yelled 'Help! Help!' at the top of his weakening voice.

There was more than a hint of desperation evident in his shout as he added, 'You daft buggers! Gaffer'll be 'ere in a minute! The last hooter's gone . . .'

Suddenly, as if in answer to George's heartfelt prayer, the loud voice of authority cut through the laughter and screaming.

'What the bloody 'ell's going on 'ere?'

The tangle of arms and legs quickly sorted themselves out, as the gaffer's demand boomed out, echoing against the iron structures around them.

Looking towards the bottom end of the shed, the girls could just make out Tom Atkinson striding towards them at a furious pace. Still sniggering, they released the captive George Leatheread, who scrabbled to his feet, red-faced and panting, his fair hair standing out on the top of his head in sheer fright. Replacing his dangling braces and putting the rest of his dishevelled clothing in some sort of order, he muttered loud curses and damnation on all and sundry. Then, after retrieving his beloved flat cap from the high beam where the girls had thrown it, he grabbed his wicker skip, and scurried off, swearing belligerently.

The unrepentant girls turned to face the gaffer who strode towards them, serious-faced and ready for a confrontation. But he represented no serious threat. They were all used to dealing with Tom Atkinson . . . he was really only a sprinter, with no staying power. 'Right then you lot! What the 'ell d'ya think you're playing at, eh?' His eyes swivelled uncontrollably as he tried desperately to bring the tittering girls into focus through the narrow surface of his tiny rimless spectacles.

'Oh come on Tommy! It were only a bit o' fun . . .' the protest was delivered on the rising crest of a fresh outburst of giggling, as the girls collapsed against each other, helpless with laughter. The surprising anger of Tom Atkinson's voice, however, caught their attention gradually as he shouted over and above the dying laughter, 'A bit of fun, eh? I'll give you a "bit o' fun"! Just look at the poor sod! You've frightened him half to death. I doubt if he'll ever set foot in 'ere again!'

As they all strained to follow the direction of the retreating George, Marcia was heard to shout mischievously, 'Don't forget your promise, George lad! I'll see you later.'

This proved to be the proverbial point at which poor George Leatheread could take no more. After darting an extremely nervous glance over his shoulder at the sound of Marcia's voice, and seeing them all staring after him with such deliberation, he completely forgot to look where he was going. In his blind nervous fear the only thought in his

59

mind was to get the hell out of there. The yawning skip-chute was a mere step away. Pushing the laden wicker skips onto the transporting chute, to be carried down to the lower level, was one of George's regular jobs. By this time he should have known instinctively the exact location of the chute; and normally he would have done. But not only did he fail to perceive the mouth of the chute, he foolishly forgot to release his hold on the wicker trolley when he *did* see the chute opening before him. Of a sudden, he was screaming like a thing in terror, as both he *and* the skip disappeared promptly down the chute and out of sight.

A split second of pregnant silence subdued the flabbergasted onlookers, before Tom Atkinson's voice called out incredulously, his bulbous eyes making crazy patterns within their sockets, 'Christ! Look what the silly sod's done! He's gone down the bloody chute . . . skip an' all!'

Marcia was doubled up in fits of laughter. She knew poor George would have landed on something soft down there. The bevy of young girls who had so enthusiastically attacked him just as enthusiastically rushed off, intent on saving him at all costs.

Even Tom the gaffer collapsed in fits of appreciative roaring laughter, before moving on, still laughing loudly, to hurry the lingering workers out.

The now diminishing clatter of clogs on the stone flag floors, and the colourful sea of moving turbaned heads, informed him that the majority were already thankfully on their way out and home.

Within ten minutes or so of the final hooter

sounding off, the factory premises at all levels were expected to be vacated, in order that all entries and exits could be tightly secured. Already the lower section workers were teeming out of the front gate in their hundreds.

By the time Marcia had finally checked for full bobbins, which were quickly replaced with empty rods ready for a clean start after the weekend, then cleared away and checked the machine off, the upper level was all but deserted.

A pleasant contented smile gently lifted the corner of Marcia's lovely mouth as she took off her soft slippers. Reaching into the locker, she withdrew her stout clogs into which she slid her dainty feet, before buckling the leather strap across her slim ankle. She thought on Polly, her eldest daughter, who had flatly refused to wear clogs . . . which she referred to as 'canal barges'. 'It's sad,' Marcia mused, 'that all the old traditions seem to diminish with the growth of our youngsters.' The slippers Marcia placed in the locker were of the type worn by almost all the working lasses here. They helped to combat the punishing demands made on the feet during a working day, when they probably covered in excess of twenty miles. Now though, Marcia's heart felt light and free, as it always did when the final hooter had blown. It was 'going-home' time.

'Go on Marcia lass . . . give us a song love.' The voice came from amongst the group of mill-hands just leaving, 'Yes, go on . . . give us a song,' they all urged in unison.

Marcia straightened up from fastening her ankle straps, her dark eyes smiling. She didn't need asking twice. Her lips parted, and from the very

61

depths of her being the happiness and inner radiance that bathed her heart at that moment came forth in an unexpectedly magnificent singing voice. Marcia never needed an excuse to burst into song. It was her pleasure—her means of escape when life began to press too hard on her. Singing was a natural extension of her own self; an intricate part of her personality. As she sang, some of the mill-hands already half-way down the stairs wended their quiet way back to stand mesmerised at the sweet sound.

Often at the end of the day, the mill-hands would hang back so as not to miss the plaintive tones of Marcia's song. The melodious voice drifted on the air, embracing and soothing their tired bodies and minds, and the lovely words

Some letters tied with blue, a photograph
    or two,
I see a rose from you, among my souvenirs,

tore painfully at their very heartstrings. They stayed until the song died away. They all loved Marcia Bendall, and never missed an opportunity to enjoy the special talent God had given her. The deep comradeship binding these mill-hands together stemmed from common hardship and common need; *no one* could express what they were feeling in the same way that Marcia could. Through her songs, she spoke for them all.

Her thoughts now claimed by immediate problems of money and family Marcia quickly made her way to the cloakroom. Most of the lights had been put out, and the mill had taken on that eerie emptiness she hated. 'What was that?' She stopped to listen.

'Marcia!'

She frowned as she narrowed her eyes to compensate for the semi-darkness. 'God! Shan't be sorry to get out of here!' she whispered to herself as she took a cautious step forward.

'Psst! Marcia.' Her heart quicker now, and still unable to perceive anyone, Marcia hurried into the cloakroom. As she reached out for her coat, a gasp of fright escaped her lips as something fleetingly brushed her arm. It was not a threatening touch; more caring, caressing. Her eyes wide and frightened, they focused on the figure which suddenly loomed before her.

Then, in that reassuring second of recognition, her nervous tension vanished to be replaced by anger. 'For God's sake, Harry! You nearly frightened the life out of me!'

Harry Fensome was a tiresome fellow. During work hours, his job was to transport the cotton from the slubbing frame where it was shaken and stretched to the spinning frames, such as Marcia's. Undaunted by Marcia's obvious anger he slid his arm around her tiny waist, quickly propelling her towards the far end of the cloakroom.

He spoke in a broad Lancashire tongue. 'Sorry love. I didn't mean to frighten you.' His hand reached across to Marcia's face, caressing the silky smoothness of her warm cheek. 'I've been hiding in 'ere for ages waiting for you to make your way up.' His hand lifted the length of hair from her shoulder, then bending down towards her, he ran his mouth suggestively along the curve of her lovely neck. 'I 'eard you singing, Marcia. You're a bewitcher, no mistake about that!'

Marcia had long fought off Harry Fensome's approaches, but she could never recall him ever having been as determined as he was now. She knew that the only way she was likely to get out of this situation was to play him along. He was far too strong for her to fight and that might just lead him into believing that she was all in favour of what he had in mind. All the same, the touch of his mouth along her neck, and the roving roughness of his hands, repulsed her.

Shaking her head free, she pulled herself up to her full height, and pushed hard against his strong broad chest. Harry wasn't much taller than her, but he was as strong as a bull. 'Leave me, Harry!' she told him forcefully, pushing hard against him. Harry, summoning the brute force within him, pushed her backwards against the coat rack, until Marcia was trapped helplessly between the coat rack and him. His voice now harsh with desire, Harry forced his mouth on hers, his probing tongue parting her lips.

Harry was nothing special; a kind of nondescript, square and heavy with regular features and the carriage of a work-weary man. His voice, however, was singularly attractive: caressing and gently soothing, with a passionate vibrancy which belied his ordinary appearance. Now, as he pulled Marcia into him she could feel the hard urgent demands nestling in his loins. Her nerves tingled and vibrated as, horrified, she felt herself responding. His voice was not unlike Curt's, she remembered.

Resisting him as effectively as she could, and alarmed at his persistent strength, she warned, 'If you're caught here like this—you'll be finished at

64

Baines'!'

'There's nobody about, darlin'. I've checked . . .' His excited whisper fanned her face. 'There's only the security-watch . . . an' he's busy supping 'is tea.'

'That may be, Harry Fensome! But I don't want to get locked up in here! I've a family waiting at home.' Marcia was fast growing unsure of her ability to defuse his obvious passions. She began to agitate and squirm, her voice reflecting the hot anger within her. 'Let me go, Harry!'

Ignoring her request, Harry stroked her hair as he whispered, 'Come on love, it won't take long.'

'For God's sake Harry! Get out of the way! I've got to get home!' Marcia was desperate as she sought to release herself from his iron grip.

Pinning her hard against the coat rack, Harry told her determinedly, 'I'll be finished in no time, Marcia . . . the way I feel . . .' He grasped her hand tightly, then guided it to the hardening bulge straining his trousers. 'Feel that,' he whispered, '*that* won't wait!' Hastily, he began to fumble at his fly-buttons, until the hard demanding member protruded from his trousers. Leaning down to blow gently in her ear, he began running the edge of his tongue around the sensitive skin.

'For God's sake, Harry! Let me go!' Marcia was about to cry out when he began to undo the belt of his trousers, and seeming confident that Marcia would succumb, he had no hesitation in using both of his large capable hands for this operation. At once, Marcia seized her opportunity. She grabbed her coat from a nearby hook and ran, the iron-clad clogs echoing a hasty retreat as Harry, still afraid to shout, called in an urgent whisper, 'Marcia! You sod . . . Come back!' Marcia, however, was well on

65

her way to the front gate. The fear which drove her gradually diminished the nearer to the gates she got, and in its place a rising humour shone in her dark eyes. 'From now on,' she told herself, 'I'll ask Big Bertha to fetch me coat!' That bloody Harry! she thought, why is it he thinks he's God's gift? Marcia was well aware that she wasn't the first Harry Fensome had tried it on with—and, no doubt, she wouldn't be the last. Cheeky devil!

The thin evening air pinched and teased at her face, shaping her warm breath into misty gyrating shapes, which hovered menacingly before melting away into the night.

As she passed through the huge iron gates and out onto Cicely Hill, the sharp colourful image of 'Hot Harry', as he would surely be known to her from now on, danced about in her mind. The thought of him with his trousers round his ankles, probably explaining himself to the night-security man who *must* have heard her beating a hasty retreat, caused her to burst out giggling. The humour of the situation, and the cheering fact that it was a Friday night, lent wings to her feet. It was only on reaching the tram-shelter that she was finally able to compose herself enough to board the tram with at least *some* semblance of dignity.

Settling back on the hard wooden-slatted seat, Marcia's mind was already dwelling gratefully on the weekend ahead. She hoped the girls had done their house-jobs, and got Barty Bendall's tea under way—she couldn't be doing with any of his tantrums!

CHAPTER FIVE

The walk from the Tram Boulevard to Regent Street, where Marcia and her family lived, took no more than five minutes—along by the shops, down Penny Street, then in past the Ship pub and over the Brown Street bridge to the little cobbled back street which had been home for Marcia for almost six years now.

Marcia had no liking for this particular journey; especially late in the year, like now. The back streets here were badly lit, with the lamps flickering ominously low, and sending out eerie shadows which made a body feel uncomfortably threatened. During the day, when God's natural light illuminated the darker corners, there was little to fear; but under the disguise of darkness, a body could be forgiven for imagining that all manner of creatures might suddenly emerge.

Marcia shivered. And she fancied it wasn't just from the cold. Night was thickening and all about her dark looming shadows moved in at alarming speed. Drawing her coat tightly about her, she hurried along—the tip-tap of her clogs on the flagstones echoing loudly into the silence, making her even more nervous.

As she neared the bridge just before Henry Street, Marcia was suddenly aware of other hurrying figures some way ahead. Judging by their yelling and laughing, they seemed to constitute a threat—at least to someone.

Some deep instinct disturbed Marcia into hastening to assure herself that what she sensed up ahead was not so. Her anxious eyes pierced the night with fierce intent, as she came close enough to identify the group of youths. Unaware of Marcia's swift approach, they were pursuing a fleeing girl relentlessly. Marcia's breath caught tight in her throat as she recognised their intended victim. 'Polly!'

The young girl fell and stumbled over the flagstones along Brown Street, her long blonde hair bright and conspicuous even in the darkness. The three brash youths pursued her with grim determination. 'Hey Blondie! 'Ave you been broken in yet, eh?' The coarse shout was followed by shrieks of raucous laughter and whistling, interspersed with cries of, 'Just let me at 'er! I'll give 'er a thrill she won't forget in a 'urry!' 'I'll break you in nice and gentle, lass.'

The young girl nervously quickened her step, her soft hair dancing out behind her, the awful fear evident in her face as she turned to assess their progress. The urgent vulgar shouts followed her as she again stumbled in her desperate haste, the intentions of her determined pursuers clear. 'A virgin's nice if you take 'er twice.' 'Let's get 'er boys! Me first,' they called.

They were coming up fast behind her. Marcia's heart thumped and leapt as she covered the few remaining yards which separated her from the loud-mouthed youths. Then, with the blind strength born of desperation, and with no thought for the possible consequences, Marcia threw herself at the nearest lad, grabbing him smartly by the collar. A hungry dog could not have held a bone tighter as she fairly shook him to face her. 'What in God's name do you think you're doing, eh?' All at once she recognised the small dark-haired lad as belonging to the Preston family in the next street.

'It's young Preston, isn't it? Isn't it?' she demanded angrily, noting out of the corner of her eye that the other two had quickly scarpered on hearing her actually *name* one of them. 'Gedoff!' the lad grumbled, his face sinking deep into his collar, 'don't know no "Preston"!' With a quick squirming action he wriggled free and was away down Brown Street before Marcia could stop him.

The smarting fear and indignation which had summoned Marcia's protective instincts towards her child still bubbled furiously as she continued on her way home, where Polly had already hurried inside.

No two houses looked the same along Regent Street. Some, like the Bendalls' home, featured iron balustrades outside, surrounding the concrete steps which led down to the cellar. The front door was reached by mounting a short flight of stone steps. Other houses were flat and just as uninteresting on the outside, with a small front door which led straight in off the pavement. Of a quiet evening, if a body walked by, they could almost hear the heartbeat of the inhabitants . . . the walls were that porous.

The interior designs varied not at all. After entering the front door, you'd find yourself standing in a long narrow corridor, which, because the houses were terraced, was devoid of any windows. The result was a long narrow tunnel of gloomy darkness. The narrow flight of stairs was situated at the far end of the passage where two doors would lead off to the right. The first door inevitably led to the 'best parlour', which was usually reserved for visitors and sitting in quietly; except in the Bendalls' case, where it remained empty and unused. The second door led to the sitting room, which in most cases was the heart of the house. To reach the tiny cold scullery, a body would need to pass through this sitting room, as the scullery was positioned at the outer back end of the house. Out of the back door, leading from the scullery, a steep run of stone steps led to the yard below; and in turn to the cellar and the only lavatory.

There were rumours that the Council had drawn up plans to acquire many such dwellings as the Bendalls', to install lavatories and such like, but up to now, these well-intentioned plans had been confined only to the drawing-board. So Marcia and her family continued to make the best of what they'd got.

What they *had* got was very little—nothing new and nothing to be treasured. Barty Bendall did however have a stalwart pride in the great brass-knobbed bed, brought from the town of Church on a flat-waggon, the very day they had moved in, after the wedding.

Marcia had been none too happy about her marital bed being the very same one in which old Mrs Bendall had departed this world. But no amount of protest or persuasion from her could shift Barty Bendall from his dogged opinion that 'It's a good strong bed! And mind, we can't afford to waste owt!' Dwelling on such thoughts never brought Marcia any comfort. Indeed, it only heightened the sense of futility which lately sought to deplete her loyalty.

Her thoughts now came back to more immediate problems. Marcia's long slim fingers closed around the brown wage-envelope in her coat pocket. One pound, two shillings and threepence, she reminded herself, being fully aware that without a further contribution from Barty Bendall, it would fall far short of their needs because the rent *alone* was ten and sixpence.

Marcia sighed as she approached the front door of No. 7 Regent Street; it was a long, deeply felt sigh, which cast a dark shadow across her lovely face. But the sigh was not born of self-pity for, above all else, Marcia had a realistic outlook on life—always fully prepared to be honourable and to do what she considered to be her avowed duty.

Marcia Bendall was a rare creature of dedication and self-sacrifice. She could lay no claim to worldly goods, but her friends were countless. She bravely fought the elements which cruelly robbed her of everything a beautiful woman should possess. In her relentless fight to keep and protect her family, she had always considered her own needs to be far less important. Her idea of contentment was to be with her children when they needed her. Most of all, she derived the greatest satisfaction out of watching them grow up strong and independent.

There were moments of great anxiety, moments when she wondered whether young Barty would learn to cope more ably with the terrible friction, which in spite of all her efforts to dispel it, often ruled his home life. Moments when she wondered whether she would ever again find the love which now seemed forever lost to her, and, most of all, when she wondered whether Polly, that poor tormented child conceived in the beauty of her and Curt's love, would ever know contentment—or even live to enjoy womanhood.

It would never cross Marcia's mind to burden her loved ones with the turbulent anxieties which so often caused her sleepless nights. All the same, they weighed heavy on her. Polly was the biggest cross she had been left to bear . . . and yet she was the very pivot of Marcia's life. Polly was a child who found it hard to give of herself. She had no friends, no confidantes, and no wish for anything other than to be ever close to her mother. All the love within her had been channelled towards Marcia with such trust and completeness that it amounted to nothing less than an obsession. It was always a great source of anxiety to Marcia, and all her efforts at drawing Polly out of herself to mix with other children her age had been of no consequence. It was sad but true that Polly's greatest friend was indeed her mother. No one would have wished it otherwise more than Marcia.

The anguish which was ever-present in Marcia's heart rose to engulf her. 'I'm only a woman,' she reminded herself, 'and God knows, I can only do my best.'

Marcia fumbled about in her pocket for the long iron key, which lay heavily immersed in the fine grubby crumbs of muck and cotton which lined the base of her pocket.

'Thar' late tonight Marcia lass?' The familiar voice penetrated the cold night air. 'Kept thi on did they?' The light from the opened door of No. 9 spilled into the darkness illuminating the short podgy figure of amiable Ada Humble as she straddled the narrow doorway before leaning down to clatter the empty milk bottles onto the pavement. 'Like as not, that silly bugger Toby'll kick 'em over when 'e gets 'ome!' she laughed good-humouredly.

Marcia couldn't see Ada Humble's face although her own was brightly visible to the other; but her mind's eye had the chubby features in sharp focus. Ada Humble was only forty-one, but looked much older. She laid no great claims to beauty and her demands were few. The great sagging belly which always looked well-advanced in pregnancy had been stretched and shaped that way by the six strapping lads she'd borne her husband Toby Humble.

The podginess of her rosy cheeks gave her a cheery clownish appearance, emphasised by the vivid colour of her round eyes, which shone bright and brown, 'like a good strong brew of tea' Marcia had often observed. But the most surprising feature about her was the red broad-brimmed trilby which had become her trademark. It had been *white* at one time. But after cadging it from the local muffin-man, in exchange for an old pair of pram wheels for his dilapidated wicker-trolley, Ada Humble had dipped it in a dye of her own making. The end result had not been the deep respectable plum colour she'd intended, but a screaming bright shade of tarty-red. It didn't deter Ada from wearing it though. There wasn't a living soul now who could ever remember Ada Humble without 'that' trilby. It was rumoured that underneath it she was as bald as a coot. But nobody could say for sure, as the trilby well and truly covered her fat little head at all times.

She was well-known hereabouts for her good

nature and bustling energy in attending house-births, and laying out the dead; and as she aptly put it, 'this 'ere cherry-red trilby will be the first welcoming thing yon newlyborns'll see—and the brightest farewell the dead 'uns could wish for!'

Folks couldn't afford to pay her for these much-needed gestures, but she was never sent off without a stout bag of flour and a big bucket of coal.

'No Ada love, I weren't "kept on". Not really.' A fleeting picture of Harry Fensome made Marcia break into a hearty smile. 'Got caught up in a last minute tangle,' she said with simple truth.

'Oh, drive me bonkers it would! Working in yon mill! All that noise, an' fluffs o' cotton up yer nose an' everywhere! Drive me right bonkers, I'm telling yer! Still, I expect it's better na' starving.' Marcia knew she meant nothing in the innocence of her remark; but she also knew that Barty Bendall's shortcomings were a matter of known fact to one and all and had been for some time now.

'Aye. 'Owt's better than starving, Ada,' she agreed, returning the other woman's cheery goodnight, as the short bulky figure retreated back into the passage before shutting out the dark night

Feeling for the large hole beneath the sneck, Marcia slid the key into place, lifted the latch and let herself in. Even before she had closed the door behind her, the uncomfortably loud volume of jazz music assaulted her ears. 'Blowed if she ain't got that blessed wireless on again!' Thoughts of the last shilling in the electricity meter drove Marcia down the passage at an urgent pace.

On coming into the parlour, Marcia saw nothing to allay her fears that Barty Bendall's tea was not yet started. Indeed, none of the allocated house-jobs had been done. The ashes from the previous evening lay grey and dead in the grate; it was painfully obvious from the odd traces of burnt-out cinders scattered immediately in front that the coconut matting by the hearth hadn't been shaken either. And there was nary a sign of the table being laid.

Marcia closed the door with noisy ceremony; but even then Polly, who had her eyes closed in blissful appreciation of the music, neither saw nor heard her mother. The big old net-fronted wireless standing in pride of place on the sideboard spouted forth obliviously. Polly, obviously unharmed by her recent ordeal, swayed in time to the vibrating rhythm. She hadn't heard her mother enter the room, and she didn't see her cross to switch off the wireless. Marcia expected that her children should all be capable of carrying out the smaller jobs of house-work allocated to them. She didn't want them growing up lazy or helpless!

'Polly! Whatever do you think you're playing at?' Marcia's voice was reprimanding, conveying her apprehension at the fact that Barty Bendall would be home in just over half an hour, 'Why haven't the jobs been done? And where are the other two?' She crossed to stand in front of the slim girl. 'And whatever took you out in the dark? On your own?'

Polly was not a beauty. Unfortunately for her, the dark captivating looks of Marcia and Curt were evident only in her sister, Florence—an incredibly lovely child. Polly had inherited the Saxon colouring of Marcia's mother, Grandma Fletcher, and in the inexplicable way that Nature weaves her creations, the fair colouring of her Grandma had exaggerated itself, resulting in Polly being almost albino. Her hair, so blonde it was almost white, hung lank and thin about her frail elfin face, and the vivid blue of her large eyes lent an almost ethereal quality to her expression. But when she spoke, the strength so obviously lacking in her appearance filled her voice with determined authority.

'It's all right Mam! They wouldn't 'ave caught me anyway!' She kissed Marcia on the cheek before rolling the hearth-mat up, ready for taking out and shaking. 'I was coming to meet you, but they were 'anging about down the bottom o' Ainsworth Street so I thought I'd better come back. Only they saw me, an' started chasing me.'

A sudden surge of guilt silenced the chastising remark Marcia had been about to deliver. If only that Harry Fensome hadn't made her late, Polly wouldn't have been worried enough to come after her. She took her coat off and hung it on the back of the parlour door. 'You'll not go that way again—promise me, Polly?' Walking over to her daughter, Marcia collected the hearth-mat from her. 'Promise?'

'All right Mam, I promise.'

'Good! Now then, where's Florence and young Barty! There's been nowt done, an' your Dad home any minute!' Without waiting for an answer, she marched through the scullery and down into the back yard, where she shook the mat vigorously. 'There'll be Hell to pay if *he* gets home afore his tea's ready,' she shouted back to Polly.

When she returned to the parlour, Polly had already raked out the dead ashes into the tin-skip ready for transporting to the cinder-heap in the corner of the back yard. 'It's not *my* fault, Mam!' There was no mistaking the indignation in Polly's voice at what she considered to be a miscarriage of justice. Hurrying past her mother and down on into the yard with her skip full of ashes, she muttered, 'That Florence and young Barty . . . they must a' gone to meet 'im! They didn't do *their* jobs!'

'Aye, well. I'll talk to them two later. And don't refer to your father in *that* tone, Polly.' Polly had never really taken to Barty—although she did believe him to be her father. And he in turn had made no real effort to get close to her, choosing instead to let the animosity between them continue to fester. It was a source of anxiety to Marcia, who was certain that Curt still somehow lingered in the lass's subconscious. Florence by contrast had accepted Barty straight off and, because of it, he made it painfully obvious which of the two he preferred. Added to which, Polly's affliction seemed somehow abhorrent to him and, whenever Marcia expressed her anxiety concerning it, he clammed up, or left the room.

Marcia glanced anxiously at the mantelpiece clock, 'You'll have to go to Skelley's Grocers, Polly, there's nowt in the cupboard!' she said as Polly returned. She collected the hessian shopping bag from the sideboard before delving into her coat pocket for the brown wage envelope. Drawing out a shiny shilling piece, she thrust that and the bag into Polly's waiting hands. 'I'm sorry love . . . but you'll have to rush! Your Dad'll be in for his tea in no time. Go on, I'll get things sorted out here.' She manoeuvred Polly towards the parlour door. 'Get gone love,' she urged her. 'Get your dad a large meat pie, if they've got one; and some bacon bits for the rest on us. Not too scrappy neither, tell him, and be as quick as you can lass.'

Marcia sensed the same old protest from Polly. 'Why should they allus have scrappy bacon bits, while Barty Bendall gets a big juicy pie all to himself?' But Polly was perceptive. Her Mam looked fair worn out. She knew when not to press a point, so delaying her exit long enough to place a kiss on Marcia's hot flustered cheek, she told her, 'All right Mam, don't you worry. I'll not be two minutes.' Grabbing her outdoor coat from the stairs where she'd thrown it, Polly scrabbled down the passage and out of the front door.

Marcia started as the door slammed hard with a resounding echo. Sighing heavily, she looked around at the awful state of the place. 'Well,' she told herself resignedly, 'no peace for the likes o' *you*, Marcia my girl!'

She set to, busying herself to straighten things up before the bad-tempered Barty Bendall swept in. 'Clamouring for *trouble* as well as his tea, I expect!' she muttered into the cold sharp air. Not one to dwell at length on any irritating setbacks, Marcia quickly got under way. Gathering up the scattered coconut mats, she carried them to the back door, where, one by one, she shook them with the greatest mettle, expelling the clinging inlaid dust in great clouds which drifted away on the gentle breath of wind. Before replacing the coconut mats, she hand-swept the oilcloth as best she could in the time. Then she quickly started a fire in the clean grate with the newspaper which had served as a tablecloth, replacing that with a

78

fresh one from yesterday, 4 October, 1937. Marcia paused for a moment as her eye caught the article concerning government measures to help the cotton industry as part of their stated policy against unemployment in the North. They had brought in what was known as the Spindles Act— meant to help the cotton industry—including the replacing of old machinery. Now, there was talk of even further help and the possibility of setting up a Cotton Board, to help stabilise prices.

'Hmh!' Marcia thought it was time the government got off its backside and taking these measures was certainly a step in the right direction. 'Not before time, neither!' she said out loud, smoothing the fresh 'tablecloth' down with the flat of her hand.

Buying a daily paper was more of a necessity than a luxury. It served as a tablecloth, fire-lighter, shelf-cover and, most important of all, the small cut-out squares would then be strung on a nail in the lavatory as toilet-paper.

After quickly rinsing the pile of dirty plates and mugs under the tap, Marcia placed them on the table. She placed the bread and jam in the centre, a pot of freshly-brewed tea beside it, together with a little pile of plates and four knives poised delicately on the top. Next she hurried out of the back door, down the long flight of stone steps to the cellar at the bottom of the yard; returning a few moments later with an armful of wood splinters which ensured that there would soon be a roaring fire to greet Barty Bendall.

All the mundane tasks completed in record time, Marcia sank gratefully into the big old rocking-chair by the fire, where she quietly hummed a tune to calm her palpitating heart and restore her flagging spirits. Here, she allowed her gaze to wander round the tiny room, the strong smell of damp filling her nostrils. It was a gloomy, depressing place, devoid of luxury or comfort in any degree. The walls were bare of ornament or picture, and here and there, large spreading patches of creeping damp wound their tenacious fingers in patterns of black and green fungus. The only daylight squeezed itself in through a tiny window, which looked out over the back yard.

The tiny parlour was filled with ugliness. All the good furniture that had belonged to old Mrs Bendall had either fallen to bits, or had been sold to keep the food cupboards replenished. The heavy brown sideboard that stood against the window, the rocking-chair in which she sat, the big square table and the few stand-chairs around it, were pieces that had been rescued at various times from local bonfires and second-hand shops, where better-off families had discarded them. The black horsehair settee, grotesque in appearance, but clean and functional, had been deftly removed one dark night from the bandaged feet of a bright Guy Fawkes destined, like the furniture, to be reduced to ashes. The Bendall children, unknown to Marcia, had spirited the settee away, cleaned and dusted it, then set it out in the parlour as a surprise treat for their Mam, who displayed the gratitude and enthusiasm that the occasion warranted. Marcia minded very much having to accept other people's cast-offs. But no one knew any better than she did that pride was a luxury she could not afford.

If the parlour was depressing, then there was no

hope for the scullery. Little more than a large cupboard, it served as a kitchen. One dark corner was graced by an old iron washing tub, topped by a huge rolling-mangle, which like everything else had seen better days. The cooker had been skilfully bartered from the rag and bone man for some valuable lead piping, which had arrived surreptitiously via the back yard wall, the source of many old items discarded by passing people. The Bendalls often found use for the more practical articles, such as the old plant pot containing a foliage plant that was close to death. Marcia had lovingly restored its health and strength, more from sheer determination than anything else. But as far as the lead was concerned, they could find no use for it except to trade it in.

The deep stone sink had survived many years, but its unquestionable ancientness was now all too evident, in the fascinating network of fine dark cracks which darted all over its much-used off-white surface. A large upturned orange box, completely camouflaged beneath a long draped cloth, served as a work surface, upon which the big old brown teapot and solitary milk bottle now stood. The plates and cups, such as they were, together with a couple of pans and a box of cutlery, held pride of place on the inside bottom shelf. On the same shelf stood an old shoe-box, inside which was kept Barty Bendall's pint mug and personal cutlery. Over on the far wall, above the orange box, Barty Bendall had fixed three plain shelves.

The bottom shelf was reserved for Marcia's collection of plant cuttings. No one else was allowed to water them; they were Marcia's pride and joy. The middle shelf held all kinds of paraphernalia. An old 'Oxo' tin filled with buttons and cottons of all colours and description; a cardboard box which held Barty Bendall's boot-polish and shining rags. There was also a pair of silver framed photographs of Barty's parents, which he treasured above all else, forbidding *anyone* to ever touch them. Nothing else that Barty Bendall owned received the same loving attention as those pictures. Nobody in their right mind would want to stay in that awful scullery a minute longer than they had to, but Marcia had known Barty Bendall to stand in there for long solitary hours, polishing the photos till they shone like sunlight. Nobody dared venture a step towards him while he was immersed in his strange occupation.

Marcia glanced at the clock—ten minutes, and Barty Bendall would walk through that door. Her heart sank at the prospect. So many things fought against her piece of mind that sometimes she felt she was fighting a losing battle herself. Polly's future was ever-present in her thoughts, and though she loved all of her children devotedly, Polly was the one who caused her the most anxiety. Polly would be ten soon; then, before too long, she would encounter that delicate period when a young girl begins to undergo that subtle change which turns child into woman.

Marcia's lovely dark eyes misted over. She prayed in her heart of hearts that she *would* come to see Polly as a woman. Suddenly, in delving into the past, Marcia had inadvertently raised wonderful deep memories that warmed her heart. A dark shadow fleeted across her beautiful tired face. She had peeped through a forbidden door which had been closed for many years now, and which had been opened by the unsettling experience on the tram that morning, leaving her restless and disturbed. The memories which could both exalt and destroy her mustn't be allowed to haunt her marriage to Barty Bendall—albeit a tragedy which should never have taken place.

But then Marcia stopped in her wandering thoughts. What would have become of them, her and the girls, if Barty Bendall had not adopted them as his ready-grown family? She *did* owe him a great deal, even if he had not kept his end of the bargain.

Forcing her attention back to Polly, Marcia wondered what would become of her child. Human relationships were at best complicated, and no one person ever completely and fully understood the measure of another. As a mother, Marcia knew more than most about her eldest daughter; but even within Polly there were depths which proved to be unfathomable. She was an unusual child, obsessed with ideas of grandeur, and driven by burning ambition far beyond her scope.

Within a family, all too often there is one child for whom the mother will weep and fear in those silent early hours. Polly Bendall was such a child. Sometimes she would appear naive and helpless, seeking comfort and security like any other child. At other times a tension, almost evil in its ferocity, would grip her relentlessly. Marcia's brows drew together in a troubled frown. Sometimes, looking back over the years, she often wondered whether it was her fault, her and Curt's? Every so often when Polly complained of 'gnawing' pains inside her head Marcia's greatest fear was that the growth had taken deep root. The thought tore at her heart like no other, and yet the frequent check-ups showed nothing. But something within Marcia made her always uneasy. All she could do was to trust in God.

Looking around her, Marcia sighed, a deep rending sigh. 'Not much of a place to bring children up,' she muttered. Then, raising herself out of the chair, she said in a typically practical manner, 'Ah well, beggars can't be choosers!' She crossed to the far side of the fireplace, where a long set of wooden doors boxed the complete alcove into a cupboard. Fishing out a low flat pair of slippers, she changed them for the clogs which still weighted her feet.

By the time she had checked that there was little Barty Bendall could find to complain about, Polly had returned. 'Dad's coming, Math. And he's got little Barty with him,' Polly told her.

'Right, lass. Is there any sign of Florence?'

'No! I expect she knows she'll cop it when she does get 'ome!'

'Polly! You leave that to me. I've told you. *I'll* be the one to take care of that!'

'I'll bet you don't.'

'Don't be silly, love. Florence knows what her jobs are, and though they're small because of her being so young, she's expected to do them, just the same as anybody else!' Polly decided not to take the issue any further, and Marcia was glad of that.

It took only a few minutes to heat the pie in the oven and fry up the bacon bits. By the time the sizzling aroma had filled the air, Barty Bendall had arrived at the front door. He had young Barty with him. It was a regular fancy of young Barty's to meet his Dad off the Corporation bus at the corner of Penny Street.

As the key turned in the lock, Marcia's breathing quickened as it always did, and her heart turned over with dread at what manner of mood he might be in.

CHAPTER SIX

The instant Barty Bendall entered the room the atmosphere was charged with fear. An involuntary shiver rippled through Marcia's slim figure, and her expressive dark eyes lost their sparkle. In spite of the forced enthusiasm, her voice was devoid of feeling, perceived only by the ever-watchful Polly. 'Hello Barty. Tea won't be long now,' she told her husband. Looking sharply at Marcia, his whole manner bristling, Barty Bendall grunted acknowledgement.

He was not a commanding figure. Indeed, Barty Bendall was quite the opposite, although his slight proud build was ever to attention, never allowed to relax. The deliberate upright carriage countered his lack of height and breadth. There was an undisputed air of discipline about him, which on initial contact invariably alienated people. The eyes carried a hypnotic magnetism which held the glance fast. Set squarely in a pointed ruddy face, the bright green eyes were uncomfortably penetrating and curiously beautiful; almost reminiscent of the eyes of a deadly cobra just before it lunges to kill. His head was virtually bald, with isolated clusters of fair hair protruding from behind perfectly-shaped pointed ears and down the short nape of his neck, which was of a red, leathery texture derived from working out of doors in all weathers.

If Barty Bendall could lay claim to anything commendable, it was his great capacity for working hard. It was a fact about which he constantly bragged; no one, family nor drinking partners, could deny the truth of it. The greatest pity of it all was that the fruits of his hard labours very rarely served to assist his family in their times of need, rendered even needier by his deliberate neglect.

Barty Bendall drank hard, swore hard, and relentlessly spouted discipline and damnation; ruling his often-servile family with a rod of cast-iron.

Marcia dished the meagre food up, while Barty Bendall instructed the children to wash their hands. Then, scrupulously checking them one by one, he directed them to sit in silence at the table. It was during this meticulous routine that Florence chose to arrive. She stood by the parlour door, her cold fingers clutching the handle, her breathing hard and erratic. A deep fearful flush spread through her lovely dark features and her body stiffened slightly as Barty Bendall's devouring green eyes fell furiously upon her. 'Where the devil 'ave *you* been till this time of night?' His voice dared the girl to answer.

'It's all right Barty,' Marcia felt the need to intervene, 'she's not been gone long . . .'

Barty Bendall rounded swiftly on Marcia. 'When I want an answer from anybody else, I'll ask for it! I was asking the girl!'

Florence's voice interrupted quickly as her exquisite dark features drew up into a nervous smile. 'I'm sorry Dad, I went to Blackburn centre to see some friends, and we forgot the time . . .' Her soft gentle voice held more than a trace of fear, and Marcia, looking at her, decided that the due chastisement Florence had earned because of neglecting her house-jobs could wait.

Barty Bendall pointed his weasel face at the girl. 'Go and wash your hands . . . at once! . . . then take your seat at the table!'

A few minutes later, the Bendall family sat solemnly round the table, waiting obediently for Barty Bendall to make the first move. It was more than they dared do to start before him. Even the table seemed to be standing to attention in his forbidding presence. The huge oak table was the very same at which Barty Bendall had sat as a child. It was as old and solid as the house itself, although they were both past their prime, and a little worse for wear. Marcia wondered whether old Mrs Bendall had set the standard by which her inflexible son had unswervingly ruled this house. If so, then she had a great deal to answer for. But the old lady had been long gone and Marcia was willing to allow her the benefit of the doubt. One thing was certain, she thought; the house had probably never played host to such an anxious family as *this*, nor the proud old table ever displayed such a meagre meal.

Barty Bendall sat now, shiny head bowed, tight little hands clasped together, chanting thanksgiving for the pittance before them. Marcia raised her head to peep at him, and even as she felt the chill of foreboding tingle through her senses at his scowling face and manner, she wondered humorously what his reaction would have been had he been aware of Harry Fensome's little escapade. The notion hardened into horror as she fully realised that Barty Bendall would probably have killed him.

Her gaze spread to Florence, who now appeared to be quite contented. She was not the sort to let her father's anger sit too long on her mind. Young Barty's little brown head was almost touching the table in an obedient, reverent attitude. Marcia thought he was screwing his eyes up just a little too tightly to be comfortable. She looked at Polly, and thought on her relationship with the man she believed to be her father. There was no closeness between these two isolated figures, each wrapped in their own special darkness. There was no sense of love or commitment which might bind them together, or soften the loneliness which Marcia knew drove them into themselves.

Marcia knew, and had long come to accept, that he had always been totally incapable of receiving Curt Ratheter's first born child as his own. Yet, inexplicably, he had great regard for Florence, who looked more like Curt's daughter than Polly had ever done. Marcia had given up trying to reason over it, but perhaps the trouble lay in the fact that Polly's personality was far too near Barty Bendall's own for comfort?

For a very long time now, since soon after they had been married, Marcia had instinctively suspected Barty Bendall's deliberate rejection of her daughter. Many times, she had fought to suppress these crucifying instincts, but their relentless persistence dogged her into finally accepting the blatant truth. Barty Bendall and Polly hated each other! And there was little or nothing she could do about it. It saddened Marcia more than either of them would ever know.

As Marcia rested her sorrowful eyes on the girl's fair head, Polly lifted her gaze. Their eyes met, and the warm smiling reassurance in Marcia's face earned an equally warm response from her daughter. Polly's face spread into a happy, loving beam, her large blue eyes eager to capture every ounce of warmth from her lovely Mam.

Marcia knew intuitively that she alone could keep her family together in spite of the undercurrent of hatred which pulled strong and spiteful.

Prominent on her mind as she searched Polly's face was a need for some kind of answer to the deep instincts within her which continued to murmur their terrible warnings. The doctor's reassurance did little to allay these instincts, and her heart trembled at every pain Polly suffered. Marcia often wondered whether she ought to inform Curt Ratheter of her fears, but then she convinced herself that, especially in the light of the doctor's reassurance, she would be using it as an excuse to contact him. That she must never do! He was lost to her now, and she had a family and husband, to whom her first loyalties must go.

A tiny shiver rippled strongly through her, causing the goose-pimples to stand out on her arms. Still sharing the secret companionship with her watching daughter, she briskly rubbed her arms in a subconscious effort to restore warmth.

The communication between mother and daughter was violently shattered as Barty Bendall's clenched fist struck the table in a sudden vicious thump. 'Is it too much to ask!' he screamed, his face tight in an effort to bring his rage under visible control, 'for some respect at the meal-table?' His green eyes flashed, then narrowed as he directed his penetrating gaze towards Marcia, who was visibly shaken. 'Have you no more sense, woman, than to sit there grinning like a fool?' he demanded in a regimental voice; then, with a shrivelling glance at Polly he added, 'and enticing *her* to do the same?'

The darkness in Marcia's eyes threatened to engulf him, as her stomach churned sickeningly at the very sight of his distorted face. She struggled desperately to control the bubble of hatred which touched her heart. For that fleeting second as she returned his glare, Marcia realised how easy it would be to hate him. Then, lowering her head, she concentrated her gaze on the teapot, unwilling and unable to contest yet another of his violent attacks.

As his complaining voice ranted on, memories assailed her, memories of love and happiness, of hope and ambition. They were all in the past . . . left behind, seemingly never to return.

The only ambitions Marcia coveted now were for her three children, who gave the only meaning to her existence. For their sakes, she would endure what she must. As for Barty Bendall, Marcia would not shirk in her duty to him. She had always been brought up to face her responsibilities, and the vows she had whispered before God in the presence of Barty Bendall were just as sacred to her now as they had been on that happier day.

As Barty Bendall's crazy rantings died away, Marcia glanced anxiously round the table. Polly's clenched hands showed white at the knuckles, and where she had bit her lip hard the fine trickle of blood quivered on the mound of her bottom lip. Her bright blue eyes had narrowed to darkened slits as she deliberately fixed them on the newspaper tablecloth. The continuing murmur of Barty Bendall's thanksgivings melted unheeded into the heavy atmosphere. Florence and young Barty had not moved. They dared not.

Barty Bendall brought the thanksgiving to an end, then reached out his short wiry arm for the salt, which he sprinkled with liberal vigour onto his food. No one moved except Barty Bendall himself. The family sat transfixed in the ominous wake of his outburst. His small green eyes swept their subdued faces. 'What's the matter with you all?' he demanded, his piping voice rising to a threatening pitch. 'Eat what the good Lord put in front of you—and be thankful!'

Marcia drew a raking breath, which she released in a weary sigh. She knew without a shadow of doubt that there would be no peace that night. Barty Bendall was in one of his moods. She started on one of her bacon sandwiches with some reluctance, her appetite dissipated beneath the ugliness of the scene. The children took their cue from their mother, tucking into their own meagre platefuls without enthusiasm.

Barty Bendall's eyes reflected satisfaction at their eventual submission. 'That's better!' he said, his voice low and triumphant. Apart from the noisy satisfaction with which Barty Bendall ate his food, the meal was continued and finished in heavy silence, of which he seemed to be blissfully ignorant.

The family waited quietly until Barty had

cleared his plate, after which he wiped the back of his hand across his mouth, and smiled a satisfied smile. 'I enjoyed that!' he said in crisp tones. Marcia could sense him levelling his glance at her, but she deliberately avoided meeting his eyes. Florence and Polly set about clearing the table, after requesting Barty Bendall's permission.

The two girls busied themselves in the scullery, replacing the condiments in the makeshift cupboard before starting on the washing-up. In the parlour, Marcia remained seated at the table, her delicate chin resting lightly on her hands, her glistening eyes filled with reflections of what might have been. Young Barty, quiet and small, lacking the natural exuberance of a five-year-old, sat beside her, straining his weak eyes to decipher the words in his precious comic, while Marcia put a loving arm round his narrow shoulders to draw him close. Barty Bendall sat in the deep rocking-chair, which he had pulled right up to the fire-graze, completely oblivious to the needs of others as he stretched his legs in front of the fire, blocking the heat from entering the room.

Within seconds of sprawling himself out in the chair, Barty fell asleep, his mouth open, and the broken rhythm of his vibrating snores filling the parlour. Marcia fixed her eyes on him, as the blank expression in them gave way to a charging, accusing glare which she quickly disguised when it seemed he might waken.

Listening to the low conversation of the two girls drifting in from the scullery, Marcia closed her eyes, and her thoughts wandered back over forbidden territory. There seemed to be small measure of happiness in her life these days, and she wondered where her path might have led if there hadn't been the children to consider. She positioned herself where she could keep a watchful eye on the girls, for Barty Bendall had instructed them to do the washing-up, and it was best she didn't interfere.

Polly stood arms up to her elbows in washing-up water, which slapped busily against the deep sides of the pot sink as she dreamily dipped the plates in. Looking out of the tiny window across the jagged skyline to the mottled sky, she touched Marcia by whispering in a soft sad voice, 'I wish I was beautiful, like you, Florence.'

How often had Marcia heard those words? And how often had she attempted to console Polly, reminding her that she *was* beautiful . . . to her Mam. She listened quietly to the two girls. 'I wouldn't stay here!' Polly continued, 'I'd take us all away to somewhere nice.'

Florence turned to Polly from her kneeling position by the cupboard, where she was having little success trying to squash the plates into the narrow opening. Her long dark hair swept across one shoulder and dipped gracefully onto the floor. Her dark wide eyes held the same beauty as her mother's, and her smile conjured up the sweeping bold looks of her father as Marcia remembered him.

Marcia warmed to the sight of her two daughters in quiet conversation, and she appreciated the effort Florence was evidently making to be patient with her older sister. In truth, her lack of maturity dictated a lack of understanding towards a complicated creature like Polly. Florence was only seven and hadn't yet reached that stage when she might come to realise that not *all* girls were the same. To Florence, the only natural progression for a girl was to get married to some unsuspecting boy, and raise a family. She had only just begun to suspect that Polly scorned these things.

Polly was still talking in an absent-minded way, more to herself than to her sister. 'I'd use my looks to get what I wanted out of life!' she continued, 'if I was as beautiful as you.' She spun round on her heel, her voice ragged, the tone harsh but determined. 'I'd have money, and a big posh house, with servants! I'd see the world and always be suntanned, and wear expensive jewellery, like the film stars!' Then as if aware of the material element in her wishes, she added sincerely, 'I'd search for all the unhappy people in the world, and make them happy forever!'

As if dwelling on this thought, Polly halted, her arms resting steeped in the now-cold water. Her dreamy eyes intensely searched the sky, before Florence's voice broke through her thoughts, 'But you *are* pretty, Polly! You're the only person I know who has lovely white hair and icy blue eyes. You're like the Vikings we learn about in History.' Marcia blessed her for that. But Polly's response reflected contempt, as she rounded on her sister.

'Don't be daft, Florence Bendall! You're only trying to make me feel better!' Her angry tearful voice rose to an accusing pitch. 'I'm *not* pretty! I'm wishy-washy and thin . . . and I've got a big nose!' Her voice, now grating and harsh, betrayed the festering hate she felt for herself. 'I wish I'd never been born!' she finished with self-loathing.

Marcia rose, unwilling to interfere, yet half-afraid of what these hot angry words might lead to. She listened and waited, absent-mindedly stroking young Barty's thick dark hair.

'You shouldn't say things like that!' Florence whispered, her soulful eyes raised fearfully towards Heaven, 'You never know who's up there, listening!' Polly stopped, calmer now, as she registered the real fear in Florence's trembling voice. The younger girl's words didn't surprise Marcia though; Florence was always pointing out to Polly the error of her tempestuous ways.

As Polly observed her younger sister gazing upwards as if the very skies were about to crash down on their blaspheming heads, she threw her head back and burst out laughing, a rumbustious laugh, which belied her delicate appearance. Florence stared at her in surprise; then with the clarity of youth, she appreciated the sketch she must have looked, and she too laughed. Marcia relaxed as the two of them hugged each other, laughing and squealing; but then, as might have been expected, Polly's raucous laughter unavoidably melted into scalding tears. So tightly was she holding onto Florence that it was only her poor sister's cry which prompted her to reduce her grip. 'Polly! You're hurting me!' Florence's cry was one of anguish.

Marcia pushed her chair back, sorry now that she hadn't intervened earlier. As she swept into the scullery, Polly flung Florence away from her and stormily headed for the door. 'I don't hurt *you*!' she cried, the sobs catching in her throat, '*You* hurt *me*! Every time I look at you! Daddy's pet. Daddy's pet!' she screamed as she tore past Marcia and Florence.

Marcia caught the younger girl to her, 'Go after her, lass, I'll finish up in here,' she told her. As Florence made her way out of the scullery, Marcia rolled her sleeves up, and prepared to finish the washing-up. Engrossed in speculating as to the latest reason for Polly's unpredictable behaviour, Marcia was not prepared for the sharp bellow which gave her a fearful start. The girls had woken him up!

At once, Barty Bendall strode purposefully into the scullery. 'What's all the bloody noise for?' His face red with fury, he continued at the top reaches of his voice, 'Can't a man get any peace in 'is own sodding 'ouse?'

Suddenly, his sharp eyes noticed that the two girls were absent from the job he had set them. 'Where's them bloody lasses, eh . . . where are they?' he demanded in a threatening tone, grabbing Marcia savagely by the arm and propelling her roughly towards the parlour door. 'You get out of 'ere! That's *their* job! I'll not 'ave them leaving their job!' With a flourish of his arm and a vicious glint in his eye, he stalked out of the scullery and headed after the girls: correctly deducing that they had disappeared upstairs.

Marcia stood looking after him, gently massaging her arm where his sharp spiteful fingers had pressed home. She felt tired after the hard day at work . . . too tired for all this bother. Now, she shuddered as Barty Bendall bellowed upstairs, 'Get down 'ere, you two! Now! Unless you want to feel the weight of me belt!'

The girls crept down the stairs; the threat of his heavy army belt across their buttocks was an all-too-real one. So far, Florence had escaped the pain

96

and humiliation of being 'leathered' by this method, but Polly had suffered the ordeal on more than one occasion. Now, as they squeezed past him, he seemed to wait for Polly, who lagged behind; then lifting his arm above her cowering head, it seemed as if he would bring its weight crashing down fit to split her head open.

Marcia sensed the evil in his intent, and moved quickly towards them. As if heeding an inner warning, Barty Bendall lowered his arm. 'You little bugger!' he blurted through gritted teeth, 'don't think I don't know you're the ringleader!'

Polly bent forward as if to defend herself, then she quickly slipped past him into the scullery, where the two girls completed the washing-up in silence.

Barty made his way back to the parlour, where Marcia, thankful that yet another dangerous incident had burnt itself out, was poking the fire. A wave of nausea swept through her as he slid his arm around her waist. 'Give us a couple o' bob,' he said in a low persuasive voice, 'an' I'll be off to the pub.'

Marcia skilfully twisted her body from his sickening embrace. 'I can't!' she told him, 'I've only got the rent and a few shillings, and I'll need that for food.' Her heart sank. What in God's name had he done with his wages? It was Friday night. Been backing horses again, I expect! she told herself . . . owed all his money afore he even collected it!

Barty Bendall pulled himself up to his full height, his nostrils flaring angrily. 'Food!' he laughed coldly, his green eyes fixing her menacingly, 'what bloody food? We never get any proper sodding food in this 'ouse!' He leaned

97

towards Marcia, his compelling glare forcing her to look at him as he thrust his hand out. 'Come on woman! Give us two bob! I haven't got all bloody night!'

Marcia's voice betrayed the awful tiredness which pulled her down inside. 'Barty, you didn't give me any wages *last* week neither. I'm having a real job to manage.' It was times like these when she wished to God they'd never met.

Barty Bendall's face glowered into hers. 'Oh, I see!' he spat out, 'being punished am I, for popping in the pub for a few jars wi' me mates?'

'No,' Marcia said firmly, stepping back from that unnerving gaze, 'it's just that you seem to be spending *all* your wages there these days!'

'What the bloody 'ell's that got to do wi' you? *You* get a wage from the mill and I don't ask *you* what you spend it on!'

Marcia looked away, she couldn't bring herself to look on his face. 'Barty! That's all I have to manage on! You know that! You don't need to ask where my money goes.'

'Come on Marcia, don't be so daft . . .' he whined, his voice growling and scraping in an effort at persuasion. When he moved towards Marcia as if to embrace her, his tone changed to one of ugliness. 'Come on!' he said as he grabbed Marcia's arm, which she wrenched away, 'I shan't shift till you give us a few bob!'

Marcia, keeping her distance, reached into her pinny pocket and gave him a two-bob piece, which he accepted with a grunt. 'This the best you can do? All right. I'll be off then. Don't wait up.' Marcia received *that* remark with the cynicism it warranted. As if she'd want to!

Barty reached for his cap behind the parlour door and wedged it firmly on his head, then without a backward glance or departing word to the children, he strode out of the house.

The welcome departure of Barty Bendall was the cue for the two girls to appear from the scullery, where the washing-up had been finished some time ago. It had only been their reluctance to venture towards the parlour and Barty Bendall's fierce temper that had kept them where they were. Marcia, grieved, knew all too well that the girls must surely have witnessed the confrontation between her and Barty.

Florence studied her mother's face, the naturally tinted skin now pinched and pale, her eyes filled with sadness. The two girls crossed the room towards Marcia, and young Barty, who had sat seemingly immersed in his comic throughout, glanced up quickly in their direction.

'It's all our fault Mam,' Florence conceded, her voice trembling with emotion. 'He's in one of his awful tempers, isn't he?' she continued, placing a loving arm around her mother's waist.

Marcia took Florence's slight hand as she sat down, pulling the girl onto her knee.

'It's nothing to do with you silly! All parents have arguments, you know.' Florence buried her head in the crook of her Mam's neck, raining kisses on her face.

'Well I *hate* him!' Polly declared in a cutting voice. 'I really *hate* him!' The vehemence so often present in Polly's voice startled Marcia. Putting Florence gently to the floor, she directed a concerned look at her eldest daughter.

'Polly! Don't ever say that again! That's your

father you're talking about!' The words stuck in her throat. Then, noting the pout of Polly's mouth, she continued firmly, 'I mean it Polly! I won't have you talking like that.' Her heart ached at the misery surrounding them, and she wished that somehow, the girls—and poor little Barty—could be spared from witnessing such scenes as the one that had just occurred.

'But he's so *awful* to you, Mam,' Polly protested, as Marcia stroked the girl's long silky hair.

'He's not always like that, lass. He can be very kind and gentle,' replied Marcia softy as she kissed Polly's head. But she couldn't remember the last time she'd been able to *talk* to him properly. In fact the Barty she'd wed soon showed his true colours—as soon as six months after their marriage when she was carrying his son. 'He's just got in with a bad lot down the pub, and we always seem to be short of money these days too.'

With the unthinking innocence of youth, young Barty ventured to pipe in. 'That's because Dad's allus getting drunk—and giving our money to the man in the pub!'

Marcia's dark eyes glinted as a vestige of loyalty prompted her to defend Barty Bendall. 'That's quite enough from *you*, fella-me-lad!' she told him firmly. 'Your father's right! Children should be seen and not heard! It's getting dark, and you're straining your eyes . . .' She snapped his comic shut. 'Come on' she said, the tiredness and anger showing in the tone of her voice, 'let's be 'aving you!' Tucking the comic under her arm, she gently levered young Barty from the table. 'Up them stairs you go!' she insisted, ignoring his protests.

Later, when he was washed and shiny, young

Barty pouted as he ambled reluctantly towards the parlour door. As if informing the girls that he wasn't blaming *them*, he ran to each in turn, and kissed them loudly. Then he slunk out, calling miserably behind him 'Goodnight!' Marcia hurried after him, her heart aching with the unhappiness of it all. She hugged and kissed his sulky little face, until he complained that she was making him all sore.

'Goodnight, God bless,' she told him, sending the lad on his way much happier.

As she returned to the parlour to eye the two girls, their stark physical contrast was more marked by their close proximity one to the other. Florence's colouring was rich and dark against Polly's angelic fairness. Anyone who didn't know them would be forgiven for denying they were sisters. Marcia continued to look at them in a searching troubled manner; then, moving towards them, she remarked curtly, 'It wouldn't do you two any harm to get an early night!' She gestured frustratedly towards the fire-grate, 'The fire's low, and we can't put any more on tonight,' she went on.

'Well, *you're* staying down, Mam. So we'll stay as well.' Polly closed in on her Mam, and put her arm round Marcia's slim waist. She walked with her to the chair, where Marcia, feeling utterly drained, sat down wearily. 'Are you waiting up for Dad?' Polly asked sharply.

'No lass. I'll just sit here quiet for a while . . . then I'll be off to bed.' Marcia felt in need of a few minutes on her own, in which to gather her thoughts.

Undeterred, Florence came and sat once more

by her feet. 'Well, we'll stay down as well,' she said decidedly.

Marcia looked first at one, then the other, as a wide radiant smile lit up the beauty of her dark gypsy-like features, 'All right then,' she conceded, 'I know when I'm beaten.'

Pointing over to the sideboard, she told Polly, 'Get the cards out lass. We'll have a game o' Snap. Just one mind you!' she added quickly. She wasn't sure whether she could stay awake that long. Florence jumped up, 'I'll get them!' she shouted, 'I know just where they are.'

Settled in their places, none of them noticed young Barty enter the room. When he spoke, he was already halfway towards them. 'Mam, can I stay down wi' you?' His big brown eyes were red-rimmed and overtired, and his pleading voice dragged sleepily, 'I can't go to sleep yet.'

Marcia's heart felt full as she gathered him into her own tired arms. No doubt it was the noisy words she and his father had exchanged which sought to upset the lad and keep him from his childish dreams, 'Course you can stay down, love . . . I'll take you up when I go, eh?' Young Barty grinned appreciatively. 'Thanks, Mam.' Safe and secure in his Mam's arms, young Barty fell fast asleep before the cards were dealt, and Marcia played best she could, while cuddling him tight. Afterwards, she crept upstairs with him and put him back to bed.

Noticing the fire low and dead, Marcia shivered and hunched her shoulders. 'Time we were all abed,' she told the girls.

'I *am* a bit tired,' Florence admitted, stifling a yawn.

'I'm just freezing!' declared Polly as she rose from the table.

After they had tidied away the cards, the girls followed Marcia upstairs, kissing her goodnight and departing on the landing, for their own room. All of the bedrooms in use were on the first floor; the cold upper reaches of the house were never used, and Marcia could remember only one occasion when she had ventured up there. It was almost like another world, cold and empty, completely cut off from their everyday living accommodation. There was an odd assortment of old Mrs Bendall's artefacts in the upper front bedroom, a busty wire dress-model and such like. Marcia left them be. Altogether, the house, being extremely narrow but very tall, boasted eight bedrooms, four on each level. Barty and Marcia occupied the front one on the lower level; Florence and Polly the second largest; Barty the third; and the fourth was a playroom of sorts, where the children could retreat, being free to make as much noise as they wanted . . . when Barty Bendall wasn't around.

It wasn't a playroom in the sense that it held numerous toys and articles of interest. In fact, the only item of any value in there was the big old sideboard which had priority in the house, as it had been there for years before the Bendall family. Its enormous dimensions intrigued Marcia, for it was too wide to get through the door, and too unthinkable to fit the window . . . so how the devil had it come into the room? Apart from that sideboard, and a scratchy square of coconut matting in the middle of the floor, the only other furniture in the room consisted of two old

103

stand-chairs. It was not a particularly pleasant room, and could certainly never be described as welcoming, or interesting to children . . . or anyone else come to that.

There was no such luxury as a bathroom, and the only lavatory was downstairs, actually outside, situated in the coal cellar behind a narrow partition.

Marcia's and Barty's bedroom contained old Mrs Bendall's double bed, a high profusely-decorated brass monstrosity, which in Marcia's imaginative mind reminded her of a polished dressed-up coffin. Either side of the bed stood a small stand-chair, upon which rested a candle, supported in a brass holder. As in all the other bedrooms, there were no carpets or matting on the floor, except for a small square of matting by Barty Bendall's side of the bed. Beside the chimney breast, there was a single huge built-in cupboard. Marcia often went to sleep to the music of pattering feet, when the mice were on the scamper.

The children's bedrooms were exactly the same, but without the luxury of the stand-chairs.

They each had a low wooden rush-seated stool situated by the bed. The permanent coldness of the rooms rendered them extremely damp, and in the winter months the biting air seeping from outside through chinks and ill-fitting window frames lost none of its cutting sharpness.

Now, with lighted candle, Marcia tip-toed into young Barty's room, tucking his sleeping form snugly into the blankets. Entering the coldness of her own room, she placed the candle in its stand, on the chair. Instantly, the light from its flickering flame spread across the high ceiling, before softly illuminating each miserable corner of the room.

While she undressed Marcia shivered violently as the cold, damp air enveloped her. Then, taking a deep breath, she dived bravely into the iciness of the sheets. Within an hour, the house was quiet.

It must have been two a.m. or later when Marcia was rudely awakened. The front door slammed heavily; then Barty Bendall could be heard swearing and blundering about in the hallway. 'Where's the bloody switch? Where is everybody, for Christ's sake!' Crashing noisily towards the bottom of the stairs, he shouted up, his voice harsh and heavy with the drink, 'Marcia! Where the bloody 'ell are you, eh?'

Marcia leaned up on one elbow, fearing, yet half-expecting the worst. 'Drunk!' she whispered into the darkness. 'Blind plaited drunk again, he is!' A rush of nausea swamped her as he continued to shout her name. This was the time she dreaded most—when he came home the worse for drink and demanded the rights of a husband. If it hadn't been for the miscarriage in the year following young Barty's birth—then only last year the girl she'd carried full term being stillborn—there would now be seven mouths to feed. Both occasions when she had suffered the loss of her babies had hit Marcia hard, but, if the poor little things had survived, then how much harder life would be now, she often reminded herself.

Marcia thanked the Lord that she had not been put pregnant since. But she thought Nature itself gave a body a certain protection—beside which, once or twice, Barty was so heavy with drink that it was not unknown for him to fall asleep on top of her, even before he had satisfied himself of the lust that put him there in the first place! At such times, when he could be viewed as either pitiful or even comical, Marcia would feel nothing but disgust for him—pushing him from her and being thankful at least for small mercies.

There was an almighty crash as something hit the wall in the front room. Barty had fallen against the sideboard, his flailing arms sending the ornaments hurtling to the floor, after which abuse filled the air and Marcia prepared herself for what was coming.

She waited, the thoughts in her mind a whirlpool of disgust and indignation. Her lovely eyes grew morose and dim, as she whispered low, 'A pig. I married a drunken PIG!'

The girls in the other room lay quiet, listening while Barty Bendall swore and shouted abuse at everything in sight. 'Shall I get me Mam?' Florence asked nervously of Polly.

'No! She must know he's drunk again! I should think the whole street knows!'

Young Barty, alone in his room, threw the blanket right over his head, and cringed well under the clothes, screwing his eyes up tightly as if to summon back the security of his shattered sleep.

Marcia lay quite still, as the disgust within her mounted, culminating in a resigned humiliation.

Sighing deeply, she swung her long slim legs out of the bed to stand upright on the bare floorboards. Slowly, she discarded her night attire; no flimsy feminine nightgown for *her* lovely figure, merely practical briefs and thick cotton shimmy. Grasping a tail end of the shimmy in each hand, she raised her arms above her head. The full, firm breasts stood out, their perfectly beautiful shape revealed, tight in the cold early morning air. She threw the shimmy over the stand-chair, then she slipped off the briefs. In all her nakedness, woman was never more beautiful. Standing there, her long thick black hair reaching down to her tiny waist, the full thighs a perfect complement to the shapely slim calves . . . Marcia's beauty was the epitome of womanhood in all its glory.

Shivering, she slithered back into bed where she lay waiting resignedly for the beast now blundering up the stairs, the tears trickling slowly down her lovely face. Her heart thumped with fear: fear of her husband Barty Bendall, and anger at herself for having failed; failed her children, failed at marriage; and most of all, for failing all the happy enthusiastic dreams of her youth.

Steeped in the realisation and misery of her dilemma, Marcia allowed herself the luxury of sending her thoughts back over the years. She was once again in Curt Ratheter's warm tender arms, and her heart sang joyfully. 'Curt,' she whispered, as lovingly as though he might be there beside her, 'I'm so sorry, my love . . . so very sorry.' The comfort she gained from these wanderings, in which she herself had been so determined never to indulge, was short-lived as Barty Bendall crashed into the doorway, where for a long moment he straddled its width. The choking sob caught in Marcia's throat as she mouthed the heartfelt words, 'God help me this night.'

She prayed that her children were asleep . . . that they hadn't been wakened by him. She could bear what she had to . . . but her compassionate lonely heart cried out for them.

As Barty Bendall used her body roughly, cruelly,

Marcia's tears ran fast down her face, and the whisperings of affection she had once felt for this man grew ever colder within her heart.

There was nothing she could do against him. He was her husband and, were she to deny him what he wanted, the ensuing trauma would be even more of a nightmare than it was now. Her opportunity must come, of that she was sure. And, when it did, she would grab it with both hands. Till then, for a quieter life and to lessen the children's fears, she would put up with Barty Bendall. But, oh, she could never again love him—not in the slightest way.

Only once before falling asleep that night did Marcia allow herself to dwell on the possibility that within the year, Curt would be given his freedom. How she wished to God she might be given hers.

CHAPTER SEVEN

Saturday was always a busy bustling time for Marcia. An easy, quiet day would have been a great treat for her after the hard sweat she'd put in at the cotton mill all week. But there was no rest on a Saturday; not with the great pile of washing that had accumulated through the week, and the mats to be beaten; the oilcloth scrubbed spotless then polished till her arms ached, and the beds turned . . . not to mention all the other in-between jobs like getting the meals and seeing to the children.

'Oh Mam—*why* can't I go to the pictures?' Florence's velvet eyes were wide and pleading as she persistently followed Marcia about the scullery. 'I've done all me jobs!'

Marcia plonked the enamel bowl on to the flagstoned floor, kneeling down on the folded rag beside it. 'Florence!' she said, exasperated, 'it's not that I don't *want* you to go to the pictures, lass . . .' She paused to look up once, assuring herself that Florence was actually listening to her, '. . . it's just that I can't *afford* to let you go.' She splashed the floor-cloth in and out of the sudsy water before squeezing it gently and slapping it onto the flagstones. 'I'll tell you what!' she offered enthusiastically. 'If you leave it till *next* Saturday, I promise you without fail that you can all go jazzbanding!'

'Jazzbanding!' Florence's eyes grew even wider, and her mouth fell open in astonishment. 'Honest to goodness? Me an' young Barty too? *We* can go jazzbanding?' She flung herself at her Mam, throwing her arms about her neck and smothering her with kisses and hugs.

Marcia protested at the assault, her lovely face smiling relief that Florence hadn't pressed the point about wanting to go to the pictures. She knew she'd need all the threepences she could muster and anyway, unbeknown to Florence and young Barty, Marcia had already decided that this year she'd allow them to accompany the neighbours' kids on their annual jazzbanding festivities.

'Jazzband Night' was always an exciting occasion for the children. Falling between Witches Howling and Bonfire Night, the ritual was charged with excitement. The children would black themselves all over their faces, necks and any other exposed parts, until all that showed was the whites of their eyes. Even their clothes were dark so as to merge into the night. Then, armed with every saucepan, frying pan or dustbin lid they could lay their hands on, they would take off in groups of sixes and sevens to bang their tin spoons or wooden sticks on their makeshift 'drums' with enormous exuberance, frightening the life out of anyone who might have been foolish enough to forget that it was Jazzband Night, and sending innocent cats and dogs scurrying away at top speed, their tails between their legs, howling and screeching to the accompaniment of the clattering music.

The destination of these spooky marauders was usually the local pubs, where they'd be sure of catching the befuddled drunks on their way home. If luck was with them, they'd be thrown half-a-crown or an odd sixpence, or even a halfpenny . . . it all added up at the end of the night. The money was gladly contributed by anyone who crossed their path, to pay for keeping evil spirits at bay; although the drunks who came upon them were invariably sozzled with spirits already.

A small frown knitted Marcia's forehead as she gently prised Florence from round her neck. God knows they've not had much of a life these last few months! she reasoned. She watched Florence charge out of the scullery towards the parlour, where Polly and young Barty were blackleading the fire-grate.

Straightening up, she tightened the turban which the excited Florence had tipped loosely askew. Then, concentrating on washing the flagstone, she revelled in the happiness of Florence's voice as she relayed the wondrous news to her brother and sister, 'We're *all* going jazzbanding this year.'

'What? Young Barty an' all?' Polly's voice piped high in disbelief.

'Yes! *All* of us. Mam said!' insisted Florence, with more than a little smugness at her first-hand knowledge of the situation.

'Me? Me an' all? Honest, eh? Honest, Flor!' Young Barty was beside himself.

Marcia waited for the inevitable, wondering whether she'd *ever* get the blessed floor washed. As she'd anticipated, the three of them charged madly towards the scullery, 'Mam! 'Ave I to take these two wi' me on Jazzband Night?' Polly obviously didn't relish the idea.

Marcia sighed and leaning back on her haunches she surveyed the three of them. 'Looks to me like you two are all ready for your jazzbanding,' she laughed. 'I 'ope you've left some in the tin.'

'Oh Mam!' Polly protested, devastated, 'I've *not* to take 'em, 'ave I? They don't know what to do!' she wailed, pointing at young Barty scornfully, 'an' he'll just be a nuisance! He'll wet 'is pants or summat . . . an' I bet 'e won't stop crying!'

'I won't! I'm *five* now!' Young Barty was disgusted at the very idea.

'Polly, when *you* first went jazzbanding, somebody had to show *you* what to do! Now don't be selfish, lass. You *can* take 'em wi' *you* . . . an' I'll be counting on you to look after the both of 'em.' She resumed her floor washing, and that was the end of the matter as far as she was concerned.

The children stood for a few seconds, looking at their Mam. There was no doubting that the conversation was over, so they left Marcia to her washing.

Barty Bendall had left the house long before, on his regular Saturday morning trip to the bookies'. Marcia was glad of that, for the house always seemed that touch less gloomy when he wasn't about.

The jobs were soon done, and the meal of hot-pot enjoyed and forgotten by three o'clock. Marcia decided to leave the darning and mending till later. It was with a great sigh of relief that she sat quiet by the fire, listing a few items of shopping for the girls to fetch from the corner-shop. Best get some food in wi' the few shillings left, she thought, afore *he* wants after 'em.

Marcia cast a glance about the parlour. Young Barty, as usual, was buried in his tattered old comic, and the two girls were manipulating their fingers into a game of 'Church and Steeple', seeing who could make the longest story. These were the times Marcia loved the most . . . her children about her, playing and content; and the luxury of a few treasured minutes' quiet when her heart could secretly embrace the memory of her beloved Curt. Curt Ratheter was never very far from her mind even though she knew that the exquisite pain of his memory was a futile, forbidden one.

Marcia drew a deep raking sigh to shake the cobwebs from her mind, before returning to her short grocer's list. Through the passage wall, which divided Ada Humble's considerable brood from the Bendalls' parlour, Marcia could hear the scuffles and shouts that inevitably accompanied the close proximity of six great gangling lads. 'Poor Ada,' Marcia mused, 'she don't get much quiet, I'll be bound!'

The house on the left of the Bendalls' was comparatively quiet, except for the odd occasion when Edith Atkinson *really* lost her temper and screamed at her sister, Sarah, more than usual. The two elderly sisters had lived at No. 5 for many years. They were long sufferers of the Humble family, whom Edith described as 'too bloody noisy by half!' At the time, Marcia couldn't help but feel it was the pan calling the kettle black.

Sarah Atkinson, at seventy-two, was the younger by six years. She was a tiny, shrivelled figure with pretty brown hair and a shawl to match; she was partially deaf and completely blind. The older one, Edith, was a huge hulk of a woman, grossly obese and extremely ugly. Her startling white hair was always piled high up into an untidy fat bun. Marcia had only ever seen Edith Atkinson's hair down once, when she wasn't surprised to see it reaching way past the old woman's thick waist. Edith's nasty narrow eyes missed nothing, and she constantly bullied her handicapped sister, ruling her with a merciless rod of iron. It was rumoured that they were 'worth a few bob' since the demise of the last of their relatives.

These two old women were the last of a long line; as they were both spinsters, hardly likely to marry now, the history of this particular Atkinson family would die with them.

In the other direction, the house next door to the Humble family had been empty since the marital break-up of the previous tenants; apparently, the young wife's close association with the previous landlord of the Ship Inn precipitated the inevitable parting of the ways, and, eventually, the end of the marriage. The house had stood quietly empty ever since; unvandalized and virtually intact, save for the odd mouse or two nibbling at the foundations, and possibly the illegal entry of ardent lovers into the lower basement in order to consummate their avowed love for each other. On the whole though, the house had stayed relatively secure.

It was common knowledge in the street that the vacant house had recently been allocated by the Corporation to an Irish family of whom nothing of any value had been discovered, much to the frustration of busy gossips; Edith Atkinson in the main. Today, being Saturday, was the day on which, according to the gist of bandied-about information, the Irish family was due to take possession. The exact time was not known, but it was reputed to be late afternoon.

Nothing very much happened these days, and life had ground down to a tired old routine of work and worry, so it was understandable, even expected, that every single inhabitant of Regent Street was agog with curiosity. Throughout the morning, curtains could be seen surreptitiously flapping, and an occasional half-hidden movement at someone's door, indicated an atmosphere of unbridled anticipation and excitement

Marcia, being as human as everybody else, was equally inquisitive. She had already alerted the children to inform her the moment their new neighbours arrived . . . so there was a constant to-ing and fro-ing down the passage to the front door. All along the street, other eyes peered through narrow letter-boxes, windows and keyholes. If Barty Bendall had been in, such 'vulgar' behaviour would never have been permitted in his household, but Saturday rarely saw him at home.

Ironically, in spite of the vigilant watch that the Bendall children executed, the Irish family chose to arrive at the very moment when all in the Bendall household were otherwise engaged.

Marcia was just finishing off her meagre shopping list for the waiting girls, and young Barty was seated at the table, having traded interest in the new arrivals in favour of his well-worn comic. His brown eyes scanned it with the utmost concentration, broken only when he felt the need to flick his head back in order to shake his abundant locks from his vision.

Suddenly, the distinct clip-clop of horses' hooves sheared the silence. 'They're coming! They're coming!' shouted Polly, her voice trembling with excitement as she leapt from the chair in a most energetic if unladylike manner. Florence and young Barty, interest rekindled, followed her at top speed down the passage and out of the front door. Marcia looked up from her list; if wasn't easy trying to make a few shillings do the job of a few pounds. Putting her pencil down with a resigned gesture she followed them.

A 'flitting', either into the street or out of it, was always a great occasion. These raw Lancashire folks were very much concerned with other folks' coming and goings. New neighbours moving in or out always supplied a fruitful source of conversation, and on this occasion the entire street had turned out, as if for an inspection of new recruits. The grown-ups filled the doorways, arms folded, women's turbaned heads nodding as they chatted one to the other while the excited screeching children ran to meet the newcomers . . .

who unquestionably accepted the part they themselves played in this all-important drama.

Suddenly, the street was alive and buzzing. The inhabitants of the old terraced houses were as varied and interesting as the higgledy-piggledy houses themselves. The eccentric of the street, old Martha Heigh, could be seen now, standing on her doorstep, stretching her neck so as not to miss anything. Martha Heigh never bothered to wash . . . or so it was told. Anyone, it was rumoured, with even half a nose could not bear to stand within range of the very nasty aroma which constantly surrounded old Martha.

She'd lived on her own in the last house along the row these thirty-odd years, since the death of her poor old father. Nobody knew her real age although folks reckoned it to be grander than eighty. She rarely ventured from the safety of her home, and the only person she had ever allowed inside it was Marcia who, to the horror of her neighbours, often fetched groceries for the old woman. Martha was as short and round as a little Toby jug, and the full-length skirts she wore did nothing to enhance her appearance. More often than not, the skirt was employed as a convenient dish rag. She'd wipe her hands on it, blow her snuffy brown nostrils on it . . . she was using it now to shine up her precious tiny silver spectacles, which were then promptly placed on her nose with delicate precision as she peered to focus.

Her hair stood out in a petrified state of attention and the nervous nodding habit she'd cultivated accelerated with excitement at the appearance of the new neighbours. The wide appreciative grin as she suddenly saw Marcia displayed the blackened rows of teeth; of the naturalness of which she was duly proud. Marcia smiled back, waving her hand in acknowledgement.

Mr Josephs, a cantankerous old busybody, hung precariously out of his upstairs window, reaching out so as to view the whole proceedings. 'Them's an odd sort o' folk!' he shouted, to anyone who might be listening, 'them's not *our* kind at all!' Nobody took much notice of his unwelcome observations, although there was a considerable degree of belly-laughter when the window-sash suddenly snapped, fetching the frame down round his ears with a noisy clatter. After bursting with abuse unfit for the ears of decent folk, he self-consciously scrabbled out from under the window-frame, and disappeared smartly inside. The ensuing curtain-shifting comfortably assured everyone that he'd elected to continue his vigilance in relative safety.

There was nothing grand or elegant in the arrival of the Irish family. The timeless method was the usual set-up. The big bay shire strapped between the shafts exerted no physical effort to pull the trailing wooden cart along the uneven cobbles, for his great strong frame and equally big heart were built for such tasks. This giant, in his gentle calmness, ignored the running, screaming children now latching themselves onto the rim of the cart to laugh and shout their 'hellos' to the new family, who greeted them with equally warm returning smiles.

The shrew-faced driver sat up front, his skinny legs dangling, reins held loosely in his bony hands. 'Come on me ol' beauty . . .' he encouraged in a thin, wiry voice, and the shire, which had been hitherto slightly confused as to whether he ought to stop, responded now to the familiar tones of his owner. The thick muscles in his chest and forelegs tightened up, as he accelerated away again, the iron rims of the wooden-spoked wheels clattering rhythmically across the jutting cobbles. Directly behind the driver sat two men, a woman and a young girl. Beyond that, the furniture was piled high, chair upon table, sideboard upon bed, boxes of linen, cutlery and crockery all balancing precariously on the peak of the confusion of paraphernalia.

The horse continued to amble slowly down the street, contentedly pulling his noisy, colourful load behind him, and the whole street was now wide awake with excitement as he pulled up outside the empty house.

'They don't look as if they're short of owt, do they?' Edith Atkinson remarked rather too loudly. Marcia supposed it was all that shouting at her deaf sister. Marcia leaned against the door jamb, her sad grey dress inadequate against the fresh biting wind, 'You're right, Miss Atkinson,' she said, 'they *don't* look short of a bob or two! I wonder what's made 'em move round *these* quarters?' Then with a rueful half-smile she went on, 'Just give me half a chance, and you wouldn't see my legs for dust!'

'Aye, well,' the big woman said loudly, 'it's too late for *me*. The only way I'll leave this 'ere 'ouse is feet first, in a wooden box!' She folded her sizeable arms in a definite gesture of acceptance, bringing her gaze down to the flagstones in an over-exaggerated sorrowful way.

'Give over!' Marcia encouraged in gentle chiding, 'you'll see *all* of us away down Regent Street!' Marcia laughed, and the old woman threw her head back, opened her wide toothless mouth and gave out a cackling bay, 'You could be right, Marcia lass! You could be right,' she conceded gratefully.

All down the street there were women chatting and children squealing, but above the sounds of their voices, fat Edith Atkinson could be heard loudly describing the scene to her poor blind sister. 'There's *two* men!' She pushed her face in front of Sarah who was desperately trying to interpret a multitude of sounds, 'I said there's *two* men, dear . . . *two*!' Her voice boomed out in an effort to penetrate the wall of deafness.

Marcia thought she looked a comical sight . . . but then, Edith Atkinson was a woman of individual taste and character. She had on an old brown overcoat against the chill air, looking every inch a general.

Her sister Sarah leaned forward towards the source of sound, her mouth open in deep concentration, blind eyes shut tight, as she cupped her ear and drew the angles of her scrawny face into a question mark. 'Oh!' she murmured in a childishly immature voice.

'Yes!' the big, ugly Edith continued at the top of her very adequate voice, 'can't think why there should be *two* men!' She seemed obsessed with the thought. Marcia guessed that her fascination probably stemmed from the sad fact that even *one* man in the Atkinson home was a rare and long-forgotten sight. 'That's very strange,' she continued.

119

Much to Marcia's dismay, Polly was the only child who hadn't rushed down the street to greet the new arrivals. She sat now, on the cold step, watching, observing the whole procedure as a cat might watch a mouse, and her blue eyes missed nothing.

The driver disembarked, and reaching into the pile of assorted articles directly behind his makeshift seat, he drew out a nosebag, stuffed with lush hay, with a teasing amount of corn thrown in amongst it. Sauntering over to the shire, he murmured quietly as he approached. 'There, there,' he breathed gently. Then, drawing level with his head, he slapped the shire affectionately on the neck. 'By Gum, thar' a good 'un! Tha's deserved this.' He slipped the nosebag carefully over the shire's nose and patted him heartily on the withers. 'Just stand quiet while we unload, me ol' beauty.' Then he wandered back to the cart, where the children were excitedly swinging on the rims, and scrambling up the huge wooden-spoked wheels, as the passengers prepared to climb down.

Marcia watched with rapt interest. They were certainly a right odd collection o' folk, she decided. The first to climb down was the woman. She was of a sort never seen round these parts before. A wild-looking gipsy-type she was, with huge black eyes and flashing white teeth set against a brown swarthy skin. Her thick curly black hair, short but profuse, was topped by a black beret leaning jauntily to one side, and casting a weak shadow across her high cheekbone. She was obviously of strong frame, clad in a thick green overcoat which tapered down to heavy knee-length boots.

Reaching up tenderly, she held out a helping

hand to the younger of the two men. The second man gave some assistance. 'All right are you, me darling!' asked the woman of the young man who took a tentative step forward. He smiled back, a weak, vacant smile.

Marcia noticed that he was very similar in appearance to the woman herself; thick black curly hair and large expressive eyes set above high cheekbones. Strangely, though, there was no vitality about him, even though he was obviously much younger than the other two adults; yet not young enough to be their son. Pale and thin, his strained expression portrayed pain and discomfort, drawing Marcia's heart out to him. His walk was slow and careful. The gipsy-lady guided him tenderly. 'Take your time Chris lad,' she told him, 'there's no hurry.' Her lilting voice was smoothing and encouraging as they started carefully towards the front door. For Marcia, watching compassionately, it was an excruciating exercise; she walked every step with him.

Most of the smaller children, usually buoyant and unbearably noisy at a 'flitting', had been strangely quietened by this slow, tender scene. They stood transfixed, captivated by the obvious physical strength of this flamboyant woman, who could so unexpectedly display such love and quiet tenderness, undisturbed and unembarrassed by the bevy of curious onlookers.

Not a word passed the thin tight lips of the pale young man. Leaning on the strength at his arm, he followed quietly, slowly. When he lifted his sad eyes for the first time to survey the crowd, they smiled encouragement at him, some of the grown-ups with heaviness in their hearts and glistening tears in their eyes at the tragic waste of a fine young man.

It was obvious to one and all that the young fellow was in the late stages of tuberculosis. There wasn't one of them who hadn't lost either close or distant relatives to that dreaded disease.

Marcia choked back the emotion filling her throat as his slow-moving gaze met hers. He responded to her sympathy with a smile before he turned away to concentrate on the path before him.

Marcia tried to imagine what he must once have been like. He still retained the remnants of beauty; his thick wild hair suggesting a hitherto boisterous, flirting nature. His large dark eyes were the most beautiful Marcia had ever seen. A strange tide of emotion coursed through Marcia's veins, and she shivered involuntarily as she speculated on the cause which had brought him down so. As if reading her thoughts, Polly asked her quietly, 'Will he die, Mam?'

She could only answer, 'If God wills it, lass!'

The woman unlocked the door, and manoeuvring the frail figure of the young man, they disappeared inside.

Marcia focused her attention on the man in the cart, noting that he was a stark contrast to the young man. He seemed a cold, calculating sort. Polly's voice broke through her Mam's studying. 'Look at 'im, Mam! He looks just like a film-star, doesn't he, eh?' Marcia smiled down at her daughter, then perceiving the very real astonishment at the man's appearance, she laughed . . . a full, raw laugh that caught the man's attention. He looked up quickly, surveying both mother and daughter.

Marcia's full radiant smile held his glance for a second, before he shifted his attention to Polly. And, of a sudden, Marcia felt afraid! In that split second, with never a word spoken, Marcia's mental assessment of this stranger disturbed her deeply. He was a woman's man. A man to be watched from a safe distance. A man who had looked at her in too familiar a fashion.

When Marcia looked up again, the man was busily handing down the contents of the cart to the eager helpful children, who deemed it a great treat to trot back and forth transporting the precious cargo into the house. She studied the man in the wake of her disturbing reaction. He was tall and slim, with long sensitive hands, almost tapered like a woman's. The 'film star' appearance was reinforced by the unreal waxen texture of his skin, and the larded-down black hair which hung over his ears in long straight strands before being swept in towards the nape of his neck by the use of what looked like a shoelace. The thick black moustache rounded his full top lip, before drooping sensuously down either side of his attractive mouth, and the effect was perfectly set off by the small impeccable knot of his creamy silk scarf, which peeped out of the top of a long black overcoat. But the most startling feature of this unusual man were the dark smouldering eyes, narrow and full beneath thick lashes and perfectly arched eyebrows. Marcia was acutely aware of his hypnotic magnetism. Without uttering a single word, he had spoken volumes.

' 'Andsome bugger, i'n't 'e?' Ada Humble was still chewing her jam-buttie, her bright red trilby tipped slightly back at a cheeky angle. 'Bet 'es caused many a stir in 'is time, eh?' she asked, searching Marcia's face for an answer. Marcia's features drew up into a frown, as she replied quietly, 'Yes . . . many a stir, I expect.' Her hand fell gently on to Polly's blonde head, where it stroked the hair thoughtfully. 'I think you'd better come inside lass . . . it's right cold now.'

'Oh no, Mam!' Polly protested, 'I'm all right, honest!' Marcia looked once more at the tall, virile man, a feeling of curiosity engulfing her. 'Very well, lass . . . but don't you sit out here too long.' She turned towards the door and went quietly into the house.

The cart was soon emptied, and the tall slim man followed the last of the children into the house.

The young girl left by the cart was a small bright creature with a happy, friendly face. Her hair had the same coarse texture as that of the young man's and the woman's, but the colouring was a light mousey hue, weaker and less striking than that of her companions.

Marcia halted in her retreat down the passage as she heard the girl address Polly in soft lilting Irish tones. 'Isn't he just a beautiful horse?' she asked.

Polly appeared to be self-conscious as she answered shyly, 'Don't know much about horses.'

'Ah, that's a shame,' the girl returned sympathetically, taking a bold step forward. At this Polly stood up, flicking her long blonde hair back over her shoulder.

'What's his name?'

'Come and look . . . I'll introduce you, if you want me to!'

As Marcia paused to watch the two of them head down the street towards the wagon a ripple of pleasure spread through her on hearing Polly actually respond positively to an offer of friendship, however vague.

'That's a grand little lass,' Ada Humble commented as she poked her head round the iron railing to gawp at Marcia, now making her way back up the passage to the front door, 'might be a little friend for your lass Polly.'

'Oh, I hope so, Ada lass,' Marcia said as she smiled warmly at the little woman, 'I do hope so.'

CHAPTER EIGHT

'Come on woman! 'As ta gone to the bloody pit for that coal?' Barty Bendall's voice grated through the air, loud and accusing. 'I'm still waiting on me sodding breakfast!'

Groaning, Marcia straightened up from her task, fetching her hand across the small of her back and rubbing the ache there. 'There's no blessed peace nowhere!' she sighed, 'Not even down in the coal cellar!' Now she turned towards the flight of stone steps which reached up from the back yard to the open scullery door, clicking her tongue against the roof of her mouth as she thought how thoroughly insensitive that husband of hers could be.

Barty Bendall's piercing glare cut through her, as she lifted her lovely dark eyes to his glowering face. Leaning on the door-jamb, his best boots half done up and the long tail of his khaki shirt flapping in the cold breeze, he told her, 'You know right well I've to be off early this morning! Promised to 'elp a mate in 'is flitting. Where's me bloody breakfast, woman!' His face was harsh on the eye, coarse and untidy, with the bristly whiskers unshaven and the boozy features distorted by a threatening scowl.

Marcia wondered why he bothered to cover up the fact that he was off to the bookies', for she knew right well where he was going, and what made it even *more* insulting was his awareness that his regular trips to the place of betting were common knowledge to his family. There were so many things she could have said—so many truths that filled her mind to condemn him. She could easily have voiced her thoughts to rile him and to challenge his lies, but to what end? It would only finish with him flinging back at her his wild, wounding abuse. Barty Bendall could wield his spiteful mouth like a weapon, battering and destroying everything within hearing and, with a man like that, there was only one of two roads a woman could take—especially when there were three young 'uns involved. Marcia believed that in choosing not to antagonise him she was doing the right thing.

'Your breakfast's on the trivet aside o' the fire,' she informed him, the quietness in her voice seeking to placate his vicious temper, 'an' there's a brew o' tea in the hearth. I expect it's curled up be now,' she muttered at his departing figure, 'but it's all there is, Barty Bendall, so you'll take it or go wi'out!'

As she came back through the cellar doorway, her voice lifting into song, the draught from her

126

movement extinguished the candle's flickering halo of light and plunged Marcia into pitch blackness. Frantically searching in the huge pinny pocket for matches, she then gingerly located the wet warmth of the candle-wick, and quickly fed the flame to it, breathing a sigh of relief at the ensuing illumination. An involuntary shiver trembled through her body as the scarpering patter of feet alerted her to the company she was keeping. She knew there were rats in the cellar! She'd seen them many a time scurrying and foraging in the wood-pile . . . 'Wouldn't fancy *them* blighters runnin' at me legs!' Marcia whispered fearfully. She would have scampered away herself, leaving them to the cellar and their futile foraging, but she had to scrape a bucket o' coal up somehow. It was a dirty, thankless task and one which Marcia despised. The wooden cellar door had long ago served as chopped kindling to warm them on a cold night, and where it had once kept the elements from invading the dark cellar, there was now just an open space through which passed the best and worst of all weather.

During the night, which Marcia had spent fitfully, waking and sleeping in spasmodic periods, the heavens had opened to deluge the earth with relentless rain. Marcia had lain silently in old Ma Bendall's big brass bed, watching the rain through the open curtains as it spat and drummed against the window panes on the crest of a noisy gleeful wind, when the strangely comforting sound of the water as it spilled over the troughing above the bedroom window somehow made the rhythmic grating of Barty Bendall's snoring more bearable.

Marcia's back and shoulders ached and pulled

as she scraped up the coal. 'That downpour hasn't made *this* job any easier!' she muttered. The rain had flooded into the cellar, washing through the smattering of coal, and spreading it thinly across the floor. But Marcia was in no hurry to climb back up the stone steps into the scullery; at least not until she was sure that Barty Bendall had departed the house. Of a sudden she was quietly laughing, saying to herself, 'Hmh! Must be coming to summat when I prefer the company of *rats* to that of my own husband.' Then, 'On second thoughts, Marcia lass . . . happen there ain't much difference, eh?'

By the time she'd collected a scanty half-bucket of damp coal Marcia could still hear him clattering and banging about through the open scullery door, so she busied herself restacking the kindling wood away from the damp hollow where the rain seemed to have settled. That done, she set the coal bucket by the open doorway, and rested herself on the rusty old chest that had belonged to old Ma Bendall.

A whimsical smile shone gently in her strong dark eyes as she thought deeply on her present station. Here she was, Marcia Fletcher as used to be, hiding down in a dark rat-infested cellar, waiting for her husband to leave the way clear for her to return to her own scullery! Yet, even in the light of her humorous recognition of the situation, her smile was tinged with sadness. 'If it were only possible to turn the clock back,' she whispered slowly, 'I'd do it right here and now!' Then, almost at once, she knew how futile such a thing would be, because she had done what commonsense had dictated at the time, and she must live with it now.

Treasured images of the homely little house in Stoneygate Street, Preston, where she and Curt had raised their lovely baby girls, filled her mind and heart with nostalgia too painful to bear. Tears welled up in her eyes. 'Oh Curt! Curt my darling, where are you now . . . at this very moment? Are you thinking of me? Of your lovely daughters? Or has our long final separation erased us all from your mind?' She thought deeply on that particular possibility, finding it so devastating that her mind quickly rejected it as being totally inconceivable. But then, she reminded herself, there could never be any future in reliving memories which were after all best forgotten . . . and yet, she could no more forget Curt and their wonderful love than she could forget to breathe.

A feeling of weariness settled on her. The past week had been hard, harder than most. One of the lasses at the mill had been taken badly, and as was always the case in such an event, she and the other hands had been called on to keep the lass's spinning machine going. They got paid no extra, but looking after a sick mate's machine at least meant her job would be there for her when she returned. While *they* were running it for her, the machine wouldn't be allocated to a newcomer. But it was backbreaking work which taxed them to their limit.

Marcia felt more cheerful as she thought of Harry Fensome. He'd spent the whole week skulking and scowling, like some dog deprived of a juicy bone; and on the two occasions she'd attempted a friendly forgiving conversation, he had stalked away, pouting angrily. 'Men!' she muttered, giggling to herself at the knowledge that the security man *had* challenged Harry Fensome . . . and according to the story which had spread through the mill with alarming speed, Harry had been hard put to provide a suitable explanation as to his obvious state of undress! The humour of the situation aside, Marcia firmly vowed that never again would she allow herself to be manoeuvred into such a situation. There were any number of such men, who were not to be trusted.

Another one was Peter Revine, the man of the Irish household that had moved into Regent Street the week before. There was something about him, Marcia had decided, that was . . . dangerous! He'd been along to the house, together with his flamboyantly attractive wife, Rosa, and their daughter Bridget. The purpose of their visit was to introduce themselves, as was the rule, and to invite the Bendalls to a 'moving in' party. The party was to take place just as soon as the woman's brother, Chris, was feeling up to receiving company. On this particular issue, it seems the folks on Regent Street had got it right. The poor young fellow *was* smitten with tuberculosis. Having no other family than his sister, Rosa, the natural arrangement had been made that she nurse him to the end. It was all very cruel to Marcia's mind.

Marcia had graciously thanked them, but the presence of Peter Revine had unsettled her. Something about him created an inexplicable trauma within her, that she neither understood nor recognised. All she *did* understand was the rush of relief on closing the door behind him.

She was thankful, however, for the strong bond of friendship which had developed between Polly and the young Irish girl, Bridget. But even the contentment she felt at Polly having found a friend was marred by the fears which gnawed ceaselessly at her unsettled peace of mind. In a determined effort now to put her worries aside Marcia sighed heavily, sliding herself down from the discomfort of the old tin chest.

Even though she'd been up, cleaning house since early light, there were still the beds to be seen to, she reminded herself. She collected the tight bundle of kindling wood and dropped it into the coal bucket. She hadn't forgotten either that today was the day she'd promised to treat Florence and young Barty to the picture house, and in a rush of foolish generosity after Polly had been subjected to one of Barty Bendall's violent tantrums, Marcia had made *her a* promise too . . . she would take her to the slipper baths for a special treat. She had since calculated that this Saturday morning's extravagance would mean tighter belts through the rest of the week, 'No matter,' she told herself stoutly, 'a promise is a promise and besides, Marcia Bendall, a little treat won't do *you* no great harm neither!'

'Mam!' Polly's anxious voice swept the yard, 'are you in the cellar?'

She slid the crook of her arm under the bucket handle. 'Good! He must 'a gone,' she said to herself. 'All right lass, I'm just coming up,' she called out reassuringly to Polly.

Polly had already sided the table, and was just putting the cups away. 'Eager to be off to the slipper baths are you, lass?' Marcia asked warmly.

Collecting the bucket from Marcia's arm, Polly exclaimed, 'Oh Mam! We haven't been to the baths for ages and ages!' She wrapped her free arm

131

round her mother's slim waist, her blue eyes bright and excited. 'And thanks for letting Bridget come, Mam,' she concluded, with a quickly delivered kiss.

'Young 'uns still upstairs, Polly lass?' Marcia asked, leaving her daughter to stand the bucket against the fireplace while she went to wash the coal-dust and black slime from her work-worn hands.

The early fire she'd lit for Barty Bendall was dying in ever-decreasing spurts of enthusiasm. 'Don't put any more coal on,' she told Polly, 'we need to save what we can, and there'll be nobody in the house for a few hours . . . and we'll make our way straight to Grandma Fletcher's after the slipper baths.' Her lovely face broke into a warm smile as she perceived Polly's pleasure at her remark. 'You love your old Grandma, don't you lass, eh?'

Polly let the bucket clatter to the floorboards, her face aglow with pleasure, 'It's looking like a right grand day, in't it Mam? Shall I go and see if Bridget's ready?'

Marcia supposed she'd better be getting a move on herself as it was already quarter to nine. 'Aye, go on then, but we've a good half-hour yet afore we need to start off.'

As she made her way towards the parlour door, Polly mentioned, 'The young 'uns went down to the toffee-shop to get some liquorice for the pictures . . . 'ave I to fetch *them* an' all?'

'I think you'd better, while I make sure everything's left tidy,' replied Marcia.

Hearing the front door close behind Polly, Marcia looked around the tiny parlour, mentally reliving the scene of the night before. As had

132

become the regular Friday night pattern, Barty Bendall had gambled away his wages. He'd been in a real bad mood on arriving home, and as usual had sought to take out his drunken vengeance on Polly but this time, Marcia had managed to get the children and herself quickly off to bed out of his way. Her heavy heart had been considerably lightened by the fact that he'd been so drunk on coming to bed that he had fallen quickly into a deep stupor. 'Will he never change for the better?' she sighed, crumpling the dirty newspaper from the table and replacing it with a clean one.

Lately the papers were filled with the anger of the Jarrow men and further news of how the depression was deepening in the North. 'Especially in *this* house—if I were to let it!' muttered Marcia, 'which I won't!' then she slid the sheets of newspaper about until the whole table was suitably covered. Afterwards she stood back to admire her handiwork, thinking how fortunate they were to afford a daily newspaper.

The rattling at the front door was easily recognisable. Marcia knew it to be the style of Ada Humble's knock. Hurrying up the passage to open the door, she greeted Ada with her usual warmth. 'Hello, Ada lass . . . out on the steps early, aren't you?' Ada Humble's bright red trilby was tipped forward at a sharp angle; Marcia at once perceived the implications of *that*! Ada's mood would have to be a dark one, and although Marcia felt in need of cheering up herself, she led the way back into the little parlour with an encouraging smile. 'Come through lass. There's a brew o' tea still warm in the pot.'

'Nay Marcia. It's kind o' you, but it's a gabbin' as

I need just now . . . somebody I can turn a thing o'er with, for I'm all out o' me own patience. I've supped tea till it's flooded me right thinking, an' I *still* can't see what's best, lass . . . an' that's a fact!'

Curious, Marcia gestured for Ada Humble to sit down on the chair by the fire, at the same time fetching a stand-chair out to sit the other side. By the look on poor Ada Humble's face, and the fact that she'd actually refused a brew o' tea, Marcia sensed the agonizing of the kindly little woman, 'You're all right Ada,' she assured her, 'the children won't be back for a while. You can bide quiet; there's only the two on us.' She leaned forward to pat the dimpled hand reassuringly. 'What's to do lass, eh? Is it your Toby come off that contraption of his again, eh?' Marcia had lost count of the times Ada's man had come a cropper on his rattling Saucy-Sally. It wasn't even as though he could *ride* the blessed thing! Toby Humble was a big blustering fool, with a kindly heart and an appetite for strong booze unrivalled throughout the length and breadth of Blackburn, even by Barty Bendall.

Marcia visualised how he'd walk his Saucy-Sally down to the pub of a night, leaning heavily on the battered frame in order to support the results of the previous night's boozing. Then when the pub turned out, there he'd be, making his usual futile attempts to cock an unsteady leg over the elusive saddle! Poor old Toby Humble would be the first to admit that the iron monstrosity had him at its beck and call, and could do with him as it liked. Drunk as he was by turning-out time, merely leaning across the Saucy-Sally and directing it homeward just wasn't enough. His two legs were

134

totally incapable of stepping one afront o' the other, and his ordinarily poor sense of direction was considerably worse for the drinking.

His good-natured but equally drunk mates would wait awhile, amused and entertained by this nightly ritual; then tucking their flat caps under their arms for extra concentration, they would step in to hoist poor drunken Toby on to the broad accommodating saddle. After fastening his hands and feet in the right position for propelling the great iron contraption, they'd launch him down the cobbled road at a gradely, death-defying pace. The shouting and cheering would be loud and encouraging. 'All right, Toby?' 'Are thi' ready then?' 'Keep thi' arms straight for'ard lad . . . bike knows its way!' Then with an almighty heave, they'd send him on his way, the Saucy-Sally riding the uneven cobbles with hair-raising speed, and poor old Toby already screaming wildly for Ada.

'Ada! Where are thi' lass! Get me off! . . . GET ME OFF!'

Ada Humble and her eldest lad, Blackie, would be on the sharp lookout for Toby's arrival. On hearing his frantic cry they'd rush out and save him. For if they weren't there to catch the poor drunken soul, he would unquestionably keep on until the deep wet cut or a solid brick wall helped him off. But even though Ada Humble and his lad, Blackie, had both offered to meet him from the pub, he'd have none of it. 'Fetch me 'ome like a common drunk! Tha'll not show *me* up, I'm tellin' thi'!' So every night he enacted his dangerous cabaret trick, and every night as regular as clockwork his faithful, loving woman and his big strapping twelve-year-old would wait nervously for

135

the frantic cries which got the whole of the street folk from their beds.

Marcia couldn't think what else might be worriting little Ada Humble; she was usually a laughing easy-going woman, who'd learned to give life a good shaking in return for every bad nudge it dealt her. Her every waking moment revolved around her man and her six great gawping lads; and even though a fair wedge of Toby's wages went on booze, he wasn't one to gamble, so they seemed to manage well enough. 'If it's not Toby,' Marcia ventured quietly, 'what is it as weights you down, lass?'

When Ada Humble lifted her head to focus on Marcia's concerned face, her chubby features glowed as fiercely bright as the red trilby atop her head, and the glittering eyes, brown and sharp as a weasel's, blinked back the full wet tears which trembled on the sparse lower lashes. 'Does ta' know, Marcia . . . thar' the only real friend a body 'as in this whole wide world.' She brought a podgy hand up to wipe away the tears, which finally spilled over onto her dimpled cheeks. 'There's nary another soul as I could confide in . . . an' for the life o' me, for all I worship the ground 'e walks on, I couldn't fetch mesel' to tell my Toby . . .'

Her sharp brown eyes grew round and fearful at the very thought, and she squeezed Marcia's hand hard. 'It's not that I'm afeard of 'im for *mesel*! It's just that 'e'd tan the bloody arse off young Blackie . . . an' I'm not saying as 'ow 'e wouldn't deserve it mind you! . . . 'e *would*!, 'e *would*, an' that's a truth!'

Marcia had to conquer a deep instinct to gather her agitated friend into her arms, but she could

136

read Ada Humble well enough by now to know that such a display of sympathy would only serve to embarrass her. Instead, she simply asked, 'Your Blackie been up to some mischief, has he? I'm sure it can't be all *that* bad, Ada! He's not a roughneck isn't your lad!' She'd always thought young Blackie to be a decent, straightforward sort.

Ada Humble smiled in sharp confirmation of Marcia's observance. 'Oh no, Marcia lass! He's *not* a roughneck, no indeed! *Never* a roughneck!' The red trilby bounced in agreement. 'Allus a little gentleman, my Blackie,' she declared stoutly, 'allus a little gentleman!'

Marcia was growing increasingly confused, 'Well, what's to do then? What in heaven's name has the lad done to cause such an upset?' she demanded to know.

Ada Humble sighed wearily, making her sagging belly shudder. 'I've 'ad that Officer fella round! More than once an' all, Marcia lass! Kept warning me like I was some criminal, saying as 'ow I'd 'ave to go to court if I didn't see to it.' Her sharp weasel eyes glittered pleadingly, as she continued, 'Court! Did you 'ear *that*, Marcia lass? Court! An' me never set foot in such a place in all me life.'

Marcia supposed she was expected to know straight away what the poor demented soul was going on about, but for the life of her, she couldn't fathom it all out. 'Ada, what "Officer" fella? An' what is it you've to see to?' she insisted.

Ada Humble looked at Marcia with a surprised expression. 'Well, what does thi' think? Our Blackie's been 'iding fro' school. Running off an' 'iding!'

Marcia was genuinely surprised. 'Blackie? Been

missing his schooling on purpose?'

'Oh aye! According to this high an' mighty Truant Officer fella, 'e's been doing it for a while now. It's the third time that bullyin' Officer's been to threaten me . . . been worriting me for a few months now. I telled our Blackie! Thi' dad'll skin thi' alive, I telled 'im! But the lad knows 'is silly ol' Mam'll not split on 'im . . . not one for tellin' tales, I'm not . . . no, I couldn't fotch mesel' to do that, Marcia lass—not at all!'

Marcia knew how serious the matter was. Her thoughts harked back to other examples that had been made of folk who were slack in seeing their children to school. These Authority narks were bad 'uns when it came to the children missing their lessons . . . and the authorities in this particular area took an exceptionally tough line on such miscreants. Marcia knew without a doubt that Toby Humble, for all his good nature, *would* skin the lad alive if he knew. He was right strict about the six Humble boys attending school, allus had been.

'Tha'll get a better education than me an' your Mam ever 'ad! *I'll* see to that,' he'd tell them, showing pride and involvement in their every little achievement.

'Oh Ada . . .' Marcia didn't wish to alarm her little friend any more than she already was, but *something* would have to be done. 'If he *keeps* missing school, you'll be left with no choice *but* to tell his Dad. What's frightened Blackie off school anyroad? He allus used to enjoy it.'

'Aye, thar' right, Marcia lass, 'e *did*! But all of a sudden, 'e's gotten this notion in 'is 'ead that now 'e's coming up thirteen, 'e should be working

138

alongside 'is Dad, an' fotching a few shilling 'ome to 'is loving Mam . . .'

Growing quiet for a while, Ada searched Marcia's thoughtful face. ' 'E'll not listen to a word I say! *Nowt* I threaten 'im with seems to bother 'im!' Reaching underneath the brim of her red trilby, Ada Humble drew out a long brown envelope which she stretched nervously towards Marcia. 'See thi' 'ere, Marcia. See this 'ere 'fficial looking letter? Well, thi' knows a poor body like mesel' never acquired no cleverness; never found no use for that there reading lark!' She nodded anxiously at the brown envelope, as she went on, 'I *knows* it's from them Schools' Officers . . . 'cause nobody ever writes to me. It's common knowledge 'ereabouts that I can't read no words . . .' The gentle pleading way she covered Marcia's long fine hand with the stout chubbiness of her own revealed the fright she had experienced on receiving such a letter. 'Go on lass; read it to us . . . an' God 'elp us all!'

'Don't worry yoursel' so, Ada love,' Marcia reassured her, her heart filled with compassion at the sight of poor little Ada Humble, frightened half out of her wits. 'You know how these Town Hall folk just love to put the fear of the Lord in a body.'

Taking the outstretched letter, she opened the envelope and withdrew the official-looking printed document. At once Ada cast a nervous eye over the upside-down emblem at the top of the page, 'I *knew* it!' She grabbed the brim of her red trilby and pulled it down hard over her forehead, as if to ward off the shock. 'It *is* from the Town Hall! What does it 'ave to say, bless us, lass!' Her voice trembled with fright.

Marcia cast a speedy eye along the wording, and with each line, her heart turned somersaults until she felt almost as desperate as Ada. She was acutely aware of her friend's increasing anxiety. 'Marcia! What's it say lass? . . . What's it say?'

Feeling physically sick, but as was her way, Marcia swallowed the hard knot of fear straddling her throat, and somehow gathered composure enough to smile reassuringly into Ada Humble's cherry-red face. 'Ada . . .'

'Go on Marcia lass! What 'ave you to tell me?' interrupted the little woman stoutly.

Marcia was frantically searching for an easy way to impart the information which had shocked even her, but there was really only one way to tell it. 'You'll not like this, Ada,' she said softly, 'you were right, lass, it *is* from the Schools' Officers. It lists all the dates of Blackie's absences from school, an' it tells as how it's strictly against the law for the children not to attend their place of learning.'

'Well, I knows all *that*, lass. They've told me all that 'afore!' The sharp brown eyes pinned Marcia's glance and held it fast. 'I'm sorry lass . . . go on . . . what else do they say?'

Marcia took a deep breath, her heart going out to the dear little figure before her. 'They've summoned you and Toby to court, Ada.' There! It was said—but she wished to God it hadn't been.

Even the bright red trilby seemed to drain of colour as the chubby face grew pale and hung loosely. 'Court! Court, did you say, Marcia lass?' she whispered. 'Nay!' She lifted her face to look at Marcia intently. 'You're never tellin' me we've to go to a *court*!'

140

Marcia's throat felt too tight to speak. She knew what such a thing meant to Ada: indeed, her *own* considerable strength might have faltered at such a prospect. She'd only ever *once* seen the inside of a courtroom, and Ada's letter had brought it all back; all the terrible pain and heartbreak. She could see it all in her mind's eye as if it was yesterday. Deliberately shutting the insistent image of Curt Ratheter from her mind, Marcia was convinced that the Humbles' court visit could never be so traumatic, although she doubted her ability to convince poor Ada of that fact.

'It'll be a harsh warning . . . to frighten you and the lad, so don't worry none,' she said comfortingly.

'You mean the *lad's* got to go to court an' all?' That seemed to be an even bigger shock than Ada herself having to go. 'They can't want an innocent young lad to step foot inside a court!'

'Yes Ada, they want all *three* of you to attend.'

'Oh Lord, Marcia lass! 'Ow will I manage to tell my man as 'e's to go to a court over summat 'e knows nowt about! 'Ow in the Lord's name will I tell 'im *that*, eh!' Getting to her feet, Ada Humble paced up and down the oilcloth in an extreme state of agitation, rubbing her hands together and moaning to herself.

Marcia felt helpless at her acute distress, and moving to wrap a comforting arm around the podgy shoulders, she told her, 'Well, at least you've plenty o' time to think about how you'll tell your Toby, because the date they've fixed for the hearing isn't till the end of January. It'll be all right, Ada lass, you'll see.' What empty foolish words they seemed, Marcia thought angrily, wondering why it was that mean-minded officials could wreak such awful anxiety amongst ordinary law-abiding folk.

Surprisingly though, Marcia's calm words appeared to placate Ada Humble, as she stuffed the letter back under her trilby, and released herself from Marcia's arm with a grateful glance. 'You're right lass! That gives me a couple o' months an' more! I'll find a way; an 'appen if young Blackie keeps regular school till the court-case, they'll change their minds, and cancel the order?' She seemed pleased at that possibility, although Marcia wasn't convinced. She would have said so, but Ada rattled on, 'I'll show this 'ere letter to 'im! That'll do it. 'E'll not want to get 'is old Mam in no bother!'

She straightened her fat little shoulders defiantly. 'I'll not let the blighters frighten *me*, eh, Marcia? Med o' stronger stuff, aren't we, lass?'

Marcia suspected the bravado was all a show, but if it comforted Ada, then she'd play along. 'That's the spirit, Ada. Don't let 'em frighten you!' Yet in spite of that defiant exchange Marcia sat quiet a while after Ada had gone; wondering where it would all end.

Less than half an hour later, with the work done, and her three children in tow, Marcia took the familiar path into town, by way of Penny Street. There was no time to go the longer way as she would have preferred, even though it was daylight; so they took the quicker route—over the little bridge along Brown Street, right on to Penny Street, by the Rialto picture house, then down to the town centre.

In spite of her anxiety over poor little Ada

Humble's dilemma, Marcia found herself looking forward to a while at the slipper baths. She'd even rescued her good brown overcoat from its safe hiding place in the back of the bedroom cupboard. She'd put it there some considerable time back, wrapped securely in a mothballed hanging sack . . . well out of sight and away from the temptation to carry it to the pawn shop, as she had done so many times before. The last time, it took Marcia almost three months to get it back, and that had been dangerously close to the 'keeping limit', before the goods were sold off.

The coat was really nothing special by other folks' standards, Marcia mused, nevertheless feeling really good in it . . . but to *her*, it was something to be treasured, kept for out-of-the-ordinary occasions, like today for instance. The feel of the soft brown wool against her skin, and the way the material gathered in at the tiny waist and buttoned sleeves, always made her feel elegant. A wry little smile lit up her lovely dark features as she glanced down at the shabbiness of her 'best' grey lace-up boots, and thought on her long black hair stuffed unglamorously beneath the black cloche hat which had been old Ma Bendall's. Hmph! Pity the rest on me couldn't be afforded such elegance, she mused.

Remembering how Curt had always loved the soft brown coat, she decided that anything else belonging to her except it could go to the pawn shop. Thinking on Curt, lifted the lightness of her step, as she anticipated the morning ahead with deliberately bright enthusiasm.

She glanced at young Barty, happily skipping along, safe in the grip of his Mam's hand. Florence and Polly were deep in the delights of what awaited them; Florence assuring Polly that 'you really ought to be going to the picture show at the Roxy', Polly quick to inform her sister in a patronising voice, 'Oh no! The picture show's all right for you young 'uns . . . but I'm too grown up for that now, and besides, Bridget's meeting us later at the slipper baths.'

Just looking on her children, and listening to their 'terribly important' conversations, warmed Marcia's heart. She knew how very much Polly was looking forward to the slipper baths; it was one of the many indications to Marcia that her eldest daughter was growing up fast.

A visit to the baths was a rare treat, and though the youngsters didn't always appreciate the luxury of a real bath and hot water from a tap, the grown-ups relished the opportunity. A bathroom, or even an indoor toilet, were not facilities afforded to the likes of Marcia's family or indeed to the vast majority of Blackburn's inhabitants.

The usual ritual was to bring in the big old tin bath, which normally hung in pride of place on the backyard wall; then, by surrounding it with stand-chairs covered with towels or sheets, some semblance of privacy could be gained. But for a girl just reaching her double years, and passing through that self-conscious period, it was less than satisfactory, and Marcia had sensed Polly's increasing embarrassment of late at what had been a normal, accepted procedure. For those fortunate people able to afford it, there was the comparative luxury of the slipper baths, housed in the centre of town, in the Municipal Buildings.

After seeing Florence and young Barty safely to

144

the picture house, Marcia and Polly made their way to the slipper baths. Saturday morning was a particularly busy time, and Marcia was not surprised to see a considerable queue. People of all ages and various sizes and shapes waited patiently for the church clock to strike ten, when the heavy wooden doors would be opened, and the bathers allowed in. Meanwhile, Marcia's busy dark eyes searched the queue. No sign of Bridget, she thought, looking up at the clock and seeing they had only a few minutes to go. She mentioned as much to Polly as they took their place at the rear of the queue. After this Polly's eyes were scanning the distance, hoping her friend would arrive before the doors opened. It wasn't long before the queue extended far behind them, and although Marcia could see Polly examining each new participant, there was still no sign of her friend Bridget Revine.

'I'll just wander to the edge of Market Square, Mam . . . to see if she's coming.' Polly was growing increasingly anxious.

'All right then, but you'll not have to be long, lass . . .'

'It's all right Mam, there's still time.'

Marcia watched her go, then amused herself by listening attentively to the loud chatter all about her. It was petty, meaningless exchange, but it cheered the waiting folk who seemed bored by the repetitive dullness of their lives.

The heavy broadness of the enormous woman immediately in front of Marcia completely blocked her view ahead. On seeing a neighbour joining the queue, the woman swung round, towering above Marcia, her voice loud and rough.

'All right are you, Peggy?'

145

'Oh aye. Not so bad,' came the reply, as the little sharp-faced woman in a green coat stretched to focus on the big woman, 'but the ol' man's off 'is food again!'

'Oh dear! I am sorry to hear that, Peggy.'

'Don't be sorry Flo! I've told 'im . . . it's all that bloody booze 'e keeps swilling down,' she cackled aloud. 'Anyroad, 'e might be off 'is bloody food, but 'e's not off me—on as often as I'll let 'im, I'll tell you!'

The big woman roared coarsely, rocking with laughter. ''Ere!' she shouted, 'if you can't handle 'im, *I'll* give 'im summat to be going on with! *My* old dear can't seem to stand the pace!' The two women laughed out loud, to the delight of the people in the queue.

From somewhere behind Marcia, a man's voice shouted, 'Hey, *I'm* going spare. I can stand *any* pace . . . come to think on it, I can stand anywhere, for anybody!' His sudden burst of infectious laughter prompted a volley of shouting, sniggering and loud guffawing, which spread quickly through the listening core of people. Marcia gave an amused smile as she enjoyed the open-hearted honesty of the people around her. They seemed happy enough, she thought, and no doubt they all had as many troubles as she did. Funny though, how folks allus managed to cope.

The loud boom of the church clock striking ten quietened the happy laughter as the heavy wooden doors creaked open and everyone shuffled forward, chinking coppers at the ready.

Within five minutes of the doors being opened, Marcia and Polly, who had had no luck in locating Bridget, were being ushered into their separate cubicles. It was an unusually busy morning but the queue was dealt with rapidly. Entrance money had been taken, towels supplied, and cubicles issued with surprising speed and efficiency.

'Numbers six and seven, lasses. Be as quick as you can, 'cause we're right pushed this morning, as you can see! Might even need to double up with you young 'uns later on . . .' The friendly barrel-shaped woman addressed herself to Polly, before waddling quickly away to collect another bather.

Polly pushed open the door to the cubicle. 'Oh Mam! I don't want nobody sharing,' she told Marcia sulkily.

'I'm sure they'll manage without asking you to share, lass,' Marcia assured her, 'so stop your moithering, an' get inside. Go on,' she urged the hesitant girl.

After seeing Polly into her cubicle, Marcia thankfully stepped inside No. seven. Crossing over to the big white bath, she ran her hand lovingly over its smooth surface, letting her fingers travel slowly up to the taps. Revelling in the rare luxury of it all, Marcia savoured the pleasure which rippled through her senses. She caressed the walls, the hand-basin, towel rail . . . in fact, everything that was unfamiliar and scarce in her own needy world. Eventually, putting the bath plug in, Marcia turned the taps on, letting her small measure of soap slither into the bath before testing the water for the correct temperature. Then, as the warm steaming liquid tumbled into the bath, she began to unclothe herself, impatient to immerse herself into the gathering foam. With slow deliberation, she lowered herself into the warm sudsy water, sighing with pleasure as it lapped and caressed

147

against her nakedness.

Outside, Bridget had reached the head of the queue. She had brought her own soap and towel. 'Just a ticket please,' she asked, as she handed the coppers over.

The cashier peered at her through tiny rimless spectacles, before turning to the barrel-shaped lady. 'Have we got any young 'uns in, Mabel?' she asked.

'Aye. We've got a couple o' lasses . . . one in six, and one in nineteen.'

'Six is the biggest one, I think,' the cashier observed, then, noticing the disappointed expression on Bridget's face, she asked her, 'You don't mind sharing do you lass? I'm afeared it's all we've got till the next session.'

'No, that's all right missus. I've had to share before,' Bridget confessed.

'Right then. Number six Mabel,' she said as she nodded smartly to the barrel-shaped woman, who in turn indicated to Bridget that she wanted her to follow.

Marcia, deeply immersed in the bath water, wasn't quite sure whether the insistent tapping was at *her* door. She slid herself up in the water, listening with sharper attention. The voice was easily recognisable as that of the barrel-shaped woman, but Marcia quickly contented herself that it was *not* directed at her.

'Open the door. You'll have to share with this lassie out here. We've got no more cubicles left this session,' came the instruction.

As the woman's voice grew more impatient, Marcia realised with a feeling of disappointment that it was *Polly* who was being summoned. 'Poor

148

lass,' she murmured, reflecting on her daughter's earlier remark about not wanting to share. She heard the distinct movement of water as Polly got out of the bath, then there was a quiet span, until the woman's voice bawled out angrily, 'Come on! Come on! I 'in't got all day, you know!' Now, Bridget's voice reached out clearly as the cubicle door creaked open.

'Oh, it's *you*, Polly!' she said with obvious relief, 'I thought I'd missed you altogether.'

The woman seemed pleased, and her voice relaxed to a pleasant tone. 'Oh, that's nice,' she said, 'it's nice if you share with someone you know, 'in't it?' She waited for the reply that didn't come. 'Right . . . in you go then,' she ordered, 'afore you catch your death o' cold.'

Marcia waited for the door to close, then she lowered herself gratefully into the water. Closing her eyes, she splashed the warm soothing liquid all over herself before working the soap up into a lather which she then spread gently, caressingly, over the soft, smooth skin of her body, then lavishly across her face. Cupping her hands, she scooped the water up and splashed it towards her face, clearing it of soap. As her coppers hadn't spread to the luxury of a softer soap for her hair, Marcia washed the heavy black strands in the carbolic, before rinsing it thoroughly.

It seemed no time at all before the great clattering handbell rattled and echoed along the corridor. 'Five more minutes,' Marcia murmured; loath to release the warm soothing water into the ungrateful drains, 'anything worthwhile in this life soon comes to an end—an' that's a fact!' In the relative privacy of the baths, she closed her eyes

149

and gave herself up to the past. The tall strength of Curt's manliness strode magnificently through her mind. How very clearly she could see the expressive black eyes, which had always been able to melt her with one passionate gaze, and how she loved the way his thick black hair tumbled disobediently over his forehead.

'Oh Curt,' she sighed from the very depths of her wretched lonely heart, 'you're not the only one who's in prison, my darling . . . but I pray God to keep you safe always.'

When Marcia emerged she was surprised to see that the door of the adjoining cubicle was still firmly closed. She'd have thought the girls would have been out long since. Tapping on the door, she called, 'Polly . . . Bridget, it's time you were out!'

'Polly's gone, Mrs Bendall,' Bridget's voice replied, 'she ran off in a temper.'

'Ran off in a temper?' Marcia could only think it was because Polly had been forced to share. 'All right lass. It's probably summat an' nowt. I'll find her, don't you worry.'

She found Polly sitting on the wall outside, looking rather dejected. When the girl turned towards her, Marcia's heart sank. Her usually pale complexion was heightened to an unnatural pink and her vivid blue eyes found it no easy task to meet Marcia's questioning gaze. A heaviness settled on her heart as she watched Polly's hand reach up to smooth the frown which had creased her forehead. Marcia had seen that frown on many occasions; she knew all too well that it signified the onset of crippling pain. Now, as she came to sit on the wall beside Polly, and with her arm about her, to murmur words of encouragement, Marcia's

150

resolve to bring Polly's check-up nearer was more determined than ever. As on previous occasions, Polly's discomfort lasted for only a few minutes. But, to Marcia, that was no compensation for the pain Polly had to endure.

After a while, Marcia reached out to clasp Polly's hand in her own, compassion in her eyes for the vulnerable child before her. 'Ready to go an' see your Grandma Fletcher, are you lass?'

Polly closed her eyes momentarily, and breathed deeply. Then, as quickly as the blinding pain had arrived it disappeared, and jumping down from the wall into her mother's waiting arms, she declared her pleasure at such a prospect. 'Oh Mam! I'm really looking forward to seeing Grandma Fletcher.'

Squashing the girl to her, Marcia said brightly, 'Oh I know you are, lass, an' there's nary a doubt that she'll be just as pleased to see *you*. You'd best find time to make peace with Bridget when we get back, eh! She was puzzled as to why you'd run off of a sudden,' Marcia added quietly.

As they turned the corner into the Boulevard, Marcia was pleased to see their tram waiting. 'Come on lass,' she smiled, placing a loving arm around Polly's shoulders, 'we've time for a cup of tea in the café, 'afore the tram leaves for your Gran's.'

Polly took the wash-bag from Marcia's hand, then looking up at her, the innocent love naked in her eyes, she said, 'I do love you, Mam.' Marcia's heart swelled at the simple truth of Polly's words and squeezing the girl's shoulders affectionately, she planted a kiss on top of the bright blonde head.

'I know you do, lass . . . an' I love you too.' All

151

the while she despaired at Polly's constant sense of insecurity, which even Bridget's staunch friendship hadn't allayed, as it might have done. But Marcia showed none of this anxiety as she ushered Polly ahead of her into the crowded cafeteria.

The many things that preyed on her mind and tugged mercilessly at her heart would never have been guessed at from the bright smile on her beautiful face as she chatted happily with her elder daughter.

CHAPTER NINE

Picking their way carefully over the jutting cobbles, Marcia and Polly made their way along the narrow back alley, aptly named 'Pickers Alley', which led to the back entrance of Grandma Fletcher's house.

Marcia followed as Polly reached the back gate first, calling for her mother to hurry up. Reaching up to undo the sneck, she grumbled irritably, 'Oh Mam! Why do they allus put 'em right at the top, so's folks can't reach 'em?'

Marcia had never previously noticed the uncomfortable positioning of the sneck. 'Go on with you!' she retorted good-humouredly, not thinking it of sufficient importance to warrant Polly's moaning. In a minute, the sneck clicked up and the old wooden-slatted door swung open. Then, holding the door back, Polly urged Marcia to come on—impatient as always to see her Grandma Fletcher.

Marcia quickly passed through with a thank you, crossing the yard to disappear through the back door of the scullery, leaving Polly still loudly voicing her opinion of 'that rotten sneck' as she made determined efforts to secure the back gate behind her.

Although the immediate yard area was Grandma Fletcher's own, the outer door from 'Pickers Alley' was also the communal entrance to the adjoining yards which ran to the left and right of the Fletchers'. Right at the very top of the open flagged area, situated beyond the last back yard, was a drab-looking group of lavatories; one allocated to each house. Marcia had always hated these cold draughty cubicles, remembering how, as a child, an urgent trip to the lavvies had often resulted in a long difficult wait; the reason being that should a neighbour find his own cubicle occupied, he would quite naturally use the one next door, regardless of which house it belonged to.

After all these years, the long trek to the lavvie didn't bother Grandad and Grandma Fletcher. They were hardened to it. But whenever young Polly came to stay, as was often the case of a weekend, there were special arrangements made in her honour. In the back of her china cupboard, Grandma Fletcher had a treasured old peepot, which had been hers as a child. It was racked and grey with age now . . . 'bit like your old Grandma', she told Polly; but 'so long as it 'olds wi'out spilling, it'll do the job!' Polly had quite grown used to the ceramic flowered peepot tucked conspicuously beneath her bed; but in spite of lengthy cajoling and persuading, she still hadn't managed to gain complete ownership of it. 'Thi' shall 'ave it when your ol' Grandma's 'ead is

lapped up ready for the ground . . . an' not afore!'
she'd been stoutly informed; until in the end Polly
gave up asking, but never hoping.

Of a sudden, Grandma Fletcher emerged from
the kitchen. The small tin bath which she clutched
awkwardly between her dimpled arms was full of
beautifully folded clothes, ready to be fed through
the mangle. On seeing her, Polly's face stretched
into a broad grin.

'Hello Grandma Fletcher,' she called, hurrying
towards the woman, who looked and smiled, a
warm beaming smile, full of pleasure.

'Hello child,' she answered. 'Your Mam's mekin'
us a brew. I thought you'd like to 'elp your ol'
Gran? Am I right, eh?' Her thick eyebrows went
up in quizzical fashion, and her bright blue eyes
grew round as marbles. 'Elp yer ol' Gran, will ye?'

One of the old breed of Lancashire lasses, she
wore a wide ankle-length full-gathered skirt; grey
in colour, and covered by a neat black waist-apron.
Her blouse, the sleeves of which were rolled up to
the elbow, was a sombre brown; wrapped around
her broad capable shoulders lay a pretty crocheted
shawl, bedecked with clusters of flowers in the
same shade of blue as her eyes. Her feet were clad
in bulky Lancashire clogs, with leather plum-
coloured uppers and the soles were tapped with
irons, which clip-clopped loudly on the echoing
flagstones of the yard. On Polly's swift and eager
agreement, she carefully bent her large frame
forwards, until the tin bath was almost touching
the ground, then releasing her grip on the handles
she allowed it to clatter heavily on the floor. The
clothes gave a short startled jump, before settling
back again into their neat sodden layers. Then,

wiping her hands down her apron, she laughed, a deep healthy chuckle, 'By the left, lass!' she exclaimed, 'I must be gerrin' old. There was a time not so long back when I would 'a thrown that tin bath o'er me shoulder, and thought nowt on it!' At which point she emphasised her words by pushing Polly playfully.

Lovingly placing her hand in the old lady's, Polly reproached her gently, 'You're not getting old! You've just got too many clothes in there.' In a spontaneous movement the old lady tenderly gathered the young girl in her arms and drew her protectively against her ample bosom.

'What a little charmer ye are, Polly Bendall,' she chuckled. 'Th'ar' a grand little lass an' thi' Mam should be proud o' thi'.' She straightened up. 'Come on young 'un, give us 'and wi' this 'ere mangling.'

Watching through the window Marcia was deeply pleased at their genuine affection for each other. The two of them working in happy unison presented an odd picture. Two generations so content in each other's company, she thought, the love and understanding between the young girl and the old woman unquestionable, loyal and very, very special. Relaxing against the kitchen window-sill, Marcia was grateful that the Lord had doubly blessed her in that dear old lady. She was ever grateful for having been given a warm, loving mother, who had stood by her through all her troubles and heartache . . . and her three children had been fortunate in having a Grandma who loved and cared for them deeply. 'And God alone knows,' murmured Marcia, 'She's had *her* fair share o' troubles—just like anybody else!' That

155

business with Curt had hurt her parents deeply. Thinking on her father in the back parlour, Marcia recalled how moody and unpredictable he'd grown. But then, he *was* in his seventies, she reminded herself. All in all, he was a grand reliable old man and he thought the world of Grandma Fletcher.

Marcia watched the antics of her Mam and daughter, as, between the two of them, they dragged the tin bath into position just underneath the mangle. The old mangle was the pride and joy of the old woman. It was far from being handsome, and had few redeeming qualities other than being 'a grand workhorse', for it was a great iron contraption, ancient and rusty. But, like its owner, it still retained much of its original beauty; evident in the intricate scroll workings, especially within the great turning wheel. To own one of these huge manacles was indeed a blessing. The alternative was to spend many back-aching hours leaning over the dolly-tub and physically wringing each garment out, until painful hand blisters called a halt.

'Right then lass. Let's 'ave this lot through the mangle and onto yon line afore it turns to rain.' Grandma Fletcher cast a suspicious eye at the dark gathering clouds above them.

'Can I turn the wheel?' Polly asked eagerly.

'Well, 'appen you'll be a lot safer doing that, Polly lass. I've known many a young unsuspecting lass lose 'er fingers through trapping 'em in these big merciless rollers.' She nodded towards the rubber clad rollers in the centre of the mangle, going on to carefully explain to Polly how the great rubber rollers could not only press almost every drop of water from a double sized bed-sheet folded at least twelve times, but once the great wide turn

156

on the cast-iron wheel started, it was nigh impossible to retrieve a sheet, bedspread, or even hand or fingers, until they appeared out of the back of the rollers and into the wicker catching basket. 'So! You just think on my gel! an' mind what ye're doing!' she warned, nodding at Polly who was tirelessly turning the great wheel.

'Yes Gran.'

'Well don't look at *me*, child! Keep your eyes on the job!' she told the girl, shaking her head and rolling her blue eyes heavenward.

Grandma Fletcher fed the folded sopping clothes in to the greedy rollers, which unceremoniously squashed the excess water out into the spill tray, before expelling the squirming flattened clothes out of its rear end into the catching basket. That done, she and Polly each grabbed an end handle, and trudged with the laden basket up to the clothes line, where the bulky garments were hung out.

'I'll 'ang the smaller things inside on the pulley-line.'

Heaving the basket up, Grandma Fletcher tucked it under her arm and strode grandly back to the house, leaving Polly to hurry after her.

'Come on, slowcoach!' she called to Polly, who was trailing half-a-dozen steps behind, 'Urry up an' close the door. It's not so warm out there!' Polly closed the door behind her and followed Grandma Fletcher through the tiny scullery and into the back living room, where Marcia had prepared to make a welcoming brew of tea.

'Finished have you?' Marcia asked of the invading womenfolk. 'Well, set yourselves down then, the tea's ready.' The smile with which she greeted them seemed happy and contented enough.

Marcia had spent all of her early life in this house, and when she left it to marry Curt that same deep contentment and belonging had coloured her own little home. Until now! Sensing herself drifting into memories and recollections which could give her so much pain as well as pleasure, Marcia quickly turned her thoughts to other things less hurtful.

She loved this house though, and treasured the childhood she'd spent within its walls. After renting it for forty years, her father had borrowed one hundred and ten pounds from the local butcher, in order to purchase it when the old landlord died.

The house was always warm, and full of lovely things. There was always cake in the cake tin, and bread in the bread-bin. Marcia always experienced a sense of security and peace here in the company of her dear Mam. The tiny scullery, with just enough room to hold a cooker, a sink, a food cupboard and two chairs set round a small table, always smelt of fresh bread, lavender, and Grandma Fletcher's snuff . . . and it had been the setting for many a heart to heart after her darling Curt had been taken away. Now, the cheery welcoming fire crackled and danced joyously in the big black iron grate. The clothes pulley-line which was slung from the ceiling above the fire swayed gently back and forth in the rising heat and, in this cosy place at least, all seemed right in the world.

Grandad Fletcher, seated in his favourite old horsehair chair, was almost entirely hidden from view, with only the sharp neb of his cap and the polished toes of his old working boots protruding from either end of the sizeable reading paper held up before him. Every now and then, a great grey cloud of tobacco smoke billowed out over the top of his paper, until the gathered fog completely enveloped him. His dog, Paddy, a hard hairy little terrier of indefinite colour, lay contented at his feet. The strong tang of pipe-tobacco filled the tiny room, flooding Marcia's nostrils with its stinging heat and making her eyes smart.

Rising from her place on the brass slipper-stool by the fire, Marcia walked over to the fire-grate, where she poured tea. When handing her Mam a cup, she nodded her dark head at the figure of her father, smiling.

'Just look at him, Mam,' she said, 'I've been talking to him for ten minutes, an' all he does is grunt.' Marcia knew of old that giving Grandad Fletcher a pipe and a reading paper meant despatching him to another world entirely!

Raising her blue eyes heavenwards and sighing in mock weariness before moving towards him and kicking the protruding boot, Grandma Fletcher demanded, 'What's up wi' thi', man? The lasses 'ave come to see us, an' all you can do is 'ide behind yon paper an' grunt!'

The reading paper was slowly lowered until Grandad Fletcher's little eyes peered over the top, lazily scanning the scene before him, then focusing directly on Marcia's smiling face, they lit up. 'Hello lass,' he drawled thickly, his smoking pipe still clenched firmly between his teeth. 'Brought the young 'un I see?' His eyes narrowed in concentration, searching for Florence and young Barty. 'Where's the other two then?' he asked, with

159

a quizzical look.

Marcia blew hard on her tea to cool it. 'They've taken themselves off to the pictures,' she answered. 'Barty gave them a few coppers in the week, an' I gave 'em the rest this morning. I promised the pair on 'em, you see.'

Grandma Fletcher paused in her hanging of the washing on the pulley-line, then with a dolly-peg bobbing up and down from her lips as she spoke, the words came out in a muffled jumble. 'Hmph!' she snorted, 'I'm surprised 'e could spare a copper! I 'ope 'e didn't leave 'imsel' short of the price of a pint!'

'Now then, woman!' Grandad Fletcher's voice boomed out firm and reprimanding, 'that'll do i' front o' the child!'

At this, Polly looked up at him. Her Grandad Fletcher fascinated her—especially that moustache of his, which drooped down either side of his mouth. The constant stream of smoke from his pipe, and the slurping filtering action when he drank his tea, had permeated the greying moustache with dark ugly stains. Polly remembered how her Mam had laughed out loud one day, when she'd told her how very much like his whiskered dog she thought Grandad Fletcher looked. Marcia had laughed because it was so true.

Marcia also could never remember seeing her Dad without his flat nebbed cap, which was always perched jauntily on the top of his perfectly round head. He had a tremendous sense of humour though, and the sudden unexpected way he would burst out singing in a flat, squeaky voice never failed to reduce folks to fits of laughter. Now, of a sudden, he lowered his eyes, released a smothered

160

grunt from the depths of his moustache, then disappeared behind his reading paper, leaving all three women quietly chuckling.

When Grandad Fletcher was safely buried once again in his reading matter, and Polly appeared to be busily preoccupied pulling out the stray hairs in Paddy's stumpy tail, Marcia became acutely aware of her Mam's constant fidgeting—as though she was deeply agitated. Then the old woman was on her feet, going to the front parlour and beckoning for Marcia to follow. At once, and most curious, Marcia followed the old woman into the front parlour.

'Set yousel' down there!' She spoke with unusual authority, which only added to Marcia's anxiety.

'What's to do, Mam? You're acting strange.'

'Just set yoursel' down, Marcia lass. We've to talk!'

Obediently, Marcia sat on the stiff upright stand-chair, which seemed fitting to the occasion.

'Now then,' Grandma Fletcher said after clearing her throat, embarrassed and unsure of how to proceed, 'your Nantie Bett was 'ere this morning!'

'Nantie Bett? She's all right isn't she?' Marcia couldn't see what was so untoward about Nantie Bett visiting *this* house! She was almost a fixture. Had been for as far back as Marcia could remember. As a toddler learning to talk, she'd found it far too taxing to refer to the dear woman as 'Auntie Betty', but her childish tongue had easily conquered the title 'Nantie Bett', and over the years the sprightly little woman had been accepted by one and all as such.

'Oh aye. She's well enough.' Grandma

161

Fletcher's frown deepened almost to a scowl; something which was indeed a rare sight to Marcia, and one which disturbed her deeply. 'She'd do better to leave well enough alone, your Nantie Bett! Should know better than to stir things up best left alone!' The tone of her voice lowered to an angrier accusing pitch. 'She's *allus* 'ad a soft spot for 'im, even more than the rest on us, an' Lord knows 'e 'eld a special place in *all* our 'earts—till the bugger proved 'isself undeserving of it!' A cold shiver rippled through Marcia's senses.

'What are you trying to say, Mam?' she asked quietly. 'Who held a special place in all your hearts?' Even as she voiced the question, the answer was suggesting itself in her fevered mind.

'Who! Oh, Marcia lass! God 'elp us all, for your Nantie Bett brought news o' Curt Ratheter!'

As the words penetrated Marcia's trembling heart, she was only vaguely aware that Grandad Fletcher and Polly had entered the room.

'Thought the pair on you 'ad gone off on a trip or summat!' Grandad Fletcher's sulkiness at having been deserted postponed the questions urgent on Marcia's mind. 'Come on Paddy!' he urged the dog, 'let's find us'selves some useful company. It doesn't befit a man biding 'ere with all these females! Come on, you lazy scoundrel!' Once he realised he was going for a walk, the dog jumped up, his pricked ears standing smartly to attention as he yapped himself into a frenzy.

'Stop that! I'll not 'ave thi' going crazy!' At once, the little dog sat obediently, silent and still as a statue. Then, turning to Polly, Grandad Fletcher asked, 'Does thi' want ter come fer a walk wi' me an' Paddy?' When the answer was affirmative the

162

little party made ready and, in a matter of minutes, they were away up the road.

Marcia thought on her mother's words, hardly able to control the excitement which surged through her veins and flushed her cheeks a warm shade of pink. What was Nantie Bett's news? She wasn't surprised by her Mam's anger, for Grandma Fletcher could be stubborn and cantankerous—steeped in tradition and having high values of loyalty. In matters such as this, she preferred to sweep things under the carpet. Marcia could appreciate the reason for such thinking as far as her Mam was concerned. But, as far as *she* was concerned, Curt Ratheter could not so easily be forgotten.

'Now then, lass!' Marcia felt her Mam's eyes on her and there was no doubting the older woman's disapproval as she went on briskly, 'I'm only tellin' yer about that scoundrel, 'cause I don't want yer telled by others! D'yer see lass!' When Marcia nodded, there came a small pause, after which her Mam spoke with a deal more tenderness, saying, 'Aw, Marcia! Marcia! 'Ow things do come back ter 'aunt us, eh?' She gave a great noisy sigh. Then, pursing her lips in that peculiar way she had when considering a problem, she reached forward to pat Marcia on the knee. 'Yer don't like yer ol' Mam calling Curt Ratheter a scoundrel, do yer, eh?'

When Marcia gave no response other than to lower her sad dark eyes, her Mam gave a second great sigh, before explaining in a quiet voice, 'Yer a lovely warm-hearted creature, Marcia Bendall! Aye! 'Appen *too* warm-hearted, and certainly too forgiving! Aw, lass . . . don't think I don't know that yer still love the fella? Ain't I seen it in yer quiet

163

sorry eyes many a time, eh? Yer *do* love 'im! An' I've no doubt as 'e loves you! But, the plain truth of it all is that yer *both* on yer married to another! Then, I'm not forgetting 'ow 'e punished you an' them little 'uns . . . all because 'e didn't 'ave the guts to tell yer about that wife of 'is in the *first* bloody place!' Realising that her bitterness was getting the better of her, Grandma Fletcher threw her two hands up above her white head. 'Aw, bugger it, lass! Yer can't blame me fer being angry, can yer, eh? An' this Barty's proved little better. But like it or not, Marcia, Barty Bendall's your legal spouse an' in this Christian 'ousehold, that's binding.' As she glanced at her daughter's troubled face, a worried little frown puckered her forehead. 'Are you all right love?' she asked, her voice heavy now with concern. 'Sitting there moithering won't do no good at all.'

Marcia looked up, her eyes glittering with tears. 'Oh Mam,' she whispered in a broken voice, 'I've been such a fool.'

Grandma Fletcher reached out a comforting hand. 'Don't look so tragic, Marcia. You did the only thing you could at the time. With folks the way they are, you 'ad no choice! Then, all that worry wi' little Polly.'

'Maybe I should have worried more about what *I* wanted! And not what *other* people thought I ought to do!' she retorted with more than a hint of defiance evident in the toss of her dark head.

'Now you know better than *that* Marcia lass! You didn't only 'ave yoursel' to think on, 'cause there were them two little 'uns. Would yer 'ave them condemned by what their father did?'

Marcia knew her mother was right, and wishing

164

it otherwise wouldn't change anything. A warm smile lit up her face as she looked on the old woman.

'You're right Mam,' she conceded, 'and where would I be now, without your help, eh?'

'Don't be daft!' came the retort, 'what's a mother for anyroad?'

'What news did Nantie Bett have, Mam?'

'Nay Marcia lass,' Grandma Fletcher said as she shifted uncomfortably, 'I did wrong! I should never a' brought the subject up. You've more than enough to worrit about.'

'Bless you Mam,' Marcia said gently, 'you know I think on him every single day as passes.' Reaching out to kiss her Mam's concerned face, she said softly, 'I know none of this has been easy for *you*, either. But it's all done and reckoned with, and we all know there's no turning the clock back, so I don't think a bit o' news concerning Curt is going to make any difference to *that*.' How calm she sounded! And all the time her heart beating like a schoolgirl's! Now, she sensed the struggle going on behind her mother's gentle blue eyes, and for one fleeting moment she felt sure that the news would be denied her. Prepared as she was, the news when it was uttered came as a shock.

'Would you believe the sly little ferret's kept in touch with 'im all this time? For six years she's been exchanging news with 'im; keeping 'im informed o' you and the little 'uns.' Her mouth set disapprovingly. 'Been to see 'im too I shouldn't wonder!' At this point, Grandma Fletcher leaned forward to place a warning hand on Marcia's. 'You'll *'ave* to forget all about 'im, lass!' she said firmly, 'I know life plays cruel tricks, but you'll 'ave to face up to it. There's too much water under the bridge. You've got a proper 'usband, an' *three* little 'uns now.' Tears glistened brightly as she told Marcia in a soft tone, 'I know 'ow Barty Bendall treats you lass,' then, encouraged by the slight rush of alarm across Marcia's face she went on, 'Oh, there's not much *I* miss, my girl! But we can't go back, lass. We 'ave to learn to make do wi' what the good Lord sees fit to give us. I think you know that much?' Her voice trembled as she brushed the flickering tears from her cheeks. 'I wouldn't 'ave told you,' she continued, 'but I thought it best, in view o' Nantie Bett's tidings.'

'Mam! What news did Nantie Bett have to tell you? Please!'

'Well,' the hesitance was still there, and the fear which marbled the old woman's voice, 'it seems as 'ow a body doesn't 'ave to serve a full sentence; not if they've be'aved theirselves.' She took a deep breath. 'Nantie Bett says Curt Ratheter could be let out any day now lass.'

'Coming out! Curt, coming out?' Marcia's eyes closed tight against the tears which spilled over. 'Oh Mam! Mam!' she cried, her heart bursting.

'Now, tek old o' yersel', think on your duties an' responsibilities. I would never 'ave told you . . . but better you know *now* than bumping into 'im unaware.' She reached forward, her own eyes moist with tears. 'Come on now lass. There's nowt to be done. As far as yer ol' Mam's concerned, yer picked two right buggers! And each in their own way is as bad as the other!'

Marcia smiled shakily. Of course her Mam was right—but only to a certain extent. There *wasn't* anything to be done! But she was grateful in her

166

heart that at least Curt was able to look forward to freedom. Only she knew just how much of a lifetime the past six years had been for him. She supposed the early release was the 'remission' the judge had mentioned, and she in her ignorance hadn't fully understood. 'I'm so mixed up, Mam,' she said softly, 'in all these years, I've not been able to forget him. There's not a day goes by when I don't think on him.' As the tender memories flooded into her wretched mind, Marcia's gentle expression slowly hardened. 'Sometimes,' she said in a harsh voice, 'I feel as though I'm being forever punished! I wish to God I'd never seen Barty Bendall!'

'Hey! Now you've got to stop that!' Grandma Fletcher's voice was firm and decisive. 'I don't like seeing you unhappy lass, but there can be no 'appiness with another woman's man—an' even if *he* were free, *you're* not!' Wagging a chubby finger, she went on excitedly, 'An' 'ave you forgotten what 'e did to you and them lasses?'

Marcia hadn't forgotten, how could she? 'But Mam, he loved us so . . . and he's been made to pay with six long years, locked away in that prison. I'm not so sure that knowing about that awful Fran Ratheter would have made any difference!' Her face became hard as she whispered drily, 'I only wish it could have all *stayed* a secret!'

'What are thi' talking about, lass!' Her face softened as she sensed the tortuous nature of Marcia's thoughts. 'The point is now, lass . . . what would thi' do if thi' came face to face wi' 'im? *That's* what preys on *my* mind.'

Marcia looked long and hard into her mother's anxious face. Yes, that was undoubtedly a

167

consideration, and what could she say? Her dark eyes grew soft as she whispered in a small tight voice, 'I don't know, Mam . . . I honestly don't know.' Her tired voice carried a world of weariness.

'Good Lord above! What are we to do? You'd better put 'im right out of your mind, girl! God only knows what Barty Bendall might do if 'e knew as Curt Ratheter was out on the streets; an' what about yon lasses! If young Polly knew the truth about 'er father, there's no telling 'ow it would affect 'er . . . she's quick-minded is that one! Too quick-minded!' Here, Grandma Fletcher saw an opportunity to change the subject, for she knew only too well how her daughter cherished little Polly. 'Ow is the lass of late, eh?'

Marcia's Mam had been right, and, at once, Marcia took up her question. 'Polly worries me. There's summat wrong, I know there is, in spite of what Dr Pitt tells me. And Barty Bendall doesn't help either. Polly has this fixation that he hates her!'

'Think what you're saying, lass. 'Ow can thi' say as Barty Bendall might 'ate the child? Didn't 'e take both them girls on an' fetch 'em up as 'is own? Polly must be imagining things! She's only a child. 'Ow can anybody come to 'ate a child?'

Marcia was adamant. 'Polly's not the only one as thinks it, because *I* do! It's not even as if she looks like *Curt*. She favours her Grandma. I think it's 'cause Polly's so close to me. We've allus been able to talk to each other; but neither on us can ever talk to him! You know, Mam, Polly never has taken to Barty the way Florence did. It's as though she *knows* he's not her Dad. And, the way she sets out

168

to aggravate him at times—well, it just drives him crazy!'

'What about Florence?'

'Oh, he's all right with her, thank goodness. She's such a naive little thing, he couldn't very well do anything else. But he hates Polly, believe me, Mam,' she added vehemently, 'and what's worse, Polly hates him.'

Grandma Fletcher remarked that Marcia must be imagining things. Then, obviously choosing to ignore such disturbing claims, she asked, ''Ow's the lass's 'eadaches?'

'Well, that's what worries me, Mam. Polly's due for a check-up in three months' time, but I intend to tek her back to Dr Pitt on Monday morning. I hope to God that tumour hasn't begun to spread. Anyway, I'd best tek her and put my mind at rest.'

'Aye, 'appen that's a good idea. I know thi' can't afford to lose a day's pay, but it's not summat as thi' can mess about with.' Lowering her voice, she reached forward. 'An' for God's sake Marcia, put that fella out o' thi' mind once an' for all! Or no good will *ever* come of it!'

A shadow of unhappiness clouded Marcia's face as her thoughts returned to embrace the past. 'I know you'll never forgive him for what he did, but I can't feel that way about him.' She lowered her eyes. 'Why did it all have to happen, Mam?' she asked wearily.

Grandma Fletcher was glad when, at that moment, Polly returned alone. 'Grandad's popped in to see a friend,' she said, running straight to Marcia for a cuddle.

'Good!' Grandma Fletcher saw her opportunity and, jumping up, she told Polly, 'There's a little

169

errand I wants yer ter run fer me, lass!' In a series of little skips and jumps, she was across the room to the cupboard which was built into the recess of the chimney-breast. Here, she clambered onto a stool and fumbled about along the top shelf until, with a whoop of delight, she brought forth a large white pot jug. All the while, Marcia and Polly had followed her furtive antics with fascination.

She descended and gingerly positioned the precious vessel on the table. Marcia couldn't hide her amusement. As her Mam frantically fumbled about in the deep folds of her dark skirt, she asked, 'Whatever are you up to, Mam?'

'Can't find me blessed purse!' came the reply, while, in the manner of a thief, Grandma Fletcher continued to pick her own pockets. Of a sudden, she began chuckling as, her face beaming from ear to ear, she whipped out a long black leather object. 'Aha! Here it is!' she cried. Then, in one devious sweep, she had Polly by the arm, ' 'Ere, lass—quick as yer can!' she urged, propelling the smiling child to the table, 'tek that there jug an' these coppers.' She thrust a few large coins into Polly's open hand. 'Get yersel' over to yon Nags Head, child.' Bending close now she whispered in Polly's ear, 'Don't go in the *front* door, mind! Go round the side—ter the Snug, an' tell yon landlord as yer Gran'ma Fletcher's sent yer. You tell the artful bugger ter say nowt to yer Grandad—but fetch me a gill o' the best—a good measure, mind! You mek sure an' tell 'im that!'

Polly had listened intently, all the while avoiding her Mam's eyes, because they were twinkling with such humour that to look on them would surely set her giggling, which would earn her a clip on the ear from Grandma. So, with the jug tucked under her arm and the big hard coppers filling her hand, Polly set off towards the front door—only to be quickly collared by her Grandma and brought to a halt.

' 'Ere, lass—'old up a minute!' She fled across the room to the cupboard from which she retrieved a blinding white tea-towel. 'Cover the jug wi' this.' As Polly took the tea-cloth, she felt herself propelled towards the front door and with every step she was given a new instruction. 'Come straight back! Yer must beat yer Grandad 'ome, 'cause 'e's a funny ol' sod when it comes ter me an' my little pleasure. An' mind yon road, child! That's a main tram route, is yon. Go on then—'urry thisel, lass!'

Meanwhile Marcia took the opportunity to gaze in nostalgia about the old familiar parlour. The sight and smell of all within it always gave her a degree of pleasure—the gramophone in its shining walnut cabinet, soft chairs covered in pretty floral material, the huge sideboard, all mirrors and polished surfaces. And, here beside her, the magnificent piano which no one could play.

The sweet pain of remembering stabbed at Marcia's heart, as she recalled her Mam's exuberance when, on the news of her and Barty's betrothal plans, she had made a most notable effort to wrestle out a tune from that lovely instrument. But, like her marriage to Barty, it had come out all wrong.

Thinking on this parlour and being taken back over the years, Marcia's thoughts drifted to other more precious moments in this very room. In spite of herself, she began to think about Curt. She

171

recalled the way he had looked on his very first visit here. Wearing a dark brown suit which looked wonderful on that tall elegant figure, he had stood there, his dark hair a mess where he had nervously run his fingers through it and on his handsome face a shy, awkward expression. In those magnificent dark eyes, such tenderness—oh, such love that even now the memory of it made Marcia's heart stand still. Of a sudden, the aching became too much, and the tears spilled down her face. Why? she asked herself, *why* did it all have to come to this?

'Hey, lass!' Grandma Fletcher's voice was soft and loving as, coming to find Marcia steeped in such pain, she bent to take her in a fast embrace. 'Yer mustn't keep on punishing thisel' love,' she murmured, rocking Marcia gently.

'How *could* he, Mam?' Marcia asked quietly, 'How could he stand in God's house and give his marriage vows so convincingly?—knowing that what he had kept secret from us could never be secret from the Almighty. *How* could he?'

'Aw, lass! 'Tis a sad fact that we all on us 'ave us crosses to bear—an' Curt Ratheter's is a bigger an' 'eavier one, 'cause o' what 'e *'imself* did! Oh, an' the scoundrel put one on *your* back too, lass. I don't think I'll *ever* forgive 'im fer that!'

Marcia wondered whether there was a small part of her also which could not entirely forgive Curt. And yet, with every breath in her body she loved him still.

'All right! I'm coming,' Grandma Fletcher cried, in response to the urgent banging on the door, disappearing in a flurry of swishing skirts and petticoats to fling it open before the froth on her

172

gill could melt. Plucking Polly off the doorstep and hoisting her into the front room, she whipped the jug out of the girl's hands. 'Thar a good lass,' she called, as she hurried away to the parlour, 'a good lass, an' no mistake.'

A few minutes later, with Marcia sitting by the fire in the back parlour where she had returned and Grandma Fletcher contentedly supping her coveted beer, all was peaceful, save for the melodic notes which drifted in from the front room, and which strangely calmed Marcia's aching heart.

Polly played without music: without knowledge, but the haunting sounds were created with love and excitement. And in the intangible essence woven into the rhythmic vibrations was something uniquely satisfying. The two listening women sat transfixed, their whole attention concentrated on the magical beauty of the strangely harmonious notes. For a little while, the whole house was filled with these wondrous sounds, urging Marcia to hum an accompaniment which added a deep dimension of harmony and beauty.

As the last note died away, the ensuing silence settled heavy and poignant, and Marcia's emotions fell away in a mingling of great happiness and terrible regret. Crossing the room, she placed an affectionate arm around Polly's shoulders, her lovely eyes wide and tearful. Now, a feeling of desperate protectiveness engulfed her, as she said softly, 'That was really beautiful, Polly. There's no denying you've a gift for music . . . a love of it, like me; if only you were given the chance.' Marcia sighed resignedly, pulling Polly into her, her painful heart grieving for lost opportunities. 'I'm not bothered about playing the piano,' Polly lied,

173

getting to her feet and placing a reassuring kiss on her mother's cheek.

'If that's what you'd like me to believe, lass,' Marcia was not unaware of Polly's transparent attempt to save her any distress.

Now, rejecting her Mam's offer of 'a fresh brew', Marcia told her gratefully, 'Thank you all the same, but we'll miss the tram if we don't go now. I don't want Florence and young Barty coming home to an empty house.'

'Right lass . . .' The old lady kissed them both, before accompanying them to the door, '. . . but mind you think on what I said! There'll be no good come of it—you mark my words, Marcia lass!' There was no mistaking the serious warning in Grandma Fletcher's voice.

On the tram ride home Marcia said very little. However wrong it might be and however futile, she did love Curt Ratheter. It wasn't a situation over which she had any control, it was just there. But for all that, guilt never ceased to torment her. In spite of Barty Bendall's impossible and often downright cruel attitude, she was obliged to him; committed not only by law, but by every sense of her moral and decent upbringing. At a time when she'd been so afraid that her two daughters would come to recognise their unusual situation—not only that they were bastards, but also that the man who had fathered them had been committed to seven years in His Majesty's Prison—Barty Bendall had been their salvation. I must never forget that, however hard I might be tempted, Marcia told herself.

Glancing at the fair-haired girl at her side, Marcia reflected on how Polly was such a strange impressionable creature that there'd be no telling

174

how she would cope with such knowledge. She shivered as she felt so many things tugging her in so many different directions, none of them offering any real comfort.

Polly's repeated efforts to draw her mother into involved conversation drew small response, except for a reluctant acknowledgement that yes, the imminence of the Bonfire Celebrations was very evident. All along the route, which carried them through lovely autumnal countryside, excited children piled up bracken, used timber, old furniture and anything else capable of burning heartily. The big day, eagerly anticipated by children and adults alike, was on 5 November, the following Friday. Marcia had not yet failed in her yearly ritual of taking the children to the festivities which accompanied the town's major bonfire, held in a sprawling area of waste ground near the heart of Blackburn. It always proved to be a magnificent spectacle enjoyed by all. Each year, Marcia herself was proclaimed the star of the show, when she would be commandeered to sing emotional heart-rending songs requested by one and all.

Staring hard at her slim wedding-band, Marcia was twisting it round and round until her finger became red-raw, her gaze so far away she seemed impervious to all around her. But Polly was not altogether blind to her Mam's unhappiness, however much she might try and hide it.

'Mam,' she said softly, reaching out and covering the long slim fingers with her own tiny hand.

Marcia turned to look tenderly on Polly's anxious upturned face, 'Yes love?' The tears hovered delicately, before Marcia's blink subdued them.

Having successfully gained her mother's attention and diverted her thoughts, even if only temporarily, Polly simply said reassuringly, 'I really *don't* mind not 'aving a piano.' She thought that revelation at least might cheer her Mam up.

Marcia laughed softly, but it was a hollow, meaningless sound. Nevertheless she answered tenderly, 'I know you don't lass. But if ever there's a chance, Polly—you shall have one!' Marcia's fervent promise to Polly was endorsed by her own deep sense of loss. Life was too short to sacrifice *everything*! Marcia knew only too well how Polly's life might be made shorter than others.

The tram shuddered to a halt and within minutes the passengers had alighted—each hurrying to be out of the cold and sealed by their respective fire-grates. It was just striking four o'clock by the big Market Hall striker when Marcia and Polly reached their front door and already darkness was thickening into a blanket of impenetrable black. Florence and young Barty had been home for the last half-hour, letting themselves in with the latch-key which permanently dangled inside the letter-box. There was no sign of Barty Bendall. That was only to be expected, for he would not leave the betting shop until the last race had been announced, then he would arrive home, either drunk on the winnings, or drunk at having lost. Either way, his mood would not be pleasant

In actual fact, it was much later than usual when Barty Bendall saw fit to make his way home. Florence and young Barty had been bathed and bedded some four hours previous, and were now fast asleep.

Polly had toyed with the notion of approaching her mother, partly to seek reassurance concerning the excruciating pains she had begun to experience, and partly to attempt to relieve her mother of the dreadful anxiety which had shadowed her face all day. Just as she made to do so, however, Polly's attention diminished because of the activity into which Marcia had deliberately plunged herself. As Marcia rushed about preparing Barty Bendall's meal, her bustle rendered a quiet intimate talk impracticable.

Marcia, in fact, had sensed Polly's worried intentions, and had purposely sought to avoid them. The guilt she'd previously experienced grew no less at her having taken such a course; but Marcia was fully aware that Polly had guessed at her distress, and the last thing she felt able to face right now was a session of Polly's alarming direct questioning. There would be time, she reasoned, and more suitable opportunity for such an exercise. Until then, it was best to let things be. At any rate, Polly would need to be told of the intended visit to Dr Pitt on Monday morning.

Only once did Marcia pause in her anxious bustling about to get Barty's meal ready. In that quiet moment, she was perturbed to see Polly looking at her in a most curious manner. She kissed Polly lightly on the forehead. 'All right Polly, lass?'

Polly's eyes swept Marcia's face with searching precision. 'Mam—are you unhappy?'

The question was delivered with Polly's usual candour, but this time, Marcia was ready for it, had been since coming home. 'Polly Bendall!' she

177

chastised, smiling disarmingly, 'how could I be unhappy when I've got you?'

For a long cool moment, Polly examined her Mam's face, and Marcia knew she was quietly considering the merits and possible implications of such a remark. She breathed an inner sigh of relief at Polly's eventual response.

'I do love you, Mam. Thank you for taking me to Grandma Fletcher's and the slipper baths. I'd best go an' apologise to Bridget tomorrow, for running off an' leaving her!'

Marcia ushered her upstairs into the bedroom, 'I think that's a right good idea lass. Now, tippy-toe to bed. I don't want you waking the young 'uns.'

Marcia found sleep elusive as she lay, eyes wide open in the engulfing darkness of the bedroom, its quietness broken only by the occasional gust of wind catching the gas-mantle in the street lamp beneath her window. Sighing noisily, she reflected on the day almost passed. Her frown deepened and the richness of her dark eyes clouded as she recaptured the events. She combed her mind again and again, in an effort to define the path of her tangled life, but the exercise was utterly futile, for every route led her inevitably to Barty Bendall, and the worries which dogged her grew out of all proportion. She would have to be firm with Dr Pitt. She prayed that little Ada Humble had found the strength to tell Toby of the impending court case. And how she'd make up for the loss of a day's pay from the mill on Monday, she just didn't know. Over and over the problems churned in her mind, until finally Marcia fell sound asleep.

Barty Bendall's drunken movements and loud vulgarity preceded his violent banging on the front door. 'Open this bloody door, woman! Come on.' His rough voice carried on the night air, prompting disgruntled neighbours to shout their angry protests. But their distress left Barty Bendall unperturbed as he continued to thump viciously on the door. ' 'Ave I to break the sodding door down? Come an' open this door!'

Marcia was rudely and violently jerked back to the ever-increasing burden of her present situation. She hurried to the door, calling out reassuringly in an effort to allay Barty Bendall's raging temper, 'For heaven's sake, Barty! Stop your rattling and banging!' But even as she pleaded Marcia knew the futility of it. If she learned nothing else, she had been taught by this man that there were times when civilised behaviour went right out of the window.

Having roused her from her much-needed rest, Barty Bendall offered Marcia no further consideration. Rough-handling her back to bed, he brushed aside her protests and rising anger before using her body for his own satisfaction and pleasure. Lying beneath the weight of his grunting drunken body, Marcia felt the hot tears of degradation and misery as they melted away into the pillow and her heart burned with loathing.

CHAPTER TEN

Sunday mornings in the Bendall household usually got off to a slower start than on a weekday. The frantic rush and commotion of a working day had no place on the Sabbath. It was the only morning when the start of the day was not heralded by the all too familiar tap of the knocker-up's long wooden stick on the front bedroom window. But, if the hurry and urgency of a normal workday had no place on a Sunday morning, then neither did laziness—with perhaps an exception in Barty Bendall's case. The swilling of booze on a Saturday night was a traditional ritual of enjoyment, and it wasn't until the following morning that the extent of penance was measured.

Marcia had eased herself out of bed just after six a.m. when everything outside was dark and quiet, and everything inside demanded her attention. Moving about carefully so as not to disturb the rest of the family, she looked across the bed at Barty Bendall. The room itself was dark; outside the window a hint of dawn was visible. For some strange reason which had always eluded her Marcia felt the need to sleep with the curtains open. Since her marriage to Barty Bendall, the need had grown into something more of a compulsion. Having the curtains open, however, never helped her to sleep easier, for her rest was ever subject to fits and starts. But during those long night hours when she lay awake, the sight of the open sky lent her a good deal of quiet contentment.

Marcia's arms moved busily, dressing her shivering body in the stiffness of a rusty-coloured jumper and skirt—a legacy from old Ma Bendall which Marcia hadn't the heart to throw out. As she dressed, her gaze fell on Barty Bendall's sleeping face and at once Marcia's heart sank. She must *not* hate him, she repeated to herself, for it would only make life that much more difficult.

A few moments later, Marcia crept from the room carrying her flat sensible shoes as she tiptoed down the stairs on gossamer steps. She felt exhausted. With so much on her mind, sleep had been nigh on impossible. She would have enjoyed a few more hours resting in bed, but with Barty Bendall lying against her, reeking of booze and liable to awake hungry to satisfy his sexual desires, the very thought was obnoxious.

In no time at all the fire was crackling and the tea brewed in the pot. Marcia leaned against the mantelpiece, thoughtfully staring into the gathering flames. She made an absent-minded calculation of the work to be done, but she felt disturbed and restless within herself, and unable to collect her thoughts.

For a long time she stood there, hopelessly lost in conflicting emotions. Her needs were just as strong as Barty Bendall's, she mused. She was young, healthy and filled with the same passions and drives as any other young woman. And, God forbid, there had been times during Barty Bendall's animal fulfilment of his sexual urges when she had actually found herself responding. Afterwards though, she had come close to being physically sick.

'It's no good, Marcia Bendall!' she chastised herself, 'your Mam's right. It's no good searching for what's past, 'cause Polly needs you now. Polly an' the other children—an' poor little Ada Humble.'

'Mam.' The voice was close by. Marcia had been unaware of Florence's close presence until a small hand slipped into hers, and leaning tight against her, the child asked, 'Can I stay down?'

Glancing at the little mantelpiece clock, Marcia realised what a short time Florence had been abed. 'It's only quarter past seven, lass. Are you not tired then?'

'No, I want to stay down wi' you,' came the firm reply. It crossed Marcia's mind that she ought to send the child back to bed. After all, they were up early enough of a weekday, but on looking down at Florence's pleading face, she was pulled up sharp. For the eyes that met her gaze were Curt's eyes, black and magnificent, and the long dark hair which hung around the child's shoulders shone with the same gleaming richness.

Of a sudden, Marcia knelt to fold her daughter in a tender embrace. 'All right then, lass. You can help your Mam wi' the work, eh?'

Florence clasped her arms around Marcia's neck, pulling her close to impart a grateful kiss. 'Thanks Mam,' she said, with a big cheeky grin.

'Back upstairs then, lass—quiet mind! Get yourself properly dressed an' sneak back down again. We don't want the whole house awake yet, do we, eh?'

When, a few minutes after, Florence came back into the parlour, she had young Barty in tow, all dressed and wide awake.

'Well, there's a fine thing! I thought I told you to be quiet, Florence!'

'I did!—but 'e *followed* me!' She stared angrily at the lad standing beside her, yet, for all she seemed annoyed, Florence kept his little hand in hers.

Young Barty's big brown eyes stared back defiantly. '*You* woke me up!' He swivelled his eyes to direct the complaint towards Marcia. 'She *did* wake me up Mam, honest! I couldn't wake up on me own!' came the heartfelt protest. At the sight of them both, Marcia's heart swelled with love for the two mites. If she needed any reason at all to put up with the life she led, well—here it was, plain as a pikestaff. 'Right then,' she said, 'so now I've got *two* helpers, 'stead o' one! But there'll be no breakfast till the pair o' you get washed!' She smiled at their long faces and moans of protest. 'But that can wait until we get the house all clean and tidy.' Her last remark was greeted by two warm bundles flinging themselves at her for a cuddle.

It was just gone nine o'clock when Florence and young Barty got down from the big table, all washed and shining, and the soldiers of bread all gratefully eaten.

'Can we go to play out now, Mam?' Florence offered herself for inspection. 'Barty's got a den to show me, where 'e's hidden Guy Fawkes.'

'But you've not to tell anybody though!' Barty reminded her seriously.

Marcia let them out of the door. As she was about to close it, Ada Humble's bright red trilby appeared by the railings. 'Marcia, 'ave yer a minute, lass?' She sounded exceedingly agitated. 'Are yer quiet on yer own, eh?'

'Yes Ada . . . Barty Bendall and Polly are still abed . . . come on in.' She sensed it was over the court business, and her heart went out to her friend. Sure enough, the swellings beneath the flabby red-rimmed eyes told their own sad story. It was obvious to Marcia that Ada Humble had been crying. Sitting her down by the fire, where she provided her with a pint mug of strong brewed tea,

183

Marcia gently accused, 'You've not told him, have you? You've *still* not told him?'

'Oh, Marcia lass!' Ada Humble sniffled pitifully, 'I've not slept a wink since that 'fficial letter come!—nary a wink! Sooner than go to court *mesel'*—let alone take my lad, an' Toby 'as done nothing! I'd gi' mesel' up for dead! Oh Marcia lass, what in the world am I to do? I'm that afeared!'

Marcia's compassion for Ada Humble's pitiful plight overrode her fear that all the noisy crying would fetch Barty Bendall from his bed. Sitting on the arm of Ada's chair, she removed the tea mug, then wrapped a comforting arm around Ada's shoulders as she told her, 'You've no right cause to be afeared, Ada lass. Them folk at the town hall have got no understanding of ordinary bodies like us.' She squeezed the little woman affectionately, her soothing voice filled with the confidence she truly felt. 'But they mean you no real harm. It just meks 'em feel over-grand to frighten folks such as us. All they're out to do is frighten you.'

'Oh aye?' Ada Humble's red trilby bobbed about fearfully. She seemed more angry than tearful now. 'Well the sods 'a' certainly managed to do that! Are they so iron-like as they 'int got no childer? or 'as they got childer as never do owt wrong, eh?'

Marcia was relieved to see Ada's mood change somewhat, because to be angry was always better than being afraid. If anybody should know about that, it was Marcia Bendall! she thought. 'That's the bone o' the matter Ada, lass! And, in all truth, the buggers are no better than us!' She walked across to the mantelpiece. 'Their offspring happen see more in attending school than ours do. I expect

184

they get better rewarded.'

'Aye well,' Ada Humble struggled out of the chair, 'we all ends up just *one* way, an' that's buried i' the cold ground wi' them worms a sucking at us! Don't mek a tanner's worth o' difference what suit you lays in, be it sack or silk—we all taste the same to them there little rascals, an' that's God's truth!'

Marcia laughed. She knew exactly what the little woman meant. 'The fact still stares at you though, Ada lass, you've to roll your sleeves up an' tell yon Toby.'

'Oh nay! I shall 'ave to tek me time on that one.' She hid beneath the brow of her trilby. 'Although I knows I *'ave* to tell 'im—I knows that!'

Of a sudden, the germ of an idea took root in Marcia's mind! *Would* they get away with it, she wondered. 'Ada! I've thought o' summat—don't know as it'll work mind, but it's worth thinking on.'

Ada Humble quivered with excitement, 'Go on Marcia lass! What's thi' got i' mind?'

'*I'll* come with you to the court! We'll say as I'm standing in for your Toby, on account of they won't let him take the day off.'

'By the left! It'll work lass—it will!' She jumped up and down with such exuberance that the red trilby performed a crazy jig all of its own. 'You're an angel—a real angel! Oh, darlin' gel! What would ol' Ada do wi'out you, eh?'

It warmed Marcia's heart to see the relief in that chubby red face. 'There you are,' she gently chastised, 'all that worrying for nothing! Once we're both there, they'll not likely cause a great fuss over Toby. They'll give you and yon Blackie a right wiggin', I expect though!'

'Aye, 'appen,' Ada conceded, then in a more

sober tone, 'All the same lass . . . you've taken a right weight off me shoulders!' Her small brown eyes glittered happily and, as though too embarrassed to go on, she changed the subject. 'It's nice to see little Polly's got a friend i' that Revine lass, eh?' Without waiting for Marcia to reply, she continued, 'Rum lot though! Can't say as I've seen the grown 'uns out on the street so much. That smarmy one—the one as fancies 'issel, well, folks say as 'ow 'es not particular as to the ways an' means of 'is living! Seems 'e 'int got no proper job, yet there's no shortage o' ready brass.' Her eyes narrowed. 'One to be watched, is that! Aye! A right bad lot if you ask me. The *woman*'s not a bad sort I think, and it seems she idolises that poor brother of 'ers. Poor lad! My troubles don't seem owt aside o' that poor bugger.'

Marcia followed the little woman's chatter with deep thought. Ada Humble had come closer to Marcia's thinking than she had probably suspected, especially where Bridget's father was concerned. 'There's a lot o' truth in your thinking, Ada,' she murmured absent-mindedly, 'a lot o' truth.'

Ada nodded, slurping her cold tea with noisy enjoyment before moving purposefully towards the door. 'Well, lass. I've two laying-outs to be done tonight, along Leyland Street, so I'd best be off to get the shrouds finished. Old folks, the both on 'em, but well loved an' respected. Blowed if they 'in't both spectacle jobs an' all!' She laughed, 'Went up to collect the shrouding sheets, an' come away wi' two more pair o' spectacles . . . I wouldn't mind, but everybody knows I can't read! I've got that many spectacles i' me old chest, if I laid 'em end to end, it's likely I'd see where I'd been afore I

186

ever got there!' She waited for Marcia to stop laughing. 'I 'in't got no 'eart to chuck 'em away, lass, nor bury 'em in yon pawn shop either. There's many a short-sighted body as'd be right glad o' them spectacles,' she finished.

When Ada Humble left, Marcia was happy to see her in a merrier state of mind than when she'd arrived. She vowed in her heart to see Ada Humble through this trying time. When it came to town hall officials, everybody had to stick together and *that* was a fact.

As Marcia closed the door behind Ada, there came such an uproar from upstairs that, fearing it would wake Barty Bendall, Marcia tore up the steps two at a time. Jerking the bedroom door open she found Polly preparing to call Florence yet again. 'Stop your shouting, Polly!' she told her, 'your Dad's still abed.' As Marcia flicked the curtains back the burst of daylight accentuated the drawn pallor of Polly's frowning face.

'Don't wake your Dad up Polly,' Marcia pleaded in a low fearful voice, 'you know what he's like if he's wakened up on a Sunday!'

An expression of defiance flitted across Polly's features, and deliberately changing the subject, she asked, 'Where's Florence and young Barty?'

'Barty *did* come in to see you, but you were fast asleep, so I told him to let you be. I thought you looked tired when you went to bed last night. You are all right, aren't you, love?' Marcia asked as she stroked the delicate face gently.

'Of course I am Mam.' Polly hoisted herself up on to one elbow. 'I think I'll go an' see Bridget,' she declared, yawning and rubbing her sleepy eyes.

'Well, be quiet coming down, Polly. I don't want

your Dad woken up. He does work hard through the week, after all!' She departed the room, leaving Polly to get dressed.

*   *   *

'It's warmer down 'ere, Mam.' Polly shivered as she entered the parlour. There was a cheery fire in the grate, and as always on a Sunday morning, the room was bathed in a warm glow. Barty Bendall always insisted that the best knobs of coal should be reserved for a Sunday, and that Marcia should make it her priority to heat the parlour before calling him from his bed. 'There's a hot pan on the hob if you want some tea.'

'No thank you Mam . . . I don't want anything,' Polly replied, walking over to the window and stretching her neck to see down into the yard below. 'I can't see them two,' she remarked, turning back to her mother.

'They're away to young Barty's den, getting Guy Fawkes ready, as far as I can gather, lass.'

Polly laughed out loud. 'I'd have thought Florence would be past that sort o' thing!'

'She's only a child, Polly! and content with childish things.' Marcia's voice was gently chiding, as she thought how old in her ways Polly was.

'I suppose so,' Polly conceded begrudgingly, shrugging her narrow shoulders, and causing Marcia to give her an anxious, penetrating look. Polly had never actually been a 'child' in the accepted sense of the word. She had always been harshly critical of any pastime which didn't explore the world of adults, and Marcia had long ago despaired of Polly ever knowing childish enthusiasm.

Only three years spanned the birth of her daughters, but Florence and Polly might be worlds apart. Florence was an easy-going child, predictable in thought and mood, but Polly was an altogether different creature. Marcia had never been able to fathom her out and yet, in spite of every conscious effort against it, her heart held a very special place for Polly.

'Why don't you find Florence and young Barty?' she asked now.

'Oh Mam! I'm too *old* to be making Guy Fawkes,' Polly responded. She threw herself into the rocking chair and settled into a gentle rocking motion. 'I wonder whether Bridget's up yet?' she asked Marcia. Then, before Marcia could give an answer, Polly was gone—leaving the rocker going back and forth in a fury, as she slammed the front door loudly behind her.

'What the bloody 'ell's going on? Who's banging the sodding doors at this time of a morning?' Barty Bendall's voice filled every corner of the house.

'Polly, you deserve a tanning for that!' Marcia whispered into the parlour. The last thing she wanted was for Barty Bendall to be woken in such a foul mood. Lately, he seemed even quicker to temper than was usual—as though something was preying on his mind, she thought. But, he never confided in her, so if there *was* something, she would be the last to know of it.

The heavy clattering of his boots descending the stairs filled Marcia with dread as she bustled about laying his breakfast, speculating as to what he might fmd to complain about on this particular occasion.

189

The parlour door was flung open with customary vigour, and in that instant, the atmosphere in the hitherto quiet parlour became ominous. Marcia was not surprised to discover that her breathing had quickened the way it always did when he was near.

As was his way, Barty Bendall snatched the stand-chair out from its place by the table, his mouth a tight thin line, his stary green eyes intent upon the bacon and fried egg which Marcia had placed before him. Settling heavily into the chair, he spoke not a word, but proceeded to wolf the food down with customary enthusiasm. When Marcia apologised for the way Polly had thoughtlessly slammed the door, he didn't look up at all—but merely grunted. Marcia thought it most strange. Normally, he would have had a great deal to say.

Stepping back against the fireplace, Marcia watched him warily, on her face an expression of bewilderment. The usual surliness and the aggressive way in which he approached his food—none of this had altered since yesterday. But there was something about his manner which struck her as being decidedly different, and it bothered her. Was he perhaps ill? she wondered. No, Marcia didn't think so, but the way he had purposely avoided looking at her, and the surprising fact that he had been in the parlour a good five minutes without actually talking to her in one way or another, left her confused and suspicious. It wasn't like him at all.

Without even waiting to wash and still not having acknowledged Marcia's presence, Barty Bendall finished his breakfast, donned his cap and coat, knotted the off-white and aged scarf about his neck in that fastidious way that was peculiar to him. Then, without a backward glance, he quickly departed.

Once outside he paused, a troubled look on his face. Then, taking a pack of five Woodbines from his pocket, he lit one which he let dangle there while replacing both Woodbines and matches in his pocket. After which, he snatched the cigarette impatiently from his mouth, then, with that deep frown still creasing his forehead he went down Regent Street and hurried the last few yards to the Lord Nelson public house. There he would stoke up with a pint or two and spend a while sitting quietly in a corner, where he might have space to think. Lord only knows, thought Barty Bendall, I've a deal to think on—what with the rumours that Ratheter was on the loose again—or would be very shortly! Dear God, wasn't life difficult enough? Barty Bendall was no fool. It was plain enough, even to a blind man, that in the six years Marcia had been his wife, she'd never really loved him. That Ratheter fellow was still in her blood—and day or night the thought was enough to send him crazy. Oh, Marcia had tried her best, he knew that. But it wasn't good enough. And the more jealous he got, the more drunk and spiteful he became. Yet, the Devil take him for it, he couldn't help himself. He wanted her to love him—instead of which he often took her against her will. He wanted to talk with her and laugh with her—instead of which he yelled and bullied, and made her cry.

It was a few moments later, after clearing Barty Bendall's breakfast plate away, that Marcia, still perturbed and curious as to his unusually odd silence, discovered what she suspected to be the reason for his behaviour. Her purse had gone from its hiding place and with it, the carefully counted shillings which were to see them through the week. The shock was so severe to Marcia's already troubled mind that she sank sobbing across the chair, still warm from Barty Bendall's presence. 'Dear Lord above,' she asked in her anguish, 'what are we to do? Where can I turn?' Barty Bendall had cajoled and threatened her many a time, intent on extracting her hard-earned shillings. 'But I've *never* known him to steal from me!' she exclaimed out loud, wiping the tears from her face. The more she dwelt on this speculation, the more convinced she became. As big a bully as Barty Bendall was, he was no thief. Pulling her weary body up, she sat stiff and uncomfortable on the stand-chair. She scanned the parlour as if looking for the answer, 'If not Barty, then who?' she demanded of the inanimate objects about her. '*Who* would take my purse, with every blessed penny that might keep us from starving?' She reflected on Barty Bendall's strange mood, and although it sorely puzzled her, she believed most profoundly that he was innocent of this particular crime. 'Must have summat pressing on 'is poor twisted mind though,' she observed, 'some gambling palaver I expect.' Of a sudden, a possibility presented itself. 'Polly! Mebbe Polly knows where it's at?' Marcia wasn't even sure what it was she was suggesting. But she felt instinctively that Polly could very well be at the mot of this mystery.

Stopping only to collect her coat and feeling very much relieved by the idea that perhaps her purse wasn't 'lost' after all, Marcia took herself along Regent Street to the Revines' house, where she intended to thrash this business out with Polly.

The first clank of the knocker brought no reply, so Marcia lifted the iron arm again, this time letting it fall with a heavy resounding clatter. It seemed like an age before she heard definite movement in the hallway. Then slowly, painfully slowly, the door opened. It wasn't Bridget, as Marcia might have expected. It was her uncle Chris—the pitiful sight of whom gave her a tingling shock.

She was instinctively aware of this sad young man's dreadful loneliness. Whether he had purposely shut out his fellow men, or whether they had disowned him, she had no way of knowing; but now as their eyes locked in mutual greeting, it was as though Marcia could see right into his very soul, and for a fleeting second which weighed heavy her own heart felt lonely too.

The young man opened the door wide. 'You're Polly's mother, aren't you? Come in,' he said gently with a weak flourish of his arm, 'you'll freeze out there.'

Marcia followed him inside.

'Mam!' Polly had been seated by the fire, but the sight of Marcia brought her running. 'Bridget's gone to church an' Chris said I could wait. He was all on his own.'

Marcia was acutely aware of Chris politely busying himself at the sideboard and she came to the point. 'Polly, I can't seem to recall where I put my purse.' She didn't want the child to feel accused so, in a softer tone, she asked, 'You haven't seen it, have you?'

'It's under the wireless, Mam . . .' Polly's tone betrayed no guilt, and the rush of gratitude and relief that flooded through Marcia made her postpone any further questioning. So, she had been right, and there would be time for questions later.

Turning to the young man who was now crossing towards them, Marcia said, 'Please forgive the intrusion. I wonder—would you please tell your sister that I'll be glad to bake a dozen barm-cakes for her party, if she's partial to the idea?'

The young man held on to the table as if for support; almost as though without such assistance he would not have been able to cover the area between them. His smile was weak, but curiously beautiful. 'They should be back any minute, and I'm sure Rosa would like to discuss it with you. Please wait!' He gestured towards the array of chairs pulled up to the fireplace.

Marcia felt she could not refuse. The room was warm and interesting. Resting on the carpeted floor were some of the lovely items of furniture Marcia recognised from the cart. But the pungent smell of medicines and rubbing-oils permeated the air like a thick choking blanket. The young man was obviously used to it, and offered no explanation or apology. In fact, by the time the three of them had seated themselves by the fire, Marcia had warmed to the comfort of the heat and the hitherto strong smell had unobtrusively mingled into the background, until she could barely detect its stinging aroma.

'Bridget and her parents never miss Sunday morning Mass.'

Marcia smiled at the young man's remark. 'Oh,'

194

she responded, 'there was a time when I too never missed Sunday Mass.'

As the young man looked on Marcia in earnest, she wondered at the parchment-like delicacy of his skin. In stark contrast, the dark wide sorrowful eyes and the thick black springy hair falling mischievously in deep waves over his forehead seemed to be the only living things about him. A surge of inexplicable sadness brought tears to her eyes as she felt that he was not long for this cruel world.

Of a sudden, Polly jumped up. 'I'm going to meet Bridget,' she told them, promptly going from the room and, in a minute, from the house.

'Your daughter's a delightful creature,' the young man told Marcia, 'and such a *beautiful* young lady—those exquisite blue eyes and that lovely blonde hair.'

For a moment, Marcia was quiet. And, when he dropped his gaze into the flames of the fire and sat in pensive mood, occasionally sighing to himself, she wondered whether Polly reminded him of someone he'd known—a past girlfriend maybe. It seemed likely, for he was obviously deeply lost in his memories. Now, he stood up as they heard the key turning in the front door lock.

'Sounds as though they're back,' he said with a half-smile, 'you'll come and talk to me again, won't you, Marcia?'

'Yes,' she nodded, her heart full, 'I will.'

Peter Revine appeared at the living room door—his tall handsome figure impeccably dressed. His devilishly beckoning eyes swept the room. Marcia, realising she was rudely staring, quickly averted her eyes though not before her

195

astonished gaze had betrayed her sneaking admiration. In a minute he had crossed the room towards her and was standing close to her chair, his voice seductive, his black eyes sweeping unashamedly across her embarrassed face.

'Ah,' he breathed, 'we have a visitor.'

'This is Marcia,' Chris explained, 'Polly's mother—and she's waiting for Rosa.'

'Oh, she won't be long,' Peter Revine assured them, 'I rushed home out of the cold. They stayed to talk to the priest about something or other.'

'Perhaps I'd best go and call back later?' Marcia felt decidedly uneasy. She was no child. But the piercing stare with which he held her gaze disturbed her deeply. This man's dark compelling looks held untold danger.

'There's no need to go,' Chris urged, 'they can't be long now. You might as well wait just a little while longer!'

'Five minutes at most.' Peter Revine undid the buttons of his black top-coat. Slipping his arms from within the sleeves, he draped the coat from his broad shoulders then carried it to the door, where he carefully hung it, brushing the hanging folds into a perfect drape. 'Now then,' he said as he turned to Chris, 'has our visitor had a drink?'

'She's had a cup of tea,' Chris confirmed, 'but I dare say she wouldn't object to another.' Leaning towards Marcia, he said, 'Please excuse me Marcia. I'm feeling rather tired just now.' Turning to his brother-in-law, he said, 'Would you tell Rosa when she comes in that I'm having a nap?'

'It's as good as done. You get your rest.' The reply was issued more as an instruction.

Chris left the room, and Peter Revine

disappeared into the scullery, only to reappear a couple of minutes later just as Marcia had decided she would go after all. She had been inexplicably flustered by the sudden appearance of this man, whose dominating presence seemed to overshadow everything around him.

'Do you like what I've done to this room?'

Marcia started at his low caressing voice immediately behind her.

'Yes,' she told him, looking around at the soft painted green shade of the walls, 'it's very pretty.' She hadn't attributed the creation of the cool colour scheme to *him*. 'Pretty' seemed a rather inadequate description. It was very attractive and inviting; but she couldn't bring herself to describe it so to him. The welcoming aspect of the room appeared to have dissipated beneath the extravagant charm of his personality.

The furniture was dark and richly decorated in a heavy, ugly manner, and, Marcia reasoned that the furniture could belong to no one else but him. Deep curving scrolls shaped like turning leaves were etched into the magnificence of the sideboard, which reached tall and sweeping to the ceiling. The huge three-piece-suite had soft billowing cushions which wrapped tenaciously around unsuspecting occupants with smothering possessiveness.

Peter Revine's black eyes flashed a look of gratitude at Marcia's obvious appreciation. 'Good!' he said briskly. Taking her by the hand, he raised Marcia to her feet. 'I can see you're a woman of taste,' he murmured.

Feeling suddenly threatened by his nearness, Marcia broke away, saying, 'I must go!'

197

So swift and decisive was her departure that he had no time to persuade her otherwise. When Marcia had emerged out onto the pavement, she felt the need to take a long gulp of air into her lungs. God! That fellow was a turn-up and no mistake, eh? Of a sudden, she felt afraid— wondering whether she was doing right in allowing Polly into that house at all.

Edith Atkinson was white-stoning her front doorstep as Marcia climbed the steps to her own front door. 'Tiresome job is this,' the big woman shouted in a voice fit to reach the deaf, 'bothersome, thankless job!' She looked about to rise from her kneeling position so as to engage Marcia more easily in conversation. But, being in no mood to exchange petty niceties, Marcia cut her short. She had Barty Bendall due home any minute; and in truth, she was still shaken by her strange experience.

'Yes, it is a thankless job, Mrs Atkinson,' she conceded, already about to close the door behind her, 'excuse me. I've a meal to be getting ready.'

The meal had been taken in silence as usual. Marcia was somewhat relieved to note that at least Barty Bendall's strange, sullen manner of this morning had given way to his usual complaining attitude. She was more used to that particular mood and was more able to cope with it.

The subject of his rage this time was Polly's absence from the table. Marcia herself was anxious about Polly's late return, but the knowledge that she was in the company of Bridget, a truly sensible creature, allayed her fears considerably.

It was well past two o'clock when Florence and young Barty eagerly raced each other to the door

198

to let Polly in. 'We were wondering where you were,' she told them, hurrying back to her place at the table, where she and young Barty were playing 'Snap' with their pile of home-made cards.

Although pleased at Polly's return, Marcia couldn't suppress a curious sense of irritation. She had found the purse exactly where Polly had said it would be, and the fact that she hadn't arrived home in time to sit down for her meal with the family had resulted in a barrage of ill-tempered abuse from Barty Bendall. As a result Marcia decided she would need to have strong words with Polly. However, she would need to pick and choose her moment, because there was no sense in riling Barty Bendall all over again. 'Where have you been all this time, Polly!' she demanded. That much she did want to know—especially after having met that Revine fellow at close quarters.

Polly gazed at Marcia's angry face. Her white hair was dishevelled and wind-blown, and her thin pale features so cold-looking that Marcia's heart turned full circle.

'Sorry Mam,' Polly said, looking truly repentant, 'I went for a walk by the Beck.'

'On your own, lass?' Polly's forlorn attitude made Marcia wish she hadn't spoken quite so harshly. If Polly had been wandering by the Beck on her own, it usually meant that she had either suffered another painful attack or she had troubles on her mind with which she couldn't cope. Marcia had come to know this well over the years. It strengthened her resolve to get Polly to the doctor tomorrow, without fail. 'I've kept your Sunday dinner warm for you, lass.' Marcia started walking toward the scullery to collect Polly's meal.

Barty Bendall was slumped in the horsehair chair by the fire, his mouth open, snores echoing around the room. In some uncanny way he still remained responsive to the activity around him, however quietly it seemed to have been conducted. Suddenly, snapping his loosely-hanging mouth shut, he sat bolt upright in the chair, his beady eyes fixed on the disappearing figure of his wife. 'Come back here!' he yelled. 'She wasn't 'ere when we 'ad our bloody meal! so she can sodding well go without!'

Marcia turned, startled at his unexpected intrusion, 'Barty!'

'Don't "Barty" me! Twist you round 'er little finger, she can! Miss 'igh and bloody mighty!' His voice rose to a high-pitched scream. 'I said she can bloody well go without!' He sprang out of his chair and rushed past Marcia violently catching his shoulder against her, causing her to lose her balance and stumble hard against the sideboard. At that moment, Marcia felt she hated him. And to think, at one time, she actually did love him a little—this beast, who was her husband!

Ignoring her gasp of pain, Barty Bendall tore into the scullery, where he grabbed Polly's dinner plate and hurled it down into the yard below, where it smashed on the flagstone, spattering itself in all directions. 'Is *that* clear enough for you?' he demanded of Marcia, striding triumphantly back into the parlour, where his gloating was somewhat dissipated by the condemning gleam in Marcia's bitter eyes.

Florence and young Barty had quickly disappeared upstairs, taking their game with them. But Polly stood by her mother, examining the rapidly swelling area on her arm where she had been thrown into the sideboard. When a dark look spread over her daughter's face, Marcia sensed trouble. At once she pushed Polly away with gentle firmness, murmuring, 'It's all right, lass. Go and see what young Barty and Florence are up to.'

Polly, however, stood firm and, stretching herself to her full height, she glared at Barty Bendall, her wide blue eyes defiant and filled with loathing. 'You've hurt my Mam,' she said simply, her voice strangely calm, and the hitherto ethereal beauty of her face stamped hard by the hatred within her. Marcia's heart contracted painfully as the loathing between Polly and Barty Bendall permeated the room until it seemed as though even the light of day shrank from it.

Now, Barty Bendall's face grew viciously dark as he walked, deliberately slowly, over to where Polly stood. 'What was that you said?' His voice was low, trembling with rage, the green eyes wild and penetrating.

Stepping quickly in front of her daughter and forcibly propelling her out of the way towards the door Marcia told her crossly, 'Polly! Do as you're told! Go and see what the young 'uns are up to.' She pushed the girl out into the hallway, quickly closing the door behind her, and turned back to confront Barty Bendall.

Polly stood in the passageway for what seemed an age, her eyes clouded, her teeth clenched. As she heard Barty Bendall's voice raised in fury, Polly grew ever more conscious of what her gentle mother had learned to endure. Her tiny fists clenched tightly. 'I'd like to kill him for what he's doing to me Mam!' she whispered vehemently.

Having said her piece and condemned her husband for the way he seemed always to set himself up against Polly—and having been quietened by the truth of his reply when he'd claimed, 'Tain't all *my* bloody fault, woman! The girl has no liking fer me at all!' Marcia watched as he settled himself back into the chair, where he seemed promptly to fall asleep again. Her eyes wandered over his face, and she wondered why in God's name their relationship had come to sink to such a level.

Feigning sleep, Barty Bendall was filled with anger at Marcia, and at Ratheter's daughter, Polly—the one who had never accepted him! Most of all he was angry with himself. He felt like a man who had burned all his bridges. But, however difficult it became to tell Marcia how much he needed her, no man could ever love a woman the way he loved her. Rather than give her up to that Ratheter fellow he'd kill the pair on 'em.

CHAPTER ELEVEN

Barty Bendall grasped his khaki overcoat from the back of the parlour door. Shrugging his sharp little body into it with military correctness, he collected the prepared billy-can and snap-tin from the table. 'I'm off!' he said. 'See me food's ready when I get 'ome.'

Marcia waited for the front door to signal his departure. 'Poor Barty,' she murmured, 'nary a cheery greeting nor a warm thought to brighten your day.' Only occasionally did she feel compassion for him, never love. It was far too late for that. Lifting the heavy length of black wavy hair from her shoulders, Marcia pinned it to the top of her head. But it wouldn't stay put, because the straight iron pins with which she sought to tame its wildness were inadequate to perform such a formidable task.

However, she eventually succeeded in shaping the long thick hair into a degree of tidiness which she thought to be acceptable. 'Can't go visiting no doctor's surgery wi' me hair draping down like a schoolgirl's,' she muttered, examining herself in the cracked mirror above the pot sink, in which she had just washed.

In spite of the anxious thoughts which had broken her sleep throughout the long night, her rich, dark eyes shone out to light her lovely face. The high cheekbones gave her features a suggestion of magnificence, and the full rich mouth portrayed something of her turbulent passions. Marcia Bendall was a woman of quality. She was a rare creature of sacrifice and loyalty, a woman who fervently believed in the hard duties of a wife and mother.

Emptying the remains of the powdered egg into the jug, she mixed it together with a measure of water until it congealed, thick and creamy. The pan was filled afresh from the tap, and boiled up on the gas ring, ready for a brew. Then, drawing her green overall tight about her, she said through chattering teeth, 'It's enough to freeze a body solid in this place!' She kept warm by busying herself with the laying of the table—setting out the plates, and soldiers of bread and margarine, ready for the children. A glance at the mantel-clock told her she'd soon have to be making for the tram. 'Better get Polly out,' she murmured, regretting circumstances which called her children from their beds so early.

'Oh Mam!' Polly winked sleepily as Marcia bent quietly to awaken her, 'I'm tired!' she protested.

'I know lass . . .' Marcia kept her voice to a low whisper, so as not to wake Florence, who could be allowed to sleep on a bit longer, 'but I've got to be going, or I'll not catch the tram!' She shook Polly with a firmness which reflected her anxiety. 'Come on! I've got to go *now*!' Satisfied that Polly was out of bed and proceeding to dress, Marcia crossed to young Barty's room, and seeing that he was content and fast asleep, she tiptoed back downstairs.

By the time Polly dragged herself in through the parlour door, Marcia had a mug of tea ready for her. 'There you are lass,' she smiled, 'you'll be wide awake after that.' Grabbing her coat from the door, she flung it round her in a hurry. 'I've left everything ready in the scullery. You've only to see the young 'uns go off to school wi' a bite in their bellies. Oh!—and see as they *wash*. An' make sure you wash *yourself* smartly lass! I don't want that doctor thinking you can't keep yourself clean!' Marcia was dreading the appointment at the surgery.

'Oh Mam,' Polly said as she wrapped her hands around the warm mug, 'do I have to go to the doctors? I don't like being looked at!' This desperate little plea halted Marcia in her tracks, bringing her quickly back to sit beside the forlorn looking girl. She knew how Polly felt, for didn't she feel it herself? Cupping Polly's small cold face in

204

her hands, she tilted it towards her, until the fearful eyes had nowhere else to look but upon Marcia's face.

'Look, Polly lass. I *know* it's not something you like, an' I like it no better. You know that, don't you?' She waited for the slight nod of acknowledgement. 'But I *want* you to see the doctor. You've not told me in so many words, but I know it's been paining you lately.'

Polly's quiet answer was hesitant, almost inaudible. 'Yes, Mam.'

'It'll be all right, Polly lass—you'll see.' She hugged her and swallowed the threatening tears which burned her eyes and filled her throat. Then, releasing the girl with a rush of guilt, she told her, 'It's best to see what the doctor has to say. Now then, please, Polly—see the young 'uns off to school, an' don't you worry none! Make sure you have some breakfast an' all! I'll meet you outside the mill gates at nine o'clock. You'll not let me down, will you?' The thought frightened her.

Polly held her gaze steady. 'No Mam—I'll not let you down,' she answered. The conviction in her voice settled Marcia's anxiety. 'Go on, else you'll miss that tram!' she added with a smile.

The smile on Polly's delicate face didn't fool Marcia, yet she marvelled at the inner strength her child had—and she saw that Polly was a girl after her own heart. Returning to clasp her daughter in a hurried embrace she murmured, 'Grandma Fletcher's right . . .' her dark eyes blurred from the swimming tears, 'you *are* a grand lass!'

Just one more minute and Marcia would have seen the tram disappear out of the Boulevard. As it was she had to run the last few yards, boarding the tram as it shuddered away.

'Thought you weren't coming with us this morning!' the conductor remarked as he rattled the handle of his machine, to produce a ticket. 'Never known you be late afore, Marcia lass!'

'Aye well . . .' Marcia had no intention of burdening others with her troubles, 'first time for everything, ain't there?'

'Well, I can't argue wi' *that*, now can I?'

As Marcia picked her way through the confusion of feet, which decorated the aisle with boots and clogs, all manner of greetings were addressed her way.

'Mornin', Marcia.'

'Couldn't get thisel' outta bed, eh?'

'Old man 'anging on to your shirt-tail, was 'e, eh?' The shouts and chuckles accompanied Marcia to the back of the tram, and she received them all with gracious humour.

'Marcia! Marcia! There's a place next to me. Up 'ere!' Daisy Forester hung over the seat, looking down the aisle to catch Marcia's attention.

'What's med you so late, Marcia? 'Ad me real worried, you did!'

'Summat an' nothing,' came Marcia's reply, as she drew in a deep comforting breath. Her lungs felt on fire and her heart was still beating desperate time, 'Oh, you know how it is, Daisy. I've to make sure everything's ready for the children—an' poor Polly wasn't too pleased at leaving her bed this morning.'

'I know just what you mean. Me own Mam's not been too well lately, an' the young 'uns look to me more than ever.'

Marcia felt so sorry for Daisy, who was still a

young 'un herself, an' bearing the load of a married woman. She reached out to collect Daisy's hand in her own. 'Never mind lass. There's plenty o' folks'd love to be surrounded by people as loves 'em . . .' She could see that Daisy's narrow little face was lost in deepest thought, and the small pale eyes were glittering with the threat of tears.

'Them little 'uns won't be long afore they're all grown up, Daisy lass, an' it's a born fact that they'll all love you the more for looking after 'em all.'

Her attempt at comforting the unhappy creature seemed to be lost. Marcia leaned nearer, anxious that something was more wrong than Daisy was revealing. 'Your Mam—she's all right is she?' She often thought that Daisy's Mam leaned hard on the lass. In fact, she'd been convinced that Mrs Forester could well be taking unfair advantage of Daisy's good nature. There had been time enough passed now for the wretched woman to pick up the responsibility of her family, and leave the poor lass to enjoy her youth. But now? Marcia wondered whether Daisy's Mam really *was* the sort who let life get the better of her. Until, in the end, she was beaten.

'Oh no, Marcia,' Daisy's quick smile flickered, 'Mam's in fine fettle! She still mopes and cries, bless 'er, but, thank God she's not any *worse.*'

'Oh, that's grand. I *am* pleased!' Marcia settled back in her seat, at once relieved. She thought that happen a good shaking might do Daisy's Mam a world o' good.

'Marcia?' There was a world of tragedy in Daisy's whisper. 'Marcia—I can talk to you, I know that . . .'

Marcia met Daisy's shy gaze. 'If you're troubling

207

over owt, you know I'll advise you best I can.' She edged nearer, aware of Daisy's anxiety to keep the conversation just between the two of them. 'It's not your Mam, an' it's not the young 'uns.' Of a sudden, Marcia recognised on Daisy's blushing face the same wonderful emotion that she herself experienced whenever she thought of her darling Curt. 'You're in love! In *love*! Aren't you, lass?'

That Marcia had *guessed* brought a fleeting expression of incredulity into Daisy's fair features. 'How did you *know*? I've never told anybody! Kept it to us'selves we 'ave. We both thought it best, 'cause o' me Mam an' all. So how did you know, Marcia?'

'It's written all over your face, lass,' Marcia told her. 'There's only *love* as can light a body's face up like that.' She smiled into Daisy's gaze, her own eyes reflecting the tears which she'd resigned herself to carry in her heart forever. 'I do *know* what it's like to be in love!' She half-smiled, her voice tailing off into the thoughts which swirled about her mind.

'Marcia.' Daisy had perceived the unhappiness in Marcia's voice. Barty Bendall was well known throughout Blackburn, and there had been numerous speculations as to the 'odd' pairing of a brute like him to such a gentle, loyal creature. 'If I looked like you, I'd *always* be in love. I've never seen *anyone* as beautiful as you. Even in the mill, in all that dirt and grime, you always look so . . . radiant.'

Now it was Marcia's turn to blush. 'Away with you!' she said stoutly, 'An' what's your fella's name then, eh?' She felt distinctly uncomfortable, and anxious to change the subject. 'Why the long face, lass? Being in love at your age! You should be singing at the top of your voice!' Marcia watched Daisy fidgeting nervously with her fingers, and she suspected the problem, but, as was her way, she waited for Daisy to tell her.

'It's me Mam! I only mentioned it to 'er just once, an' that were about five months back, when I first met 'im.' She shook her head, recalling the terrible memory. 'Oh, Marcia! If you'd 'a seen 'er! It was awful!' The nervous fidgeting became an agitated hand-wringing.

'You really love this lad?'

Daisy was crying now, the tears running helplessly down her tragic face. 'Oh Marcia, Marcia . . . I *do* love 'im with all my 'eart! An' 'e loves me.' She wiped her face with the back of her hand, sniffed hard, and sneaked a surreptitious glance around the tram to assure herself that nobody was looking. They were all asleep. 'I know I'm not that old . . . not yet, Marcia. But, every day's exactly the same! I see lasses o' my age, going out, enjoying theirselves. I met Ginger at the market. He runs a fruit and veg stall—does all right too! I told me Mam that, because I thought it'd mek 'er feel better, but she shouted an' screamed. Said as 'ow I was an ungrateful wretch! Said I only wanted to dump me responsibilities! Oh Marcia!' she sighed wearily, 'sometimes, life seems to be going past me like it 'ad skates on! We love each other, me an' Ginger, an' we wants to get married, but, I'm so afeared! What would me Mam do? An' who'd look after the young 'uns?'

Marcia examined the girl's peaked features. And they told their own story. So! It was no wonder the lass was frightened half out of her wits.

Squeezing the fidgeting fingers reassuringly, she whispered, 'But you'll have your *own* babby to take care of soon, won't you lass?'

Daisy was past being surprised at Marcia's uncanny perception. For a while, she just fell silent. Then, a smile lighting up her face, she said, 'You're a one an' no mistake! You *knew*! Oh! we're that pleased an' excited, Marcia. Ginger's got a little 'ouse 'is folks left 'im, an' it's just waiting. But me Mam says she'll do away wi' 'erself if I leave 'ome!'

'Well you're right about life whizzing past on skates! Nobody knows what you mean any more than I do, lass! Life has a cruel way o' doing that.' Marcia understood from bitter experience just how soul-destroying it was, to be made to choose between misguided loyalty and what was truly in your heart. She couldn't bear the thought of young Daisy having to face such a choice in the wake of her Mam's heartless threat. And she couldn't not do her best by the lass. 'Daisy lass, a body can find a whole lifetime o' misery packed into just one short day!' she told her. 'But happiness and true love are precious, elusive things, that don't come our way too often—mebbe just the once in a whole lifetime. Your Mam had her chance. She had the love of your Dad, and the joy of bearing his children. She'll always have her memories.' As she spoke, Marcia realised just how much she had in common with Daisy's Mam, but God forbid that she should ever rob one of *her* children of the love of a partner, or of the happiness that came with such love. 'Your poor Mam, she's letting her treasured memories bring her misery and sorrow. And she's letting that sorrow turn her into a helpless invalid, looking to you for compensation. It doesn't work out that way, Daisy, not for her, and not for you. She needs to find strength and comfort in the fact that at least she had somebody to love, and who loved her. When she brings herself to face *that*, believe me, she'll be a different woman.' Marcia felt in her heart that what she was about to advise this poor little lass was right. 'You go and marry your fella, Daisy! Marry him and thank the good Lord for sending him to you. Your Mam'll 'appen disown you for a while, but I'm thinking it's just what she needs to be made to do for hersel' and cherish the young 'uns your Dad left in her charge.' She kissed Daisy on her tear-stained face, patting the back of her hand confidently. 'Go on lass! Be brave and grab that chance of happiness with both hands!'

Daisy started her crying and sniffling all over again . . . but the tears this time were tears of joy, 'I will! Oh, Marcia, I know you're right. I *will*! I'll fetch my Ginger 'ome this very night, an' we'll tell me Mam together.'

By the time the tram had disgorged its tired cargo into the sharp morning air, Daisy was already bright and full of exciting intentions, and Marcia felt confident that all would be well. And, as the surging mill-hands rounded Cicely Brew, the familiar thick, acrid smoke from the mill chimney mingled with the morning air, stinging the nose and clinging to the throat like dry sawdust. There came that usual bout of coughing and throat-clearing, and from somewhere in the middle of it all a shout was sent up.

'Hey, Marcia! Stand thi'sel right there an' give us a chance to catch up!' Big Bertha squashed and pushed through the teeming multitudes before drawing alongside Daisy and Marcia, breathless and bent double. Catching hold of Marcia's shoulder, she leaned against her, puffing and gasping at the air. 'My God! It's been a long time since I ran like that! An' by me ol' Dad's memory . . . it'll be a long time . . . afore . . . I runs like it again!'

The three of them saw the funny side of the situation. Big Bertha—nose running dewdrops and fighting for breath—was a thing to behold! In a chorus of laughter, they proceeded towards the mill gates.

As usual, the frantic hurry to get their cards clocked in before the hand swung past six o'clock resulted in a heavy crush of bodies, all pushing and shoving, shouting and laughing.

'Here, Elsie.' A batch of yellow cards would appear from nowhere, as they had done every morning as far as Marcia could remember. 'Shove these in while you're at it, lass!' The cheeky instruction, which meant a frustrating wait while Elsie casually clocked half-a-dozen cards through the timer, brought a battery of protests.

'Cheeky sod!'

'Who the 'ell keeps doing that, eh?'

'Whose bloody cards are they? Give us a look!' But Elsie, loyal as they came, would have none of it. Keeping her hand over the cards, she'd have them in and out of the timer in record speed. The mill-hands had come to accept the exasperating routine as inevitable, deciding that their only salvation was to get to the timer before the dreaded Elsie. This practice unfortunately served only to increase the death-defying crush.

212

Marcia and Daisy were fortunate in having Big Bertha alongside them, for she acted as a sort of battering ram holding the minions back by a gigantic spread of her strong arms.

'Come on Bertha! Stop bloody showin' off!'

'You're nowt but a great bully. I'd soon 'ave thi' away fro' there, if thi' were ticklish, eh?'

'Hey! Big 'uns like you should learn not to tek advantage!' they'd shout good naturedly. But Big Bertha took no notice. Graciously ignoring the few 'shorties' who dived through under her arms, just occasionally, when the pushing got a bit cheeky, she'd yell 'Piss off!' at the top of her voice. And they did!

Marcia had Polly constantly on her mind. She'd have to find Tom Atkinson. She'd need to leave about five to nine, if she wasn't to keep Polly waiting in the cold. She confided her intention to Big Bertha.

'Well o' course I'll keep your machine going for you, Marcia lass.' Big Bertha waited for Marcia to hang her coat on the peg, then she grabbed her in a friendly hug. 'You tek care o' that smashing little lass o' yourn! An' don't fret about nothing!' she declared stoutly.

'Girls!' the shrill voice pierced the air, ' 'Eard the latest, 'ave you? Marcia! Marcia lass, *you'll* 'ave a laugh at this, seeing as 'e's chased you up 'ill an' down dale ever sin' 'e clapped eyes on you! Are you ready, girls, eh!'

The suspense was unbearable, as the response came back quick and demanding, 'What's up?'

'*All* the fellas fancy Marcia, you bloody cloth 'ead! *Who* is it you're talking about?'

'An' what are you talking about, Maggie Clegg.

Out wi' it!'

Maggie Clegg, a slim girl with waist-length dark hair, hoisted herself above the colourful turbaned heads to stand on an upside-down bucket, where swaying and staggering in a dangerous manner, she spouted her news out to the great delight and amusement of all present. 'Tomorrow morning at six we shall have a *new* member of the female brigade! I 'ave it on the authority of a certain Mrs Arkwright, as buys 'e sausages in the same butcher's as me, that Mrs HARRY FENSOME has caught her randy old man keeping company wi' a floozy from the weaving shed!' With a wink and a naughty whisper, she concluded, 'The floozy being compensation o' course, on account of 'e couldn't get nowhere with our razzling beauty, Marcia! Anyway! Old Ma Fensome's coming *'ere* to work, so's she can keep an eagle eye on 'im! Poor ol' sod! That's *'is* share o' spare oats gone for a bloody tumble, eh?' she roared.

The news was greeted by a hubbub of cheers and laughter. 'Marcia! what d'ya think o' that, eh? Best news you've 'eard for a month, ain't it?' someone called out. Then, 'Aye! Come on, Marcia lass . . . gi' us a song. We'll *all* be glad to get shut o' that one's wandering eyes! Can't bend ter pick up yer bloody slippers, wi'out 'is gawping up yer arse!'

For a few moments, Marcia's immediate problems disappeared beneath the bevy of calls and her own passion for losing herself in the heart of a song. 'A song,' they demanded, 'one as fits the situation!'

Of a sudden, Marcia felt herself lifted from the ground. In a moment the lasses were carrying her bodily over to the upturned bucket which Maggie

Clegg manoeuvred beneath her dangling feet. At once the enthusiasm grew wilder.

As the feet started stamping, and the hands came together in rhythmic beats, Marcia began.

Who were you with last night (Harry
    Fensome)
Out in the pale moonlight.
It wasn't your sister, it wasn't your Ma,
Oh! Oh! Oh! Oh!—Ha, ha, ha, aah.

By the end of the first verse, not a mill-hand stood silent. The thunderous clapping and shouting was almost drowned beneath the roar of voices which took up the song.

Who were you with last night (Harry
    Fensome)
Under the moon so bright—'
Are you gonna tell your missus
When you get home—
Who you were with last night.

Quickly now, Big Bertha caught Marcia by the waist to pluck her from the conspicuous position in which the mill-hands had affectionately placed her. The singers at the door fell quickly silent, and the silence spread through the gathered crowd like a breaking wave.

'What the sodding 'ell's going on 'ere?' came an angry voice.

With whispers of 'It's the gaffer!', the mill-hands scuttled in all directions, to the tune of hearty chuckles.

'You!' Tom Atkinson's dislocated eyes spun in

every direction as he tried to fix his glance on Marcia and Big Bertha. 'I'd a' thought you two might 'ave 'ad a bit more bloody sense! I'll dock ten minutes from all your sodding cards, I'm buggered if I won't!'

'Hey! Just don't rush yer fences, my lad!' Big Bertha straightened herself up to him, the sight of which seemed to have a devastating effect on poor Tom, as his eyes continued to execute their fearful dance, and his voice fell away to a stutter.

'Little Marcia, 'ere,' she began, and Marcia decided to let Big Bertha defend her, 'she were wi' *me*! All as we were doing were 'anging us coats up, an' we got swept up that corner there, like corks in a tide! Now you can see as there were no way through that rampaging mob, can't you, eh! In fact, Tom. if you 'adn't come along to rescue us, as sure as fate we'd 'a' suffocated!' Her eyes grew wide and fearful at the very thought—the sight of which made Marcia back away to hide herself in Big Bertha's green overall, where she fell into a fit of helpless giggling, as did all the girls looking on. What a liar Big Bertha was, when she'd a mind.

'Aye . . . right. Well!' Tom shuffled awkwardly from one foot to the other, his one stable eye flitting suspiciously over Big Bertha's face, and the other spinning uncontrollably. He backed away. ''Appen we'll overlook it, just this *once*, mind yer! Aye!'

As he moved away Big Bertha grabbed Marcia out from behind her. 'Go on lass!' she shouted, while Tom was still in earshot, 'you're all right now. Bit of a shock, eh lass, being squashed agin' the wall like that!' The two of them crept away, doubled up laughing and tears rolling down their

216

faces.

Marcia thought better of approaching Tom Atkinson straight away about leaving early, although as she passed him to get to her machine, she had the distinct feeling that he'd mistaken the tears of laughter in her eyes for tears of distress at having been 'squashed against the wall'. In a small pathetic voice he enquired, 'All right are yer, Marcia?'

Seeing her chance, Marcia replied in as trembling a voice as she could muster, 'I think so, Tom.' Then, after a bit of coughing and a few pitiful expressions, Marcia was told, 'It might be a good idea if yer tek yersel' off early, eh?' Then, when she quietly thanked him, she could see Big Bertha out of the corner of her eye—hiding behind one of the machines and waving a triumphant fist in the air. It was all Marcia could do not to burst out giggling.

CHAPTER TWELVE

Polly stood in the cold morning air, braced defiantly against the strong biting wind which buffeted mercilessly against her. The long white strands of hair lifted and danced, revealing the frozen pinkness of her small numbed ears, and as her eyes glittered with tears of cold, Polly's stiff fingers left the warmth of her pockets to clasp the worn gaberdine mac tightly around her shivering form. Now she drew herself into the hiding place, her eyes narrowed against the whipping gusts to focus intently on the activities being played out three or four hundred yards up the High Street at the foot of Canal Bridge.

The tram had glided to a halt and the noisy, bustling schoolchildren surged forward, pushing and shoving each other so that no one could actually board.

'Give over pushing! You silly blighters!' The tram conductor's voice yelled angrily as he thrust his arms into the heaving mass of excited bodies, grabbing first one child then the other, and swinging them easily off the tram. With the threat that he would leave them all there if they 'didn't stop acting daft!' the children at last organised themselves into at least some semblance of order. 'Right! That's better!' The conductor's face registered smug satisfaction as he watched them climb aboard, and much to the amusement of some of the cheekier children, he kept injecting chirpy comments into the proceedings. 'Now then. Why couldn't you 'ave done that in the first place? Eee, I don't know! Is this how you behave at home?' he wanted to know.

Polly grimaced appreciatively as she saw the last passengers onto the tram then, opening the small white note clutched in her stiff fingers, she looked at it for a moment, having no need to read it, for she knew its contents by heart. It was intended to have travelled on the school tram via Florence, whose purpose would have been to deliver it to the headmaster's office. The note read:

Dear Mr Wiggins, please excuse Polly Bendall's absence from school today. She has been in some considerable pain of late, and I am anxious that she visit the doctor. She will be back at her desk tomorrow without fail.—Mrs Bendall.

Polly watched the breeze carry the piece of paper away. She saw no reason why old Wiggins should know about her being in pain. It was none of his business! Now, as the tram moved off, Polly watched it from a safe distance. Afterwards she turned and headed in the opposite direction, towards Cicely Mill and her Mam. A little while later, as she drew up towards the top of Cicely Brow, Polly stopped to gaze at the mill from there.

The sprawling ugliness of the wide Victorian monument fascinated her. Her eyes swept the building, before coming to rest on one of the multitude of small narrow windows which almost completely covered one wall. She knew it to be the one nearest to her mother's spinning machines because the bottom corner was broken; smashed by a flying bobbin which had suddenly taken off and launched itself through the air, as if in a final desperate bid for freedom, only to be unceremoniously retrieved and thrown contemptuously into the rubbish skip.

Polly eased herself into the arched recess carved within the depth of the mill wall—all the while keeping a wary eye on the over-zealous gatekeeper. The eagle-eyed monster had hauled her out on more than one occasion, when she'd crept beyond the big gates to wait for her Mam. But she was safe enough tucked into the big wall. From here she was able to monitor the main doors through which her Mam would appear any minute.

Inside, Marcia slipped her card into the timer. A quick calculation told her that she'd lose more money than could be afforded, but, in the face of Polly's increasing pain, it wasn't even worthy of consideration.

A strangely exhilarating sensation swept through her as she emerged from the relative darkness of the mill into the grey daylight behind the wide doors. She felt free! This would be the very first time since starting here that she hadn't spent a full weekday harnessed to the relentless demands of her spinning machine. As the gusty breeze blew against her face, Marcia greedily breathed it in. She'd been used to entering the mill in the dark and emerging at the end of the day, still in the dark. Daylight was something she only ever enjoyed on a weekend.

'Mam! Mam, I'm over 'ere!'

Hearing Polly's voice, Marcia fastened the coat about her, knotted the scarf under her chin, and headed for the gates. 'Good grief, lass,' Marcia said as she pulled the girl towards her by the length of her open lapels, 'your neck's all exposed to the cold! Where's your scarf?' She retrieved the brown woollen square from Polly's pocket, instructing, 'Here, put it on where it'll do some good! It won't keep you warm in your pocket, lass!' She watched while Polly obediently wrapped it round her throat, being most careful under her Mam's scrutiny to tuck the end in securely.

As they made their way towards Cicely Hill, Marcia remembered the note. 'Did you give Florence that note for Mr Wiggins?' she asked.

Walking backwards and facing her Mam, Polly lied, 'I couldn't, the wind just snatched it from me 'and, and it blew it right away up the road!'

'Then I shall have to write another one, shan't I?' said Marcia. There passed between them a knowing look, followed by a span of silence. Then they both burst out laughing. 'You little scamp,

220

Polly Bendall!' Marcia chastised, making to grab her.

But Polly sped away, half-running half-skipping down the compelling steepness of Cicely Hill. It was one of those exaggerated gradients where in order to climb to the top, you'd need to lean forward at an unnatural angle. Conversely, to reach the bottom, you would be faced with the uncomfortable choice of either running freely without concern for your ultimate safety, or leaning backwards and negotiating the steep fall painfully slowly. Marcia chose the latter, but Polly ran like the wind was on her tail. She flew and leaped, she screamed and shouted as she tore headlong down the steep brew, the wind in her face and her sheer ecstasy finding expression in the whooping and hollering as she threw up her skinny little arms and let herself go. Marcia's heart raced with her. Oh, to be so young and carefree again, she thought—for a minute she almost added 'and healthy'. But, to look at her darling Polly now, she observed with a deep pang of regret, who'd ever think there was anything wrong with her?

As Polly sped away ever faster, Marcia became frantic. Across the bottom of the brew ran Eanam—a very busy tram route.

'Polly!' she shouted, her heart fearful, 'Mind what you're at, lass! Grab hold o' summat!' There were enough lamps lining Cicely Brow which Polly might have used to check her flight. Instead though, she went hurtling into a body coming in the opposite direction.

Of a sudden, the very air was pummelled out of his chest when Polly collided with him, head on. Now, they stood facing each other—Polly too out of breath to voice an apology, and the man staggering, cap askew, legs splayed, mouth hanging wide open and emitting wheezes like those from a broken whistle.

'Bloody 'ell,' he moaned between heaving breaths, 'You've bloody winded me!'

The shock in his face was too quickly replaced with anger, as, without warning, he grabbed wildly at Polly. 'Yer sodding little 'ooligan!' he shouted.

Polly darted skilfully in and out of the infuriated man's reach. 'You little bugger!' he called out, tormented and in exasperation, 'I'll find out which school tha' goes to! I'll 'ave 'em lay bloody nine-tails on thi!'

Polly was already speeding out of earshot. 'I'm sorry Mister,' she yelled in the wind, 'An' I don't go to school! I've left! So there's nowt you can do!'

By this time Marcia was almost upon them, her chest tight and breathless from hurrying in the face of the wind. Before she was able to say a word, he began pointing at the disappearing Polly most angrily. 'Little sod!' he told Marcia. 'Did you see that?'

'Yes,' Marcia confirmed, her eyes following Polly, who was now waiting along the road. 'They've no respect these days,' she announced in a detached manner, her courage having deserted her, 'no respect at all, I'm afraid.' A few moments later, she was giving Polly a piece of her mind.

If there was one shop Marcia could never walk by without pressing her nose to the window, it would have to be Billy's pawn shop. This aladdin's cave was easily identifiable from a great distance by the three enormous brass spheres which protruded stiffly from a sturdy bracket above the doorway. Now, she and Polly surveyed the numerous articles laid out in the window; rings, musical instruments, shoes, false teeth and paraphernalia of all shapes and description. All of these items represented a varying degree of heartache and sacrifice for their owners, who brought their precious belongings to Billy when times became so hard that their only salvation was to pawn perhaps a treasured brooch or a Sunday-best one and only suit, for a few paltry pence. A more valuable article such as a wedding-ring might produce the staggering sum of four shillings. The problem lay in recovering the goods, which called not only for the production of the sum lent, but a handsome interest charge for Billy's trouble as well.

Fearing that they might be late for surgery, Marcia took hold of Polly's hand. 'Come on lass!' she told her. 'We don't want to miss Dr Pitt.'

As they drew near to the surgery, Marcia sensed a sullen resistance in Polly's step. 'Please Polly,' she said, though she could understand the lass's apprehension, for wasn't her own heart sad and reluctant, 'we've to let him see you. There'll be no resting till he does.' She released Polly's hand, and placed a reassuring arm around her shoulder. 'It's best to see him, darling—an' I'll be there with you all the time.'

'Promise, Mam?' Polly was close to tears.

'I promise, of course I do!' As they rounded the corner, Nab Lane was immediately facing them. Marcia had always liked this little lane and she'd often thought about the person responsible for its design, certain that whoever it had been had possessed a heart filled with romance. Nab Lane was delightfully picturesque and so uniquely Lancastrian—with its cobbles and fluted lamps—and the way it sort of curved out of sight. It was so narrow that a body could stand in the centre of the cobbled road and touch the walls on either side with his outstretched arms.

All too quickly, Marcia and Polly found themselves almost on the doorstep of the doctor's surgery. A monstrously ornate Victorian building, it belonged entirely to an eccentric old woman, known as Miss Gladys, who was renowned for her surprising knowledge of religious matters, and being the appointed recruiting officer for the gathering of lost souls. But she was well intended and was invariably treated with the regard and courtesy befitting a woman of her age and disposition. In her generosity she had allocated the doctors three ground-floor rooms at the back of her grand old house, all rent free—'in the interests of the poor folk' she'd say to one and all. Marcia guided Polly ahead of her, down through the little back gate and along the side of the house towards the waiting surgery. With every step her heart was in her mouth.

'It's Mrs Bendall, isn't it?' Miss Gladys emerged from a small brick-built shed, the luxurious home of the little white terrier which hid behind her to yap ceaselessly at the intruders, and her grey wiry head nodded up and down, while the little pink eyes regarded Polly. 'Would this be little Polly?'

'Good morning, Miss Gladys,' Marcia replied. 'You're right as usual. This *is* my Polly—although not so little now, eh?'

The pink eyes disappeared beneath a broad beaming smile which rolled up all the loose skin in her face, 'Knew it was! Just *knew* it was.' She reached into her coat pocket and withdrew a sickly green lollipop, which she happily thrust into Polly's hand. 'You be a good girl! Go to church regular and take good care of your soul! The Lord above will take good care of your poor little body.' With that parting gift, she trotted away through the gate, the small dog tight up to her hurrying ankles.

'She's crackers!' Polly placed the sickly green lollipop on a nearby window ledge.

'That's enough o' *that* kinda talk, young lady!' Marcia chided. Miss Gladys might be crackers, but Marcia wasn't having it said in such a disrespectful tone. 'I've brought you up to know better than to be rude! Kindly keep your thoughts to yourself, my girl!'

'Sorry, Mam.' Polly looked suitably regretful, as a result of which she was allowed to lead the way through the thick heavy door into the surgery.

As usual when Dr Pitt was on duty, attendance was considerable. Marcia nodded to one and all, easing herself onto the very edge of the corner bench, and gesturing for Polly to sit on the small stool beside her. It always struck her as being odd that folks who would stand outside on the flagstones to talk for hours on end suddenly became mute and nervous on passing through that surgery door. She was acutely aware of several pairs of eyes looking her and Polly over. But the instant she looked up to communicate, they'd all be looking elsewhere! It amused and entertained her—the shifting glances which darted from one unsuspecting victim to another became 'the dance of the eyes', and she found herself joining in the game whereby she would rest on a disinterested face, then, when they looked up, she would quickly shift her attention to someone else. She felt like a naughty child. After a while, Marcia turned towards the enormous middle-aged woman squashed up against her.

'Been waiting long, have you?' Almost at once, everybody stared at her as if she'd committed a crime.

'No,' the woman sighed heavily, 'but I wish 'e'd get a bloody move on!' There was a bout of loud coughing and throat-clearing before the room settled back into an even more uncomfortable silence, when Marcia scowled threateningly at the rising laughter on Polly's upturned face. Polly grabbed a comic from the shelf and buried her fair head in its tattered pages—sniggering quietly to herself.

Marcia busied herself making a mental note of her position in the order of things. She was the last one in, so there was no one to be counted after her. There were nine bodies waiting—she counted five men and four women, all bent and weary, as if awaiting execution. She had no way of knowing which one of them preceded her, and it was always helpful to be able to keep your eye on the body in front, especially in the event that someone else might come in. It was easy enough to count up to your turn, as long as there wasn't infiltration of new folk. Marcia knew the confusion it would cause.

'Excuse me,' she ventured, as all eyes turned to her, 'who was the last one in before me?'

There was a flurry of waving arms and a gabble of voices, as each questioned the other.

'*I* were last.' It was the self-pitying voice of the

amply-proportioned woman.

There followed grunts of, 'Aye, that's right.'

'Well, I must be afore you.'

'I stopped counting a while back.'

'I'm next!'

A slight argument arose as to who was third, but eventually it was amicably agreed on, and everyone settled back to their job of looking suitably ill, and for a while all was silent again.

Marcia looked around the room. It was a cold forbidding place, which always made her feel distinctly uncomfortable. The walls were painted in a depressing shade of dirty green, and the coconut matting which covered a large area of the brown oilcloth was shaggy and pitted with bits of mud and dried-up leaves. There was an old wooden trolley beneath the reading shelf, on which rested a tin bowl for anyone likely to be sick, a child's clog, minus its button, and, stuffed right underneath, a large flowery hat. Marcia had never yet seen a fire lit in the grate, because, like now, it was always stuffed full of old newspapers, then covered with a piece of oilcloth for tidiness. The narrow wooden benches which ran two-thirds of the way round the room were hard and uncomfortable, polished thin and shiny by the neverending stream of visiting bottoms.

'I'm fed up, Mam.' Polly shifted uneasily. Marcia glanced down at the anxious face and the eyes filled with dread.

'I know, lass—I know,' she whispered.

Polly sighed and returned to her comic. A feeling of helplessness engulfed Marcia. Whatever the doctor had to tell her, Marcia knew that she would have to be ready.

So much had happened since that day when she and Curt were told of the 'dormant tumour' threatening their newly born babe. How they had clung to each other, their tears of joy turning to tears of sorrow and fear. A deep longing washed through Marcia 's senses as she thought on Curt. If only Curt were here now, to give her strength. She hadn't been too surprised to learn that Nantie Bett had kept in touch with him, and she was glad. It must have been a comfort to him, for while she still had their girls, he had no one. But their sacrifice of each other had at least brought her children into a legitimate family unit, recognised and accepted by neighbour and friend alike. The fact that Florence and Polly would not grow up beneath a hostile cloud of gossip and suspicion was a compensation for which Marcia was ever grateful. Yet, as obliged to Barty as she was and however hard she tried, Marcia could not quiet the excitement in her heart whenever she thought of her darling Curt—not a minute of the day or night was spent without the warmth of his love drawing her towards his memory. Curt Ratheter would be with her till the day she died. No power in God's heaven, or on this earth of purgatory, would ever alter that fact.

'Mam,' Polly gently prodded Marcia's arm, 'it's us.'

Marcia collected her wandering thoughts. She hadn't noticed that their turn had come round. 'Come on then, lass.' Taking a deep breath to still the flutterings of anxiety which had tightened her throat, she urged Polly forward. 'Let's see what he's got to say.'

The examination was long and exceedingly thorough. At the end of it, Doctor Pitt sat at his huge roll-topped desk, thinking deeply, while Marcia sat opposite folding and unfolding her hands in nervous anticipation, with Polly standing beside her, a small arm draped round her shoulders. Marcia endured the silence with remarkable patience as she stared at his dark bowed head and old stooping shoulders and wondered with trepidation what he was pondering so very deeply. She forced herself to concentrate on the heavy swing of the pendulum in the clock on the wall, allowing the resounding tick to penetrate her mind to the exclusion of all else.

Finally, Doctor Pitt looked up. 'I'm not sure,' he said hesitantly, then nodding at Polly, he suggested, 'would you like your daughter to wait in the other room?'

'Yes,' Marcia agreed, 'go on lass. I'll not be a minute.' By Polly's pleading glance, she knew the lass wanted to stay. If the news was good, then there'd be no harm in Polly's staying, but—she daren't even think on it. 'No. Find yousel' a comic and don't worry, love—I'll be straight out.' She waited for Polly to close the door behind her, then turning to Dr Pitt she asked, 'She'll be all right won't she Doctor?' Her heart wouldn't stop fluttering as she waited for an answer.

'Well now,' said Dr Pitt as he leaned back frowning in his deep leather chair, 'she *may* be all right. There's nothing to suggest that anything's changed dramatically. But I'm not too satisfied. There's something not quite right, Mrs Bendall. There's a deep area of tenderness which seems to be giving her a lot of pain, and although it's to be expected to a certain extent, I'm not happy about it.'

Dropping into deep thought again, he nodded as if replying to himself, 'Yes! I'd like her to see Mr Morton at Blackburn Infirmary—as a precautionary measure, you understand. He's a specialist in matters like this.'

Marcia wanted more reassurance. 'As a precautionary measure? You don't think there's anything for us to concern ourselves about then?'

'Mrs Bendall! As far as *I* can tell, except for an increase in pain and the tenderness which she'll probably always have, things are very much as they were.' He leaned forward, letting his voice drop to almost a whisper. 'But, believe me—trust me—Mr Morton will be able to put *all* our minds at rest. You'll feel much happier if she sees him, I'm sure?'

'Yes, of course. I'm sorry.' She *wasn't* sorry! She resented him. She resented them all!

'Now! You're to worry about nothing! And, as far as payment is concerned, there's no need to fret. Just keep up the shilling a week to the Friendly Society and it'll all be taken care of,' he promised. Marcia was thankful for that at least.

'I'll write for an appointment with Mr Morton and, until she sees him, I'd like you just to keep an eye on her. Now I've prescribed some tablets that Polly can take when she has these attacks. Keep them away from the other children.' He smiled at her, 'but I don't need to tell *you* that, do I?'

Outside in the fresh air, Marcia related the information to Polly, keeping back as much as she felt necessary, 'So that's all he said, Polly lass, just that he'd like you to see Mr Morton at the Infirmary, to see if they can put a stop to all these headaches you've been having.' Marcia only wished that was all. She felt no less apprehensive

230

now than when they'd arrived at the surgery. Now, they'd got to go through the whole thing all over again.

For a time Polly fell into a quiet mood, which Marcia didn't like for it seemed to shut her out. Whatever she herself was feeling, Marcia knew she had to impart comfort and confidence to Polly, so, placing a gentle hand on her shoulder, she turned her round to face her, saying gently, 'I expect it'll be *weeks* afore you're able to see that Mr Morton. They're very busy, these specialists.'

'I'll tell you what, Polly Bendall!' Marcia went on, smiling brightly. 'I fancy a walk out to Freckleton!' She crooked her arm under Polly's miserable little face, her voice belying the wretchedness of her own feelings. 'Would that pretty blue-eyed lass want to take me by the arm?'

Marcia couldn't really afford to walk out to Freckleton because, if she was to keep up with the financial burden placed on her, she really ought to get back to the mill. But she knew the wide-open fields and tree-lined avenues which belonged to that enviable outer part of Blackburn was one of Polly's dream places. She had often talked to Marcia of the bright-eyed squirrels she'd seen, and been enthralled by the majesty of the old oak trees which lined the avenues. There was a freedom there—and open fields, and the smell of blossoms instead of dry choking smoke. Marcia had little hesitation! The cotton mill would be here long after they were dead and gone and it was *now* that mattered.

Polly looped her arm through her Mam's, and laughing, she said, 'Oh, Mam! I do love you!'

231

CHAPTER THIRTEEN

All along Regent Street there was an air of excitement. Sour old Miss Atkinson was walking about with an unusually cheerful expression and she had actually been heard to sing on her way to the shop that morning! There was an almost unbelievable rumour abroad that smelly Martha Heigh had defied her own ruling and broken the tradition of nigh on forty years, because, the story went, she had been seen with a clean shawl about her shoulders, and the small brown blemishes over her face *weren't* freckles after all, for they'd promptly disappeared beneath a deluge of soap and water.

Ada Humble had filled her washing line from one end to the other, delighted at the numerous shirt-tails that pranced in the drying breeze—telling the world and its neighbour that she was the proud custodian of seven darling men.

There wasn't a front step from one end of Regent Street to the other that hadn't been meticulously white-stoned, and the afternoon air was alive with the bright optimistic chatter of women and the delicious aroma of freshly baked bread and sugar turnovers.

There was a simple and fitting reason for all this jubilation. Today was Wednesday, and this evening would see the residents of Regent Street loaded down with their own special results of a day's baking, and all heading towards the house of the Revine family. Today was the day of the 'moving-in' party; a well-loved celebration which had been sadly missed, due to the long-staying habits of the settled folks hereabouts.

'You'll have to move yoursel' quicker than *that*, Polly!' Marcia lifted young Barty away from the fresh barm-cakes which sat cooling on the lower shelf. 'And *you*, you rascal!' she scolded as she ushered him out of the scullery and back into the parlour, 'fingers to yoursel'! You'll get yours when we set down for us tea.' She watched as he included himself in Florence's newly started game of Snap, then she turned her attention to Polly's efforts at getting the tea ready. Marcia wasn't really looking forward to the party, although in normal circumstances she would have been as excited and enthusiastic as the next person, but she'd been baking since she'd got home from the mill, and her body was bone-tired. Also, her mind was greatly troubled. She couldn't rid herself of an awful feeling that somehow, somewhere, catastrophe was quietly brewing.

'I've only to mash the tea now, Mam,' Polly said as she washed the big brown teapot under the tap, 'then it's ready.'

'Be quick then lass.' Marcia lifted out the last tray of barm-cakes, 'An' make sure you swill them tea-leaves down the drain holes. You'll put your Dad in a right sour mood if that sink gets blocked up again.'

'Hmph! 'Tweren't 'im as unblocked it *last* time!' Polly retorted, ' 'cause he made you grovel about in it!'

'That's enough!'

'Anyway, he's allus in a sour mood!' Young Barty, as usual, couldn't resist sliding a truth into the observations. But, just now, Marcia had neither

233

the time nor the inclination to entertain such comments even though she had secretly to concede their accuracy.

'Not another word,' she scolded, 'or there'll be no party for the Bendall children *this* night!'

At this Barty fell into a sulk, and Florence declared that she was going upstairs to comb her hair. Polly finished laying the table in silence, a tight obstinate set about her mouth. Marcia continued about her business, thinking sadly how even the mere mention of Barty Bendall's name infected the very air with a disease that touched them all.

It was seven-thirty when the parlour door burst open to admit him, and her first glance assured Marcia of the sour mood on which young Barty had commented. His whole attitude was one of aggression, evident enough when he slammed the door behind him, threw his cap and overcoat on the doornail, and strode angrily across the parlour to his seat at the table. The ensuing silence was nerve-racking. Marcia collected his hot-pot from the kitchen, and placing it in front of him together with his freshly-baked barm-cake, she said 'Hello, Barty'—forcing a bright smile, and pleased to see that at least he hadn't been on the drink.

His response was a cursory grunt, as, at the same time, he assessed the situation around him. The storm in his sharp green eyes heightened when he noticed the three children along the settee, all newly-scrubbed and dressed in their Sunday clothes. Marcia herself was looking especially beautiful in a light blue blouse of her own making, and a full darker blue skirt. Her long wavy hair shone sleek as the blackest coal, and her eyes

234

sparkled deep velvet brown.

As she turned away from his withering glance Barty Bendall grabbed her arm, and demanded to know, 'What the sodding 'ell's going on 'ere?' With every word, he yanked hard at her wrist, until Marcia thought she would cry out. 'Am I to eat me tea on me bloody own? An' what the 'ell are *you* lot poshed up for? What's going on? I'm asking you! What the bloody 'ell's going on?'

'We've 'ad us tea,' Polly piped up, a deep scowl etched across her face.

'One more word out 'a *you*, an' you'll feel the weight o' me bloody belt!' His piercing glare was meant to rivet the girl to the seat, but Polly's answering look was dangerously defiant.

Marcia took the opportunity to wrench her wrist from the vice-like grip of his fingers. 'We sat round this table for nigh on half-hour, waiting on you to come home,' she told him, rubbing her wrist and preparing herself for a set-to. 'The moving-in party at the Revines' starts at eight.' She turned towards the three children, conscious of their anxiety. 'They're excited,' she continued. 'They've never been to such a do.'

'Be buggered to the Revines an' their sodding party!' he yelled. 'An' look at you!' His eyes swept her furiously from head to toe. 'Done up like some bloody street-woman!'

Marcia knew well enough when he was about to get really nasty, but she was determined that the children would have their little treat. God knows, she thought—they get few enough. Crossing the parlour with determined swiftness she ushered the children out into the passage, her expression communicating to them that they do her bidding without question.

'Go next door to Ada Humble's. Wait there till I fetch you.'

'What about you?' Polly asked as she moved with frustrating slowness.

'Do as I tell you!' Marcia shoved her out and leaned on the closed door, thankful that Barty Bendall hadn't jumped up to drag them back. At the same time, she wondered why, because it wasn't like him to let her get the better of him in front of the children. She waited for the front door to slam before returning to the table, where—for what must have been less than a minute, but seemed a lifetime—she poured Barty Bendall's tea, sickened by the revolting noises which accompanied his obvious enjoyment of the hot-pot. Apart from an occasional sideways glance at her as she cleared the table, he spoke not a word. To Marcia, it was more unnerving than having him shout at the top of his voice. She was used to that but not this 'silent treatment'. She thought better than to speak—convinced that a word from her would be akin to a match against a powder keg, but she knew it wouldn't be too long before he approached her. He'd left her alone now for a while, and it wasn't like him to go long without his 'rights'.

It was when she stood by the pot sink, her sleeves rolled up for the task of washing the plates, that she sensed him standing behind her. She could remember the time, so long back, when his nearness might have produced a little measure of contentment in her heart, but now the feel of his warm breath against her neck repulsed her. When his small groping hands touched around her waist, then sought a way in to her breast, Marcia had to set herself against running from him, the nausea rising to choke her.

'I've need of a few bob.' His voice scraped low against her ear. 'But that can wait, eh? Come upstairs wi' me first.'

Pulling forward to free herself from his groping fingers Marcia told him fiercely, 'I've no money! None at all.' Now, Barty Bendall caught her roughly by the shoulders, swinging her round, and causing the unbuttoned blouse to pull open revealing the magnificence of her firm youthful breasts, as she stood before him, defiant and incredibly beautiful.

Pinning her against the sink, Barty's glittering green eyes bored into the loveliness of her face. Then, with a low growl catching in his throat, he brought his open mouth down on her breast before pulling her to the floor, fired by her aggressive resistance.

The strongest fear in Marcia's cold heart was that the children might return. For herself, there was no feeling! She'd borne the driving weight of Barty Bendall's basic passions before, and there was no doubt that she would again. But it was a plain and shattering truth that each time he sought to possess her body he drove her further away in spirit. He seemed like a man possessed as he took her—all the while murmuring words of love, but loving as though he hated. Until, finally, her ordeal was over.

Leaving Marcia to brush and straighten the blouse and skirt which she'd so lovingly made, and which were now creased and soiled, Barty Bendall returned to the parlour to don his cap and overcoat. She didn't even look up, for doing so would have betrayed the disgust and loathing she felt.

'Well! Give us a few bob then . . . I 'in't got all bloody night!' He had asserted his authority—had shown her whose woman she was. Now he'd be away—to do some thinking.

Marcia lifted her eyes to meet his and the naked accusation there seemed to affect Barty Bendall in a surprising way.

Marcia couldn't remember a time when she had seen even a slight flicker of embarrassment on his weasel face. But as she looked on him with bitter eyes, a pink shadow flushed his features—then, just as quickly, it matured into the redness of rage. 'Come on!' He strode towards her, hand outstretched, manner threatening. 'A few bob. Now, I tell yer.'

Marcia stood her ground, telling him, 'If you can't look after your own needs on a man's full wage, what makes you think I can keep us all fed, clothed and sheltered on a *woman's* wage?' She turned from him. 'There's nowt left.'

'Nowt left, eh! Well, *o' course* there's nowt bloody left!' He brought his hand up to swipe at the barm-cakes, sending them flying from the shelf. Those that didn't roll across the floor landed in the sinkful of washing-up water. 'Nowt left 'cause you've spent the bloody money on *them*!' Kicking at the broken barm-cakes as they rolled about the floor, he strode out towards the passage. 'Go to your sodding party, and make no apologies for *me*!'

For a long time after he'd gone Marcia stood quite still, her eyes gazing over the floor at the shattered remnants of her hard day's work, and her mind alive with the memories of these past moments. She felt dirty—used, and the ever-present regrets which ate away inside her never seemed so sharp. If only she knew what to do for the best. Thoughts, frightening in their insistence, rushed through her mind. She was sorely tempted to go upstairs right now, pack the children's things and go back to her Mam. But then she remembered how very much Grandma Fletcher had already done. Also, she reminded herself of the way Barty Bendall had taken her and the girls on, affording her children the valued respectability she was afraid had been denied them. How many men would have done the same? And, in spite of his vindictive tongue and vicious ways, never once had he used the past against either her, or the girls. She had little if no choice in the way of her future. Her place was here and her loyalty was to him—in spite of everything. If she spent the rest of her life in regret, then that would be the price she'd have to pay. There was nothing to be done, for it had all been decided by circumstances out of her control.

So, she gathered up the scattered remnants of her baking, with the grim resolution hardening her heart.

'You've made your own bed, Marcia Bendall. Now you'll have to lie on it!'

She hoped and prayed that Curt might find more happiness than she had done. Her lips moved in silent prayer as she begged that Polly be allowed the same healthy chance afforded to any child. 'Don't make her pay for what Curt and I did,' she pleaded. 'Let *me* pay. Help poor Polly find peace and contentment.' Her sore heart was filled with a fierce hope and belief that God would not take her poor child from her, for there would be no great purpose served by such cruelty. Yet, deep within Marcia, a terrible fear lingered—a mother's fear for her child, an instinct that already, Polly seemed to be drifting from her.

Kneeling on the floor, amidst the ruins of her hard work, Marcia cried bitterly. She cried for the hopelessness of an empty marriage—for what had been lost. And for her children, Polly in particular.

Later, when she had tidied the mess up, Marcia washed her face and prepared to collect the children from Ada Humble's.

First though, she dabbed a little cold water around her eyes to reduce the puffiness, then, her cheeks pinched to bring back the roses, she brushed the long hair into smooth dark waves. Feeling somewhat better, she left the house.

She took a mental stock of herself as she tapped on Ada's door. 'Might not be as fresh and respectable as I was,' she smiled to herself. 'But who's to notice?'

Polly noticed. By the concerned look with which she greeted Marcia, so did Ada Humble. But, in that particularly thoughtful manner of folks hereabouts, she made no comment, except to tell Marcia breezily, 'Come in Marcia lass! We're all ready an' waiting your inspection!'

Laughing at the insinuation that she had been appointed overseer, Marcia followed Ada Humble's bright red trilby as it waddled busily down the passage and into the parlour. The Humbles' back parlour was always in delightful disarray. Marcia could never recall even *one* occasion when she'd been made to feel uncomfortable or unwelcome, either by Ada herself or by any of her considerable brood. Thinking on the atmosphere in her own parlour, especially in the presence of Barty Bendall, Marcia considered the busy, noisy, crowded Humble home to be the happiest she had ever set foot in—certainly the happiest in all of Regent Street.

'Right then, you lot!' Ada Humble positioned herself next to Marcia, by the door. Her commanding voice, strengthened by years of yelling at her rumbustious offspring, rose above the excited chatter which reverberated round the room in a noisy crescendo. While she waited, Marcia took pleasure in the air of contentment here, and the strong sense of that unique bond of love which drew this family together.

The little parlour was a vivid reflection of Ada Humble's seven special men. The walls were painted in a strong shade of brown, dashed here and there with a dab of sunshine orange, and the ceiling was still the mucky colour it had been for the past seven years. On the far wall, positioned high up, away from the reach of curious fingers, hung a picture. It was Ada's pride and joy, referred to most lovingly as 'my soldier'. Toby Humble looked suitably resplendent in his 1915 khaki uniform and long droopy moustache, the stern expression on his face not unlike that of the man's in the recruiting poster—the only thing missing being the caption which read 'Your Country Needs You!' The picture itself was quite ordinary, but to little Ada Humble, it was the greatest treasure in all the world.

Around the mantelpiece ran a corded garland of deep green, with big hanging silky bobbles which danced and bumped in the rising heat from the cheery fire. All along the mantelpiece stood a varied selection of little china dogs, some smiling, some howling, and some sitting on their haunches displaying silly expressions of self-importance. But they were Ada's cherished animals, for each one had been purchased at some time by one or other of her lads. The furniture was old and battered, but it didn't seem to matter that the brown settee had a busted spring, or that the stuffing had completely escaped from beneath the seat of an armchair, collapsing the seat like a deflated Yorkshire pudding. Ada was content to describe them as being 'lived in'. The place was an absolute shambles. Shoes and boots covered the oilcloth from one end of the room to the other, and there wasn't a chair nor article of furniture that hadn't been used as a clothes-horse.

'Line up then!' Ada was still issuing instructions. 'Let's be 'aving a look at you!' Satisfied at the shuffling and pushing that took place under half-hearted protest, Ada turned to Marcia. 'Right then Marcia, lass.' Her proud face was as red as the trilby which sat on her head, in as jaunty a fashion as Marcia had ever seen, and she thought it strange how that little red trilby reflected Ada's every mood by the way it sat on her head. 'What's the verdict, eh?'

Marcia stepped forward, feeling for all the world as though *she* was the one under examination, for no fewer than eleven pairs of eyes descended on her at once, all eager that she should find no fault with Ada's presentation. Toby headed the line-up, which started by the scullery door, stretched right round the back wall, and half-way to the fireplace.

242

'Looks right grand my Toby, don't 'e, eh?' Ada was hopping excitedly from one foot to the other. 'Not coming to the party! *Won't* come to the party, but it's no matter, so long as 'e goes to the pub looking as smart as the rest of us!'

'Stop thi' gabbing, wife.' Toby was eager to be away on his Saucy-Sally and off to the company of his drinking pals. 'Leave Marcia to 'er own reckoning!'

'Aye! Right 'usband, I'll do that. 'E does look grand all the same, don't 'e?' she whispered into Marcia's armpit, for she came no higher than Marcia's shoulder.

Marcia thought Toby did look nice. He was a tall, slim man, slightly bent at the shoulders and slow to walk, but his face had a quick smile about it that enveloped all present in its warmth. There seemed to be a special twinkle in his light brown eyes and a cheekiness about his face that suggested a certain 'naughtiness' in past youth. Casting her eyes along the line, Marcia took pleasure in each and every one of Ada's brood. There was Blackie, a grand-looking lad of dark strong features, all smiles and well turned out; then to the left of Blackie there came Edward, the freckled-faced one, Jimmy the giggly one, and Berty, the sad-eyed one who never had much to say for himself. Then came the twins, Freddy and Joseph, whose goals in life seemed to include the daily collection of the most peculiar things—such as the one-legged frog which now lived in a box beneath Joseph's bed, or the half-a-flute, from which Freddy produced the weirdest most fearsome wailing imaginable. On the end of the line in order of age came the fair Polly, with eyes as blue as a summer sky, then the

243

dark-haired Florence of fiery looks and haughty countenance. Right at the very end stood young Barty, with brown saucer eyes and dark unruly hair—looking every inch a little gentleman, all freshly scrubbed and standing to attention.

Marcia loved them all, thinking that a better gathering of gradely creatures would be impossible to find, and she said as much to her friend. 'You've done yourself proud, Ada Humble!' she laughed, 'what a motley crew they are!'

'There you are!' Ada cried, allowing the line to stand at ease, 'I told you! There's nowt better than a collection o' smart-looking folk, that's what I say—an I'm proud o' the lot of yer!' Of a sudden, she was sniffling. 'Right proud, I am!' she finished in a trembling voice.

'Well, now that you've put us all at us ease, Sergeant Major,' Toby Humble said as he bent his head towards the red trilby to kiss the chubby face beneath it, ' 'ave I got thi' permission to be off to yon pub?'

'Aye, 'course thi' can be off to yon pub, Toby Humble. But mind you watch what you're up to!' A deep frown wrinkled her forehead. 'Will you not leave yon bike at 'ome, Toby? I'm allus afeared you'll come off it.'

'Get away wi' you! I'll do no such thing!' He disappeared through the door still tutting and moaning.

Less than ten minutes later the house was securely locked, and the whole procession of party-goers were on their way to the Revine household. The scene which greeted them on being received into the parlour was one of excitement, music and merry laughter. Bridget collected their coats, and hung them along the passage wall together with the countless others.

'I was getting worried,' she told Polly, 'thought you weren't coming!'

Polly followed her into the front parlour. 'Not coming! I've been right looking forward to it,' she said positively.

'Go on you young 'uns!' Ada Humble propelled the children after Polly and Bridget, 'in you goes— and mind you be'aves yersels!'

Marcia accompanied young Barty and Florence into the front parlour. In spite of a bright cheery atmosphere radiating from the noisy festivities, she felt uncomfortable—apprehensive. She dismissed the notion that it might be due to Barty Bendall's abuse of her. No! There was something else, something here in this house. Her thoughts flitted back to Peter Revine and at once Marcia knew why she felt so uneasy.

'You'll be Polly's mother? Though you look so glamorous I wasn't sure.'

Rosa Revine was decked out in a gaudy patchwork dress which flounced as she walked, the bright scattered colours eye-catching and blinding in their profusion, and Marcia thought it well-suited to the flamboyant nature of the woman. Holding out the tray of bread-pudding, silently thankful that Ada Humble had been thoughtful enough to share the results of her labours, Marcia exchanged greetings in a light, happy manner.

'Hello Mrs Revine,' she said—correcting herself when the woman insisted, '*Rosa* if you please.'

Marcia nodded towards the back parlour, from which emanated gales of laughter. 'Sounds as though the party's well under way?'

Rosa Revine collected the tray from Marcia's hands and squeezing past the tight groups of children she placed it on the long table by the window, resting a large knife on top of it. 'That's right,' she said, 'and none enjoying it so much as *your* old friend.' She led Marcia through to the front parlour. 'Will ye look at that?' she said.

At that point, the half-inflated balloon escaped from Ada Humble's hands, taking off on a crazy flight. Swooping noisily up and down, in and out of the crowded tables, it bombed and dived at the children, who screamed and hollered with the utmost delight.

'Catch 'old on it!' Ada Humble's bright red trilby could be seen bobbing and jumping, pouncing and running, until the whole place was in a tumultuous uproar. The cry went out from all directions, 'Catch 'old o' that balloon!'

As Marcia fell into a fit of laughter, there came a familiar voice in her ear. 'I'm away 'ome!' It was Martha Heigh.

'Oh Martha. You did come after all.' Marcia had wondered whether the hermit-like character would actually bring herself to leave the 'safety' of her little house, even to attend anything as exciting as a moving-in party.

Martha grunted, collecting up the folds of her skirt with which to shine her spectacles before promptly edging them back on to her nose. 'Aye. But I'm straight off home now,' she whispered, 'I don't like it here. No, I don't like it at all.'

With that she was gone, leaving Marcia wondering what it was that the eccentric old lady didn't like. In truth she would not have minded going home herself.

During the rest of the evening, which in actual fact turned out to be more pleasant a prospect than Marcia had anticipated, she noticed Peter Revine engaging Polly in frequent conversation, which disturbed her. But, as long as she had them in sight, she didn't intervene.

'Mam!' Florence was calling from the doorway, clutching young Barty by her side. At once, Marcia hurried over to them. 'What's to do, lass?' she asked, her dark gaze going from one to the other.

'He keeps falling asleep!' Florence complained as she rubbed her eyes wearily. 'An' *I'm* tired, Mam, I want to go.'

Marcia gathered the sleepy boy in her arms and placed him on a nearby stand-chair, where he sat in a hunched, exhausted fashion. 'Sit with him, darling,' Marcia told Florence quietly, 'and I'll fetch our Polly. It's time we were *all* abed.'

At first glance there was no sign of Polly. Marcia excused herself as various people called for her attention. A ripple of horror travelled her senses as her frantic search alerted her to the sudden disappearance of Peter Revine. They had both been there earlier—by the scullery door. Of a sudden though, and much to Marcia's relief, Polly appeared as if from nowhere. On her Mam's urging that they were all about to leave, she gave a bright smile and was in the passage waiting, almost before Marcia had finished speaking.

'Where've you been, child?' Marcia asked Polly, at the same time gathering Barty into her arms.

'Just talking to Bridget's Dad,' Polly answered in such a matter-of-fact voice that it made Marcia think she was a fool to imagine things. All the same, she had no liking for that Revine fellow.

'Merciful heavens! Will you just look at the time!' Ada Humble rushed into the passage just as Marcia was about to open the front door. 'Blackie! Quick, lad. Your Dad! 'E'll be on 'is way 'ome—and nary a one on us ter watch out fer 'im!'

Marcia couldn't help but smile at poor Ada Humble as she grabbed Blackie from his jelly trifle, recruiting him to gather their scattered tribe. It was a certainty that Toby would never be capable of lifting himself from that Saucy-Sal—not if he'd had a pint or two he wouldn't. Now, though, she had her own brood to think on. With young Barty asleep in her arms, and the two girls in tow, Marcia proceeded down the passageway towards the front door—from where there came a sudden knocking!

It was an unfamiliar knock, loud and authoritative, the sort of knock which by its very nature put the fear of the Lord into a body's heart.

'Open the door, Polly lass . . .' Marcia held her breath and the sense of impending doom which had haunted her all evening rose in her breast to stifle and choke her. When Polly had done so both she and Florence took a step back at the sight of the dark-clad constable towering above them.

'Good evening!' he said to Marcia in a low kindly voice. 'Is there a Mrs Humble here?'

Marcia's heart fell like a stone.

CHAPTER FOURTEEN

Marcia was bone-weary! But the day was not yet over and there were still some fifteen minutes to go before the machines were shut down, after which there was planned a little celebration amongst the mill-hands on this floor. For, at long last, Daisy Forester had stood up to her Mam. Today was her last day at Cicely Mill—and, soon, she would be wed.

But poor Daisy was cheated of her little celebration because even as Marcia was lifting her hand to throw the switch which would close down her machine, there came an almighty noise from some way up in front—a great screeching, jarring noise, which was unlike anything she'd heard before. Then, of a sudden, it was like all hell let loose! Folks ran in all directions and even Tom Atkinson, who judging by the heightened colour of his face and the wild look in his eyes, could go down any minute with a heart-attack, pelted past Marcia's machine.

By now most of the machines had ground to a halt. But, where normally at this time of day there'd be a swell of laughter and a good deal of chatter, there was only hushed silence. When Marcia emerged from changing her slippers for shoes, she saw little groups of mill-hands standing about and conversing in whispers. From a distance, she could see young Daisy crying, with old Bertha comforting her. Some of the other women were stark-eyed, with their hands flattened over their mouths as though to stifle any sound that might come out.

Going to where old Bertha had young Daisy enclosed in her arms, Marcia asked in a soft voice, subdued by the sight of wretched faces all about her, 'What is it, Bertha? Whatever's going on?'

But Bertha could give no answer, except to shake her head and gently to lead away the trembling girl in her arms. As she passed Marcia she whispered, 'Come away, lass. Come away!' As Marcia made to follow her—thinking something really bad must have happened to dash poor Daisy's plans—there came a flurry of activity from both behind and in front of her.

Tom Atkinson walked about, going from one little group to another, gently moving them on and telling them, 'Tek yersels off home. There's nowt to be done 'ere!' His face looked totally drained of colour and his shoulders stooped as though pressed down with a great weight.

When the two dark-suited fellows came hurrying by her carrying a rolled-up stretcher and looking grim, Marcia's eyes followed them and, almost involuntarily, she took a few paces forward. What she saw came as one of the worst shocks she had ever experienced. It was Maggie Clegg's machine around which all activity was taking place—bright chirpy Maggie Clegg's machine, splattered from top to bottom in great splashes of blood standing out scarlet and horrifying against the white cotton bobbins and the great iron struts, which Maggie knew like the back of her hand. From the huge cogs and rollers which ran this monstrosity, there hung ragged hanks of hair—Maggie's hair that was once long and jet-black, and which now was crimson and split asunder.

Of a sudden the two men were lifting what was left of Maggie before, with touching reverence, they wrapped her up and placed the bundle on the stretcher. It didn't move at all when they carried it past Marcia. For long shocking moments, Marcia stood stock-still, her wide-open eyes following that bundle. She saw it go from the factory floor—then, in her mind's eye, she saw it being carried into the ambulance some long way down—saw it riding to some awful dark and cold place, which Maggie would have hated. All the while, Marcia's horrified imagination saw Maggie Clegg's bright bubbly face, her laughing dark eyes and, just for a minute, there, Marcia could hear her shouting, 'Give us a song, Marcia!' And she sobbed. She sobbed as though her heart would break.

When some long time later she began her way home, Marcia knew that, come what may, she could never, *never* go back to Baines' cotton mill.

As Marcia walked away from one dark, forbidding Victorian building, Curt Ratheter walked away from another some thirty miles away in Manchester. As he paused before moving on, his face grim and gaunt, his tall, slim figure dressed in the garments in which he had been arrested—brown cord trousers, dark navy jacket and checked shirt—he might have seemed to any unknowing passer-by to be a fellow on his way to work. Yet, were they then to look closer they would see the pale haggard face, the sad brown eyes and that weary stoop to his shoulders and they might well have changed their minds.

Before he lost sight of it he stopped and turned about to look at the great iron-studded prison doors beyond which lay the awful place that had been his domicile for six years. In his mind's eye, he could recall the very day, the exact minute, when they had brought him here. His heart had been heavy with thoughts of Marcia then and it was just as full with love for her now. With love and with deep painful regrets. He waited a moment, letting that terrible sensation of loneliness subside a little. It would never leave him, he knew. Not as long as he lived.

Fishing an envelope from his pocket, he withdrew from it a letter, which he then carefully unfolded and read for the umpteenth time. The letter was from his father—explaining how he and Fran had got back together for good, since Curt and Fran's divorce. Would Curt come to the wedding? Would he forgive and forget? Never! thought Curt. But at last he was free of her. She had vented her spite on him, shattered his life and now, this final humiliation! How blatant they were, the pair of them, to think he might even contemplate attending such a ceremony.

Well, to hell with them both! They deserved each other. Yet, what had *he* got left? He might be released from prison, but never from the nightmare which had cost him his Marcia.

Having read the letter again, Curt's arm dropped to his side, and as it did so, the letter fluttered to the ground, was picked up by the wind and after a moment, when it merrily played with it, was sent flying high into the air before disappearing out of sight.

Curt stood there, quite still and steeped in thought, his face a serious study as he looked first one way and then the other. The road to the right would take him far south to the Bedfordshire brickworks and a new life. To the left was Blackburn, where thanks to Nantie Bett, he knew Marcia and his two daughters to be living. Straight on would take him along the road to Accrington and to Fran Ratheter.

After long agonizing moments, when his every instinct beckoned him towards Blackburn and the woman whose image had kept him sane these past lonely years, Curt stood up tall, thrust his hands into his pockets and, with a sigh which reached every corner of his being, turned right.

He had saved every penny of the meagre wages he had earned these past six years. It wasn't a fortune, but it was enough to get him started again. Yet, for every step he took further away from Marcia, the deeper she became engraved in his heart. If he had not reminded himself time and time again that she was married—even though Nantie Bett had a poor opinion of Barty Bendall— Curt would have beaten a path to Marcia's door. But then, he told himself, even if she was free, there was no way of telling whether she had ever been able to forgive him for the pain and humiliation he had put her through. He was an outcast of his own making and, if any man ever deserved the love of a woman such as Marcia, it was not he.

CHAPTER FIFTEEN

The big day had arrived—a day when the Bendall children would not be quietened. That very evening the big bonfire would be lit and, following the tradition which had evolved over many years, it would draw great numbers of folks hereabouts, from their cosy firesides. It would light up the skies over Lancashire like some gigantic fiery beacon. Even Marcia—for all that she had been staggered first by Toby Humble's accident, then poor Maggie's—was looking forward to the celebrations. Besides which, the innocent laughter of the children was always infectious and heart-lifting. Strange, she thought, how through the eyes of little ones the world seemed a better place.

Marcia had been up since six o'clock that morning, preparing breakfast for her own and Ada Humble's family, making sure that they were all washed and dressed, with socks on the right way round, shoes on the right feet, and hair combed into some pretence of tidiness. It was a mammoth job! On top of that, she had elected to supervise the housework in the Humble abode *and* take on all the washing. Blackie had shown himself to be a thoroughly reliable young man, taking over the considerable responsibility of minding the house, and seeing to his five younger brothers; even though he missed his Mam more fiercely than perhaps anyone could guess.

Poor Toby Humble had lain at death's door for nigh on three full days now, and his devoted heartbroken woman had refused to leave his side. She'd sat by the hospital bed, her fat little fingers covering the pale stillness of Toby's work-worn hands, and all that could be got out of her was a broken declaration that 'It's *my* fault,' over and over again, until even the familiar bright red trilby seemed to have faded to a dimmer sadder shade.

Now, the scene that greeted Marcia as she

254

entered the back parlour was a noisy happy one. Grandma and Grandad Fletcher had come over and with them was Nantie Bett, a gangling woman of awkward shape, and confident manner. Her square blunt features had a perpetual joyous expression about them, and the brown speckly eyes set beneath a thatch of dark grey hair missed not a thing. A family outing to the bonfire celebrations was a very rare treat for her and, like everyone else, she was excited and full of enthusiasm.

Young Barty jumped off Grandad Fletcher's amply comfortable lap to bound energetically across the room to his mother on her return from the market, where she'd been spending a few coppers on some fresh vegetables. 'Mam, Mam, Gran and Grandad are coming to the bonfire.'

Marcia swooped him up in her arms and kissed him. 'That's nice,' she told him, replacing him on the floor before crossing first to Grandad Fletcher, then to her mother, to greet them with a light peck on the cheek. For Nantie Bett, who sat fidgeting on a stand-chair, there was an extra special hug, for Marcia had not forgotten how the old lady had kept in touch with Curt. She hung up her coat and shrugged her shoulders wearily.

'Polly love. Go and wash yourself and don't forget your legs! Your Dad'll be in for his tea in a minute. It's best if he doesn't see what state you're in.' She shook her head. 'Good Lord! When I went out not an hour ago, you were quite presentable.'

'Mam! I'm not a baby! I know what to do.' Polly was most indignant. All the same, she wasn't allowed to go until she'd explained to Grandma Fletcher that she and Florence had been down in the cellar 'playing shops'.

255

Now, when the key rattled impatiently in the front door, Grandma fidgeted nervously, while Grandad concentrated on watching her with interest, before she blurted out, 'We'll go and sit in the front parlour while Barty 'as 'is tea.' She would have risen from the chair at once, if Marcia hadn't stopped her.

'You'll do no such thing! Barty won't *eat* you, you know!' she said with a soft laugh. But by the apprehensive look on Grandma Fletcher's face, it was painfully obvious that she feared him.

Marcia understood the reason for her Mam's anxiety. Curt Ratheter was uppermost in her mind, she knew. Patting her Mam's fingers, Marcia told her firmly, 'It's all right Mother; there's nothing to worry about.' Grandad Fletcher had grown suddenly quiet and Nantie Bett excused herself on the grounds that her presence, like her loyalty, belonged elsewhere. Then she disappeared into the scullery.

The atmosphere in the room grew ominous as Barty Bendall's footsteps resounded down the passageway to bring him suddenly to the open doorway, when all eyes turned in his direction.

The short authoritative figure was bundled in a heavy overcoat buckled at the waist by an evil-looking metal clasp, one swing of which could gouge a man's eye out. His green eyes darted round the room, frowning in the gathering before him. 'What the bloody 'ell's all this, eh?' he blurted out, taking a step forward as his frown grew darker.

'It's Mam and Dad, Barty. They've come over to the celebrations. Oh, and they've brought Nantie Bett too,' she added with a rush of pleasure.

256

'What bloody celebrations?' He strode into the room and slammed the door shut behind him, before taking off his cap and coat and throwing them over the nail in the door.

'The bonfire celebrations in town,' Grandad Fletcher offered, '*I* was all for giving it a miss; but you know what these women are like.' He gave a small nervous laugh as Barty Bendall glowered at him.

'Oh aye? I thought your old woman didn't like bonfires?' His cutting tone was final enough for Grandad and Grandma Fletcher to know that they had been dismissed from the conversation. He deliberately turned his back on them, an action which forced Grandma Fletcher to mutter under her breath, 'Surly bugger!'

Being used to Barty Bendall's manner, Marcia shrugged saying, 'I'll give Nantie Bett and Florence a hand with the tea.' At this Barty crossed the room with surprising and frightening speed to grab hold of Marcia by the shoulder; causing her to gasp as he pounced on her so unexpectedly.

'Who's in that bloody scullery, did yer say?' he demanded, his bulbous eyes raking her face, 'Who is it, eh? Florence is it? Is it?' With a spiteful twist he released her and disappeared into the scullery. Marcia feared her parents would be tempted to have a go at him. However, the way her Dad was pretending to help young Barty read his comic soon told her of his intentions. Her Mam though was red in the face, her mouth set tight and, by the look in her angry blue eyes, she wasn't too far off exploding. Quickly now, Marcia's expression warned her not to interfere.

Of a sudden, there came a volley of abuse from

257

the scullery, finishing with 'bloody folks everywhere! Pushing Florence before him, he emerged from the scullery, saying, 'Go an' get the lazy bitch down, an' tell 'er to be bloody quick about it!' Rounding on Marcia he screamed, 'This is a bloody fine thing to come 'ome to! House full o' sodding visitors, and no bloody tea ready!' He gave Nantie Bett a scathing look as, her face stiff with anger and disgust, she reappeared to resume her place on the stand-chair.

Now, Florence and Polly appeared at the door. Florence moved in front of Polly as if to offer a degree of protection, but Polly pushed her gently to one side and, crossing the room determinedly, she brought herself to stand to within four feet of Barty Bendall, where she stood upright and defiant, her bright blue eyes staring unafraid into his.

The momentary hush was charged with a current of awful expectancy, as Polly met Barty Bendall's savage stare.

Then, of a sudden, all the more frighteningly because it came in the wake of such ominous silence, Barty Bendall leaned towards the girl, and in a thick trembling voice he told her, 'You! You're a lazy baggage! A no-good, useless piece of work!'

When Polly's answer was to turn away from him with a look of disgust, he gave out a scream like that of a madman, at the same time aiming the crippling weight of his work-boot full and hard in the small of Polly's back. The impact sent Polly sprawling across the floor with such suddenness that there was no time to protect herself from the glancing blow as her head caught the sharp corner of the table.

Of a sudden, everything happened at once. Marcia's piercing scream mellowed into a terrified sob, as she reeled forward to grab hold of Polly, who appeared lifeless and who was now lying sprawled out on the floor, her face a ghastly colour. At once Grandad Fletcher got to his feet, to meet Barty Bendall's glaring eyes with a forthright stare of heavy disapproval.

'What kind of man d'yer call yersel', Bendall?' he asked in a low accusing voice.

Barty Bendall appeared unrepentant as he retorted, 'What kind o' *man*! The kind o' man who's fed up to 'is back teeth wi' troublesome bloody kids an' moody women—that's what!' His still angry eyes swept the hostile faces in the room as he continued to screech and threaten, 'What's all the bloody fuss about anyway? She's *pretending*, I tell yer! An' if she don't soon gerrup, she'll likely feel the weight o' me bloody belt on 'er arse!' When he saw that he'd gone too far, Barty Bendall ripped off his hat and coat from the nail, and stormed away down the corridor. 'I'm off to wait for the bloody pub to open. I might get summat to eat down *there*!' he yelled, slamming the front door behind him.

'Lass. I didn't know. I didn't know.' Grandma Fletcher helped to get Polly to her feet. And, with only a slight graze to show on her forehead, Polly appeared none the worse.

'I'm all right Gran,' she murmured, walking slowly but steadily, and reassuring her mother also that she was perfectly unharmed.

The tears still wet on her face, Marcia took the girl in her arms, and for a long moment, she just held her tight, speaking not a word. 'Marcia, lass—

I've seen enough to know that ye've a real heavy cross on them shoulders o' yourn,' Nantie Bett said in a shocked voice. 'Sit thi' down lass. Me an the young 'uns, we'll mek a strong brew.'

Marcia, still silent and shocked, helped the white and shaken Grandma Fletcher back into her chair, then for the first time for as long as she could remember, she watched her Dad place a comforting arm around his wife's shoulders. For a long poignant moment, the only sound which disturbed the quiet thoughts of those in the parlour was the insistent ticking of the clock on the mantelpiece. Until, beginning in a soft slow whine, young Barty's crying became hysterical, shaking them all and moving Marcia to take command of the situation before the whole evening was completely ruined. Gathering the lad into her arms, she told him, 'If you can show me a great big toothy smile, I just might find you an extra copper or two, for the fair tonight!' It took only a minute for little Barty to oblige.

The celebrations were due to start at seven o'clock, and, at last, they were all ready. It was a noisy excited group which tumbled out of the Bendalls' front door, and Marcia thought it was just as well that a couple of kindly neighbours had elected to take the Humble brood to the fair. She dwelt for a minute on poor Ada, and hoped that all was well.

'Polly! Wait for me!' Bridget's voice halted Polly in her tracks, as she turned and waited for her young friend to catch up, 'Ooh Polly, I'm so excited! It's going to be fine! I've never been to a big bonfire night before!'

Marcia's parents went on ahead with the

children while Nantie Bett hung back, close to Marcia. The slip of paper she thrust into Marcia's hand was seen by no-one. Not a word passed between them, but the look on Nantie Bett's face was quickly perceived by Marcia. Nodding her head, she clenched her fist around the paper, drawing it surreptitiously into her pocket, where it would remain safe until she could read it in privacy.

When Grandma Fletcher looked round to see Marcia's smiling excited face, she thought it was because of the fun they were all looking forward to at the fair. Only Marcia and Nantie Bett knew the real reason for that special glow in Marcia's lovely eyes.

*   *   *

'The Fair! Mam! I can 'ear the fair! I can smell the baked tatties!' Young Barty's feet barely touched the ground, and his little flat cap bobbed about excitedly as he hopped and jumped, ears straining, towards the tinny rhythmic tones wafting towards them on the breeze. In that miraculous way that children have, young Barty had opted to put the distasteful memories of the earlier scene out of his mind; 'Oh go on Mam! Please,' he insisted, *'please* let me 'ave a ride on the 'orses.'

Florence hurried to keep up. 'Yes, and can we all have roasted chestnuts?' she pleaded.

'We'll see,' Marcia laughed, afterwards brushing her fingers over the deep indentation where her ring would normally be nestling; albeit uncomfortably. Thank God Barty hadn't noticed. Her blood ran cold as she imagined Barty's

261

reaction should he discover that she had pawned her wedding ring. Ripples of panic ran down her spine as the image of his face grotesque and distorted with rage loomed in her mind. 'Pop-Shop Billy' had given her a good price for the wedding-ring—four shillings would ensure that the children found this a night to remember. She had been determined to brighten their lives by whatever means she found at her disposal. It would be almost impossible to retrieve the ring, but she would tackle that problem when the time came.

As much as she hoped and prayed that all would be well, and they could enjoy the bonfire celebrations the way they had planned, Marcia was plagued by the earlier scene, when Polly had cracked her head on that table. Polly had assured her that the blow had done no harm, but still Marcia was not convinced. The sheer determination however that it would not spoil the evening, either for her children or their visitors, quelled the endless anxieties which flooded Marcia's mind.

As they approached the waste ground where the bonfire was held, Grandad Fletcher could be heard emitting snorts like an old steam train labouring to pull out of an uphill station, as he rubbed and clapped his hands together in an effort to keep warm. His old woolly muffler was tightly wrapped round his upturned collar, and the ancient neb-cap had been lugged down to meet it, so all that remained visible was his bright button-red nose and sprouting lengths of greying moustache. Walking with an odd swaying gait, he gestured for the rest of the party to hurry themselves. At once, Grandma Fletcher hurried along behind, pulling her shawl tighter about her and the ankle-length skirt slapping from one side to the other as she quickened her pace. Her iron-clad clogs made a peculiar determined tapping noise. 'Don't push us!' she told her husband with some impatience, 'We won't miss 'owt. Don't worry!' By now she was quite breathless and somewhat out of patience.

Now, everyone started talking at once, as they hastened towards the increasing volume of noise and bright lights filling the sky with a rosy glow. As the family turned the corner on to Ainsworth Street, the whole colourful scene lay before them like the setting on a stage, only this was *real*!

The music filled Marcia's soul with joy as she perused the busy scene. It seemed as if the whole world and his friend were here to enjoy the festivities. The area was decked from one end to the other with twinkling lights and from every corner there came the shouts of excited stall-holders clamouring for attention. There was no official entrance as such, but the positioning of stalls and stages dictated points of access, and flanking every path colourful enterprising characters had set up their varied diversions. At the junction where the stalls split away to either side, a little wizened man had placed his barrel organ in a shrewd position, so that anyone emerging from Ainsworth Street had no choice but to pass him before reaching the centre of activity.

'Good evening one an' all!' His voice was an odd grating squeak which seemed to suit his tiny size and general set-up. Fascinated at both his goblin-like appearance and whole unusual ensemble before them, the little party ground to a halt.

'Mam! Just look at that!' Polly's voice was

tremulous with the eager excitement of a child, 'That's a *monkey*!' The incredulity in Polly's voice caused them to stare all the harder.

'That's right lass. You're looking at the gamest little monkey in Lancashire!' The wizened man stepped forward with the monkey squatting skilfully on the bony protrusion of his shoulder and the light from a corner street-lamp illuminated the weird pair. Marcia couldn't help but notice the striking resemblance between the monkey and its shrunken owner. They were both of the same scrawny appearance, and even the cheeky red cap perched jauntily on the monkey's head was identical to the one worn by the man. 'I'm tellin' you,' he continued to squawk, 'there's no monkey in the whole of Lancashire—perhaps the whole world—as can do tricks like my Jasper 'ere!' He swung the monkey by the length of its confining lead to land with a soft thud on Polly's shoulder. His quick jerky movements startled her into springing forward, whereupon the monkey flew into the air, emitting a series of jabbering squawks and chatters, before landing squarely on the side of the barrel-organ.

'An' that there organ's the finest in the land!' laughed the tiny little man, his bony chest swelling with pride. The chattering monkey, eager no doubt to reinforce his master's sweeping statement, took hold of the handle and proceeded to turn it at a curiously dignified pace, whereupon a lovely tune floated out of the organ, full of jolliness and laughter, and as colourful as the organ itself. It was a musical machine such as Marcia had never seen before. Standing some four feet tall and shaped like a miniature piano, the whole of its body was festooned with swirling garlands of bright coloured patterns. The entire contraption was supported by two gigantic wheels, painted in circles of bright green and deep orange diamond-shapes.

Young Barty was beside himself with excitement, 'Oh Mam! Mam! Let me 'old 'im! I want to 'old 'im!' he shouted, jumping up and down and waving his arms in the air.

'Is there *anything* you don't want to do?' asked Marcia squeezing his hand lovingly.

'Course you can 'old 'im, son. Just put your arms out an' call 'is name—Jasper.' When young Barty did as he was told, the wizened man jerked the end of Jasper's lead. Unfortunately, as the monkey landed full in his outstretched arms, young Barty found it all too much. With his eyes tight shut, he let out such a fearful scream that they were all convinced he'd been bitten! The terrified monkey shot into the air like a catapult, whizzing over Florence's head to seek the relative security of his master's shoulder.

Slipping the wizened man two large shiny pennies, Grandma Fletcher led them away, towards the central bonfire area. 'Come on then. Let's be 'aving you! Night'll be gone afore we start, and there's me itching for a go on yon merry-go-round.'

The image of Grandma Fletcher whizzing through the air on a wooden dobbin horse was so ludicrous that they all collapsed into helpless laughter.

'Hey, come on! This is summat I've got to see for meself!' Grandad Fletcher was all fired up at the very thought of it.

''Ello Marcia lass. Barty not wi' thee?' Jim

265

Rawlinson was a burly coal-humper—a right enough fella, but known throughout Blackburn as a bit of a trouble-maker when he had a drink inside of him. Marcia thought the least said, the better.

'No, not tonight Jim. 'Appen he'll catch us up later,' she said, moving on.

'Oh, I see. Thar' singing aren't thee?'

'Aye. A bit later.'

'Well I'll not be going 'ome till I've 'eard thee. So long lass.'

'So long Jim. I'll tell Barty you asked after 'im.'

'Yon fella looks a right 'andful!' Grandma Fletcher watched him go.

'Poor old Jim. It's the drink as has 'im by the throat. He's not a bad 'un really,' she told her Mam.

They were standing now by the huge box-van which also served as a generator to convey the announcer's voice throughout the sprawling length and breadth of the area. It was from this van that Marcia's voice would be piped out on the open broadcast. The man and woman busily occupied with all the gadgets strewn about the van floor turned as they recognised Marcia. The man was nondescript, one of those people whose face could belong to a thousand others, but the woman was striking in appearance. Her broad Lancastrian accent belied her appearance, because she had dark swarthy skin and a wild mop of jet black fuzzy hair, which seemed totally out of place hereabouts. Her voice was coarse and loud, but genuine in its welcome.

Striding towards the open end of the van, she called out in amplified tones, 'Marcia love, get yoursel' up 'ere, an' give this mike a try! We can't seem to stop the bloody feedback. It's done nowt but screech its damned 'ead off all night!'

'Now what do *I* know about mikes an' electric things, Sal,' protested Marcia.

'Never mind that! You don't 'ave to know 'owt. *We'll* set it up. Just get yoursel' up 'ere an' give us a voice level.' She noticed Marcia looking at the rest of her family with concern. 'Hey, fetch 'em *all* up 'ere. The more the merrier,' she chuckled.

'Oh Mam! *I* don't want to go up there,' Polly complained. 'Can me and Bridget go and 'ave a look round? We'll come back when you start singing.'

Marcia reckoned on there being a good hour yet before she was needed to sing, and she'd been looking forward to seeing the fairground with the family first. Her fingers reached around the note in her pocket. Also she *had* to find a quiet minute in which to read Nantie Bett's little letter. 'You sort it out, Sal,' she decided, 'I'm going to wander round for a while—show the young 'uns the fairground. You'll be all right, won't you?'

The woman's features broke into a wide grin, 'Go on then . . . I'll call you on the tannoy when we're ready.' She turned to lose herself amongst the twisted confusion of cable and gadgets.

'Oh Mam,' Florence moaned, 'I wanted to go round on me own!'

'Well you're *not* going on your own!' Marcia considered the lass far too young for such an adventure. But now, Nantie Bett stepped forward to grasp the girl's hand.

'Us old 'uns can take the young 'uns round,' she told Marcia, 'It'll be a treat, eh?'

'That's right,' Grandma Fletcher sealed the

suggestion with her approval and the matter was settled. Marcia would go with Polly and Bridget, and the remaining five were to stay as a party.

When Blackburn Town Hall officials put on the celebrations for the annual bonfire, they really meant business. It seemed to Marcia that every nook and cranny was bursting at the seams. There were more people here than she could ever remember before, and more vendors of all descriptions were peddling their wares, or calling out for eager members of the milling crowd to 'Come and have a go!' There were shooting-ranges; catch-a-goldfish stall, candy-floss and toffee-apple kiosks; roll-a-penny chutes, and many more.

At the core in the main central area, mile upon mile of cable hung in gigantic rings, from which were suspended myriads of bulbs of every conceivable shade.

Right in the very centre stood the bonfire. No ordinary bonfire this! It was all of twenty feet high and more, with a base circumference which would easily have swallowed the downstairs area of Grandma Fletcher's little terraced house. If you stretched your neck up into the night, to look beyond the mountain of timber, rags, paper, furniture and anything else that would produce a crackling flame, you would be rewarded by the awesome sight of Guy Fawkes. A monstrous creature, seated in a great wooden armchair, he claimed pride of place right on the very highest plateau. From there, he could survey the gathering admirers below.

His proud reign was doomed to a short duration however, for within the hour both he and his ragged castle were destined to be reduced to smouldering ashes. The haughty look on his cloth face betrayed no sign of concern, rather a proud inner knowledge that at least he had been King for a day.

As Marcia and the girls leaned over the rope barrier which had been erected with the intention of keeping would-be foragers and happy wanderers at bay, Polly appeared to be lost in a reverie as she kept her eyes fixed with fascination on the Guy Fawkes.

Marcia, watching Polly's thoughtful expression, wondered what was going on in her daughter's mind. She followed Polly's gaze, above the piled-up pyre, to the dark sacrificial figure seated on his deathly throne and, for just the fleeting span of a heartbeat, Marcia thought the painted features bore a striking resemblance to Barty Bendall, his dead gaze falling on them like blasphemy from hell. It occurred to her then that Polly might be imagining the very same thing.

'Come on lass,' she said as she turned Polly away from the bonfire, 'there's lots to see yet.'

Polly turned, seemingly alert—but the depth of her thoughts was still there in the glazed surface of her eyes. 'Oh, sorry Mam. I were just thinking.' Now, she shivered and seemed in a hurry as she pulled Marcia along. 'Let's go an' see how much the candy floss is,' she said. They quickly made their way across to the toffee-apple stall, where the spinning drums of pink candy-floss threw out a sweet aroma, and where Marcia was content to stay back and let the children enjoy themselves. But even now, she dared not retrieve the letter from her pocket, for she knew that were Polly to

269

notice there would be difficult questions to answer. There would be time enough later, she thought.

Her rambling thoughts were alerted by the lively discussion taking place. 'How much for a go?' Polly asked the lady on the hoop-la stall.

'Three hoops a penny!' the dumpling-shaped lady yelled out in a gruff voice. 'Come on, don't be shy. Try your luck.'

'I'll 'ave three.' Polly held out a penny, which the lady quickly seized before thrusting three plate-sized hoops into her hand. The small wooden stands which held various prizes each had a spike protruding from its centre. The hoop had to swing over the spike and come to rest round the entire stand before the challenger could claim the prize. The trouble was, the hoop had barely enough manoeuvring space, and it became a rare event to see a challenger actually collect a prize. But human nature being what it is, people still queued ten deep to try and prove their superiority.

Marcia watched as Polly surveyed the collection of prizes, which included watches, Woodbines, and generous piles of coppers. Her eager expression changed to one of sharp determination as her eyes alighted on a large shiny pile of threepenny bits.

'Polly,' Marcia read her thoughts, 'you'll *never* hoop that!'

Bridget had also followed Polly's gaze and was equally sure. 'It's too far away,' she said, 'and just *look* at the size of that stand. It's a cheat!'

The gruff-voiced lady stepped back to allow Polly an unobstructed view of the table. Her certainty that this slim white-haired girl would go away empty-handed betrayed itself on the squashy dimpled smugness of her face. 'Go on lass. Tek your time,' she said with her chin receding into three and her fat arms folded. She looked like a Buddha, Marcia thought.

Polly transferred the hoops into the tight grip of her left hand, then she stepped forward until her taut body contacted the rail. For what seemed an age, she fixed her narrowed eyes on to the stand holding the threepenny bits. With her whole body held completely motionless, it seemed as if even the natural function of drawing breath was suspended. Until, with slow deliberation, she took one of the hoops in her right hand, and lifted her arm to take aim. The hoop spun into the air, sailing happily on a straight path towards its target, and, to everyone's amazement, it landed fair and square!

There was a dense hush of disbelief, before the watching crowd realised what had happened, then suddenly, everyone started shouting and hollering at once.

'Ey, she's done it! She's bloody well done it!'

'I don't believe it! I saw it but I don't believe it!'

'Come on lady! She's beat you tonight by 'eck! Give the lass 'er prize.' The dimpled puffy face thrust itself into Polly's line of focus. The tight expression was grudging.

' 'Ere, 'ave you done this afore?' she demanded, obviously looking for an excuse not to pay out.

'No! She has not!' Marcia stepped forward, telling the woman, 'You'd do well to give her the prize without sulking!' She was justly proud of Polly's achievement, and she wasn't going to stand by and have it belittled.

'Ey lady! What the 'ell do you think you're playing at? The lass won fair and square!' came a protest from the back.

'That's right. Pay up and shame the devil.' The crowd was up in arms; one shouting above the other. Polly looked the lady straight in the eye and said quietly, 'No missus; I 'aven't done it afore. But even if I 'ad it'd mek no difference.' The quiet controlled firmness of her voice had an odd sobering effect on the crowd. The shouts reduced to murmurs of:

'That's right!'

' 'Course it meks no difference.'

The gruff-voiced lady was quick to realise the folly of betraying her grudge in front of a crowd of potential customers. 'There you are then lass, you did well, an' there's your prize.' When Polly took the little pile of threepenny pieces, there went up a roar of approval from the crowd.

'I'm going to buy you summat special,' she told Marcia.

'Are you love?' Marcia hugged her. 'That's nice,' she said. Then, over the air, came the announcement, 'I hope as you're all enjoying yourselves on this fine crisp evening. We've ... a ... great ... many ... treats lined up for ... you ... th ...'

There followed a low whistle, then the voice was clear once more. 'Sorry about that. We've fixed it now, so you're all right! Right then, as I was saying, we've a lot of exciting competitions and events lined up for your entertainment this evening. It'll be about an hour before we send yon dastardly Guy Fawkes to his well-deserved end, so enjoy the fun of the fair till then. After the bonfire, the fair will close down, and the drinks will be dished out from this 'ere trailer. So stay with us, because someone most of you know and love will be wringing your hearts with her lovely singing— Marcia Bendall! She'll be with you in about ten minutes. Marcia, don't forget—ten minutes.'

Marcia's heart swelled with a deep surging pride, as every man jack around her cheered their hearts out, calling for her, urging her to sing this song or that. Telling Polly and Bridget to stay in the lights from the stall, where she could easily find them later, she started her way back towards the van. The conversation followed her.

'I didn't know your Mam could sing.'

'There's nobody as can sing like my Mam, Bridget!'

As Marcia came up into the shadows alongside the huge van, she drew herself into the gap between the front cab and the actual container, where she brought Nantie Bett's note from her pocket. The light around her was dappled with shadows, so she moved into a stray beam of light from the nearby wrestler's tent. Was it from Curt, she wondered? Now, as she looked down on that extravagant scrawl, she knew at once that it *was* from him, and, trembling deep within herself, she pressed the note to her lips and closed her eyes.

A great happiness seized her as she went on to read it, yet, even as she read, she was desperately afraid.

The note read:

My beautiful darling Marcia,
The years have been hard and lonely, and how I endured those endless hours without you, only God can tell, for I never will know. The hardest thing of all was steeling myself

273

from coming to you the moment I was released from prison. Thanks to Nantie Bett I know your every move. When I learned of your marriage to Barty Bendall, I was inflamed with terrible rage and blind jealousy, but then, I came to be thankful, thankful that you had found someone to love and protect you and the babies, and I was so grateful. But the thought of you in another man's arms drove me nearly crazy! Oh, Marcia, can you ever find it in your gentle heart to forgive a very foolish and weak man? I had intended to leave Lancashire without seeing you, my love. But I can't! Do you see how weak I still am? But, if I am, then it's because I love you so very much, my darling. When you sing tonight, sing for *me*, because I'll be there, listening, watching you, and always loving you. Be happy in your marriage. Forget me—even though I can never forget you! May God keep you and our daughters safe.

Yours forever,
Curt.

For a long while Marcia stood in the darkness, the note pressed to her breast, its words burning her thoughts, and the bitter tears flowing down her face. Her heart was so full, yet, at the same time, so very empty. After a while, when she had composed herself, she returned the note to her pocket and walked away.

'You had me worried!' Sal told her as she helped Marcia into the van.

'Sorry,' Marcia replied, positioning herself in

front of the mike, 'I forgot the time.'

The van had been adapted for this particular use, and the main panels along the side were fixed to a row of hinges. This enabled the entire side of the van to be lowered outwards, so that from her position, the audience could see Marcia without obstruction, and she in turn enjoyed a panoramic view of them. She was talking to them now, deliberately concentrating on what she must do. 'I'll sing *all* your old favourites, but first, I know you won't mind if I sing a special one for a . . . dear friend here with us tonight.' If Curt *was* out there, she wanted him to know she had read his note. 'Danny Boy' was his favourite song. 'I know this song is very special to him,' she said. Then, remembering how she used to croon it to him she added, 'And to me.'

The waves of music rode out on the night breeze as Marcia picked up the cue to mingle her clear lilting voice with the melodic rhythm. Without effort, the voice surpassed the music, reaching out to tug at those hearts, all tuned in on the same emotional wavelength. And, as Marcia's eyes roved across the sea of faces, her gaze came to rest on the bright red trilby which stood conspicuous amongst the listeners. It struck her heart cruelly, for fixed around its base was a broad span of black ribbon, stark and fearful against the gaudy crimson. For one painful moment Marcia's voice faltered, as she looked upon the tragic face of little Ada Humble. The small round eyes, drained now of their sparkle, glittered in terrible sorrow as they gazed on Marcia. Her heart already aching, Marcia could not contain the tears which flowed down the strong lines of her beautiful face. Toby was gone—

Ada's face told all.

Everyone was familiar with the powerful words of 'Danny Boy' but never before had they heard it sung in such a way. The song became a story, and the story breathed life, and Marcia Bendall's voice was never more magnificent.

For a few precious moments time rolled back and once again, each heart knew the joy of embracing a loved one. They knew also the despair when one was taken.

There was nary a sound from the four hundred-strong audience. Even the stall-holders and fair-folks had brought their churning machinery to a halt, so as to concentrate on the heavenly voice.

Marcia's caressing words bathed the cool night in a soft gentle warmth, weaving a magical spell. 'But come ye back when summer's in the meadow, or when the valleys they are white with snow.' Her lovely voice rang out clear and fine, as now the folks began to sing along with her, until the chorus swelled so strong that it could have been heard many miles away. 'For I'll be here in sunshine or in shadow—Oh Danny boy, oh Danny boy, I love you so . . .'

In Marcia's heart, 'Danny' could have been Curt—it could have been Ada's Toby, and the words of the song had never moved her so deeply. When her sad eyes scanned those faces all reaching up to her, she saw one other who stabbed at her heart. It was an old, old man, who appeared to be isolated from the crowd—a small solitary figure lost in his thoughts, his face creased in anguish. But through the tears which ran heedlessly down his face, there shone a defiant pride which lit up his features with a haunting beauty, and which made Marcia wonder whether he also was thinking of his loved one, now gone from him.

When the song drew to a close, the crowd stood transfixed, then, of a sudden, the silence was broken. The cheers that had caught in the choking fullness of their throats broke through in waves of shouts and whistles, all praising Marcia and all wanting more.

'God bless you lass.'

'Give us another song, Marcia.'

'Sing your 'eart out, lass. We've got all night.'

Marcia obliged with two more songs, then she hurried from the van to search for Ada, only to find that Blackie had taken her back to the infirmary chapel, 'to be wi' my Toby for a while longer.'

All the while she was searching for Ada, Marcia looked for Curt but he was nowhere to be seen. He saw her, though. It took every ounce of his self-control to stop from running to take her in his arms. When he left, he would leave his heart with her, but he did not expect to be back—ever. Marcia had her new life and he must make his own way, as had been his intention before he thought to say goodbye to Nantie Bett. Now, he went quickly, before he changed his mind.

'Your Mam! I can't believe it. Why isn't she on the stage?' Bridget was awestruck by what she had just experienced.

'I asked 'er that once,' Polly said, brimming with pride at Bridget's remark, 'but she just said that God gave 'er a singing voice to share with friends and loved ones.'

'But she could be *rich.*'

'Mam says if your heart's full of love, you'll always be rich.'

'I can't understand that!'

'Neither can I,' Polly's expression betrayed a certain amount of confusion, 'but one day Bridget, *I'll* be able to give me Mam anything she wants.' Her eyes grew hard and determined. 'And *nobody* will ever be able to hurt her! Nobody!'

*   *   *

There were still hundreds of people thronging the fairground, so many of them eager to stop and talk to Marcia that it was some time before she could concentrate on her search for the family.

Hoisting herself on to the steps of the merry-go-round, she scanned the crowd. Over by the roll-a-penny stall, there stood a familiar dominating figure in the shape of Grandma Fletcher, but, Marcia couldn't be sure. She recognised no-one else, so quickly began her way towards the distant stall.

'Mrs Bendall!'

The sight of Bridget running fast towards her gave Marcia a fright. 'Bridget!' she said as she looked beyond the breathless girl. 'Where's Polly?'

Bridget took a few seconds to recover her breath. 'Isn't she with you? I thought she was with you?' she asked.

Marcia forced down the creeping sensation of alarm as she replied, 'No. I haven't seen Polly since I left for the van. How did you two get split up?'

Now, Bridget's expression became thoughtful. 'Well, I was told me mother wanted me.'

'Where were you standing? Who told you your

mother wanted you, eh?' Marcia demanded.

'My Dad! My Dad came and told me,' Bridget said as she indicated their position at the time. 'We were just standing there.'

'Your—Dad? *He* told you?' A chilling sensation in the pit of her stomach caused Marcia to curb the suspicion in her voice. She didn't want Bridget upset 'All right, Bridget,' she said quietly, placing a hand either side of the girl's shoulders. 'I expect she's found her Grandma Fletcher, or she's just wandering around on her own. You know what Polly's like.'

'Yes, I'll bet she's gone back to aggravate that hoop-la woman.' Bridget giggled at the thought, 'I'll go and see.'

'No,' Marcia said as she kept her grip on the girl, '*I'll* go and see. *You* find Grandma Fletcher and the rest on 'em. Whether or not you find Polly with 'em, tell Grandma Fletcher that I've gone home, an' I'd like her to follow me! Right? Have you got that? I want them to find their own way home.'

'Right. But if Polly's *not* with them?'

'The same!'

Marcia left Bridget to carry out the errand, while she headed for the nearest exit. She didn't need to search anywhere else, because her instincts drove her back to Regent Street, her expectations fearful. Hastening along the nigh-deserted stretch, Marcia couldn't ignore the terrible warnings which whispered to her, reminding her of suspicions she had entertained ever since setting eyes on that man. She prayed it was just the over-protective instincts she'd always held where Polly was concerned.

By the time Marcia reached Regent Street, her

279

conviction that Peter Revine had enticed Polly from the fairground was somewhat weakened. She began to think she might have acted hastily. Supposing she was wrong? What if Polly really *had* gone to the hoop-la stall—or was even now on her way home with the rest of the family? All the same, there was something sinister about that Peter Revine. It was there, lurking in the depth of his black piercing eyes. She felt sure he had drawn Bridget away from Polly!

Shivering, Marcia began fumbling in her pocket for the front door key—she had it in mind to check and make sure Polly hadn't just brought *herself* home and gone straight to bed, for the mood often took her that way.

But then she heard the quiet noises some short way along the street. She could see little in the soft flickering glow from the gas-lamps, so she followed the sound. Marcia was astonished to find Polly and Peter Revine scuffling about on his doorstep, he with his arms about her, and she protesting that she 'must go back to me Mam!' In her voice a trace of panic could be distinguished.

Quickly, Marcia was between them, plucking Polly from his grasp and accusing him furiously, 'What the hell's going on here?' She felt Polly sidle behind her and, when there came no reply from the man who even now was turning his black charming gaze on Marcia herself, she pulled her out, at the same time giving her a shake and demanding, 'What in God's name d'you think you're doing, Polly! Whatever possessed you to leave the fairground?' She could feel the girl trembling beneath her fingers.

'I'm sorry, Mam,' Polly said, starting to cry.

280

Fixing her eyes on Peter Revine she said in a loud accusing voice, 'It were 'im! Bridget's Dad! He said Chris weren't well, an' 'e wanted to see me right away. He told me he'd already asked your permission—and you said it were all right!' Of a sudden she was sobbing and clinging to her Mam. 'Only when we got here—he grabbed me. He frightened me!'

In a low, terrible voice, Marcia told him, 'It's plain to me what your intentions were, Peter Revine! An' I'm damn sure the police will see it the same way!' Still he gave no answer, although, at her threat, the smile had slid from his face. The smell of stale booze which thickened the air about him told Marcia he was well the worse for drink.

Now, as Marcia began to lead Polly away, there came another voice into the gloom—a voice Marcia recognised even before she saw its owner. 'Are ye having trouble, Marcia Bendall?' Rosa Revine had also returned home early, having discovered that her husband had left the fairground 'with a fair-haired young lass'. Now she stepped in front of Marcia, her face serious and her sorry eyes going from Marcia to Polly. After casting a scathing glance at her husband who swiftly disappeared inside the house, she again looked at Marcia, as she pleaded, 'Don't go to the police. Please?'

For a minute, Marcia was speechless! There had been no explanation requested. No angry protests at her husband's innocence. Only this heartfelt plea that she should not go to the police. It was almost as though Rosa Revine *knew* what had happened here—or, God forbid, what might have happened if only she hadn't come on the scene!

281

Inside Marcia was boiling. She was trembling from head to toe—whether it was with rage, fear, or both, she wasn't sure. But it was a fact that, for two pins, she'd be straight off to the constabulary this very minute, if it weren't for two things. One was that her entire family would know of it. The other was that Polly was obviously greatly distressed by the fright she'd had.

'Please, Marcia,' the woman asked again, 'you won't go to the police, will ye? Ye have my word that it won't ever happen again!'

Marcia felt sorry for Rosa Revine. God knows, she thought, Barty Bendall's no blessed angel, but accosting young girls in—that way! Well, it was a terrible thing. Of a sudden, she pulled Polly past the unfortunate woman as she told her in a whisper, 'I'm sorry, Mrs Revine.' Then, when she saw the woman's face fall desolate she added, 'I shall have to think on it.'

As Marcia hurried Polly away, Rosa Revine turned to look on them both, her eyes flat and empty, her fists clenching and unclenching and her mouth set in a grim angry shape. 'God help us!' she muttered, lifting her eyes to heaven, 'will there *never* be an end to it? Are we always to wander like gypsies from one place to another? Oh, Peter Revine, I should hate you for your black treacherous heart! But I can't help it if I still worship the ground you crawl on.' Then, with her face still as black as thunder, she hurried into the house after him.

Only when Polly had repeated her promise did Marcia quietly close the bedroom door behind her. For a long time, she kept a lonely vigil on the stairs, hating the lecture it had been necessary to

282

give poor frightened Polly—yet knowing it was called for, in view of what had taken place this evening. How she wished she had a good man to lean on in situations like these. How she wished Curt could have been here to handle it all. She had to smile though, because, if Curt *had* been here, he would likely have thrashed the fellow within an inch of his life. It stabbed at her when she recalled how much he had loved little Polly. Now, reading his letter over and over again, Marcia felt suffocated with sorrow until the tears ran down her face to stain the words he had written. Then, she gathered herself together and took the letter downstairs, where she carefully slipped it out of sight beneath the oilcloth. Mam an' the others'll be here soon, she told herself, better make them a hot drink before they get the tram back to Church. It was good to have something to take her mind off other, disturbing thoughts; not the least of which was that she feared she was pregnant again.

CHAPTER SIXTEEN

The watery early morning sunshine filtered into the miserable room, disguising the wintry bite still in the air. Blinking towards the window, Marcia realised she was alone in the room. Barty Bendall hadn't been home all night!

Slipping quietly out of the bed, she wondered whether he'd collapsed drunk on the downstairs sofa. It certainly wouldn't be the first time he'd done that, although she had to admit that it was more gambling than drink that caused these terrible rages of his. Not *just* the gambling, because there was something else, something eating away at him—driving him like a thing possessed. What it was, Marcia couldn't even begin to fathom. He'd said nothing about it to her but then, she reminded herself, he hadn't confided anything in her these past five years.

Quickly dressing, Marcia pushed the distasteful thoughts from her mind. If he didn't want to talk about it, there was nothing *she* could do.

She felt surprisingly refreshed, in view of the previous evening's trauma, and the fact that it had been late by the time she'd finally crawled into bed. Nantie Bett and her parents had caught the last tram in plenty of time, and young Barty, together with Florence, had gone to their beds full of excited chatter and uncomfortable from too much candy-floss.

Before falling asleep, Marcia had made herself two promises. One was to take in dressmaking, which would provide those few shillings to keep their heads above water. The other was to see Nantie Bett, because, God forgive her, she wanted to hear of him from the woman's own lips. She shivered as she thought what Barty Bendall would do if ever he was to discover what her intention was. All the same, it did not dissuade her, for she did need to satisfy herself that Curt was all right. After all, he'd been more of a *real* husband to her than ever Barty Bendall had been.

Of a sudden, the cold rush of air that entered through the open window fair took her breath away, and, filled with an urge to get things done quickly in order to slip next door to Ada Humble, Marcia now hurried downstairs to get a fire going.

Later, sitting in front of the fire, watching the leaping yellow flames and enjoying the crackle and explosion of burning wood, Marcia felt strangely at peace with herself. There seemed to be an easiness in the house; she wondered fleetingly whether it was because of the absence of Barty Bendall or whether it was due to the fact that with the arrival of morning had come the revelation that she was *not* pregnant, as she had feared. Oh, what a weight off her mind *that* had been! Whatever the reason for the quiet atmosphere, she didn't dwell on it too long. It was enough that it was so.

More than once her eyes gazed on that square of oilcloth under which she had hidden Curt's note, but Marcia made no move to unearth it. There was no need, for weren't the words written on her heart?

The charcoal-burnt kettle started to splutter forth its newly boiled contents, spitting impatiently into the fire until Marcia lifted it out using a cloth wrapped round the handle. Then, with the fire dancing cheerfully, and the freshly-brewed tea keeping warm on the hob, she lost no time in tackling the household chores one after the other. As she busied about, she allowed herself the luxury of imagination and forbidden emotions. She imagined her poor tormented Polly to be well and strong, free from pain and discomfort. She imagined Curt would walk in at any moment, his tall manliness filling the room with warmth and love and his dark handsome smile falling on her the way it always did. Now, she imagined that poor Toby Humble would be away on his Saucy-Sal tonight, the same as usual—there being no truth in the idea that he was lying stiff and cold in the chapel morgue. This day-dreaming could only be short-lived, however, and of a sudden reality flooded back.

Tears blinded her until she could hardly see the flagstones as she continued to scrub the scullery floor with mechanical vigour, her thoughts filled with a kaleidoscope of images: Polly's pain-racked face, little harmless Ada Humble sitting quietly by her man's side, knowing he was gone forever. And Curt, Curt with his wonderful dark eyes which had so often gazed with tender intimacy on her face— *his* image, above all others, was fierce and persistent, looking at her from his prison cell, where his love for her and the spite of his legal wife had put him.

Now, Marcia shook the cruel images away. There was no sense punishing herself for a tide of events which she had been helpless to stem. Deliberately now, she began humming a tune to herself, as she embarked on a strip-out wash at the pot sink. Afterwards, looking in that part of the mirror which wasn't cracked with age, she said aloud to herself, 'Dreams ain't for the likes of you, my girl! And, if you look about hard enough, you'll always find there's things to be grateful for— you've got your health and strength! You have a roof over your head and the ability in your fingers to earn a few bob.' Here she smiled, a deep contented smile as she wagged a finger at herself. 'Oh, and Marcia Bendall! Just think on them delightful little creatures all abed and sleeping to their hearts' content. If you're of a mind to count your blessings, my girl, *there's* three worth a fortune!' At this, she launched into a beautiful rendering of 'Irish Eyes' and, having finished the brushing of her long dark hair, she tied it neatly back, turned from the mirror and got on with her daily routine.

Deciding to leave the children in bed a while longer, Marcia made her way to Ada Humble's door. A respectful knock brought the tousled-haired Blackie to greet her, and Marcia ached at the sight of his woeful face, swollen from the crying. 'Come in Mrs Bendall,' he said as he threw the door open and turned to lead the way down the narrow passage to the back parlour, 'Me Mam's not in.' He waited for Marcia to sit on the tall stand-chair by the door, then edging himself into one of the armchairs by the fire, he whispered, 'She's gone to fix it for me Dad to come 'ome.' Saying such poignant words proved to be more than his sadness could cope with, for now his voice rose to a terrible wail of, 'Oh, Mrs Bendall, what shall we do, eh?' The pain inside him twisted his features into a strange lopsided shape. 'Oh, what shall me poor Mam do—now me Dad's gone, eh?' He looked at Marcia as though *she* had the answer.

'Blackie, Blackie!' Marcia rushed to gather him into her arms, but a boy almost a man was not to be subjected to such comfort, and with a shrug of embarrassment, he pulled away from her.

'Me Mam says it's 'er fault! Over an' over again she keeps blaming 'erself! But it's not 'er fault! I should a' been watching for 'im—me Mam were looking after all them bloody kids! So, it's *me* that's to blame, not 'er!' He paced the room as he spoke.

'Nobody's to blame, Blackie,' Marcia said. She knew something of what he was going through, but she felt helpless to relieve his pain. 'Your Mam'll be looking to *you* now.'

287

'She can rely on me Mrs Bendall!' Stopping in his tracks, he brought himself round to look down on Marcia, his face set hard and grim. 'I'll not be going back to that school neither. I'm needed 'ere. *I'm* the man o' the 'ouse now. There's nobody to look after things, only me, an' I'll 'ave more to do than sit in yon bloody school! I'm getting meself off to fetch a worker's wage in! 'Cause I've to watch out fer me Mam an' the little 'uns.'

Horrified, Marcia rose to face him. 'Blackie! You mustn't talk like that. You *have* to go to school!' She voiced what she knew was on *both* their minds, 'your Mam's been called to court on account o' you not going to school! And she *still* has that ordeal in front of her. If you stay away from school now, it'll only mek things a lot worse.' Marcia sensed that she was losing the argument. 'I *mean* it, Blackie! Besides which you know how much your Dad wanted a good education for you.'

'What use is an education, eh? No bloody use at all! 'Ow am I gonna 'elp me Mam by learning about Nelson an' maps, an' things as 'ave no use at all for a fella like me. It won't feed the little 'uns, an' it won't put coal on yon fire!' The determined set of his face hardened. 'No! I'm to fetch a wage-packet 'ome! When the authorities know about me Dad, they'll be med to see sense!'

Marcia could see the logic of his argument. It made more sense than having a big lad sit behind a desk all day, scribbling and chanting, yet she knew only too well that these school officers could see nowt but their own pitiful importance.

'It's not the time to talk on it just now,' she told the agitated lad, 'you get a brew ready for your Mam, an' I'll tek the twins off your hands. I've been promising myself to take the children round to Blakewater Brook—your two'll be that much more company, eh?' She shook his arm in a friendly fashion, her bright warm smile melting the stern lines of his dark frown. 'Go on, Blackie lad, you get 'em dressed an' fed, an' I'll be round for 'em in a little while.'

Blackie bent to place a quick embarrassed kiss on Marcia's face. 'My Mam loves you, d'ya know that?' he asked, the tears glittering afresh in his sorrowful eyes, 'an' I can see why!' Then, as an afterthought, he added, 'Them Revine's 'ave gone, did yer know?'

'Gone?' Marcia answered, astonished. 'Gone where?'

'Dunno! Me Mam noticed this morning, she thought she'd 'eard a 'orse an' cart in the street, somewhere's in the early hours. An' sure enough, she told me afore she went—they've gone! Bag an' baggage, just skulked off in the night wi' nary a word to a soul!' He looked directly into Marcia's wide eyes. ' 'Ow d'yer reckon that, eh?' he asked.

'I've no idea, Blackie,' she lied, knowing full well that it must have something to do with that business with her Polly, and happen her own threat to go to the police. She recalled the look in Rosa Revine's face and was sorry. All the same, Marcia was relieved to have them gone. It was yet another blessing to count, as far as she was concerned.

Later, having returned to her own home, where for a while she sat by the fire, thinking, Marcia picked up her cup of cold tea and emptied it down the sink. 'No use moping! I'd best get the children ready,' she said aloud, thinking how she was beginning to talk to herself too much. They did say

289

as how that was a sign of either growing old or mad. Well, she weren't old—not yet, so she'd best watch herself, she laughed. Glancing round to satisfy herself that the work was done and the table set, she made her way towards the parlour door.

Even before it actually happened, she knew. In that uncanny way she had of perceiving the presence of Barty Bendall, Marcia instinctively backed away from the door. In that same split second, Barty Bendall kicked open the living room door, his green eyes heavy from lack of sleep and bloated from too much drink. Now, with chilling directness, they fell on Marcia. Moving purposefully towards her, he slammed the door shut behind him, stemming the blast of cutting cold air which still whipped in through the gaping front door. 'Well now—if it isn't the harlot herself!' His evil grating voice, low and deliberate, warned Marcia of the impending scene. But she had never seen him as threatening as this, and it put the fear of God in her. Retreating from his steadily approaching figure, she said nothing. Some quiet voice deep inside warned her to stay silent.

In a moment though, and without warning, his hand was round her throat, squeezing so hard she felt the blackness rushing up to meet her, and instinctively her wild thrashing hands tore at his face, until she forced him to relax his deathly grip, giving Marcia a chance to flee.

'Leave me Mam alone! Leave 'er alone, you rotten pig!' Polly's face was ashen as she rushed to her mother's aid.

Leaning on the table for support, Barty Bendall stared wildly at the pair of them. The sight of Marcia cradling Polly as she gasped the air back into her depleted lungs seemed to infuriate him further. 'You think I'm blind, don't you? Or mad? Yes, you could bloody well say I was mad! *Furious*, more like!'

He turned towards young Barty and Florence, who were cowering in the open doorway. Raising his voice, he ordered, 'Shut the bloody door and get yourselves in 'ere. You're all in on this! Don't think I don't know, you rotten bastards!'

'What are you talking about? In on *what*?' Without even thinking, Marcia's glance fell on the square of oilcloth by the door. Surely to God he didn't know about that? No! He couldn't! But she had entertained so many disloyal thoughts of late that her heart trembled with guilt, and that guilt was written on her face.

Barty Bendall's answer was to plunge towards her, before gripping her by the arm and forcing her into the nearest chair. And, straightaway, Polly was there, the look on her face terrible to see. Barty Bendall watched her with a half-closed smile on his face, almost inviting her to challenge him, but quickly Marcia gestured the girl to stay where she was.

'That's right Marcia my love.' The drunken Barty Bendall leaned forward, as though to slobber kisses on her, but stopped close to her white shaking face, his green eyes boring into her. 'This can only be settled by you!' His hand came up roughly under her chin, as he tipped her head back and held it at his mercy.

'What is it you want Barty?' Marcia's voice was uneasy, but delivered in a controlled effort to calm him, and it seemed to work, for he snapped his hand away from her.

Young Barty was shivering, partly from cold and partly from the sight he was made to witness, as Barty Bendall grasped him by both arms and whirled him roughly to seat him on the table, where the lad cried loudly for his mother.

'You don't want *her*!' Barty Bendall turned to Marcia, who was now on her feet. Lunging his leather neck to its full reach towards her, he spat out, 'At least *this*!' He shook the lad violently, then crushed him to his side, '*This* is mine!' Young Barty was crying hysterically now, as with deliberate calm his father crossed to the door and turned the key, to lock it, after which he strode back to the horsehair chair, and threw himself down into it. 'You might as well all sit down! Because *nobody* leaves 'ere until I get some answers!' he declared, waving a hand towards the chairs.

Gathering young Barty up into her arms, Marcia wiped away his tears and spoke softly to comfort him. She ushered the two girls towards the stand-chairs by the door, her fears for their safety paramount.

'Barty, let the children go back to bed.' Her voice was deliberately steady and she hoped it might instil some measure of calm into Barty Bendall. But the ensuing shout came so unexpectedly that Marcia was visibly startled, and young Barty resumed his crying with more lust.

'Don't sodding well ignore me, woman! For two pins I'd throw the bloody lot o' you out on the street! And shut that kid up!' The veins on his neck pumped in and out, as though about to burst. Then, grabbing a stand-chair, he dragged Marcia and the clinging lad towards it, at the same time pushing his face close to hers, as she was thrust into the chair. '*Nobody* leaves this room until I get to the truth! Is that understood?' He crossed to the fireplace where he stood with his back to it, arms folded behind, legs astride, his vicious eyes sweeping the room and resting on everyone's face in turn. As he met Polly's defiant gaze, his eyes narrowed a warning.

Only the ticking clock and young Barty's quiet sobs broke the silence. Then Barty Bendall continued, his voice unusually calm, but shot with a low threatening tone. 'Last night, I happened to come across a mate I 'aven't seen for a long time.' His darting gaze continually fixed them all in turn, in a penetrating, methodical manner, and nobody ventured a muscle, 'Jim Rawlinson? Remember my old mate, do you? Well, this 'ere mate passed on some very interesting information.' He paused, as if half expecting some confession of misdemeanour, and when no such 'confession' emerged, his sharp weasel face puckered in angry impatience.

Marcia was now convinced that he knew nothing of the note—or of Curt being at the fairground, for, if he had *really* received any information concerning Curt he wouldn't be just standing there threatening them. He would all but have flayed them alive by now.

He knows nowt! Marcia told herself in a rush of relief. His next words however, aimed directly at Florence, sent a chill through her heart.

'Did anyone ask after thi' Mam last night—at the fairground, eh?' His voice dropped to a menacingly suggestive level. 'A *man* for instance— a tall dark-'aired fella?'

Florence was quick to answer, 'No, Dad!' and it

293

was plain to all that the child was shaking in her shoes.

Moving swiftly across the room, Barty Bendall grabbed Florence by the arm and expelled her furiously into the hallway. 'You get out!' he told her, before slamming the door shut behind her, 'there's nowt you can tell me!'

Rushing towards Marcia, who put down young Barty on his feet and told him to scurry towards Polly, Barty Bendall grabbed her hand and spread the bare wedding finger in front of her face.

'D'you think I'm bloody blind, woman! Did you really think I wouldn't find out as you pawned your wedding ring? *My* bloody wedding ring!' He held her hand in a fierce relentless grip, enjoying the discomfort on Marcia's face. 'An' that's not all, is it eh? Eh? It seems a mutual acquaintance of ours might be out o' jail! Roamin' the bloody streets!' He gave her hand a spiteful twist. 'I only 'ave to add two and two up, don't I? I'll tell you this, Marcia Bendall! I'm going to watch you like a 'awk, an' if I 'ear so much as a whisper that you've seen 'im,' here his eyes narrowed to thin cruel slits, 'I'll swing for you both! Mark my words 'ere and now, I swear on my mother's grave, I'll kill you both!'

A ripple of cold horror shuddered through Marcia's being. She knew without a shadow of doubt that Barty Bendall was capable of doing just that, for he was never one to make idle threats.

Of a sudden, the ominous silence which fell was shattered by the loud thump which rattled insistently on the front door.

Barty Bendall flung Marcia's hand out of his iron grip, and straightened himself up. 'That'll be

294

Jack!' he said.

Florence had closed the front door, shutting out the peering faces of neighbours who had gathered outside. Now, she sat huddled fearfully on the stairs, as Barty Bendall strode past her to answer the door. 'Oh, 'ello Jack. You're early,' he greeted the burly fellow warmly.

'Aye well. First race starts at eleven-thirty. We want to get there in good time.' He looked at Barty, still in his coat and cap, and said, 'Anyroad, it looks as if thar' ready.'

'Oh aye,' Barty Bendall winked and laughed before lowering his voice, 'spent half the night in landlord's back room, tekin' 'em all for a bob or two.'

'Thi' always were good at cards. Hey, by the way, what's going on outside? The whole bloody street's out for summat!'

Barty Bendall dismissed it with a sneer. 'Tek no notice! They're a nosey lot o' sods round 'ere.' He turned with a purpose. ' 'Ang on a bit, Jack. I'll not be a minute.' Whereupon, he pushed his head inside the living room doorway, and when Marcia looked towards him, he held her eyes fast with his own, his voice low and insistent. 'You've not 'eard the last of it woman—think on. I meant what I said.'

Much as she loathed to ask, Marcia had no choice. 'You've not given me any money. I can't manage without some money from you,' she told him, afraid that she might have made a wrong decision in leaving the cotton mill. As yet, she had only a few odd orders for shortening dresses, or lengthening them, but the word had been spread and Marcia felt sure the work *would* come in.

Barty Bendall took a threatening step forward, then through gritted teeth, he told her, 'It were *your* bloody idea to give up the mill! An' that's just a bloody shame! Because you're getting nowt from me! I'll tell you where the money's gone!' He produced a small shiny object from his coat pocket. As he held it up for Marcia to see, she recognised it at once as her wedding ring.

'See that! *That's* where the money's gone! An' if you all go bloody 'ungry this week, you've only yourselves to blame!' He strode towards her, his face triumphant as he grasped her hand and forced her fingers apart. First he cruelly thrust the ring down to the base, then he warned her in a low trembling voice, 'This ring 'ad better stay where *I* put it! I took you on when nobody else wanted you, *or* your brats and never you forget it. I'll chop your bloody finger off, afore I'll see it without that ring again!'

Polly hardly noticed him as he passed her to leave with big Jack Tanner. 'What did 'e mean Mam? All that talk about a fella—and everything?'

Marcia drew Polly towards her as she told Barty, 'Go and fetch Florence in, love,' then turning to Polly she said simply, 'Don't worry, Polly. Just trust me, please? I don't want you bothering your head about anything.' Marcia thought how very pale her daughter looked, and how brightly the blue eyes shone as they gazed on her in such adoration, and she wondered whether she would ever be worthy of such profound love. 'Bless you, Polly Bendall! What would I do without you, eh?' Marcia forced a smile. 'I've set the table, so you three get your breakfasts eaten, then we'll see what we shall see, eh?' She must erase the awful scene from *all* their minds. And, like it or not, when there was a private moment, she must also destroy Curt's letter.

*   *   *

Marcia watched the children as they chased each other up and down the cobbled banks. Perched on an old beer-barrel which someone had tipped over the bridge-wall to its last resting place, she pulled her coat tight about her and marvelled that the youngsters didn't seem to feel the cold. Sitting there, listening to the water gurgling over the shiny washed cobbles, she felt far removed from Regent Street, even though it was only minutes away. Blakewater Brook was a special place to Marcia, for its quiet atmosphere had always been able to soothe her. She recalled the time when Barty Bendall first brought her and the two small girls to live in Blackburn. Whenever her memories of Curt pressed hardest, she would always find her way to Blakewater and some sort of peace. She had never been able to understand why. Perhaps it was the rhythmic slapping sound as the water splashed against the jutting stones, or that sense of total isolation which always enveloped her as she looked back at the steep descent from the street to the bowels of the brook.

There was nothing of any striking beauty along Blakewater. If anything it was a lonesome, unattractive place. According to local gossip, there were plans afoot to fill the brook in, and redevelop the entire area. Marcia hoped there was no truth in such rumours.

The main access was a narrow footpath which followed a downward line in the shape of a long slithering snake. On the right as you descended was the prettiest little arch-backed bridge, spanning the brook from a lofty position some fifty feet above the water. On the left, the red-brick wall reached higher and higher the further down you went, until it seemed that the whole sheer face of it would fall like a pack of cards to crush everything beneath.

The discoloured trickle of water followed a long meandering path, threading in and out of the steep sloping banks on either side and over the round shiny cobbles which formed the banks and which were worn smoother each year beneath the constant licking of the water. Some folks abused Blakewater and all along its shores lay remnants of discarded debris, old shoes, tin cans, and the odd dead rat here and there. But in spite of all that, Marcia loved it.

As always, she stayed far longer than she had originally intended, gathering the children together only when young Barty complained about his 'frozen fingers'. Rubbing the stiff little hands between her own, Marcia called, 'Come on you lot! Let's be making tracks homeward.' Her voice echoed along the high surrounding walls.

It was a happier group of children that rushed to gather about her and as they picked their way back up the narrow path, Marcia felt thankful that she had been able to replace their brooding thoughts with more agreeable memories.

On arriving back in Regent Street, Marcia left her own children to climb the steps to the front door while she took the Humble twins home.

Blackie ushered them into the passageway and Marcia was grateful that he appeared to be less emotional and more able to cope. In answer to her concerned question regarding Ada, he answered in a calm, controlled manner, 'No, she's not back yet, Mrs Bendall. I thought she *would* a' been by now.'

'These things all take time, Blackie . . .' She could picture little Ada Humble sitting somewhere quiet, taking the time to gather her strength before bringing Toby home.

'Look lad, I'll take the twins back wi' me, shall I?' she offered, and, in Blackie's resolute smile, Marcia perceived his strength of character when he replied.

'No thank you, we've to learn to cope on us own now. We'll manage.'

'If you say so, lad, but I want you to promise that you'll fetch me the minute your Mam comes back, and even *afore*, if you need anything,' insisted Marcia.

' 'Course I will, and me Mam'll probably send for you anyway, 'cause you're the only one she'll really want just now.'

Touching his hand in a fleeting gesture of comfort, Marcia told him softly, 'No lad! It's *you* she needs most of all. Although sometimes a woman can say things to another woman that a man might not understand, it's you your Mam will rely on now,' she assured him, 'and your Dad would be right proud o' you.'

After he'd closed the door behind her, Marcia stood for a moment, pondering on the turn of fortunes in the short span of a single day, and coming to the conclusion that sometimes there seemed to be no justice in the world.

The house struck cold as Marcia flung wide the front door to let everyone in, and the damp air

299

filled her nostrils as she followed the children into the house.

'Brrr! it's freezing in 'ere Mam!' Polly jostled her way to the fireplace. 'I'll mek a fire and brew a pot o' tea.' Meanwhile, young Barty had rooted out his tattered old comics and Florence had fallen into the nearest chair. 'I'm tired!' she moaned, pulling up her legs beneath her.

'Tired! Give over, Florence!' Marcia rebuked. 'You're not old enough to be "tired"! Go and give Polly a hand with that coal.' Reluctantly the girl complied with her mother's instructions, leaving Marcia to take the long bolt poker from the grate and proceed to jab it noisily in and out of the fire-bars, until the dead ashes had all been forced into the bottom tray, leaving only reusable cinders lying in the grate. That done, she went to the scullery to retrieve a pile of old papers and a box of matches.

In no time at all their joint efforts produced crackling warmth, which melted their frozen joints. 'Florence, there's half-a-crown in my purse on the sideboard, tek young Barty with you to the corner shop. Wait a minute—I'll write down what I want.' After listing a few meagre necessities, Marcia ensured they were well wrapped up before telling them to hurry and reach the shop before it shut.

Gradually the room was beginning to feel more comfortable as the heat from the fire radiated through the air. Marcia looked around her at the bleak bareness of the room, thinking how she despised the place for it had always seemed so full of unhappiness. Well, maybe not in that first year up to little Barty's birth—but it had been downhill from there. Taking her empty mug into the scullery she busily pottered about, laying out a newspaper tablecloth for Barty Bendall's next meal, and ruminating on how, as a rule, after his morning's betting spree and a bout with his mates down the pub, he'd turn up about one o'clock demanding food, with little or no thought about how it had been provided. She glanced at the mantelpiece clock to see that it was already ten past one and there was no sign of him, and frowned. She wouldn't really care if he *never* walked in through that door again! She cast a dark glance at the wedding band on her finger, suddenly loathing the sight and feel of it.

Later, Marcia told Polly about Bridget having moved from the area, and, as she'd suspected, Polly took the news badly—first running out and down the street to see for herself, then returning in tears, to throw herself into Marcia's arms. 'Bridget was my best friend!' she cried, 'an' now I've got nobody!'

'You've allus got *me!*' Marcia smiled, drawing the lass into her arms, 'an' you've got your brother and sister.'

'But it's not the *same*, Mam!' protested Polly.

'Oh, Polly,' she began, 'I know how much Bridget meant to you, darling. But, you know, we *all* lose somebody we love; it's a fact of life, and when it happens, we struggle against the truth on it, and we fight an' kick, but, it changes nowt! They've gone, an' we're left behind to see it through.' Marcia felt the anger leave her daughter and she reached out to wipe away the flowing tears from Polly's face. 'It's a sad, cruel world we live in, Polly lass, but for all on us, at some time or another, there's a little share o' love an' beauty, that meks it all worthwhile.'

CHAPTER SEVENTEEN

The deepest of winter had passed. Now, it was one of those bright, crisp January mornings, when the whole world appeared to sparkle with trembling anticipation. The birds lifted their newly-discovered voices to herald the promise of spring and the flower buds just emerging from months beneath all the heavy settle of winter peeped out with tentative curiosity. But Regent Street and the drab greyness of its surroundings looked no different year in, year out. There were no seasonal changes, each day being a continuation of the day before, and even the birds sought brighter climates. Marcia, like the birds, had chosen to leave the wretchedness of it all behind, because she and the children were on their way to Corporation Park.

The sharp clean breeze teased about her beautiful face, lifting the stray lengths of her rich black hair, and urging her to walk a pace faster. 'I do love these sort o' days,' she said, 'won't be long now afore it's spring.'

'Well, I can't say as *I'm* all that excited about it, Mam,' Polly answered as she tucked her hair inside the deep security of her collar. 'It's right nippy!'

'Give over, Polly!' Marcia protested tenderly. 'It's a *beautiful* day.' Whereupon Polly lowered her gaze and concentrated on the path before her. Florence and young Barty were skipping happily a few yards ahead, anxious to get to the park as quickly as possible. Every now and then they broke into a little friendly race towards the huge iron

302

gates which were only a few steps away.

Corporation Park was an oasis on the outer rim of Blackburn town. It was a place where everyone, young, old, rich or poor, could come away from their two-ups, two-downs and the towering shadows of the old cotton mills. It was a huge rambling paradise, acres of flowers, lawns and magnificent views, the whole securely encompassed within a wrought iron palisade of ten feet high, in places, punctuated here and there with tall ornate gates, through which in the course of a year there passed many thousands of people.

The interior was a landscape gardener's dream, boasting undulating green banks covered in graciously weeping willows and gigantic spreading rhododendrons, which in early summer blossomed proudly in gorgeous shades of purple and red. Everywhere there were sprawling reserves of natural beauty, where man had cleverly allowed nature to merge with his own hand, until the two created a unique and breathtaking splendour.

Feeling rather taxed by the long uphill walk, Marcia and the children turned into the main arched entrance and through the great iron gates, where Marcia collapsed onto the first bench she came to, all the while keeping the others in sight as they wandered over to the fountains.

The fountains were always a source of fascination to Marcia's children. 'Do you know a little lad was drowned in these 'ere fountains?' Polly asked of Florence, who appeared entranced by the whole thing.

'No.'

'Well 'e was!' Polly stood just ahead of Marcia, lost in admiration of the great lions before her.

The fountains had taken years to complete and the end result was truly remarkable. The large, twisting rose shaped pool in the immediate foreground provided an overspill receptacle for the even larger cameo pool directly behind. The two great lions were sculpted into a pair of rising columns nigh on thirty feet high, situated to the left and right of the cameo pool. They were utterly magnificent, proud and commanding. The grey stone heads were enormous, painstakingly detailed to capture the fury and royalty of the beast. For a while, Marcia sat in awe at the sight and sound of thousands of gallons of water frothing and tumbling from the open mouths of the snarling lions into the swallowing depths of the pool below.

''Ave you ever seen a *real* lion, Mam?' Polly asked.

'No, never!'

'Neither 'ave I!' Polly dragged her eyes away from the spectacle before her to look into her mother's face with that odd determination that Marcia had come to recognise, but never to understand. 'That's one o' the things I'm going to do when I get the chance. I want to see *everything* and go *everywhere!*'

Quietly Marcia examined the strong blue eyes, glinting with desperation for everything the world had to give. She reached out in an involuntary gesture, as if to calm the raging torment which she knew existed beyond that blue wall. When she spoke, her voice was filled with total belief. 'I know you do Polly.'

At this, Polly turned away to gaze intensely into the frothing water.

Marcia knew instinctively that her daughter's

torment, and consequently her own, was not yet over. These last two months had brought little peace, in spite of the fact that Polly's frightful attacks hadn't accelerated. The specialist's examination could neither deny nor confirm a deterioration in her condition, and so arrangements were under way to admit Polly to the Infirmary at the soonest possible date, in order for a more detailed examination to be undertaken. It had been a hard thing for both Polly and Marcia to accept, and, thinking on it, Marcia closed her eyes for just a moment, allowing the playful breeze to blow coolly on her face.

'Poor Polly,' she mused sadly, 'It's all so unfair to someone so very young! And she does miss that little Bridget.'

Marcia sighed, a heavy raking sigh which left her weary. She herself had missed the uplifting company of the mill-hands. But at least there was a deal of dressmaking to be done, now folks knew she was turning her hand to it.

Of a sudden, Marcia stood up and sought to leave her thoughts behind her. 'Come on then,' she said as she waited on the wide walkway which cut through the heart of the park for many winding miles, 'let's make our way up to Badger's Den.' Quickly Florence and young Barty appeared from behind one of the ornate bridges which straddled various areas of water and shrubbery, and running along in front they left Marcia and Polly to follow slowly on behind. Lost in the beauty which surrounded them on every side, neither were in any immediate hurry. There was little verbal communication between them, for each was preoccupied with her own private thoughts. Marcia wondered what possible choices lay ahead, for she sensed that things couldn't go on as they were, and although she herself would deny it to the last, she speculated whether she disliked Barty Bendall every bit as fiercely as Polly did.

However, wandering about in the glory of Corporation Park, Marcia found it difficult to dwell on the darker side of life, for there was so much beauty around her, and there had to be hope. Without that there was nothing at all. All the same there was no one Marcia could really turn to. She grew angry on recalling the cruel indifference of Barty Bendall when she'd attempted to discuss Polly's imminent admission to the Infirmary. She didn't really care too much when he turned his spite and viciousness onto her, but Polly was only a child.

'Mam,' Polly's voice broke in, 'the young 'uns want to go to the sandpits first.'

'I don't mind, but what about you, Polly?'

'I'd like to see the sandpits as well.'

'Right,' Marcia decided, 'the sandpits first, then Badger's Den.'

The meandering walkways, which in the summer gave forth an abundance of scent and colour, were a delight to linger in. At this time of year, the golden hues and tints of browns and yellows greeted the wanderer at every turn. Primrose Way carried the little party into the quieter, older part of the park. It was an uphill path, twisting and turning in and out of the overhanging branches, arriving at the highest point possible before merging with the broad flatness of a more open footpath, which led to the sandpit. Polly had taken charge of the picnic bag from her mother when the uphill struggle seemed to be taking its toll. At the top of the path, they paused.

'Phew! I'm worn out!' Marcia said, puffing and panting, her breath shooting out in little puffs of white vapour.

'It's right steep is that!' Young Barty took only a minute to regain his breath, at which point he prodded Florence hard in the ribs before running at full pelt from her to jump knee-deep into the sandpit.

Marcia looked vivacious as she stood recuperating. The cool wind had blown her long black hair into wonderful disarray, and her flawless skin was now flushed with a soft pink glow. She felt exhilarated by the climb and wonderfully free from the encumbrances of the unseen chains that bound her. Noticing Polly, who was still clawing for breath, Marcia trembled as she observed the change in her daughter's features, for the skin seemed stretched over the sharp delicate features like a shrinking mask, its quality that of fine alabaster. Then as Polly lifted her eyes to smile at her, Marcia's breath caught fearfully in her throat. The blueness which had been so vivid seemed to have drained away, leaving behind an almost ethereal transparency. The white eyelashes fluttered nervously as Polly's thin lips moved stiffly.

'Can we sit down a minute, Mam?' she asked in a breathless voice.

To Marcia, the awful recurring nightmare that had stalked her restless sleep these past years never seemed nearer than it did now. She eased Polly onto the stump of a felled tree. 'We'll bide here my lass,' she murmured, taking Polly into her

307

arms. 'Tek yer time, darling. Just rest a while an' get your breath back, it's as pretty here as anywhere else.' Leaning over to brush her lips against the pale forehead, she asked, 'Have you any pain, lass?'

'No, Mam,' Polly's attempt at laughter produced only a small broken noise, 'I've just run out of puff, like a broken-down old train.'

'Mebbe we shouldn't have come this way,' Marcia told her, angry with herself for having been persuaded up the steepest path. 'We'll not go to Badger's Den, eh? We'll spend us time at the sandpits.' She squeezed Polly affectionately. 'Then we'll mek our way back down.'

'Oh Mam.'

'No buts, my girl!' Marcia said adamantly. 'We'll go no further than the sandpits!' She had always marvelled at the speed with which Polly's attacks left her, but this one, although apparently free from pain, seemed to hold the girl in its grip for an endless time. Yet, when it finally subsided, it left no trace of its severity.

'You're sure you're feeling better? You don't want to sit here for a few minutes more?'

Polly's slight colour had returned, and she was looking for mischief. 'No, I'm off to aggravate them young 'uns.' She saw the concern in her Mam's eyes, and was quick to assure her, 'Don't worry Mam—I'm all right, honest! It were just the steep climb that got me all breathless.' She gestured to far beyond the sandpits where Florence and young Barty played happily, and where the shrubberies fell away against tall, stately trees which scraped the sky. 'Look at that, Mam! I bet there's all manner o' little animals in there!'

Marcia watched her heading towards the sandpit, then she followed as far as the bench which skirted the play area. The bench on which she was resting nestled cosily in the folds of a tall, rambling laurel hedge. From there the sandpit dipped into a hollowed-out crater at the foot of the crag, so while Marcia could see her children by stretching her neck and maneuvering her position, she was perfectly camouflaged from their view. Now, she leaned back against the hardness of the seat, feeling strangely quiet within herself. It wasn't often that she could allow herself the luxury of coming to the park, for her long days at the sewing and the demands of her domestic duties swallowed up her life in its entirety. All manner of things she had planned, but none had come about—such as that long talk she'd meant to have with Nantie Bett for instance. Today was a special treat, and one in which Marcia wallowed shamelessly.

From that very day when the tiny damaged bundle had struggled to survive the awful complications of her birth, the tiny creature that was Polly had held a special place in Marcia's heart. It didn't mean that she loved her other children any the less, but only a mother could know the special searing joy that comes with the birth of a first child, and when that child is damaged, the natural instincts of protection take on a deeper significance. There had always been an unspoken understanding between them, a bond of comradeship that had survived through early diagnosis of the lurking tumour, through the bad time when Curt had been taken from them, and through all that had dogged them since. In

Marcia's pursuit of security and happiness for her children she had always known that Polly's happiness and peace of mind would be the hardest to win. The bond between mother and daughter had proved flexible enough to withstand many atrocities.

Yet, even though Marcia had tried so desperately to understand the inner battle she knew constantly raged within her daughter, its cause and consequence still perplexed her. Often, when she'd felt that Polly needed help most, Marcia had discovered that, even for her, there was no way through the barrier with which Polly protected her inmost feelings, so Marcia had clung to the fervent hope that all would be well in the end.

Closing her eyes, she stilled the rising worries that churned through her mind. The gentle sunlight fell upon her face as she gave herself up to its soothing caress, and she counted the blessings she had. They may have been relatively few to someone who knew nothing of a woman like Marcia Bendall, but to her, each blessing was a joy to cherish. She remembered the burning, deep love once shared with Curt. She embraced the love of her own darling parents, and the children she had borne, and her heart swelled with gratitude.

How far away seemed the strong comfort of Curt's loving arms, and how desperate her own terrible loneliness at times. She had twice set out to visit Nantie Bett in pursuit of news from Curt, under the pretext that he had every right to be told of Polly's predicament. Inside though, she had already decided that Curt had been through more than enough, but she would have given a great deal to share her anxieties with Polly's father.

On the two occasions she'd started out to Nantie Bett's, it was only to turn back at the very last minute. If it proved to be necessary to contact Curt, then that would be time enough . . . As for herself, Marcia had resisted the many urges to retrieve Curt's note from beneath the oilcloth where it had lain hidden since the night of the bonfire. But she couldn't bring herself to destroy it, even though every word was written on her heart. There never was and never could be any future in their love for each other, for their chance had gone, and time had moved them both apart, to where their paths might never cross again. All the same, there was nothing to deny her the wonderful pleasure she experienced on holding his memory close.

A short distance away, Curt Ratheter stood undecided. Now that he had come this far, should he approach his darling Marcia or should he have the strength to turn and walk away, now that he had seen her and the girls? But, somehow, when he'd seen them emerge from that miserable little house, he stayed a few paces behind them—on the slimmest chance that he just might get to talk to Marcia alone. Now that the chance appeared to have presented itself, the doubts began setting in. What would her reaction be? Would she turn from him? Did she still love him? Or would she always blame him for having ruined both their lives, shattering that wonderful happiness they had shared together? His heart told him that she loved him as much as he still loved her. His head told him that he was asking too much, and that he should go now.

Satisfying herself that the three children were safe, Marcia leaned back against the bench, closing her eyes and letting the warm memories invade her fevered mind. So real was the pleasure she felt within her that she could almost *feel* Curt's nearness. She shivered lightly, the urgent pounding of her heart echoing so thickly in her throat that she could hardly breathe. An inexplicable compulsion within her caused her eyes to open without her having consciously willed it. The tears were already warm in her eyes, although she knew not why, and the surging sense of great joy carried her along on a wave of anticipation. When of a sudden the murmured words reached her, she was startled. It was almost as though Curt was here beside her.

'Marcia! Oh, my own darling Marcia!'

The ecstasy within her became almost too much to bear. Her eyes flicked upwards and there was Curt! Not a dream! Not a figment of her imagination! But her own dearest Curt, warm and real, and close enough to touch! She was filled with excitement and fear.

'Curt,' she whispered, afraid to chase away what might be only a shadow. Holding out a hand, she stood to face him. 'It *is* you—it *is*!' The tears spilled down her face. 'Oh, Curt! Curt!' She was both laughing and crying, and strangely embarrassed.

'Marcia—just as I've always remembered you,' he murmured, his black eyes intent upon her, devouring her loveliness with passion.

Marcia could barely focus on his face—that handsome face whose every line she knew so very well.

Curt Ratheter stepped forward, the tears glittering, then, the barriers between them in disarray, he caught her into his strong arms. Marcia offered no resistance—she had none to offer. Her thoughts swirled in a turmoil of great fear and heavenly rapture. How could she not thrill at the strength of his arms, at the touch of his mouth as it came down against her lips to stir the very fibre of her heart? She was his! This was *her* man, hers! And she loved and needed him more than words could ever tell. She gave herself up to his arms, to his kisses, to the love which had always held them fast, and she experienced such great pleasure that it made her reel.

Yet all too soon her happiness became marred by the ever-present knowledge that it could never be. The sadness returned to her eyes, dimming the light of love which had shone so fiercely in the radiance of the moment, and freeing herself from his arms, she drew an agonizing sigh.

'Curt—no!' She retreated to the bench, her gaze imploring him to understand.

These last long years had left their impression on the man who, in Marcia's eyes, would always be her true husband. The figure still carried the same tall confidence, in spite of the slight stoop about the trim shoulders, which maybe no one but Marcia would ever have noticed, and her heart was pained by the years he too had been locked away. Now, when he crossed to sit beside her, he took her hand tenderly into his own.

'I've been a little way behind you all morning,' he told her, 'but I had to wait 'til you were alone.'

Marcia prayed she could be strong. 'Curt,' she said as she slid her hand away from his, 'please—

please understand. I mustn't see you ever again.' Her fear was not for herself, but for him. She had not forgotten what Barty Bendall had threatened.

'You can't say that, Marcia!' His voice grew excited. 'Fran and I are divorced, I've been south, Marcia, and I've been promised work and a tied house! I've also saved a little money. Oh, darling— how I do love you! Say you'll come with me, you and the children—to a new life.'

'No, Curt! We can't.' Marcia's voice was torn with anguish as she pleaded with him. 'Can't you see, my love, there's nothing for us now. It's too far in the past. Too much has happened which could hurt us all, and even if *you* are now free, I'm very much married!'

'If I thought you didn't love me, Marcia, didn't want me, I'd go now and you'd never see me again. But I know different. You and I are as much in love now as on the day when I first saw you.'

Remembering seemed to revive old fears and Marcia longed to hold him to her, to comfort him in his painful memories. But she dared not, or she also would be lost! He bowed his head as if to escape the unbearable memories, then, of a sudden, he wrapped both his hands around her slim fingers, raising them to his lips, and caressing them most tenderly.

'I *know* you're not happy with Barty Bendall,' he said softly.

Now, she gazed at the face of her beloved Curt, and the rush of emotion filled Marcia's throat with choking tightness. 'Don't talk about it, my darling,' she whispered, 'for it can make no difference, don't you see that? He's my husband, and I have to stick by him. You and I must let the past go for

314

ever.' Her voice was heavy with the love she felt for him, as she caressed the dark, loving features whose every line was etched in her memory. Meeting his strong, steadfast gaze, her heart cried out to him. Oh, how she loved this warm, caring man, and how jubilant she would be if only they could be together again. But there was still too much against them! How could she uproot the children? And if she did what madness would Barty Bendall be driven to? Then, on top of all that, she and Curt would be in no better position than before, for Barty Bendall would never allow her the freedom to marry Curt. If anything, he would go to extreme lengths to prevent such a thing. The very thought of his manic temper and what he might do terrified her.

Then, there was Polly. Polly, who was already suffering and afraid of what the future held. How in God's name could she subject Polly, or the other children, to such a future that frightened even her? Dear God! It seemed every way she turned, there was no help—no easy way. Yet, as God was her judge, Marcia was sorely tempted to throw all caution to the winds and to take what Curt offered with open arms. At once, Curt perceived the great love she held for him. It was all he needed! Catching her to him with the fierce hunger on which he had survived these past years, he found her mouth eager and fulfilling. The desperate love between them flowed and bound them together, and a great happiness filled their souls, as they each surrendered to the all-consuming emotions which would not be denied.

The tears, hitherto borne alone, flowed down Marcia's face as she told Curt everything, how

Barty Bendall had grown insanely suspicious, how she was afraid he would do something terrible, and how he hated their daughter Polly with a black consuming passion. Yet even then she could not bring herself to tell him of Polly's imminent admission to the Infirmary. All the while Curt listened, he tenderly wiped away the tears from her sad, lovely face. 'I daren't leave him, Curt. I am afraid. Oh, I know in his own way he loves me, or he wouldn't have taken me on with two children when he knew all about you. I've never lied to him about my love for you.'

Her voice was low and broken as she told Curt decisively, 'I am indebted to him!'

'No! You owe him nothing, Marcia! He's used you all these years. Do you think I haven't made it my business to find out?' His voice softened as he reached down to smother her upturned face in tender reassuring kisses. 'You don't owe him anything, my love. You've worked hard, long hours to feed and clothe the family, while he's boozed or gambled his wages away. Don't feel obliged to him.'

Now Marcia sensed that her future, and that of her children, lay with Curt. But she couldn't shake off that deep-rooted anxiety, for he did not know Barty Bendall as she did.

'Curt, will you promise me something?' she asked. The look on his face prompted her to repeat her plea. 'Please!'

'What am I to promise?'

'Don't come after me again. Leave me to sort things out. To decide what I must do.'

'I can't promise *that*,' Curt said incredulously. 'I could *never* promise that.'

316

'You have to, Curt! It's the only way.'

'No!' He got to his feet, drawing Marcia up into his arms with fierce possessiveness. 'I won't promise anything but this.' His eyes shone defiantly. 'I'm coming to claim you Marcia, for you belong to no one but me. You and I, we belong together and there can be no compromise. I want you, I want our children, it's all that's kept me going these long dark years. Will you take the children, darling, and stay with your mother or Nantie Bett—until I secure us a home?' His passion thickened his voice. 'Marcia, I mean to fmd us a new life, away from memories of the past. I'm going this very day to secure a house and a job. When I have them safe, I'm coming straight back for you and the children.'

Marcia wanted so many things. She wanted to tell him how impossible it all was, how she feared for him and how Barty Bendall would hold her fiercely to the vows which bound them. But more than anything else, she wanted to believe that all would come right in the end. Yet, in the darkest depths of her heart, she believed it to be a lost cause. Seeing him now, tortured by the circumstances which held them apart, and yet so determined to bring about their reunion, the past seemed to roll away, and all that remained, all that mattered, was their undying love and those three precious children. 'If only there was a way,' she murmured against his mouth.

'There *is*, my love—there is *always* a way.' Curt kissed her once more, a tender kiss, a kiss filled with promise, then, turning to watch the children who played unaware of anything but their own enjoyment, a smile of pleasure lit his face. 'How is

Polly?' he asked. Then, when she assured him that the girl was well, he went on, 'Our daughters have grown lovely in your care, and you have a son.' He kissed her dark, tearful eyes. 'Your son, my son, it's all the same, my darling. How could I not love a part of you as though it were my own?' As he moved away, he reminded her, 'You *will* take the children to your mother's or to Nantie Bett's?'

She shook her head and replied firmly, 'No, Curt! I won't do that.'

He knew from old that there was no changing her mind, so, after a moment's hesitation, he told her, 'Very well, sweetheart, have it your way—but as soon as I have it all arranged, I'll be back for you. Remember that!' Then he was gone.

Marcia wondered afterwards whether it hadn't all been a dream, brought on by her own desperation. Yet she knew it was no dream. It was reality and, up to now, reality had been a cruel nightmare.

Now Marcia quickly composed herself at the sound of Polly's voice, and her spirits lightened at the sight of her daughter's glowing face. Obviously the fresh clean air up here was doing her some good. 'Polly, enjoying yourself, are you, lass?' She returned to the bench to examine the contents of the picnic-bag, thinking it odd that she could do something so mundane, when every part of her was still trembling with excitement.

When an hour later they started to make their way home, Marcia felt happier than she had done for a long, long time. She would count the days until Curt came back.

'Come on Florence,' Polly called, grabbing her loitering sister by the arm, and compelling her to

318

join in a race down the steep walkway. 'Last one to the bottom's a real stinker!'

As Marcia followed, urging young Barty to be careful in his hair-raising pursuit of the two girls, she pondered on other families they had encountered in the park, families complete, where the father sat his children on his lap, or played silly games with them, just to amuse, and her thoughts kept coming back to Curt, dwelling on the heaven of being in his arms. She remembered every word he'd said and she lived and re-lived every stirring emotion until her head spun and her joyous heart turned somersaults. There was a deep lurking fear too, which tempered the ecstasy within her. But for now the fears and doubts could wait, for there was room only for tenderness, for the delicious feelings which put the flush of youth upon her lovely face, and the gaiety of spring in her step.

All the same, the nearer she got to home and Barty Bendall, the deeper her heart dragged, and the more she realised how dreadfully complicated her life had become. She hurried after the others, her senses still reeling from the memory of Curt's touch.

CHAPTER EIGHTEEN

'Come on lass, get your coat done up. Polly and young Barty are waiting to go!' Marcia was in a hurry.

'Oh Mam!' Florence stood sullen while her Mam buttoned her coat right up to the neck. 'I 'in't even finished me soldiers!' she moaned. But

Marcia would not be moved, as now she hurried the protesting child along the passage towards the front door, where Polly stood, holding young Barty with one hand, and with the other holding open the door. 'You had time enough, lass! If you'd been hungry enough, you'd have finished!' she told her.

'Come on you!' Polly ushered Florence through the door, before turning to give her Mam a quick cuddle. 'She'll 'ave us miss the tram!' she complained, pulling a wry face. Bending to kiss them all one after the other, Marcia watched as Polly grabbed Barty's hand on one side, then Florence's in the other, after which she marched them down the street, tutting and moaning all the way.

After waving them out of sight, Marcia headed for Ada Humble's door. Blackie answered her light firm tap.

'Hello Blackie, lad,' Marcia said. She thought he looked unnaturally troubled for a lad of his age. 'Cheer up young 'un,' she told him, 'it'll not be so bad, you'll see.' Yet she herself was troubled, for today was the day Ada and her son were summoned to appear in court.

'I'm not bothered for mesel' Mrs Bendall,' Blackie replied, opening the door wider and stepping back to let her through, 'it's me Mam. She's not been the same since we lost me Dad.' The tears were not very far from filling his eyes. 'What can I do about me Mam, eh?' he asked. 'What's a body supposed to do?'

'I'll not come in, Blackie,' Marcia told him, 'I've to tidy up yet. But, tell thi' Mam I'll be ready for off in about an hour.' Now, she lowered her voice and smiled gently into his troubled face. 'Hey!

Think on what I said—it'll *not* be so bad. An' your Mam'll feel a lot better when it's all over. Losing your Dad was a shock to all of you, I know, but your Mam needs a bit o' time to get used to it, that's all—a bit o' time, eh?' Turning to leave, she remembered how much responsibility Blackie had taken on since Toby's death, and her heart went out to him. 'The young 'uns all gone off to school, have they, lad?' she asked, trying to take his mind off the ordeal yet to come.

'Aye! I 'ad 'em away bright an' early this morning.'

'You're a right good lad, Blackie. A blessing to your Mam, that you are. I'll be waiting ready for you then, in an hour,' she added, as she turned away.

Quickly returning to her own house, Marcia left the front door slightly ajar and made her way back to the parlour, feeling far from being as confident as she might appear to Blackie. His school attendance had gone from bad to worse since Toby Humble's death, and even though he'd been badly needed by a grief-stricken Ada, Marcia knew that the school authorities wouldn't allow that fact to soften their hardened hearts. She felt sure that at the very least they would impose a crippling fine on poor Ada. Well, she herself didn't have much, but whatever she could spare, it was Ada's! Now, as she set about clearing the breakfast things away, she assured herself, 'Before this day's through, we shall know the way of things.' Yet, somehow she was not comforted by the thought.

It didn't take long to wash the few cups and plates, and set the parlour and scullery at least *looking* tidy, Marcia being of a mind that a quick 'lick-over' wouldn't harm anything once in a while. She didn't have the time this morning to scour and scrub. Gathering the remnants of her dressmaking paraphernalia together, she shoved it out of sight behind the armchair. 'I shall need to work that bit harder tomorrow,' she muttered, as she hurried into the scullery.

The splash of the cold tap water on her bare skin sent a shiver from the nape of her neck right down to her toes. 'Lord love us!' she exclaimed, 'that's enough to give a body an 'eart attack.' Quickly now, she dried herself and put on her best blue blouse and skirt. Catching the long black hair in to the back of her neck, she twisted its thickness into a single rope, twining it round and round, before draping it upwards to the top of her head, where she secured it with a considerable number of long hairpins. A glance at the mantel-clock told her that Ada and Blackie should be along any minute, so she lost no time in bolting the back door, and fetching her best cloche hat and brown coat from upstairs.

No matter how many times Marcia walked over the oilcloth where Curt's note still remained hidden, the thought of it always wrenched at her, yet not once had she taken it out to refresh her memory of its contents, for she knew them so well.

Regarding Curt's plans, Marcia had little hope. But deep down inside, she harboured just a faint suggestion of that forbidden emotion, which although she consciously rejected it, coloured her every dream.

Now Marcia put just enough water in the pan to make a small brew of tea. 'There's time enough for a warming drink afore we need to face them hard-headed officials,' she consoled herself, still not admitting that the nervous flutterings in her stomach had anything at all to do with the prospect before them. She knew just how heavy it had sat on Ada Humble's mind, and she pondered on the cruel twist of fate which had removed not only her need to tell Toby—but also poor Toby himself.

By the time Ada arrived, all done up in her black grieving coat and the sash of black ribbon still tied smartly round the red trilby, Marcia had just tipped the boiling water on to the tea-leaves. Spilling in a tip of condensed milk and the merest sprinkle of precious sugar, she handed Ada a mug, and gestured for her to sit down.

'We're all right for five minutes,' she told the grim-faced Ada, at the same time looking about for Blackie. 'Where's the lad?' But Ada appeared not to have heard her, and Marcia didn't bother to repeat the question. She just surmised that Blackie would be along shortly. All the while she sipped her tea, Marcia was acutely aware of Ada's preoccupation with her own thoughts, and she felt indescribably sad at the plight of her friend. Ada Humble had changed so dramatically that Marcia was forced to wonder if she hadn't in effect died along with her beloved Toby.

'Ada.' Marcia leaned forward, moving her eyes over the weariness of Ada's quiet face. 'Ada lass,' she repeated, touching the official-looking letter in the little woman's hand, 'is this for the court? I'll tek care on it, shall I, eh?' She waited for Ada's response, which, when it came, was a hesitant half-hearted smile.

Lifting her unhappy eyes to look at Marcia's face, she shook her head, and seeming suddenly to

323

be aware of what was going on, she exclaimed, 'God love us, Marcia lass, I be forever dreaming lately! Forever wandering off on me own, wi' no thought for 'owt nor nobody!' She held out the letter. 'Just shows 'ow bloody daft I'm getting, lass—'cause this 'ere letter's not for the court! Blackie 'as *that*! This 'ere letter was lying on your mat as I come in.' She thrust the letter into Marcia's hand.

It was from the specialist at the Infirmary, and as Marcia read it, her mouth went dry and a great lump straddled her throat. Polly was to attend two weeks tomorrow, and must expect to be there for at least a week. There was a list of things to take, night-clothes, toiletries and so on, together with the letter itself. At the bottom of the letter was the name of the Honourary Consultant who would be attending Polly.

'All right are you, lass?' Ada Humble enquired as she noticed how Marcia's face had grown still and drained of colour. 'Nowt wrong, is there?' she asked anxiously.

'It's from the Infirmary, Ada. Our Polly's to go in two weeks tomorrow.' Marcia didn't wish to go into details, for it would serve no purpose. She had been expecting the letter, and yet in a foolish way, hoping it would never come. 'She's to have closer examinations and tests.' Then something prompted her to ask of Ada, 'Ada, I'd be right grateful if you'd not let on about this to anybody, especially not our Polly, eh? I'd like to give her a few more days afore she needs to start bothering about it.' God! she thought. It seemed she was allus borrowing time, one way and another.

'O' course, Marcia lass, o' course,' Ada was

324

quick to assure her, 'I'll say nary a word! Nary a single word, bless your 'eart.'

As the two anxious women exchanged glances of a kind only created by mutual suffering, the sound of Blackie making his way down the passage brought the exchanges to an end. Ada got to her feet, straightened her trilby and told the approaching Blackie, 'Right then lad! Let's go an' see what's the worst these 'ere 'fficials can do to us, eh?'

As Marcia pinned the cloche hat on tightly and eased herself into the warm brown coat, she felt pleased that at least Ada appeared to have rediscovered some of her fighting fettle. But then, if it involved the punishment of one of her precious boys, Ada's protective instincts could be frightening.

By the time they had threaded their way across town to the magistrate's court, Marcia could see that Ada Humble's show of bravado back at the house had lapsed into a nervousness which made the little woman's voice stutter, and caused her to fidget frantically with her fingers. 'Oh Marcia lass,' she said as she tugged at Marcia's coat sleeve, an imploring expression in her small round eyes and a fearful tear in the voice, 'I can't see as 'ow an ignorant body like me can tek 'erself in there! I'm not crafty enough to face yon 'fficial folk. Why, they'll swallow me whole. Nay lass,' she pulled away, the trilby shaking like a jelly from the trembling of her head. 'I can't do it, lass—I'm afeared! Shameful coward that I am, I'm too afeared.' Her voice broke into a pitiful plea, as she went on, 'God love and save us, me two feet are set 'ard to these 'ere flagstones, an' I can't shift 'em neither back'ards nor for'ards.'

'Would you send me in there on me *own*, Ada Humble?' Marcia demanded, threading her arm through the crook of Ada's elbow, and with a determined tug propelling them both forward. 'If you don't go in to face 'em now, Ada lass,' she told her in a stout voice, 'they'll never leave you be. Let's have it done an' over with.' She gave the little woman an encouraging squeeze. 'Aw, it'll be all right, lass. You've faced a good telling-off before, haven't you? Come on, where's your fettle?' she teased.

Marcia didn't care for the tomb-like atmosphere of the magistrate's court. She liked it even less when Ada and Blackie were taken to sit before the bench, and she was directed to a pew some distance away, but she took refuge in the fact that she had both them and the proceedings clearly in earshot and view, so the occasional expression of encouragement was still possible.

The courtroom was a cold echoing place, with high-reaching walls and a deep domed ceiling decorated with thin stroking patterns which seemed to point downwards like the accusing finger of God, although Marcia was of the opinion that the guilty folk were not poor frightened creatures like Ada Humble, but the stern-faced men who sat in judgement on those lesser mortals than themselves.

'Everyone stand.' The ringing tones of the court usher disturbed Marcia's ponderings and now she rose to her feet in response—a quick glance at Ada Humble telling Marcia that she was still in a state of acute nervousness.

Marcia took stock of the situation. There were

326

half-a-dozen spectators in the pews behind her and she felt nothing but disgust for these low creatures. Ahead of her, there were long benches to the right and left, and set high upon the far rostrum which ran right along the back wall was the magistrate's bench, overlooking the entire proceedings. Above the magistrate's bench hung a magnificent crest, depicting all manner of savage beasts, whose glittering eyes by some strange trick of light seemed to devour the insignificant figures of Ada Humble and her lad, Blackie.

The man who had been appointed to defend the offenders waited, his sheaf of papers resting before him. On the opposite bench were two serious-faced officials, who occasionally shifted their beady eyes in superior assessment of all before them. One of these gentlemen held a sheaf of papers in the grip of his long sinewy fingers.

When the time came for this particular fellow to speak, he launched into the details of Blackie's continuous and downright rebellious attitude to school. He described in the grandest terms how Mrs Humble had been constantly warned that her son's persistent truanting would result in serious repercussions, and he told how she had deliberately ignored such warnings. He concluded by reminding the magistrate's bench of the very strictly-upheld law which required all children to attend school as long as they fell within a particular age range, and how for the last four months right up to the very day, Mrs Humble had completely ignored all requests to send her son to school! Therefore, it was only left to surmise that the rebellious attitude of the son had been learned by example, from the mother.

327

Marcia's heart sank at the ferocity of his onslaught. He was obviously intending a punishment more severe than a reprimand, and seeing the stiff serious expressions from behind the magistrate's bench, Marcia was already calculating how Ada's fine might be paid. Now she cast an anxious look at tired Ada Humble and her strapping son Blackie. Ada had fixed her gaze on the floor, her short chubby hands moving one over the other in an absent-minded attitude, and at once Marcia realised with horror that her obvious inattentiveness might be construed as reflecting that 'rebelliousness' claimed by the prosecution! In truth, Marcia knew that Ada had merely lapsed into the dream world to which she often retreated since Toby's death, but these hard-hearted folk here weren't to know that.

Blackie was not near enough to his mother to console her. He stood some four feet away, tall and upright, with straight broad shoulders. Marcia felt proud of him. As she lifted her gaze to his face, she was astonished to see that Blackie was crying. The tears tumbled down his face, yet he stirred not a muscle as he continued to gaze adoringly at his distraught mother.

With the defence solicitor's explanation of 'young Humble's' deep sense of family commitment, and his desire to leave school early in order to help support the considerable Humble brood, Marcia found herself relaxing. She listened compassionately as he went on to describe how since his father's fatal accident, and the consequent mental and emotional stress of his widowed mother, Blackie had taken it upon himself to adopt the role of father to his five younger brothers. There was every justification, he argued, to allow Blackie Humble to leave school officially, in order for him to take up his position as the main breadwinner. In his passionate conclusion, he summed up Mrs Humble's hitherto unfailing execution of her wifely and motherly duties, being a well-known and respected member of the community.

An uncomfortable silence settled over the courtroom as the magistrate's thin bony face twisted itself into an expression of painful thought. Then calling the same man to attention, he asked in a sharp voice, 'May we ask the reason for the non-removal of Mrs Humble's head-piece?'

Marcia hadn't thought of that! She'd been so used to seeing that bright red trilby atop Ada Humble's head that it had become part of the little woman herself, yet by the tone of the magistrate's voice, he was pompous enough to consider its presence as a deliberate mark of disrespect.

'We would beg the court's pardon,' the young man returned, extending his apology to include a reminder of the recent death of Mr Humble, and of the accused's condition of mourning. 'It is meant in no way as an affront to the court or its proceedings.' But the magistrate was obviously not placated. In fact, judging by the sour expression on his face, and the sharp way he turned to consult his colleagues, Marcia felt almost as though Ada's red trilby had suddenly become the issue, and not Blackie's truancy.

After a flurry of murmured discussion, and a short withdrawal to the chambers, the three elderly benchers returned. The central magistrate addressed himself to Blackie.

'Have you anything to tell the court?' Marcia silently willed him to give a good account of himself, as Blackie straightened his shoulders and cleared his throat.

'Please sir, I was the one who kept running away fro' school! Me Mam 'ad nowt to do with it. She celled me time an' time again, *threatened me! Telled me* to get to school!' He cast a sideways glance at Ada. 'It's *not* 'er fault, sir, not at all!'

The magistrate sighed, a heavy noise which reverberated round the room. 'I'm afraid it is to do with your mother, young man. The law makes your school attendance the sole responsibility of your parents—in *this* case, the sole responsibility of your *mother!*' He dismissed Blackie with a curt nod, before turning to the impassive Ada Humble. 'Is there anything *you* would like the court to take into consideration?' he asked in a stiff upright voice, his small eyes boring into her face, and his head leaning forward the better to hear her answer.

Marcia thought her heart would stop as Ada kept her gaze fixed to the floor, and the magistrate's words fell on deaf ears. There was a damning awkward silence, as the magistrate impatiently tapped his pencil against the bench.

Moving quickly to touch Ada Humble on the arm in order to gain her undivided attention, the one who had spoken on her behalf whispered an urgent repeat of the magistrate's question. Marcia breathed a sigh of relief as the little woman looked up to meet the impatient stare of the magistrate's beady eyes. 'Please Ada,' she whispered below her breath, 'say the right things, lass.'

'I do beg your pardon, your Honour.' Ada

shifted uncomfortably, and it seemed as though all present in the courtroom relaxed. 'My Blackie's been a right godsend since—since.' It was obvious to Marcia that Ada couldn't bring herself to say it, but she continued in a steady voice, 'I needs the lad at 'ome, I *really* do, sir.'

'Are you saying then, Mrs Humble,' the magistrate's voice cut in short and impatient, 'that you will make no effort to see that he attends school?'

'Oh no sir! I'm *not* saying such a thing. If you says 'e still 'as to go to school, then I'll tell 'im so! But 'e sees it as a downright waste o' time sir, an' I do need the lad at 'ome!'

'Thank you Mrs Humble.' As the magistrate turned to his colleagues for further consultation, Marcia caught Ada's eye with her persistent gaze, and the little woman's face creased into an acknowledging smile. Marcia began to relax. Surely, she thought—after the solicitor's plea that 'the boy should be allowed to leave school early, because of the extenuating circumstances', and the polite request by Ada that she badly needed Blackie's help—the magistrate would comply with such a reasonable request.

But the magistrate's response was such that Marcia was riveted to the spot. As he delivered the court's judgement, the gasp of horror which escaped her lips was easily heard by all, and she found herself gripping the bench so fiercely that her knuckles shone white through the skin, and her fingers grew numb.

'It is the law, Mrs Humble. The law of the land, which states quite categorically that your son *must* attend school. By your own words, you stress your

331

preference for him to stay at home from school, and from the evidence before us, it is clear that you made no real effort to secure his school attendance in the past, therefore it is our confirmed belief that you intend to make no real effort in the *future*! It is our avowed duty to uphold the law, and it is our responsibility therefore, to deliver the only decision possible. Your son *will* attend school. We are also extremely concerned that he has been expected to take on the considerable duties of a father to his five younger brothers. I am afraid that there is much here to disturb us. As a result, we are imposing an order that Blackie and the younger children be taken into immediate care, and you Mrs Humble, for breaking the law in persistently depriving your son of his rightful education, shall be sent to His Majesty's prison for six months.'

'No! No! You can't!' Blackie ran from his place, first briefly to gather the stricken figure of his mother into his arms, then to rush at the magistrate's bench with the seeming intention of vaulting it to catch the thin bony neck in the crush of his hands.

As for Marcia, she felt paralysed with shock. She wasn't even aware of the tears which ran down her face and trickled into her open mouth. Then, as the numbness wore off, to be replaced by an uncontrollable bout of trembling, she got to her feet, keeping her eyes fixed on Ada. By the time she had negotiated the steps leading into the square open area at the front, the benchers had vacated their high vantage points, Blackie was held in the grip of the appointed welfare officer, and Ada—flanked on either side by official figures— was being gently led towards a flight of stairs which took her out of Marcia's sight.

'Sorry.' The constable set himself across Marcia's path. 'You can't go any further.' He gestured to the nearest bench. 'If you'd like to wait here, I'll enquire as to whether you can see her later.' He was not unsympathetic as Marcia collapsed onto the bench, still knocked sideways from the totally unexpected development.

It was two hours later, at ten minutes to one, when Marcia was shown down into a long narrow room at the foot of the stairs, where the kindly constable ushered her into a large wooden chair. 'She'll not be a minute,' he informed her, stepping back to take up his dutiful place by the wall. Sitting there in that cold impersonal room, Marcia still couldn't fully comprehend what was actually happening, so steeped in shock was she, and all the while, the magistrate's voice echoing in her mind: 'Six months in His Majesty's prison.' Dear God, how could it be true?

The slow distant footsteps drew nearer up the passage and into the long narrow room, and now there was a low murmuring of voices—after which a female official appeared at the door to address Marcia. 'No more than a couple of minutes please.' She stepped aside to allow Ada Humble's entry, then, after seeing the little woman to her chair at the opposite end of the table to Marcia, she backed away to stand by the door, her eyes watchful.

As Ada Humble raised her head, Marcia reeled under the impact of that desolate look as she implored, 'I 'ope the Lord can see 'is way to forgive me, Marcia.' Then, her voice breaking under the dreadful sobs which shook her cruelly, she cried over and over again, 'My Toby! Oh, my babies! I've let 'em all down, an' I'm a bad worthless woman! A bad worthless woman!' The tears ran fast and furious down her face and her sorry eyes never left Marcia's compassionate gaze.

'No Ada, lass!' Marcia's frantic efforts to comfort the little woman seemed hopelessly inadequate. She knew instinctively that Ada Humble would go on punishing herself. She looked at that poor creature, and she thought she would never again see such suffering.

When, later, Marcia turned to thank the constable who saw her out, she was not surprised to see the glint of tears in his eyes also.

Marcia could never remember that journey back to Regent Street. It was only the bright chatter of the homecoming children that pierced the anguish within her. Yet at the same time, the conspicuous absence of the noise which usually heralded the return of the Humble brood only served to deepen Marcia's realisation of the full horror of this day. She told herself that, however desperate were her own troubles, they paled beside those of little Ada Humble, who had lost her husband, her children, and was cruelly locked away.

CHAPTER NINETEEN

'You'd best swallow one o' your tablets afore going out.' Marcia was pleased to see Polly looking a good deal brighter than she had been on first waking. 'No sense leaving 'em to lie there, when they can be doing you some good, lass,' she said cheerfully—laughing out loud when Polly took the tablets and gingerly swallowed them, complaining that they 'tasted like poison'.

'Never you mind that, Polly lass!' came her Mam's retort, 'It's better than putting up with a miserable head!' She rose from her place at the table, a look of concern on her face. 'Have you any pain now, lass?' she asked softly, stroking Polly's hair.

'No, Mam, none at all,' came the answer.

'Aw, that's good.' Marcia quietly collected the breakfast things together, casting a keen eye over young Barty as he dipped a toasted soldier into the mug of cold tea, and telling him in no uncertain terms, 'Stop that at once, fella-me-lad!' She took the mug from him as the bread slithered out of sight, only to pop up again as floating debris. 'Barty, I've asked you afore *not* to do that. It's disgusting!'

'Well.' Florence pushed him in a playful manner that wasn't fully appreciated by young Barty. 'That's 'cos *he's* disgusting!'

At this Marcia gave a long sigh. Carrying the plates out to the scullery, she told her noisy brood, 'If you lot are wanting to catch the early show, you'd best be making a move.' When there came an offer from Polly to help with the washing-up, Marcia replied warmly, 'No, that's all right lass. Get yourselves off. The coppers are on the sideboard.'

Later, with the work done, and Barty's breakfast ready, Marcia topped up the fire with the few splinters in the grate: stopping for a while to relax before the cheery glow. She still couldn't accustom herself to the silence which had settled over the Humble house, because normally on a Saturday morning, the dividing wall between the two houses would tremble from the barrage of noise which filled the air and echoed down the street. 'Strange,' she said softly, 'it's the awful stillness that's so deafening now.' She sat for a long quiet moment, scanning the flickering flames which licked the chimney back.

During the week, since Ada Humble's imprisonment, there had been various comings and goings to and from the Humble house, mostly health and welfare people, collecting items belonging to the children, or just busybodies appointed to keep an eye on the place. Marcia had gone out of her way to avoid them, for the grudge in her heart was still too raw, too painful. She feared the urge to say what was on her mind. Her only concern was for poor Ada, and the six lads who had been removed to a children's home 'for their own good'. She had made several attempts to see Ada Humble, but there were rules and regulations which had to be observed. No visitors for a fortnight, and no letters out until the business of paper and stamps had been 'satisfactorily arranged'. Marcia had listened patiently to these explanations, eventually coming away with the conviction that the world was full of fools.

Marcia had written to the Governor's office, only to receive a curt reply that, no, she could *not* send stamps, writing paper, or anything else that might represent collateral. Now all Marcia could do was to wait until Ada sent her what was called a 'visitor's pass' on receipt of which she would be allowed the privilege of a visit. Thereafter the visits would take place just once in every fortnight. And still no pass had arrived! Dark anger and frustration at such rigid application of what Marcia considered to be an inhuman system shone from her brooding eyes. 'Poor Ada,' she murmured into the fireplace. Never a night went by that she didn't remember the little woman in her prayers. The sound of Barty Bendall thumping down the stairs got Marcia quickly to her feet.

'Is me breakfast ready, woman?' He seated himself in his place at the table from where, with his braces dangling and the collarless neck of his brown shirt flung open, he glared at Marcia. 'I said *breakfast* woman! Where's me bloody breakfast?' His top lip drew back over his small even teeth, putting Marcia in mind of her Dad's terrier. She hoped his temper might be markedly improved once he'd eaten his breakfast, so with a little smile she bustled into the scullery calling over her shoulder, 'It's ready.'

Unfortunately, his temper was not improved upon having wolfed down his breakfast. Marcia had a mind to start up a conversation—*anything* to ease the tension between them. But she was put off by the way he kept looking at her, in that same staring quizzical fashion with which he'd been regarding her these past weeks. It was most unnerving.

Conversely though, the house had grown more peaceful.

If Marcia craved anything besides the passionate love and tender companionship which had been hers and Curt's, it was the need to talk to someone, to really *talk*, about her concern for Polly, about poor Ada Humble, about the future, if there was any! And about all those little mundane things that make up a day.

'Barty,' Marcia said as she eased herself into the stand-chair where she could look at him. She felt tired, tired in her mind and tired in her heart. She knew, as Barty Bendall must know, that there had to be some effort made, by one or both of them, to break down the barriers which drove them further and further apart. 'Barty, have you got a few minutes? There's something I . . .' She stopped, as he looked up to stare into her face, his eyes alive with animosity. Just a mere second of looking back into those terrible eyes was enough to convince Marcia once and for all that whatever she did and however hard she tried to see any goodness in him, there wasn't a single thing she could do to change him. Barty Bendall was a tyrant and somehow every effort made only seemed to antagonise him.

She remained seated a moment longer, her eyes torn away from that piercing glower which she knew still held her in its grip. Now, with her head bowed, she told him gently, 'Barty—I can't live this way.' She felt desperate! All of her lonely life stretched before her—all the dreams, the regrets, the heartache. 'Please, Barty,' she said forcing herself to look at him, 'won't you even try?'

The look which bored into her was strange to Marcia—a cunning, secret look which disturbed her. Then, without saying a word, he turned and headed back upstairs.

When he had gone Marcia stood, her hands on the table, head bowed. She knew the futility of it all, and she had never been more convinced than she was now that Barty Bendall must be suffering from a kind of madness; yet in some inexplicable way, he always managed to make *her* feel like the guilty one. His bawling and shouting was less frequent these days, though, and Marcia was grateful for that, but these morose and silent moods of his were far more frightening. She recalled his look just now, and she shivered deep within herself. 'Oh Curt!' she sighed, 'what's to be done?'

Immersing herself into the business of tidying away Barty Bendall's breakfast things, she allowed herself to think longer on Curt. She wanted him, here and now! In the darkness of her wretched heart, she cried out for his strength and the fullness of his love, but she knew she was only fooling herself. *She* was committed to another. There were children involved, loyalties and moral observances. And there was Barty Bendall. She dared not contemplate what he would do were he to discover that she and Curt had seen each other, had embraced and even dared to make plans for a life together.

The obstacles were insurmountable, and she knew she would have no peace until she accepted that fact

The parlour door swung open as Barty Bendall returned to collect his cap and overcoat, which he donned in a great hurry, before striding away towards the front door. He'd talk this bloody business over wi' Jim Rawlinson down at the Lord Nelson! At least he'd got a friend in that one!

From inside the parlour, Marcia became curious as she heard the door open and his gruff voice telling someone, 'I suppose you'd best go through!' Who her visitor might be, Marcia couldn't begin to guess. She had the notion that it was possibly those busybodies from the council, so when Big Bertha and young Daisy appeared at the parlour door, she rushed forward excitedly, the unexpected arrival of the two mill women giving her a flurry of pleasure.

'Well! You're a sight for sore eyes, that you are!' she declared happily. 'Come in, do.' She quickly drew them to sit by the fire. 'Sit yourselves down there. I'll brew a pot o' tea an' you can tell me all about the old faces, eh!' While she bustled about the scullery, the lively conversation ran on in the usual flippant manner that characterised the down-to-earth easy attitude of the mill-hands.

Handing them each a mug of tea, Marcia inquired of young Daisy, 'Things working out all right, are they, lass?' She thought the young girl fair glowed with health and happiness.

Big Bertha roared her familiar laugh, leaning over to pat the conspicuous bulge jutting from beneath young Daisy's tightly-fitting coat. 'Look 'ere Marcia lass!' she cried gleefully, 'be popping out like a pea fro' a pod any day now, eh?'

'Give over embarrassing the poor little thing!' Marcia chastised, aware of young Daisy's acute self-consciousness. Turning to Daisy, she asked, 'How's thi' Mam? And that young fella o' yourn?'

'They're grand, Marcia,' Daisy quickly forgot her embarrassment as she went on to tell Marcia of her Mam's new fella. Afterwards she reached out to squeeze Marcia's hand. 'We've a lot to thank you for, Marcia Bendall!'

'Marcia!' Big Bertha said as she leaned forward. 'Is it right what they're saying about Ada Humble, lass—they've tekken 'er boys away, an' put 'er in prison?'

Marcia nodded, seeing in her mind's eye that little woman with those small round eyes mirroring her unbearable sorrow.

'Lord love us!' exclaimed Big Bertha and the look on Daisy's face was one of astonishment

'That's terrible!' she rejoined, in a shocked whisper.

To this Big Bertha added the further opinion that, 'There ain't no bloody justice in this world!'

An uneasy hush fell, when every thought was for Ada in her predicament. Now, Big Bertha asked in a quiet voice, 'If thi' gets a chance, Marcia, lass—pass on our regards.'

To this Marcia readily agreed, anxious now to change the subject. When, with a knowing laugh, she enquired after 'Hot Harry'—curious to know how he might be faring since his wife started work at the cotton mill—Daisy began sniggering, and Big Bertha's answer was to roll about laughing and slapping a hefty fist against her leg. After making several attempts to catch her breath she suddenly blurted out, still roaring with laughter in between. 'Follows the poor sod everywhere, she does! Can't even go for a quiet piss wi'out she's waiting on 'im as 'e comes out!'

'Poor old Harry,' Marcia commented, unable to stem a little giggle. All the same, though, she did feel just a bit sorry for him.

'Getting on all right wi' that dressmaking lark, are you?' Young Daisy looked around the room for signs of Marcia's new occupation. 'Amazing i'n't it, eh . . . how soon word gets about?'

'Not so bad,' replied Marcia, fetching a roll of half-finished skirts from behind the armchair, 'can't say as I've owt left over after feeding us and paying the rent, but we get by. I go out one morning a week and collect the work, then deliver it the same morning the following week.' Having shown the women the kind of work she was doing, she then rolled the heavy serviceable skirts back up and replaced them behind the chair.

'Look, lass!' Big Bertha stood up and lifted her coat to reveal her ample girth. 'If you 'as a tape big enough, get that measured, an' do us one o' them panelled skirts, like what you just showed us.' She hopped about impatiently. 'Come on then! Treat me like a proper customer if thi' doesn't mind!' She looked a real study as she stood there, with her coat hitched up and her face going a bright shade of purple where she was holding in her breath in order to reduce the size of her stomach. Unfortunately, all that happened was that her chest was pushed out to enormous proportions and, all in all, she looked exceedingly uncomfortable.

Young Daisy giggled helplessly as Marcia ordered Big Bertha to breathe properly. When Bertha did, her stomach straightaway popped out like a great balloon.

'Don't know what *you're* sniggering at, young Daisy!' Big Bertha snorted good-humouredly, 'if we set about measuring you we'd need a barger's rope!'

Sitting by the fireside, supping tea and exchanging lighthearted chatter with two pals, proved to be just what Marcia needed. By the time she rose to accompany them to the door, her face positively glowed with pleasure, and she felt a degree of peace and contentment which had so long been absent. 'Bless you both for coming to see me,' she said as she embraced each of them in turn, 'I do miss you. But I don't regret leaving the mill.' Even then, she couldn't bring herself to tell them about Polly, for talking about it seemed to make it too real.

'You tek care o' yersel', Marcia lass,' Big Bertha said, squashing her against her bosom, 'an' we'll come an' see you again.'

' 'Course we will,' young Daisy added, 'but we might bring a little 'un with us next time.' She patted her swollen tummy.

Marcia waved until they disappeared round the corner towards Brown Street. It was then when she turned to go back inside that she caught a movement out of the corner of her eye. Approaching rather hurriedly from the far direction of Regent Street was a short sturdy woman, and judging by the confident style of her step, together with the expensive cut of her tweedy clothes, Marcia believed her to be one of the welfare bodies who had been keeping an eye on the Humble abode. She somehow thought she'd seen her once before, going *away* from Ada's house. Now, anger rose in her throat as she deliberately turned away from the woman and stepped back into the passageway. 'I want no truck wi' *you* lot!' she muttered under her breath, preparing to close the door behind her.

'Mrs Bendall! Wait a minute, please,' the stranger called.

When Marcia swung round at the sound of her name, it was to find the woman already on her doorstep. 'Mrs Bendall, I must talk with you!' Of a sudden, her voice had dropped. Also she was eyeing Marcia in the strangest way. Beneath that quiet pained look, Marcia felt uncomfortable—apprehensive.

'Can we go inside, please?' the woman asked

softly.

Somewhere deep in the pit of her stomach, Marcia sensed this woman to be the bearer of bad news. A curt nod of the head indicated that the woman should follow.

Once inside the parlour, Marcia declined the suggestion that she should sit down and, even before the words had been uttered Marcia knew, as though deep down inside her she had already been preparing herself for something of this very nature.

'I'm sorry, Mrs Bendall. Yours was the only name we had—the only visitor Mrs Humble had requested.' The words were clear enough, and each one registered on Marcia's shocked mind with startling clarity. 'It was peaceful enough at least,' the woman continued, 'she just seemed to give up—wouldn't talk. She just went away peacefully.'

The cloud of sorrow which gathered to blind Marcia gradually hardened into seething anger. *Ada was dead!* They had *killed* Ada Humble! These bungling, hard-hearted officials! 'Get out,' she told the woman in a fearfully low and trembling voice. Then, when the woman made no move, only to widen her eyes in disbelief, Marcia repeated her instruction—this time in a wild scream as she lunged at the creature. *'Get out of my house!'* If the woman had not then scrambled to her feet and hurried away up the passage with as much dignity as she dare, Marcia would have forcibly ejected her onto the flagstones.

Long after the woman had wisely retreated, the little house echoed from the deep sobs of anguish which rent the air.

Marcia was past sleep. The night spent in Ada Humble's parlour had been a long lonely one, and even during the four hours she'd been relieved by Mrs Atkinson, she hadn't been able to close her eyes in comfort, just returning to her own parlour, where she'd sat still and quiet, her unseeing eyes staring into the cold emptiness of the fire-grate. Every now and then, a shuddering snore from Barty Bendall upstairs had startled her from the depths of gnawing memories, the discomfort of which had urged her back to the vigil by Ada's side.

The last neighbour to pay respects to poor Ada Humble had gone over half an hour before. There had been a steady stream of sad-eyed visitors since before six o'clock that morning—all making their way to the Humble house, before starting out for their work at the mill. Marcia was glad they hadn't forgotten. There wasn't a single family within a five-mile radius that hadn't benefited from Ada Humble's services as baby deliverer, comforter, friend and official mourner. Now it was their turn. They had shown their appreciation by donating whatever their lean purses could afford and with this money had been bought the beautiful walnut and brass casket in which Ada Humble would be laid to rest beside her beloved Toby.

'Strange,' Marcia mused, 'sitting here in Ada's little house, and not being deafened by the noise of that great rattling family.' It was an eerie experience, and one which badly unsettled her. Now, her glance fell high on the wall where Toby's picture still hung, and she crossed to stand beneath the portrait.

'Well, Toby,' she murmured softly, 'we 'in't got your little woman down 'ere no more, so, it's to be hoped she's up there, holding fast to you.' The tears in her eyes grew steadily, until two large pearl-shaped tear drops spilled over the long lower lashes to trickle down her face. 'Tek good care on her, Toby Humble,' she whispered in a broken voice, at the same time reaching up to tip the picture into her grasp. She carried it back to the little polished coffin by the window where, for a moment, the pain which sat in her breast like a solid shaft caused her to avert her eyes from the familiar face which she knew was only an arm's reach below her. Instead, she forced herself to concentrate on the heavy dark green curtains which had remained drawn these last twenty-four hours, ever since they had brought Ada Humble home for the last time. Now Marcia's gaze travelled along the gleaming chrome trellis which proudly bore the weight of that tiny, polished wood coffin. Of a sudden she was staring at the inner silk which lay ruffled over the little figure in white billowing folds, and slowly she reached out to touch the podgy fingers, folded in perpetual prayer. In the silence of that room the choking sob which caught in Marcia's throat seemed to startle even herself.

Crossing the still hands, she marvelled at their cold parchment beauty, then withdrawing her touch, she focused on the large cross on the wall over the head of the coffin, as though drawing strength to look again on Ada Humble's face. The arch of flickering light from the half-circle of tiny candles which cradled the head of the coffin drew her eyes down, and her stricken gaze alighted on the ever-familiar lines of the little woman's face.

The bright red trilby—which Ada's insensitive ''fficials' had taken from her—Marcia had gently placed over the wispy stumps of hair and ragged bald patches which Ada Humble had managed to hide from the curious world for so long. It made a stark contrast against the soft silky whiteness of the pillow. As Marcia dwelt soulfully on the dear face, a sick fury tugged at her senses. Half seeing through the misty veil, she leaned forward to place a gentle kiss on the alabaster forehead. 'I know you'd not want yon town hall folk to tek your Toby—your "soldier",' she whispered, 'so *you* tek him, Ada lass, for he belongs to nobody else.' She removed the frame from around Toby's picture, then slid the rolled up picture gently underneath the long shroud and out of sight. Somehow, the act gave her a feeling of pleasure.

The rustle of movement echoing down the passage announced Mrs Atkinson's early arrival. 'Go on, lass,' she whispered, 'it'll soon be time. Remember they're fotching 'er at nine o'clock.' Mrs Atkinson was already done up in her heavy black, ready for the journey to the church and the funeral.

'I'll go an' get meself washed and ready,' Marcia replied in a whisper, 'I'll not be long.'

'That's right. Get thisel' ready an' I'll bide 'ere quiet like.' She sat down stiffly on the upright stand-chair at the foot of the coffin.

The cold air in Ada Humble's parlour had been so penetrating that Marcia didn't notice the slicing dampness on entering her own house, where she wasted no time in stripping down to the skin and indulging in a thorough top-to-toe wash. Barty Bendall's breakfast things were still scattered about the table, as though he'd rushed off to work in a great hurry. 'If he was late, I'll be for it tonight,' Marcia told herself, dreading the prospect of another awful scene.

Marcia was not upset by the fact that she had nothing black. 'Ada'll understand,' she promised herself, donning the dark blue skirt and grey jumper, afterwards pinning a broad band of black woollen cloth around her coat sleeve. Then, pulling her cloche hat on, she examined herself in the mirror. 'It ain't what a body *wears* to a funeral,' she told her image stoutly, 'it's what's in a body's heart as matters!'

At the foot of the stairs, she suddenly realised that she hadn't got any coppers for the collection. 'That won't do at all!' she said, remembering how she had given the children the last bit of brass in her purse, and hoping at the same time that her mother had not been too worn out by a day and night of her three grandchildren. But Grandma Fletcher was a good woman, and she also had a liking for Ada Humble. Rummaging in the drawer, she found a threepenny piece, 'It's better than nothing,' she said, staring at the coin.

As Marcia went out of the door, she thought again on her Mam—she thought briefly on Nantie Bett also, and wondered whether there was any more news of Curt. For Marcia found herself thinking more and more about his promise to come back for her.

CHAPTER TWENTY

'Don't try tekking the entire blessed world on thi' shoulders, lass.' Grandma Fletcher reached up to place the freshly-washed cups onto the shelf, 'Yer no'but a youngster thisel' yet!' she went on. She turned to where Marcia was peering out from the scullery window, a far-away look in her eyes.

Satisfied that the children were happily playing in the yard, Marcia turned to smile warmly at her mother. 'I wish I *was* still a youngster, Mam,' she told her, leading the way into the parlour. 'I'd mek a few changes in my life, I'll be bound!'

'Aye, an' we all know what *sort* o' changes, don't we, eh!' She cast a quick knowing glance in Marcia's direction, 'Aw, lass! Get that bloody Ratheter outta yer mind! I know Barty Bendall's not what we all hoped, but the fella's still yer husband when all's said and done! Oh! I in't forget what yon Curt Ratheter did, my girl, an' I'm never likely to, I can tell yer!' She finished with a disapproving shake of her snowy white head. Then, on seeing Marcia's downcast expression, she quickly added, 'Sorry lass. That were a heartless thing to say, I know. But, to my mind, the marriage vows is sacred!'

'It's all right Mam . . .' Marcia dropped into a chair opposite the rocker where her Mam was now settling herself. She was only too well aware that Curt Ratheter would never be made welcome in this house! 'But as God's my judge,' she went on, 'I'd give almost *anything* to turn the clock back.'

'Well that's one thing as you *can't* do, lass!

Time'll march on with or without us, we've got no say in the matter. It's just a pity as we couldn't start out wi' as much wisdom and experience as we ends up wi'. I dare say we'd *all* on us mek a few changes then, eh?' With that, Grandma Fletcher fell silent, gently rocking to and fro and softly humming to herself.

Marcia's thoughts ran on as she gazed deep into the crackling flames. 'That Blackie, Mam,' she said. 'Oh, you should a' seen that poor Blackie.' In her mind's eye she recollected the awful look on his face as he'd stood in the church, his hard glinting eyes never leaving Ada Humble's coffin for one moment.

'What'll 'appen to the lads now?'

'I don't know, Mam. I expect they'll be kept in the children's home, till they're old enough to fend for themselves.' Marcia had little knowledge of these things. 'It's Blackie as sets heavy on my mind. He was allus a sociable, warm sort o' lad, but summat's happened to him, Mam. I can't quite put me finger on it, but he seemed harder in the face— terrible bitter, like.'

'Aye, I expect 'e's old enough to feel it deeper than the young 'uns. I didn't know the family all that much—an' only Ada, through you, but I'm told 'e doted on 'is Mam an' Dad.'

'He did. He idolised them! I only hope the good Lord sees fit to help him through this awful time.'

'Oh, 'e'll not forget, lass! 'E'll never forget. A body 'as to learn to live wi' summat like that. If 'e comes to be able to live wi' it, that's enough to see 'im through!' Grandma Fletcher straightened her shoulders, and sat up straight, her expression firm, her voice chastising, as she declared in a stout voice, 'As for thisel' Marcia Bendall! Thar' to stop thinking on it.' She reached out to poke the fire, her agitation finding an outlet as she prodded and stirred up the coals. 'God alone knows where yon man's got to! Playing dominoes at ol' Jack Merriman's I expect!'

Marcia was relieved that the subject had been changed, and she wasn't ignorant of the deliberateness of such a move. Ada was gone now, gone to her Toby, and in the end she supposed the children would come to no real harm. Children were a resilient lot. All a body could do was to pray for them.

'You're right, Mam,' she conceded, 'fretting on such matters can only do a good deal of harm.' She got up and wandered over to the back window which overlooked the yard, pushing the matter of the Humble family from her thoughts. It was done, and there wasn't a thing she could do to change it! Like so many other things in her life, it was out of her control. Now, her heart filled with pleasure as she watched the children laughing and playing. How like Curt young Florence was, she mused— the same dark striking handsomeness, the infectious laugh. Curt—where was he right now? This very minute? She supposed that Curt was still down south organising that 'new life' he was so excited about. Of a sudden, Marcia's back stiffened. God! The letter—Curt's letter! She had intended to destroy that, but what with one thing and another it had slipped her mind. What if Barty Bendall was to come across it, she tormented herself. But how would he? It was well hidden and he would have no need to go looking.

All the same, Marcia was filled with dread at the

351

consequences should he ever find the letter, for, try as she might to hide her true feelings from Barty Bendall, Marcia knew he sensed how very deep went her love for Curt Ratheter. She knew also that a black need for revenge had festered in him. Over the years he had let it grow out of all proportion, until, with the news of Curt's release from prison, it had spilled over to engulf him. These past weeks he had been little short of a madman! More and more Marcia had come to see the impossibility of her life with him.

Yet her mind was torn between the magnitude of her love for Curt and the unquestionable loyalty she owed to Barty Bendall and their marriage vows. 'Sacred' vows, as her Mam had so rightly pointed out. Vows which dictated that she must make at least one final effort to try and achieve some semblance of normality between her and Barty Bendall. She owed it to the both of them. Above all else she owed it to the children, for they must not go on being subjected to that terrible atmosphere of hatred and fear which reigned in the Bendall household.

'What's to do, lass?' The voice was soft and concerned, as Grandma Fletcher touched her daughter on the shoulder and, turning to see the love in those bright blue eyes, Marcia was tempted to pour out her heart—to tell her Mam of Curt's letter, to confide how she had *seen* him, to tell how he had held her in a way Barty Bendall never could. She wanted to reveal how there might be the opportunity of a new life for her, with Curt and the children. All of these things she was tempted to say out loud. But could not, for there was little anybody else could do about her dilemma.

'Nothing, Mam,' she lied with more than a small measure of shame. 'I was just watching the children.'

Grandma Fletcher looked deep and long into Marcia's sad dark eyes. 'Can't tell me, eh?—or don't want to! All right then lass, but remember, I'm 'ere if you should ever need me.'

'I know that, Mam,' Marcia said as she leaned over to kiss the anxious face, 'bless your old heart.'

In that characteristic way she had of knowing just when to change the subject, Grandma Fletcher looked across the backyard to where Polly was sitting on an old discarded chair. 'That little lass 'as it on 'er mind about going in that Infirmary—won't talk on it though! Clams up whenever I mentions it, poor little mite. When is it she goes? A week today?'

'Monday next, that's right, Mam.' Marcia looked across at Polly, and her heart ached at the sorry forlorn little figure she was. 'It is preying on her mind, an' you're right. She seems to have closed in on herself. Even I can't get through to her.' Marcia despaired of the way Polly had distanced herself.

'I'll be glad when it's over, Mam, and I'm fetching the lass home from the Infirmary,' she said, wrapping her hand over the comforting fingers which now gripped her shoulder, 'she *will* be all right, won't she Mam?'

'Well, o' *course* she'll be all right. All the same, it'll be a blessing when it's done with.' She grabbed up her long skirts and propelled Marcia away from the window. 'Now give us 'and to get a bite to eat.' Her face twisted into a quizzical expression. 'Tha's not about to rush away are thi'?'

Collecting the home-baked bread and preserve,

which she carried to the parlour table, Marcia assured her, 'No Mam, we've got half an hour or so.' The letter was still on her mind. It must be destroyed this very day. 'But I do want to get home afore Barty Bendall,' she told her.

Florence and young Barty had worked up a healthy enough appetite, tucking in to hot muffins with such unbridled enthusiasm that Grandma Fletcher found it necessary to warn them against choking themselves. Polly nibbled her way through a slice of home-baked bread, after which she excused herself from the table.

'Hey!' Grandma Fletcher would have none of it. 'What's ailing thi'? A grand lass o' your age can do better than that! What say thi' tried one o' me special hot muffins, eh?'

'Aw, Grandma,' Polly said, 'it's not that I don't *like* your lovely tea—honest!' She crossed to hug the ample hips. 'I'm just not hungry.' No amount of chastising could persuade her otherwise.

Rising to collect the dirty plates, Marcia declared, 'You'll have no objections to lending a hand with the washing-up then, will you?' She thought to draw Polly away from Grandma Fletcher's well-intentioned bantering.

At that moment, there appeared a small round figure at the door leading into the parlour. 'Well, I'm jiggered! If we in't got the Bendall brood for tea!' Nantie Bett stood there beaming. She caught the embarrassed young Barty into her arms, covering his scarlet face with sloppy kisses, which he promptly wiped off.

Florence looked on in horror before diving at Nantie Bett and delivering a quick kiss to the face which leaned towards her. At least *that* way, she could dodge back quickly!

Marcia allowed Nantie Bett her pleasure, returning the bear hug and kiss with generosity. After which there came a volley of protest and long faces from the children, who were instructed to reseat themselves at the table. 'While our Nantie Bett 'as a bite to eat, we shall all keep her company!' declared Grandma Fletcher. ' 'Tain't manners to let a body eat on her own!'

The moans became cheers when Nantie Bett loudly protested, 'Get awa wi' thi' Fletcher! What does thi' tek me for, eh? I wants nobody gawping at me while I mek crumbs o' thi' muffins!' She turned to the children and commanded, 'Get thi'selves out i' that fresh air. Go on! Be off wi' thi'!' She began chasing them, sending the little folk before her in fits of giggles.

Only Polly stayed behind, her face a sorry little picture as she began to make her way to the scullery. When Marcia followed, it was to see Polly making a start at the washing-up. 'No, lass,' she told her lovingly, 'you go an' set in the fresh air. I'll see to this.'

Without saying a word, Polly turned to look at her with a revealing look, which told Marcia of the fear Polly had of her imminent admission to the Infirmary. 'Go on, sweetheart,' she encouraged, bending to kiss her. 'We shall be leaving for home very shortly.'

Later, when the time came to say their merry farewells, Marcia's heart felt lighter for having visited. It always did her a power of good to see her dear old Mam. Now, as she ushered the children outside, she told them, 'Come on, don't be dawdling!' There would be hell to pay if Barty

Bendall's tea wasn't ready when he got home. Besides which, she *must* destroy Curt's letter.

'I'll walk as far as the top o' the road wi' thi' Marcia,' Nantie Bett said. She hustled herself out of the door, and as she did so, Marcia saw the warning look which her Mam cast upon the little woman.

With the children in front, as Marcia and Nantie Bett made their way to the top of the road—during which time the conversation covered Ada Humble's demise, Polly's condition, and the usual unimportant pleasantries concerning everyday life—Marcia got the distinct impression that Nantie Bett was working up to impart her own piece of news. Finally, Marcia could bear it no longer.

'Have you heard from Curt?' The question was delivered with hesitance, and perhaps a trace of regret that even now, with so many other matters weighing on her mind, she craved news of him.

Having reached the point where she must take leave of the little group, Nantie Bett brought herself to a standstill. The expression on her craggy face as she looked round towards Marcia was a mixture of loving anxiety and relief that Marcia had broached the subject first.

'I very nearly kept mesel' fro' talking of it, Marcia,' she said in an intimate voice, inclining her grey head towards the children, 'but *yer* not unaware o' my affection for Curt, an' if anybody's a right to know o' Curt's business, it's you! Did yer know Curt's been gone these last few weeks, searching out a job an' a fresh start?' Without waiting for a reply, she went on, 'Well, 'e's back! An' I've a strong feelin' ye'll be 'earing from 'im,

356

lass. So think on, eh? Be ready wi' yer answer—an' Lord 'elp yer to mek the right decision.' There she vigorously shook her head, at the same time placing her hand on Marcia's and saying, 'Y'know, lass—sometimes it's more wrong than right ter do it all by the rule-book. Life's too short an' precious to throw away. Just think on that!'

The minute Marcia came into the parlour she knew something was wrong. Things were out of place—chairs had been moved and something indefinable made her tremble in her shoes, as now she felt her eyes drawn to the spot where she had hidden Curt's letter.

'What's wrong Mam?' Polly, who had left the children playing on the flagstones outside, had followed her Mam indoors, and seen the colour drain from her face.

In spite of the fear which gripped her, Marcia forced herself to smile at Polly. '*Nothing's* wrong, child,' she said, putting her hands on Polly's shoulders and turning her about, 'go and fetch the young 'uns in, would you, lass?'

Quickly now, hardly daring to look, she swept across the room and fell to her knees at the spot where Curt's letter had been secreted. She pulled up the edge of the oilcloth, she pushed her fingers far beneath, in the faint hope that it might have slipped further in, and, when she saw that there was nothing there but bare floorboards, her heart sank like a lead weight inside her.

It was gone! The letter in which Curt had poured out his love for her was gone and with it, any hope she might have had for a quieter life.

Gripped by a dreadful premonition, Marcia swiftly returned the oilcloth to its place and replaced the chair over it, all the while cursing herself for having kept the letter in the first place. It had been a foolhardy and dangerous thing to do—but it had brought her such great comfort. Now she dreaded to think what else it would bring.

Some time later, when the children were all washed and abed, and even Polly had lapsed into an exhausted sleep, Marcia could not bring herself to go up those stairs. As it was, she could hardly sit still, for several times she had got out of the stiff horsehair seat to pace the floor. Up and down she had gone, the heart trembling within her, for she knew there was something terrible brewing this night. Barty Bendall had not come home at tea-time, and already the darkness was closing in outside. Marcia had visions of him sitting in some shadowy corner in one of the pubs he haunted, poring over Curt's letter, his heart growing blacker at every word, and downing pints of booze which would sink him ever deeper into the hatred and jealousy which had marred their marriage almost from the beginning.

Marcia had toyed with the idea of taking the children back to Grandma Fletcher's but two things dissuaded her from doing so. Firstly, there was her Mam's unforgiving attitude towards Curt Ratheter and she knew she would take on about that letter. Then Marcia believed that, having brought this particular trouble down on her own head, she must face it as best she could—however much the prospect frightened her!

When it was pitch black outside, and the mantel-clock had struck first one, then two in the morning, Marcia sat hunched in the chair, shivering and making every effort to keep her weary eyes open.

358

When the clock struck three, she forced herself to go and look outside—but still there was no sign of him. When the clock struck four, and the daylight was just beginning to peep over the house-tops, Marcia was unable to stem the tide of sleep which threatened to wash over her. Curled up on the settee, a coat flung over her, she lost herself in fitful, restless sleep.

Disturbed from the sleep which had partially refreshed her, Marcia blinked at the searing brilliance of the naked light bulb. She hoisted herself up, bleary-eyed and not yet fully awake— but at the sight of Barty Bendall a state of panic at once enveloped her.

'I said get up! Up I say! Afore I lay your skin open wi' me sodding belt!' His shouts seemed to shake the house to its very foundations. Then, as Marcia scrambled to her feet, he crossed to the bottom of the stairs, where he yelled, 'You bloody kids! Get down 'ere, *now*.'

Instantly, all three children began making their way down, whereupon Barty Bendall came back into the parlour to fix Marcia with that spiteful green glare. '*You!* Stay right where you are!' he growled, looking more repulsive than Marcia had ever seen—with the bottom half of his face covered in coarse gingerish stubble and those glittering eyes marbled with rivers of little pink blood-vessels. His hair was unkempt and, down the front of his half-open shirt, spread a dark misshapen beer-stain. His gait was unsteady, as though he'd been downing liquid courage all the night long. And—the sight of which turned Marcia's heart over—he had clutched in his square, stocky fist that piece of paper she had so frantically searched for earlier. Curt's letter!

Now, on seeing him, the children hesitated at the parlour door, involuntarily moving closer to each other, the two younger ones never taking their frightened eyes off him. Polly, ever-defiant, mocked him with her gaze.

'*Move* yersels! Come on, get in 'ere!' He took a pace forward and, at once, little Barty ran to the outstretched arms of his mother, who seated herself in the tall stand-chair by the scullery door. Florence would have followed him, but Barty Bendall blocked her path. 'No!' he bellowed, 'You—over there!'

He gestured impatiently towards the horsehair armchair, then took an unsteady threatening step towards Polly. In a slurred voice he told her, low and thick, 'An' *you*! You little swine! You stay just where you are—the further you are from me, the better for all of us.'

Marcia watched, ever ready to act as Polly straightened her slight shoulders. Then, her head drawn back, she met Barty Bendall's stare with equal challenge. Judging by the girl's erratic breathing, Marcia perceived that the brave outward stance belied the fear which Polly must be experiencing. The sight of Barty Bendall in one of his rages was enough to strike fear into the heart of anyone, she thought—but let him try and touch any of my children, that's all!

Of a sudden, he had swung round and was loudly abusing her. 'My own bloody wife! Carrying on behind me back!' He thrust the letter in her face. 'Yer nowt but a bloody trollop! I ought ter say to hell with the pair on yer—but so help me, I can't!' Here, his voice broke and Marcia took the opportunity to try and save the situation. In a soft voice she called his name, but it seemed only to rile him further.

'Shut your lyin' bloody face! You've told me nowt but bloody lies all along!' He turned to Florence, who for the first time since Marcia could remember looked terrified of this man whom she knew as her father. His clenched fist crashed down hard on the table. 'An' *you*, you little bitch! You knew! You *all* knew!' He swung round towards the fireplace, grabbed the end of the mantelpiece cloth and ripped it down with a vicious tug which sent ornaments, clock and all, crashing to the floor. Stretching the cloth taut between his hands, he crashed and fumbled his way towards Polly. As he did so, Marcia got to her feet, ready and watching.

Polly didn't flinch as the epitome of everything vile confronted her. When his voice dropped to a grating level almost inaudible to the others, his eyes narrow pools of green liquid, as he murmured 'You—', Polly kept steadfast, her gaze never leaving his face. 'You never 'ave liked me, never wanted me!' he went on, 'Just like yer Mam, eh? Can't get 'im out o' yer system!' Only then did Polly's gaze wander, to flicker uncertainly at Marcia's concerned face. His lips curled tight over his small even teeth. 'No use lookin' at 'er! Why! I could do for yer now—an' there i'n't a prayer could save yer!'

'Oho!' He stretched the mantel cover tight in his fists.

'Barty!' The scream was a desperate plea as Marcia dropped young Barty into the chair, 'Leave her alone! It's nothing to do with her! It's nothing to do with any of 'em. Let 'em go back to their

361

beds. Please! I'll do whatever you want of me. Please Barty—leave the children alone.' She came towards him and as she did so Barty Bendall lashed out to strike her, which only served to unleash the fury pent up in her for too long. As she launched herself at him, the stench of stale booze filled her nostrils, heightening the revulsion she felt. And when with a roar like a bull, he sent his fist flying into her body, Marcia fought like a tiger—convinced that she was fighting for Polly's life!

The ferocity of Marcia's onslaught when she pulled at his hair, punched and scratched at his face and made every effort to draw him away from Polly, only served to excite him more, whereupon the cruel blows he brought to her head and body landed with crippling viciousness.

Marcia felt her senses swamped by the painful blackness which smothered her, and as she slithered seemingly lifeless beneath the vile and terrible beating, she prayed he would spare her children.

A chilling silence settled over the room, as now Barty Bendall stood over Marcia's crumpled form. When, of a sudden, young Barty's whimpering grew to loud fearful sobs, he yelled, 'Get out of 'ere! *All* of yer!'

Florence, her face stark white against the black frame of long hair, quickly grabbed the sobbing boy by the hand, dragging him out into the hall, her words of caution to him also rapidly deteriorating into helpless crying.

Polly made no move, except towards Barty Bendall. When, in a voice terrible to hear, she told him, 'I hate you!' her vivid blue eyes held his astonished stare with such naked loathing that it struck him silent for the merest second. Then, he was crashing towards her, the back of his hand raised to land across her face. But Polly was ready for him. Skilfully ducking out of his way, she ran beneath his arms to grab him round the middle. With a roar, he thrashed about, punching at her back and making every effort to loosen her grip until of a sudden he plucked her from him, to send her crashing through the air and into the sideboard, where her head hit the corner with a sickening thud. Slithering to the floor, Polly lay deathly still, the trail of blood from the wide gash spreading into a thick dark pool. Barty Bendall's wide staring eyes filled with a look of abject terror at the sight of that still small figure.

Looking wildly about him, he emitted a sharp cry, like that of a trapped creature and, blundering in his haste, he made for the door—only to run straight into the confining arms of a burly neighbour.

'Oh no you don't!' the fellow cried, grappling with him, 'the police are on their way!' But he hadn't reckoned on how desperate Barty Bendall was, as, viciously now, he thrust his fist into the big man's groin. Then he took the opportunity to break away down the passage, quickly dodging between the gathering neighbours and out of the front door.

Miss Atkinson pushed her way through to the living room, where Florence and young Barty stood trembling, silenced by the scene before them.

As the horrified neighbour gathered the children to her, her shocked whisper echoed down the passageway. 'God help us all! He's killed 'em both!'

CHAPTER TWENTY-ONE

Grandma Fletcher rammed the pinch of snuff up her nose, then proceeded to cough from its penetrating strength. 'Come on, lass. Drink that tea, an' stop your moithering.'

'I'm not moithering Grannie! I'm just fed up waiting.' Florence propelled the old wooden rocking-chair back and forth. 'She's been gone *ages*!' she complained.

'Nay, lass. It just might seem that way to you.'

'An' why could Barty go, an' I *can't*? I'm older than 'im.' Florence wouldn't be consoled.

'Because you went last time! Now behave thisel'.'

'Hey,' Grandad Fletcher said poking his hairy face over the top of his paper, 'does thi' want to come wi' me an' Paddy for a walk in this grand spring sunshine?'

'No, Grandad. I want me Mam to come 'ome!'

'Oh well.' He disappeared behind his paper again, the clouds of smoke from his pipe belching over the top, until even he had to come up for air. Wafting the smoke away with his folded paper, he got to his feet. 'All the same, me an' Paddy's going for a walk.' With a mischievous twinkle in his eye, he concluded, 'Up to yon toffee shop.'

In a minute, Florence had scrambled down from the chair and was at his side, 'All right then Grandad. But we won't be long, will we?'

'Well, it depends on 'ow quick thi' make thi' mind up. Yon shop's got 'undreds o' toffee jars, all crammed an' spilling o'er!' He was still listing

364

the endless delightful choices, when Grandma Fletcher heard the door close behind them.

She was glad of a quiet minute to herself. Now, she stared into the cheery blaze of the fire, a thoughtful expression on her face. Occasionally a long drawn-out sigh escaped her. After a while, she got to her feet, gathered the folds of her ankle-length skirt into her hands, and pulling the grey shawl tighter round her ample shoulders, she went over to where a picture hung askew on the far wall. It was a framed print of Jesus. But even the great wisdom which shone out of its depth offered no answer to her quiet question, 'What does Thi' mek of it all, eh? What's to be done?' Nodding her grey head, she sighed resignedly, after which she bustled about collecting tea cups, all the while muttering, 'It's a rum old do, an' no mistake. Aye! A rum old do!' She busied herself in the kitchen, her low mutterings mingling with the muffled rattle of crockery being washed rather too vigorously, as all manner of past events paraded through her troubled mind.

Almost four weeks had gone by since that unforgettable scene at the Bendalls' house. After Marcia and the desperately ill Polly had been rushed to the Infirmary, the house had stayed securely locked, and as far as could be told by busy neighbours, nary a soul had set foot in the place.

Grandad Fletcher had insisted that Florence and young Barty should come to them and when two weeks later on 2 April 1938 Marcia had been discharged fit, there had been no question but that she also should come and join the children.

'Who the devil's that?' Grandma Fletcher wiped her hands on her pinny and scuttled towards the

365

front door, a look of relief spreading over her anxious face on opening the door. 'Aw, lass—it's you!'

'Sorry Mam!' Marcia was pale and visibly weary. 'I didn't want to go round the back, in case that Foster woman was there. She stops me every time.'

'That's all right love. She's a nosey old bugger is yon—although I reckon she means well. I've told her afore not to keep stopping you!'

Marcia nodded, ushering young Barty in before her. 'He's been as sick as a dog, Mam.'

'Aw—poor little chap!' Grandma Fletcher looked down at the lad's thin, drawn face. And her heart hardened against Barty Bendall because of the nightmares he'd caused the little fellow. 'Oh, well,' she said cunningly, 'If tha's been sick, tha'll not want a rosy apple I've been saving.'

Young Barty threw his chubby arms round her thighs to hug her tight. Bending down to pick him up, she asked, 'Shall I give it yon dog next door? 'cause 'e's right partial to big rosy apples.'

'No, Grannie! It's mine!' His face crumpled into a grin, and already there was a touch of colour returning to his cheeks.

'Oh, right then. I'll send yon cheeky dog on its way!'

'Where's Florence, Mam?' Marcia felt swamped with guilt at having to leave the children during her long anxious vigils at Polly's bedside. Yet a great surge of gratitude lightened her weary heart. If it hadn't been for Curt's strength and the comfort of his constant presence by Polly's side—Marcia shivered inwardly—she couldn't bring herself to think how she could ever have coped. She knew also that she could leave it no longer. Grandma

Fletcher would need to be put in the picture!

Grandma Fletcher put young Barty down, and whispered in his ear, 'Tha'll find it in me sewing tin.' And as they all went through to the back room she answered Marcia, 'She's gone wi' 'er Grandad up to yon toffee shop.'

Satisfied that young Barty was settled eating his apple behind a tattered old comic, Marcia hung their coats on the kitchen door hook before returning to sit by the fire, where the dreadful pain and trauma of the last few weeks showed clearly on her lovely but tired face.

' 'Ere you are lass,' Grandma Fletcher said as she handed her a pint mug of tea, 'get that down thi'.' She watched as Marcia smiled at the enormous mug, yet accepted it gratefully. 'Now then. What's the news about yon poor lass?' she went on.

When Marcia looked up with a forlorn expression, to say, 'Oh Mam—I daren't think about it. I feel sick to my stomach when I think what I've done!' she swiftly retaliated by telling her. 'Stop that sort o' talk! you've no call whatsoever to blame yersel' my girl!' Then she went on in softer tone, 'Polly's a game little soul. She'll be all right with the 'elp o' the Lord, an' yer mustn't say as it were *your* fault! You did all you could. Oh, I know yer did wrong wi' that letter from Curt Ratheter an' all! But, if yer ask me, Barty Bendall's been coming unhinged fer a long time—judging by what ye've telled me, lass.' She reached a comforting hand out, 'Look love, yer not to dwell on owt else, but Polly gettin' better. An' Lord willin', she'll be up an' about in no time!'

Marcia's dark eyes were shot with the rawness of

misery as they pleaded for reassurance. 'Oh Mam—if only I could be that sure.' Although she prayed like she'd never prayed in her life before, Marcia dared not allow herself to believe what her heart wanted to. Polly was ill—desperately ill, and even the doctors held out little hope. 'If only I could be sure,' she murmured again.

'Well you *can* love! Now then, 'ow is she today? Tha's been gone a long time.' For the first time, Grandma Fletcher's voice faltered, and under the pretext of blowing her nose, she took out her hankie and surreptitiously wiped a trembling tear away. 'Four hours tha's been gone, lass—I 'ad no way o' knowing.'

'I'm sorry Mam. I left young Barty with Mrs Atkinson. I didn't really want him to see Polly— not yet.' Her jaw set hard as she attempted to stem the threatened sobs. 'Oh Mam, she's so ill. She looks terrible, I just couldn't bring myself to leave her.' Polly's small white face loomed ever-present in Marcia's mind. 'I can't even tell if she knows I'm there! She lies that still, with her eyes never opening.'

'What does the doctor say?'

'He had a long talk with me—but to tell the truth Mam, I don't understand all them long-fangled words. I asked him in me own way, and from what I can mek out, the tumour was more deep-rooted than they'd thought. Y'see—they don't know enough about these things, nor how exactly to treat them—but they consider the operation to be "a qualified success". Anyway, she's off the danger list now. She's still very ill, and they've moved 'er into a little side ward on 'er own.'

'Oh, that's a blessing, love. But, why 'asn't she wakened up?'

'According to Dr Tomlinson, she *has*, but she keeps drifting in and out of consciousness all the time.' Marcia's voice fell to a whisper as though she had stopped addressing Grandma Fletcher, and was talking to herself. 'Looks like death—that still.' Grandma Fletcher strained her ears to decipher Marcia's mutterings, before accepting it might be best to leave the lass alone for a few minutes.

Of a sudden, the door knocker sounded. Grandma Fletcher said in a sigh, 'That'll be Father.' Pausing to pat Marcia on the shoulder she told her in a stout voice that didn't fool Marcia for a moment, 'Don't fret yourself, lass. All we can do now is pray.'

Marcia smiled ruefully, as her Mam hurried out to the front door. 'Seems to me,' she murmured into the warming flames, 'that when it comes right down to it, praying's not enough!' Yet even as she uttered the words, she knew that praying was all she had left to cling to. *She* was no doctor! She couldn't cut away the malignancy that was eating into Polly's poor suffering brain. She couldn't even offer her daughter the love and reassurance which spilled from the fullness of her heart, and though she'd sat endless hours by Polly's bedside, whispering tender words of comfort, Polly was so steeped in coma that she showed no response at all. Even though the doctors assured her that there was definite movement towards consciousness, Marcia couldn't see it. What was even more alarming, she couldn't *feel* it, couldn't *sense* it within herself.

369

She thanked God with all her heart for sending Curt to share her lonely vigil although she knew her Mam wouldn't see it that way, and so far, she had managed to keep them apart. But now, she must tell her.

During those long days when she herself had lain in the Infirmary, her still painful ribs cracked by Barty Bendall's merciless beating, and her face so swollen she could neither eat nor see, Marcia had thought long and hard about Barty Bendall, asking herself what manner of man could lose his senses so completely? She'd tried so hard to hate him for what he'd done to Polly. But she found herself pitying him. Had *she* been to blame in some way? Had those years with Barty Bendall been so overshadowed by her love for Curt that his mind had faltered?

Marcia didn't know—maybe the madness had *always* been in Barty Bendall. In spite of her avid belief that she had made every effort to bring contentment to their marriage, Marcia wondered what else she could have done. She wondered also where he might be now, and she was filled with remorseful guilt.

The return of Florence thankfully stemmed her punishing thoughts. 'Are you staying home now Mam?' Florence had thrown herself into Marcia's arms and was looking at her appealingly. Marcia knew how hard all of this was for Florence and little Barty, and her heart went out to the lass.

'Yes love, but I'll be going back after tea.' Marcia was hurt when Florence pouted her lip and pulled away, remembering how she had not once asked after her sister—almost as though she couldn't bring herself to say Polly's name.

'Oh! Will you be long?'

'No love, I won't be long. They don't like visitors to stay too long at night.' She was gladdened by the spontaneous kiss which Florence now planted on her lips.

'Oh, that's all right then,' she declared promptly, proceeding to share her toffees out with young Barty, who was seated on the floor, sorting his 'Snap' cards out, ready for a game with his sister.

'Mam!' Marcia's call produced Grandma Fletcher from the scullery, where she had been testing the progress of her bacon and onion dumpling.

'Yes, lass?'

'I wondered if you and Dad wanted to come and see Polly tonight?' Only Marcia and Curt had been allowed to visit Polly up to now.

Grandma Fletcher's response was immediate and enthusiastic. 'Oh we'd love to come, lass, but did you ask the doctor?'

'Yes. He said it'd be all right if we went in two at a time . . . I'll stay outside while you and Dad go in, then one of us can change over. Mrs Atkinson's already said she'll look to the young 'uns.'

When Marcia asked her father whether he also would come to see Polly, she wasn't surprised when he answered quietly, 'No, love. I'd rather not. I'll stay 'ere with the young 'uns.' His dislike for infirmaries was well-known and Marcia didn't condemn him for it. 'You tell the lass I'll see 'er when she's ready fer coming 'ome, eh?' he told her, looking greatly relieved that nobody was going out of their way to persuade him otherwise.

Marcia felt bone-weary, her head was throbbing and she was desperate for a few hours sleep. 'Can I go and lie down upstairs for a while, Mam?' she enquired.

'I've 'eard you, lass—pacin' round an' round that blessed floor at all hours when yer shoulda been sleepin'. You go and get some rest,' her mother answered.

Once in the privacy of the little back bedroom, Marcia lay across Grandma Fletcher's big old bed, and, with eyes gratefully closed, she uttered a heart-felt prayer. In her desolation, and in spite of all her parents had done to help, she felt utterly alone. Although Curt's love and support brought her immeasurable comfort, with Polly as close to death's door as she would ever be, and Barty Bendall still on the run from the police, there could be no peace, and now Marcia had begun to wonder if there ever would be. Yet the knowledge that Curt was even now at the Infirmary did give her a warm feeling. He was a pillar of strength to her. It was he who had insisted that she should return home for at least a couple of hours in order to 'get some proper rest'. And now Marcia did just that.

Downstairs Grandma Fletcher tutted, 'I don't know! If she's not careful, yon lass is going to mek 'erself right ill!'

'Aye,' rejoined the old fellow, ' 'tis a worrying time for 'er. What wi' young Polly at death's door, an' Barty Bendall 'aving disappeared.'

'Hey!' Grandma Fletcher pulled him up sharply, giving him a warning look and shifting her glance sideways to where the children were playing. 'As thi' no more sense?' she demanded.

A sheepish embarrassment coloured his face, and pulling his neb-cap forward, he hoisted himself out of the depths of his chair with a noisy grunt. 'I think I'll just pop across an' 'ave a word wi' Tom.'

'A crafty out-of-hours pint yer mean!'

'Away wi' you woman!' he rebuked, hurrying to the door as if afraid she might somehow attempt to stop him, 'that's more than the fella's licence is worth!'

'Just mek sure you're 'ome in time for yer tea.' Grandma Fletcher's raised voice fell on deaf ears, as she knew it would, for he was already out of the door and away.

It wasn't until five-thirty that Grandad Fletcher returned, wandering in through the back door just as Marcia was putting the last of the tea things away. Judging by the deep lustre in her smiling eyes, the sleep had done her a world of good. 'Oh there you are Dad. Mam's left your tea warming in the fire-grate. She's just getting herself ready.' A thoughtful look came to Marcia's face, 'I want to get back to Polly,' she added in a low voice.

' 'Course you do lass. You two get gone. The young 'uns will be fine wi' me.'

Marcia pecked his cheek. 'Thanks, Dad. I've told 'em they're to go to bed no later than eight o'clock,' she reminded him.

'Stop your moithering! I can manage them I tell you. We'll listen to yon wireless, see what this 'ere bloody Hitler fella's up to!' His voice took on a note of concern. 'What wi' Austria being swallowed up—signs of unrest all over Europe, and talk in this country of Home Guard an' air-raid precautions, well, folks is gettin' tetchy an' that's a fact!'

'Stop frightenin' the young 'uns!' Grandma Fletcher scolded him from the kitchen doorway.

She already had her heavy shawl about her shoulders. 'Get yer coat on lass,' she told Marcia. 'We'd best be off!'

Marcia gave Barty and Florence a hug and kiss, saying, 'Grandad promises, if you're good, you can listen to the wireless.' This seemed to compensate for any misgivings about their Mam's departure, as now young Barty slipped his arms around Marcia's shoulders.

'Mam—will Polly be better soon?' he asked quietly.

Marcia was not expecting such a direct question from young Barty, and it showed in the rush of tears which swam in her eyes. 'Oh Barty—I hope so,' she whispered in a trembling voice. Then, quickly regaining her composure, she told him reassuringly, 'Of course she's going to get better. I'll give her your love.'

The gas lamps had already been lit, and the light from the pub across the road lent a cheer to the sharp spring evening, as Marcia and her Mam stepped out into the street. They had timed it right because there was a tram already waiting at the stop to carry them almost to the Infirmary door.

As they alighted opposite the grey and archaic building which was the Infirmary, Marcia hesitated before crossing to the main entrance.

'What's to do, lass?' Grandma Fletcher asked.

For a moment Marcia seemed lost for words, before replying softly, 'Mam, don't be shocked at Polly's appearance. I was sick to my heart when I first saw her, but I'm used to it now. Just be prepared, eh?'

The old lady gripped Marcia's hand. 'Hey! I'm an old soldier, so I'll not be shocked. Just as long as she gets better and comes 'ome—that's all as matters.'

Marcia nodded, but made no attempt to move. 'Mam,' she said as she put her hand in the older woman's arm, 'there's summat else you ought to know.'

'Oh?' Grandma Fletcher didn't care much for the tone of Marcia's voice. 'Summat else?' she was eyeing Marcia in a most peculiar manner—almost as though she's guessed, feared Marcia.

'Curt's here.' There! It was said. And judging by the astonished look on her face, it had come as a complete surprise to Grandma Fletcher.

'Curt Ratheter!' she exclaimed. 'Yer tellin' me as the fella's *here*—wi' Polly?' The disapproval showed in the tone of her voice and the firm set of her jaw.

'Yes. He's been at Polly's bedside every spare minute, Mam. He's been nearly out of his mind with worry. Mam! Polly's *his* daughter, and Barty Bendall nigh on *killed* her!'

'Oh I know what Barty Bendall's done, love. I *know* full well what 'e's done, an' the good Lord'll see 'e suffers for it, but it were the *tumour* as nearly took the lassie's life—not Barty Bendall.'

'Aye, it *were* the tumour Mam, but it was Barty Bendall who triggered it off. Curt's scoured the streets night after night, looking for him.' Grandma Fletcher was visibly taken aback at the unusual force of animosity in Marcia's voice. 'I've told him *not* to look for Barty Bendall. But to tell you the truth, Mam, I wouldn't care if he was lying dead in some gutter, for what he's done to Polly.' Even as the words left her lips, Marcia realised that she still wasn't ready to forgive Barty Bendall,

375

in spite of the fact her hatred of him for what he had done to Polly was tempered with a measure of guilt.

'Oh lass. God forgive yer!' the older woman said, plainly upset.

'No Mam. It's Barty Bendall who wants forgiving, and it won't be *me* as forgives him. Not as long as I live!'

Grandma Fletcher gripped Marcia's arm and propelled her across the road. 'Come on lass. It'll do no good to keep thinking like that! No good at all.'

The anaesthetic stench of the Infirmary enveloped them as Marcia pushed open the heavy inner doors. Everywhere there was a sense of urgency, as busy white-coated doctors and 'slips-o-lasses', as Grandma Fletcher insisted on calling them, hurried back and forth, intent only on the task in hand. Grandma Fletcher's clogs echoed on the stone flag floors as she and Marcia hurried down the corridors. 'I never 'ave liked the smell o' these places,' she told Marcia in a loud whisper, as she scurried to keep up with her daughter.

Of a sudden, Marcia stopped near the wide glass doors which led to the side wards. 'We're 'ere Mam. You stay there—I'll not be a minute.' She studied the span of the windows in the small office opposite. 'I'd best mek sure we're all right to go in, first.'

As she hurried away, her Mam followed her every step. She watched with acute interest as the kindly face of the duty nurse appeared at the door to greet Marcia, after which there was a quick exchange of words, and a nodding of heads, before, smiling, Marcia hurried back to Grandma

376

Fletcher.

'We can go in,' she confirmed, adding in a warning voice, 'Curt's already with her—he's been here all day.' She pushed open the door and waited until Grandma Fletcher drew level with her. 'Remember what I said. Be prepared.'

The kindly old features betrayed only the slightest hint of the very real apprehension she was feeling. 'Go on lass. It's time I saw me grandchild,' she declared, in as stout a voice as she could muster.

A deep common love for the girl lying hurt in there strengthened the intensity of their emotions as the two of them went in silently. Once the wide glass doors had swung shut behind them, they found themselves in a rectangular hallway. The three doors to their left each led to a tiny side ward, and quickly now, Marcia led the way through to where the antiseptic aura permeated the air and stung their nostrils. 'Polly's in here Mam.' As Marcia reached out towards the handle of the second door, she observed with absent-minded interest how odd it was that the forbidding quiet of the place induced them to whisper.

Now as the two women entered the room, the brilliance of the corridor lighting gave way to a softer light. But it was not so soft that Marcia didn't see the stiff look on her Mam's face as Curt Ratheter rose to greet them! The years of imprisonment had robbed nothing from his dark handsome looks—although his strong black eyes were now shadowed by dark heavy circles. The firm lines of his features had been sharpened by anxiety and loss of sleep.

He moved two stand-chairs towards the bed and

gestured for the old lady to sit down.

Ignoring him altogether, Grandma Fletcher shuffled her way round the far side of the bed, where she took Polly's small hand in the rough strength of her own. All the while, Marcia watched, her heart sore as she realised that in spite of herself, that dear cantankerous old soul was suffering the same degree of horror that *she* had suffered when first she'd looked on the small still figure of her daughter.

Turning now to Curt, Marcia took his outstretched hand, their eyes meeting in a blend of love and despair, as he told her tenderly, 'I'd better leave for a while. I'll go downstairs and see if I can get a cup of tea.' Then, with a wistful glance towards where that grand old lady was bent over the bed, he murmured, 'She'll never forgive me, will she?'

Marcia didn't speak. She merely responded with a reassuring squeeze of the hand before making her way across to the bed, and, as her Mam looked up to her, Marcia cried out silently at the pain on those dear familiar features. Now, when she spoke to Marcia, it was in a broken tearful voice. 'Oh lass! Marcia lass!' She reached into her shawl for a hankie, then clumsily wiping her face and making every effort to minimise her obvious distress, she shuffled round towards a stand-chair—never once taking her tear-filled eyes off Polly's inert form. She pulled her shawl about her, as though deriving small comfort from it, and quietly sat down.

Marcia moved closer to her daughter, where she clasped the hand which rested on the outer cover. She sank into the chair, pulling it ever closer, until her own head was almost touching Polly's. Her

378

busy loving eyes moved across her daughter's face looking, searching for life—a flicker of an eyelid, or a suggestion of movement at the mouth. But the face remained like a grotesque mask, almost unrecognisable as the tiny sharp features that Marcia knew and loved. The shape was lost in the mass of bruises, which disguised the strong line of the nose and the fine tapering forehead—these dreadful bruised lumps of flesh had been caused by the surgeon's probing knife, as he'd cut into the skull to root out the invading tumour. The stark whiteness of protective bandages made a poor substitute for the fine flowing hair, which was lost to the nurse's shears.

The minutes ticked by, and in the half-lit solitude of the tiny room, Marcia's tears fell with heart-rending anguish. She told herself over and over that this was Polly lying here. Polly, who had never been allowed a moment's peace. 'Is it *my* fault?' Marcia had to ask herself. Now, as many times before, she questioned her every move, every decision. Had Polly been born only to carry the burden of a sin which had been committed in love and ignorance? The child, Polly, had been conceived in the strongest love possible between two people—two people who were not man and wife! Marcia tortured herself with self-recrimination, which she knew in her heart was unfounded. And, in the midst of it all, there emerged a strong undeniable belief that whatever had been determined as Polly's fate, could not be attributed to, or influenced by her, for there was a greater influence at work, a power of destiny, over which neither she nor Polly had any control.

'Oh God,' Marcia's voice was fraught with

desolation, as she whispered the words which shouted in her heart. 'Hasn't she suffered enough? She's not yet a woman. Let her be! Let her live!'

Seeing how desperate Marcia seemed, Grandma Fletcher came to help her to her feet. 'Marcia lass—I'll sit here for a while. You go an' find Curt,' she said. When she saw that Marcia would not be easily persuaded to leave Polly's side, she insisted quietly, 'Go on, lass! I'll stay wi' Polly.'

Downstairs, in the comforting enclosure of Curt's arms, the flood of despair found its outlet. With the tears streaming down her tragic face, she asked him, 'Why? Why, Curt? Why is she being punished? For God's sake tell me. Is she paying for our mistakes?' Marcia was torn apart by the desperate love she felt for Curt, and a deep rending sense of the helpless guilt which constantly plagued her.

'Marcia. There's no blame, no sins to be answered for.' Curt's voice was calm and reassuring, as he tilted her face towards him. 'You mustn't punish yourself, you know. And Polly is tougher than you think. She'll emerge stronger than all of us.' His eyes dimmed sadly. 'We have to believe that, my darling.'

As her questioning gaze met the determination of his own, Marcia believed him. She clung to his every comforting word—drawing from him unflinching belief in Polly's full recovery. 'I hope you're right,' she said, 'I pray you are, my love.'

Curt gathered her closer to him. 'Believe me my darling, Polly has more guts and determination than we give her credit for. I've watched her these last weeks. Sitting in the twilight of that room, I've been awed by the powerful sense of survival that

380

seems to fill the room like a living breathing presence.' Here, he bent to kiss her. 'Our daughter's a *fighter*!' he told her, 'She won't give in so easy!'

Curt and Marcia sat for a while, quiet and secure in each other's arms, until Marcia said, 'I must go back to sit with Polly.'

Curt lifted her head, drawing her gaze towards him as he whispered, 'I love you so much, Marcia—so very, very much.' Then he brought his lips down, tasting the bitter-sweet salt of the tears which had dried on her mouth. 'You go back to Polly now. Watch her closely, my love, and you'll feel the strength in her. Be cheered and warmed by it, my darling.' He stood up above her, stretching his long legs which were cramped by his tireless vigil by Polly's bed. As Marcia surveyed the long lean stance of his body, her heart opened to his every word, as she told herself that he alone would be her salvation and Polly's protector. It was Curt they must look to now, and they would grow in the strength of his love. She felt a strange sensation of peace within her as Curt drew her to her feet. 'I'll be back later,' he told her, kissing her full on the mouth, before turning and going from the room.

Marcia drew in a deep raking sigh, then hurried back to the ward, and Polly. The second she stepped inside the tiny room, her senses tingled. Something had happened, she knew! Grandma Fletcher was on her feet, by the bed. 'Look!' she whispered urgently, 'God's been good, lass—the child's awake.'

Marcia's heart almost stopped as she leaned over the bed, and at once Polly's hand reached up slowly, painfully, to grip her fingers with gentle determination. When she felt those small warm fingers entwining hers, Marcia cried heartfelt tears of gratitude. 'Polly, oh Polly! God bless and love us,' she sobbed, holding Polly's hand in an iron grip as she showered kisses on the poor swollen face. Turning to hug Grandma Fletcher she cried, 'Oh Mam! Mam! She's going to be all right, thank God!'

Grandma Fletcher lifted the back of her hand to wipe away the tears with embarrassment, and sniffling hard, she smiled into Polly's searching eyes. 'Aye lass,' she rejoined happily, 'Thank God.' Then as if to caution the exuberant Marcia she went on, 'Gently, though, lass. There's still a fair way to go.'

CHAPTER TWENTY-TWO

The whole town of Blackburn was buzzing with talk about the Bendall family—of how the man of the house was on the run, with the authorities searching high and low for him. There had been neither sight nor sound of the fellow since that shocking business when he'd gone completely crazy—attacking both wife and daughter so viciously that the one was kept in the Infirmary some while, and the other had been at death's door ever since. It was agreed by one and all that Barty Bendall had been going steadily downhill these past years. First, there'd been the gambling and the drinking—then, of a sudden, his mind seemed affected, when he'd sat in the corner of the Lord Nelson, with such a black moody face as would put the fear of God in a body.

Of Jim Rawlinson, who knew Barty Bendall better than most, they would ask, 'Gone off 'is rocker, ain't 'e, Jim?'

'The fella had his reasons, I'm thinking!' he would reply. When he thought on how his old drinking pal had a wife who craved another, Jim Rawlinson wasn't surprised that he'd gone 'off 'is rocker!' All the same, he had little to say on the subject of Barty Bendall—for hadn't he himself stirred up muddy waters there? Oh, no! Jim Rawlinson figured the best thing HE could do, was to keep his trap well and truly shut now.

Barty Bendall pounded the cellar floor in the empty house in Regent Street, and, as he paced back and forth, his green eyes darted wildly about. When he reached the shaft of gaslight which filtered in through the dust and grime of the low casement window, the blade of the knife in his hand glinted. Thrusting the knife into the long pocket of his old great-coat, his low mumblings droning incoherently through the rankness of the damp, dark air, he turned sharply toward the narrow door which led to the pavement steps, and strode out into the night, leaving the cellar door creaking back and forth in the gentle evening breeze. On this miserable night, Barty Bendall had in his crazed mind the intention of an even darker and more terrible deed.

*   *   *

The Infirmary grounds were all but deserted, with only the odd visitor or two to disturb their serenity. Barty Bendall's slight figure, shrouded in his black

383

great-coat, attracted no special attention as he passed through the main doors and on towards the inner sanctum. The night-sister immediately recognised the name 'Polly Bendall' and assisted the man who wished to visit his daughter, by pointing out the location of her ward.

'But you do know you've not to stay long?' she warned, 'and no more than two visitors at one time.' When he nodded she added, 'Good! Your daughter's coming along nicely you know. The doctor's very pleased with her progress.'

Barty Bendall followed her instructions as he made his way to Polly without further challenge. Keeping his right hand over the weight of the hidden knife, he turned the handle and entered the small inner corridor. The first ward appeared to be empty, then, as he stepped stealthily inside the small interior of the second ward, he wasn't sure whether or not the small figure lying deep inside the covers was Polly. Creeping silently nearer, he leaned over to examine the face more closely. As he did so, a tight horrified gasp escaped from the back of his throat. His hand involuntarily gripped the knife in his pocket with shocked reflex and, without thinking, he stepped back a pace.

As he stood staring down at the swollen face, a small moan rent the still air, and Polly slowly opened her eyes, a swift surprise clouding their blueness as they struggled to focus on the unkempt face of Barty Bendall.

Her initial stab of fear mellowed into a strange confusion of pity and wonder, as she continued to search out the intruder's features.

Barty Bendall's vivid green eyes, now bitter with tears, locked into hers. Then, with a tormented cry, he quietly hurried away—the knife still held fast in his pocket.

Outside, from the camouflage of his hiding place, Barty Bendall waited and watched, until the arriving tram clanged to a shuddering stop to expel its passengers.

Curt stepped lithely from the tram, then, turning, he held out a hand to assist Marcia down the steep step. Worry and illness had taken their toll of Marcia, and Barty Bendall was visibly taken aback by the drawn weariness on her lovely face.

As he watched the strong, lean strength of Curt Ratheter's dark features, he emitted a low growl and his eyes brimmed with fierce hatred. Now, as Marcia and Curt approached the main entrance, he could hear them clearly.

'Don't fret about the future,' Curt was saying, 'I'll take care of you, of all of you.' When back came Marcia's observation that it was still too early for them to be making firm plans, he was quick to reassure her, 'But we're not only thinking of ourselves. Polly, Florence and young Barty, they all deserve better than they've had.' He pulled Marcia to him. 'But of course, you're right, my darling. It *is* early yet.' There, in the darkness, he gathered Marcia into his arms and kissed her long and tenderly.

As he moved back, to gaze down on that lovely face which he adored, Marcia smiled up at him, her heart heavy with love. Then, somewhere out of the corner of her eye, there came a flurry of movement. In a second she saw the danger—having time only to cry out 'Barty!', before the lunging figure emerging from the shadows launched itself at them.

As the utter madness on Barty Bendall's face revealed itself, Marcia's terrified screams muted the dull thud with which the glinting blade thrust into Curt's struggling body. Instantly, Barty Bendall pitched towards Marcia and in that moment she was convinced that she was about to die. Until, of a sudden and with incredible swiftness, he lifted the blade again to bring it down hard and straight into the depths of his own tortured heart.

As he sank to the ground, Marcia's screams alerted a bevy of white-coated nurses, some rushing to help Curt, others making for Barty Bendall's crumpled body.

Dazed and trembling, Marcia watched as they bundled Barty Bendall onto a mobile stretcher, then, when someone spoke to her, she followed the two male nurses who had taken charge of Curt. She would have gone straight into the emergency cubicle with him, had not the nurse kept her back, saying, 'No dear, it's best if you come with me, you've had a bad shock.'

Marcia gave little resistance, for she was emotionally drained, and shivering violently, feeling first hot and then icy cold. Her heart shrank within her as the awful scene relived itself in her mind. Over and over again, she murmured with horror, 'Dead! They're dead!' The rising hysteria was quickly intercepted by the prompt action of the nurse, as she injected the soothing, quieting liquid into Marcia's veins.

*　　　*　　　*

It seemed only a minute to Marcia, but it was in

fact sometime later when she opened her eyes. 'Curt?' His was the first image that came into her mind.

'It's all right, dear, sit yourself up. I'll get you a hot drink!'

Marcia grabbed the arm of the retreating nurse. 'No!' she protested, 'I don't want a drink.' She gripped the sofa for support, as the sudden rise to her feet rendered her dizzy. 'Curt and Barty?' She was almost afraid to ask.

'I'll get the doctor, you just sit still a minute.' Marcia's dark eyes were tragic as they gazed after the disappearing figure.

'Now then, Mrs Bendall, you are not to get yourself in a state.' The doctor was at her side in no time. 'How are you feeling?'

'*I'm* all right, but I want to see Curt—and Barty.'

How could he be so calm, when such a terrible thing had taken place, she wondered. 'Please!' she pleaded, 'I must see them!' She made an effort to get to her feet, but the effects of the drug were still heavy on her.

'Mr Ratheter is conscious—he will be fine,' the doctor assured her, 'but he'll have to stay at the Infirmary a few days.' Marcia's heart leapt, only to sink at his next words: 'Mr Bendall—that's your husband isn't it?' When she confirmed that yes, he was her husband, the doctor's face told Marcia everything. 'I'm sorry,' he said gently, 'we've done all we can.'

'Is he?' she breathed, fearing the word 'dead'.

'No, but it's only a matter of time.'

At this, Marcia got to her feet, her head spinning, as she told him, 'I've got to see him! Please, let me go to him.' She watched as the

387

doctor nodded agreement to the nurse. Marcia followed the white-coated figure down the long narrow corridor, until, a few moments later, they turned into a brightly lit room, where the nurse stood back and beckoned Marcia towards the bed situated under the window.

As she looked down at the prematurely aged face of Barty Bendall, Marcia reproached herself. The wicked features had relaxed in that quiet moment before his life and his torment were over. 'I'm sorry, Barty,' she murmured, the tears spilling down her face. 'Oh, I'm so sorry!'

The sudden movement of his hand interrupted her, as, weakly, it motioned for her to lean towards him. When she did so, he spoke in a broken whisper, barely audible. 'Marcia—not your fault. Mine! I only ever loved two people in all the world,' he went on, 'my father—an' you!' The gathering clouds in his eyes grew ominously dark. 'I always hated Polly,' he said in a fainter voice, 'Polly—never mine—always *his*!' His voice broke as he turned his eyes to her and in all the time Marcia had known Barty Bendall, she had never seen such softness as now in those sharp green eyes. 'Polly? She won't—die, will she?'

Placing a comforting hand over the white knuckles, and even now cringing inwardly from the touch, Marcia whispered kindly, 'No, Barty, God willing she won't die.' Beneath her hand the fevered grip relaxed, as the light of life slowly faded from his eyes, and, with his last dying breath, he pleaded, 'Marcia, forgive me.'

Marcia allowed herself to be led away when the nurse told her, 'There's nothing to be done now, dear, come along.' At the door, she turned to take

388

one last look, and whispered tearfully, 'Forgive?—don't we *all* need forgiveness, Barty?'

Sometime later Marcia was allowed to see Curt, who, according to the doctor, had suffered only minor wounds to his neck and chest. When she opened the door he asked at once, 'Barty? He's—gone, isn't he?'

Marcia's answer was written on her tear-stained face. She crossed the room and came to sit by him, until, with a moan, he drew her close. There was no need for words.

For a long long time they stayed quiet in each other's embrace, too filled with emotion to speak. When the nurse came to tell her, 'You'll have to leave now, Mrs Bendall,' Marcia felt stronger within herself.

Treading the deserted corridor towards Polly, Marcia asked herself many questions. Could she have stopped any of this? How much of it *was* her fault? Would she ever completely be rid of it all? But no answers were to be had.

CHAPTER TWENTY-THREE

Barty Bendall was finally laid to rest in the solitude of the little churchyard not far from Grandma Fletcher's home. Marcia had chosen a secluded corner, beside a tall spreading cedar tree, not far from the resting-place of old Connie Bendall herself.

It was a well-attended service, with big burly navvies shedding genuine tears at the demise of their 'mate', and big Jim Rawlinson never once able to look into Marcia's face.

The little house in Regent Street had stayed securely locked, so Barty Bendall had not lain overnight in the parlour, as was the tradition. Instead the church had opened its doors throughout the night before the service, when the brass-handled casket lay open beneath the compassionate figure nailed to the cross. Respectful visitors, mostly drinking cronies and work-mates, had come to take a last farewell look at the face which, in spite of the fury which had so often filled it, had finally succumbed to perpetual stillness.

Marcia and Grandma Fletcher had stood alone at the head pew, representing as they did the only family Barty Bendall had. Grandad Fletcher kept the children home—and it was not considered right that Curt Ratheter should attend.

Curt had recovered quickly, and during the weeks following his release from the Infirmary, he had busied himself for the new life on which he and Marcia had decided to embark. He had finally secured a job in a large brickworks company, some two hundred miles south. With the job came a tied cottage on a nearby estate.

Polly's strength grew day by day, and within a month of the delicate, experimental operation to stem the rapid growth of the tumour, she was sitting up in bed, excited by the prospect of a new life in a new place. Never once did she mention Barty Bendall.

Marcia had been disturbed by the reluctance on Polly's part to accept the friendship Curt had gladly offered. Polly was always polite, but distant and wary. Marcia often perceived in her quieter moments a fleeting glimpse of the old Polly, trying to come to terms with all the changes in her short, eventful life. It seemed to Marcia that Polly had taken all of these recent events too deeply into herself. In her most fervent prayers she asked, 'Let her forget, dear lord. Please let her forget.'

By the time Polly came home, spring had just begun to blossom into summer. Hurtful memories had become less painful, miraculously blurred by the passage of time. From the dark bitter experiences there had emerged a kind of rueful peace, a platform on which to build, and gradually, very gradually, Marcia found herself able to look forward with quiet optimism. Gratefully, she now embraced the unfolding year, with revived faith in its promise of new hope for the future. Yet she knew Polly found it more difficult to shake off the nightmares which still woke her from her sleep in fits of terror.

One of Grandma Fletcher's proudest possessions was her long Victorian mirror. It had somehow arrived at her home via some distant relative, and the reflection it produced now was blurred with age and marred by careless handling from former owners. Polly loved it and spent many hours admiring herself from head to toe.

Now, the taller, slimmer Polly stared back through the shadowy hairline cracks which cut irritatingly through the reflection of her naked form. 'Mam,' her voice interrupted Marcia's dressing, 'am I beautiful?'

''Course you're beautiful, Polly lass.' Marcia had noticed how conscious of her appearance Polly had become. The quick reassuring smile which lit Marcia's loving expression camouflaged the dark fears which still lingered in her mind. She thought on the doctor's warning, a severe caution that had pierced her and Curt's joy at watching Polly regain her vitality—'the tumour is malignant and deep-rooted,' he had told them, adding that Polly would need to be monitored constantly. And there would always be the possibility of further surgery.

The unexpected blow had devastated Marcia. The wonderful new-found love between her and Curt was overshadowed by the fact that in spite of all the surgeon's skill, Polly's tumour had not been completely removed.

That part of Marcia which had been released from a futile cruel marriage wanted so much to launch itself into the new life which was opening out to her. She was so very much in love with Curt—Curt, who had been constant and strong in his love and devotion to her and the children—Curt, who was all she would ever want in a man, and who, like her and Barty, had suffered because of the strength of their love.

Yet, the happiness she craved was not yet within her reach, for how could she grasp at such happiness, when Polly seemed doomed to live each day immersed in shadow. She looked across at Polly, marvelling at the change in her. Her cheeks weren't flushed with a healthy hue, but then Marcia reminded herself, they never had been. But there was an intangible quality of maturing womanhood about her that seemed to belie the destructive presence of any tumour. Marcia wondered whether the doctor had been wrong, yet she knew in her heart that no mistake had been made.

She and Curt had decided that Polly would be

better knowing just enough for her to attend regular examinations, and Polly had accepted this as routine procedure. After long deliberation, Marcia had brought herself to live each day as it came, being grateful for whatever happiness came along. She still concerned herself, though, about Polly's nightmares, and the fact that occasionally she would fall into one of those deep dark moods that instinctively took Marcia back to that little house in Regent Street, in Blackburn—back to Barty Bendall!

Polly's voice echoed her disgust. 'If only my hair would grow quicker!' she said. She tugged at the straight wispy clusters of fine golden hair which protruded sadly from various areas of her head, leaving between a series of ugly, shiny patches. 'It meks me look like a scabby donkey, Mam!' she protested. All the same, in spite of the fine stubbly growth covering the jagged scar, Polly was growing into a little beauty.

'I'd much rather you stayed here with your Grandma,' Marcia told her now, changing the subject.

'No! I'm coming wi' you, Mam.' Polly moved across to Grandma Fletcher's big old brass bed, reaching for the garments she had previously laid out ready. 'I want to come wi' you!'

Sighing, Marcia began to make her way downstairs, 'Come on then!' she said, 'there's a lot to be done this morning.'

As Polly came into the parlour, Grandma Fletcher had to pop in her own twopenn'orth. 'Ready at last? I should think so too, lass! I'll bet ye've been parading yersel' in front o' yon mirror again, eh?' She knew nothing of the seriousness regarding Polly's condition. Curt and Marcia thought it best not to burden her with such information.

Running to the old lady, Polly threw her arms around the ample shoulders, then, with just a hint of embarrassment at the teasing remark, she declared, 'Well! What if I have?'

' 'Ere! I don't want me mirror getting any more cracks, do I?' The wise old face creased with laughter at the mock horror on Polly's face as she added, 'but I expect somebody's got to use it. I don't fit into the blessed thing! It's too long and thin!' At this point Florence and young Barty rolled about in fits of giggles. 'Hey!' Grandma Fletcher assured them with a serious expression, 'I'm not kidding, tha' knows!' at the same time giving Marcia a crafty little wink.

Smiling, Marcia gave Florence and young Barty a kiss each. 'We'll not be long,' she told them. Then turning to Grandma Fletcher, she added, 'we shouldn't be too long afore we're back, Mam. Curt's coming round later, to sort out the date for the registrar and he's fetching Nantie Bett with him.'

Grandma Fletcher's face tightened as she glanced sternly at Marcia. 'I don't go along wi' no registrar business! Don't seem like a proper wedding to me!' Realising the children were paying more attention to what she was saying than to the game they should be playing, she quickly changed tack. 'Aye well, there's a lot o' sorting out to be done, an' that's a fact! Now don't push yoursel' to get back in too much of a hurry. Mek sure as you do a proper job, lass. We don't want to be hearing no more from Regent Street, once that key's been 'sent back.'

The house in Regent Street had been shut to the daylight for a long time now, and Marcia would much have preferred it to stay that way. But the furniture had to be cleared, and she had a particular ghost to lay! Her glance fell on Polly's face, and noticing the slight apprehension colouring the pale features, she asked, 'Polly, are you sure you wouldn't rather stay here with your Grandma?'

'No Mam!' Polly led the way to the front door, as if to assure Marcia that she had no intention of staying behind. 'Come on,' she urged, 'or we'll miss that early tram if we don't get a move on.' Marcia followed, thinking Polly also might have ghosts to lay. Once outside, encouraged by Polly's enthusiasm, and cheered by the warmth of the sun on her face, together with the wonderful prospect of seeing Curt that evening, Marcia's mood lightened. 'Let's get on with it!' she told Polly, laughing.

*　　　*　　　*

'Mind yer backs! I say, mind yer backs!' The tram conductor's penetrating voice pierced Marcia's ears as she followed Polly to a double seat. No sooner had they sat down than he was standing in front of them, impatiently flicking the heavy metal ticket-dispenser which hung from a thick strap of well-worn leather slung round his neck. 'Tickets please! I say, tickets please!' His irritating habit of repeating everything inevitably jarred on the nerves, although Marcia couldn't help but smile at Polly's quiet whisper that, 'I wish he'd stop shouting, Mam!'

Fishing fourpence out of her purse, Marcia requested two returns to Regent Street, Blackburn. She winced as he repeated her request at the top of his voice: 'Two returns to Regent Street, there yer are then, lass.'

Thanking him for the tickets, Marcia turned to smile at Polly. 'I expect there's many an early morning when he wouldn't be heard, unless he shouted.' She looked around at the surprisingly large number of passengers, it being too late for the mill and too early for shopping.

As the tram trundled along its predestined lines, Marcia lapsed into silence. The nearer they got to Regent Street, the more she brooded. She hadn't set foot inside Barty Bendall's house since that terrible day, and she wasn't looking forward to the daunting prospect with any enthusiasm.

They watched the familiar signs come and go and both mother and daughter experienced relief at the knowledge that it was to be for the very last time. Marcia's thoughts turned to Polly's attitude towards Curt. It was odd how even the presence of a man, any man, seemed to unnerve the lass. Polly hadn't yet been told that Curt Ratheter was her real father, for both Curt and Marcia thought it too early after her operation for such an enlightenment. She had seemed, though, to accept their forthcoming marriage with enthusiasm as had all the children. But Marcia had noticed how on several occasions, if Curt got too close to Polly, she would withdraw within herself, retiring to a safe distance. And it wasn't just Curt, Marcia recalled, it was the same with Grandad Fletcher, and any other man who got within touching distance of her.

Marcia could understand it in a way—what with Barty Bendall's viciousness and later, being prodded about in the Infirmary. It was little wonder that Polly had become such a private person. All the same, it was a source of anxiety for Marcia, who now believed that Polly's scars were nearly all on the inside, and she chided herself for having allowed Polly to accompany her this morning.

'You needn't come in, you know,' she suggested, 'by the time we get there, Mr Grady should have it all organised. I've only to collect some money from him, and mek sure as everything's tidy an' locked up after he's gone.' Marcia waited hopefully for Polly's reply. She'd much rather the lass sat in Mrs Atkinson's till the job was done.

'No, Mam. I want to come in.' Polly would not be moved.

Mr Grady's horse and cart stood outside, surrounded by hordes of excited children. The beds had already been loaded and Mr Grady and his strapping son were struggling out through the front door with the solid weight of the sideboard. Marcia and Polly stood well back, while the two men manoeuvred the awkward article down the stone steps and on to the light side of the cart. 'By 'eck!' Mr Grady's round face was a puffed-up red ball as he turned to greet them, 'yon sideboard must weigh a bloody ton!' He tipped the end of his neb-cap backwards, saying, 'We've nearly done, Mrs Bendall, just one or two more bits and bobs. The three piece is the biggest thing left now.' Marcia followed him as he went inside.

Polly was close behind. Once inside, she made towards the scullery, while Marcia took herself

397

down the empty echoing passageway, leaving Mr Grady moaning and shifting. She carried on up the stairs and into the front bedroom which had been hers and Barty Bendall's. It was stark and empty, reeking of damp, and so cold as to make Marcia draw her coat more tightly round her. The floorboard, where her side of the bed used to be, showed a little blob of candle-wax, grown hard and pointed like a frozen pyramid, and over by the window there was a wide halo of creeping damp which had spread outwards from the frame until its dark tenacious fingers were already touching the adjoining walls.

Standing there shivering, Marcia half-expected to sense Barty Bendall's presence, but he was long gone and, strangely enough, so was the aura of fear and hatred—only a chilling emptiness was left, causing her to turn quickly from the room.

'Nearly done, Mrs Bendall.' Mr Grady was busy collecting all the artefacts from the scullery shelves and arranging them carefully in the bottom of a spacious orange box. Marcia's wandering gaze fell on to the silver-framed photograph of Barty Bendall's parents. And, as she continued to look on it, his last words came into her mind: 'I only ever loved two people in all my life, my Dad and you.' The memory filled her with a sudden surge of compassion. Reaching down, she collected the photograph and held it reverently between her fingers. 'Real old silver is that—should fetch a few bob,' Mr Grady piped up.

'No, Mr Grady, not this. Mr Bendall wouldn't want this falling into the wrong hands,' she answered smiling. Leaving no room for argument, she carried it away into the front parlour, where she stood holding it and gazing out of the window across Regent Street, until Mr Grady had finished the moving.

Some short time later, when he'd paid her the sum of three pounds, seven shillings and fourpence halfpenny, Marcia watched as horse and cart ambled away out of sight. Then, collecting the photograph, she made her way out through the scullery, down the yard steps and on into the cellar. There was an old copper boiler on the far side of the cellar and behind that the wall fell into a hidden recess. Marcia eased the boiler away from the wall, and pushed the silver-framed photograph deep into the dark gaping hole, then, sliding the boiler back, she returned to the house feeling as though she had finally laid all the ghosts to rest.

Locking all doors securely behind her, Marcia made her way to Miss Atkinson's. As she stood waiting for a response to her knock, she looked anxiously up and down Regent Street, expecting to see Polly. She'd left the house some short while before, saying she was going out to 'have a last look round'. But, as yet, and in spite of the fact that Marcia had warned her not to be too long, there was still no sight of her.

'Hello, Marcia, lass!' Miss Atkinson's broad homely face stretched into a welcome as she opened the door to Marcia. 'I thought it best to keep out from underfoot while the stuff was being tekken out,' she explained. Then, 'Oh, fetched the key, have yer?'

'I'm grateful to you, Miss Atkinson,' Marcia smiled, 'you giving it to the rent-man will save me a trip to the Corporation offices.'

'Coming in for a while, eh?' She stepped back to

allow Marcia access.

'No, thanks all the same.' She was beginning to worry about Polly, convinced she should have found her way back by now. 'Young Polly's wandered off, so I'd best find her.' But Miss Atkinson was eager to talk.

'I 'ears as 'ow yer off to mek a fresh start— London i'n't it? That's grand, eh? Fancy that, London!'

Marcia smiled patiently. 'No, Miss Atkinson, not London. It's a little place called Ridgmont, about forty miles this side of London.'

'Oh, Ridgmont eh? Well, that sounds right nice.' Her expression grew serious. 'Well, let's hope as all goes well. As God's my witness, I don't know 'ow ye've put up wi' it all these years,' she tutted loudly, 'dreadful goings on!'

'There's a rent book and five shillings back rent in there,' Marcia swiftly interrupted, pointing to the envelope in Miss Atkinson's hand, 'I'd best get and find Polly.' She turned in the direction of Blakewater Brook, for both she and Polly had some wonderful memories of that quaint little place.

'Aye, off yer goes, lass,' Miss Atkinson called, 'an' God go wi' yer an' all, eh?' Marcia didn't look back. Instead, she waved her hand in acknowledgement, quickening her steps and wondering whether they'd make the midday tram.

Blakewater was deserted! Marcia had searched the banks at least half a dozen times before she had to admit that she must somehow have missed Polly. 'There's nothing for it,' she murmured crossly, 'but to mek me way back to Regent Street. She's mebbe waiting there.' She was angry at Polly for having wandered off, but, deep in the pit of her stomach, Marcia was also afraid.

Back in Regent Street there was no sign of Polly. Investigations at Miss Atkinson's and the corner shop, where Marcia was convinced she'd find Polly at one or the other, proved fruitless. At a loss as to what to do next, she stood before Miss Atkinson, the both of them gazing up and down the street.

'What about young Bridget's old 'ouse,' Miss Atkinson suggested, 'appen she's wandered i' there?'

'No, I've been there—looked in all the windows,' Marcia told her.

'Well! would the lass 'ave gone back into your old house? Or, mebbe she was still in there when you come out, eh? 'Appen upstairs?'

Good Lord, Marcia thought, asking Miss Atkinson for the key back—that was a distinct possibility! The lass could have been in the cellar, the bedroom—wandering about stirring up memories best left behind.

She found Polly on her knees in the back parlour, and it was plain to Marcia that the lass had been crying. 'Aw, sweetheart,' she said, half smiling and feeling greatly relieved at having found her, 'you shouldn't be in here on your own!' Falling on her knees beside the small, bowed figure, she wrapped her arms about her. 'What is it, lass! You tell your Mam, eh?' she said, stroking that savaged little head. When there came no reply, she tilted Polly's head upwards towards her and it clutched at her heart to see those bright blue eyes swimming in tears.

'Was I horrible to him, Mam?' she asked in tearful voice. 'Was it my fault that Barty Bendall

401

went mad?' She began trembling and in a moment was sobbing uncontrollably.

'Aw, lass! Lass!' Marcia held her tight, rocking her back and forth, protesting that what happened was nobody's fault, least of all hers—and pacifying her every way she could. But Polly would not be pacified, and Marcia knew that the lass was tormenting herself in just the same way that she had done for so very long. In spite of everything Marcia said, Polly continued to sob as though her heart would break—until Marcia began to suspect that it went deeper than bad memories. She wondered with horror whether Polly had overheard anything? Some little unguarded conversation between her and Curt, which might have told Polly the truth of how desperately ill she was.

'Come on, my girl,' she said, pulling the sobbing little figure to her feet and making towards the passageway, 'we'll set in Miss Atkinson's a while. There's plenty of trams—we'll catch a later one.' She was desperately afraid that Polly was working herself up into a dreadful state.

It was just as Marcia went to open the door that Polly slumped in her arms, uttering a strange moan as she did so. 'Polly!' Marcia caught the girl tight to her, half shaking her, half crying herself.

The surge of fear which raised the skin all over Marcia's body set her trembling. Leaning forward, she urged, 'Polly, try to put your arm round me. We've got to get you to Miss Atkinson's.' The tears choked her voice and blinded her eyes. When she looked at Polly's face, and saw the thin crimson rivulet which trickled from the corner of her mouth, her heart stood still, and, taking Polly's limp body into her arms, she found the strength to lift her bodily, all the while praying as she had never done before. Ever since Polly had been born, there had always been the terrible fear of a day such as this. Marcia knew that. But she would not accept it. Her darling Polly would be all right! She would! She would! Marcia said it out loud, over and over.

Miss Atkinson collected Polly from her mother's arms and laid her gently on the sofa, before running, for the first time in her life, down to the shop where an ambulance was summoned on 'one of them telephone contraptions'.

The ambulance arrived with great urgency to transport the unconscious Polly and Marcia to the Infirmary. As they sped through the narrow streets, Marcia sat on the stretcher, holding Polly close to her breast, her eyes never leaving the small delicate face, some deep thinking part of her grown deathly cold.

Of a sudden, the blue eyes which had so often lighted Marcia's days with their merriness, and just as often plunged her into terrible despair with their defiance, opened to look at her. 'Aw, sweetheart,' she murmured, stroking Polly's high white brow, 'lie still now—you'll be all right.'

'I'm dying, aren't I, Mam—like Barty Bendall?' whispered Polly.

'No, Polly lass,' she told her in a firm quiet voice, the tears streaming down her face, 'you're not dying!'

Polly managed a weak smile. 'It's all right, Mam. I don't mind, not really.'

'Ssh, child,' Marcia could hardly talk for the lump which blocked her throat 'you're not to think such things!'

Now there came a little choking sound from Polly, a sound like laughter, but which was not. 'I'll be an angel, eh, Mam,' Polly whispered, her fingers clasped into Marcia's, 'and angels don't cry, do they, Mam?'

At that moment, Marcia knew that Polly was going from her. Holding on to her every ounce of courage, she grasped the child to her as though she would never let loose. But all of Marcia's love, her stout courage, could not sustain that flickering life, as it trembled in her arms, then slipped away. For a long heartbreaking moment, Marcia could not bring herself to look down on her daughter's face. When finally she did, there was no holding back the avalanche of sobs which cascaded from her.

'Oh, my darling, darling baby,' she cried, every word the greatest agony she had ever known. Gathering up the small still figure, Marcia buried her head in that pale delicate face, and was enveloped in such searing grief that it drained her mind, her heart, her very soul, of all else.

Together, Polly and Marcia had travelled to the boundary of infinity, and only she had returned. On the bright sunny afternoon that Polly died, part of Marcia went with her forever.

Part Three

1938
Marcia's Last Love

CHAPTER TWENTY-FOUR

It was a beautiful July day. Spring had finally surrendered to the heat and glory of a radiant summer, and the song of the joyful birds rose in harmony to greet the morning. It was early yet and the day was quiet, save for the smooth flowing organ music which wafted from the church to caress the ears of the small group which stood by the carefully-tended grave.

'I miss our Polly, Mam,' Florence said as she leaned against her mother, safe in the curve of her arm.

'Is she never coming back, Mam?' Young Barty's face and perplexed question caused Marcia to draw him closer. With a loving arm around each of her children, she gazed down towards the disturbed earth beneath which Polly lay.

'No love,' she replied, her voice gentle with care, 'she'll not be coming back.' In her heart of hearts though, she knew that Polly, poor tragic little Polly, had never left her and would *never* leave her.

Of a sudden, a small jenny-wren alighted on the sheaf of flowers which Marcia had rested on the nearby bench, and young Barty, with the innocent resilience of youth, quickly chased it away to retrieve the flowers which he returned to his Mam. 'Mam, can I go in the church an' listen to the organ?' he asked.

'Only if you promise to be very quiet,' Marcia told him, turning to Florence, who was gazing still thoughtfully towards the ground. 'Go with him, lass. I'll not be long.'

Left alone, Marcia knelt close to the grave, still clutching the colourful flowers in her arms. For a long while, she just knelt, her memory filled with the image of Polly's bright blue eyes—not the sad pained eyes, but the eyes of a baby, of a toddler, of a laughing child, and her aching heart grew peaceful beneath their gaze. Now, the beautiful organ music flowed over her in soft soothing waves, and as the melody permeated her consciousness, Marcia came to recognise the song. It was a song she had always loved. With an instinct as natural to her as breathing, Marcia allowed her magnificent voice to mingle with the tones of the organ in its rendering of 'The Old Rugged Cross'. As she sang, the strange sense of peace which dulled the sorrow within her lent an almost ethereal quality to her voice as it soared above and beyond the music, to fill the air with special beauty, even surpassing the songs of the birds.

Curt trod the ground softly as he approached. The sound of Marcia's singing brought him to stay beneath the spreading arms of a hawthorn tree, where he stood captivated by the paradisiacal grandeur of her song.

'So I'll cherish the old rugged cross, till my trophies at last I lay down.' Now, she was on her knees, her fingers touching the earth. 'I will cling to the old rugged cross, and exchange it some day for a crown. He'll call me some day, to his home far away—where his glory forever I'll share . . .'

The exquisiteness of Marcia's singing brought a few worshippers from the church to stand in the great entrance arch, where they listened in silent reverence, as Florence and young Barty moved towards their mother. Curt crossed their path and bade them wait. As he stood holding the children, his eyes shone with pride and emotion, and the love he felt for the kneeling woman strengthened his avowed determination to bring joy to her life— to make such a wonderful future for her that it would erase all the terrible pain she had suffered.

When she had finished singing Marcia felt stronger in herself than she had ever been. Detaching a sheaf of flowers from her arms, she arranged them carefully in the granite vase; and remembering Polly's last words to her she whispered, so quietly that no one else could hear, 'You're wrong, Polly my lass, for angels do cry— sometimes.'

Now Curt reached out to bring Marcia to her feet. 'Oh, Marcia.' He shook his dark head, seeming unable to utter anything further. But the depth of his love shone at her, as now he caught her fiercely to him, embracing her for a moment in the haven of his arms.

'Curt,' Marcia said as she pulled away, gesturing to Florence and young Barty who had found great amusement in chasing the birds, 'will you start back with the children?' She raised the remaining flowers in her arms, 'I've to take these. I'll only be a minute—I'll catch you up, eh?' She lifted her face, brushing her mouth against his. And, as he gazed on her radiant face, she thought how strong and handsome he looked now, compared to the lean haunted man who had been released from more than one prison—a prison of physical confinement, and a prison of his own making!

'We'll wait for you by the gate, Marcia love,' he nodded. As she walked away, Marcia was poignantly aware of Curt's bowed head over Polly's grave, and the resonant murmur of his quiet voice as he said a little prayer.

Heading over the grass towards the gravelled footpath, Marcia thought over the last few months. She hadn't been able to forget the horror of Polly's death—she believed she never would, but with the passage of time she'd found the painful grief less severe. Curt had been her mainstay, falling in with whatever made her life bearable.

They had been married for two weeks now. The ceremony had been a quiet, intimate occasion, with only the closest of her old friends beside her. Since then, because of Grandma Fletcher's unwavering bitterness towards Curt and because of the need to finalise matters down south, Curt had occupied himself in planning the new life which the brickwork owners, in their compassion, had kept open for him. He'd spent a week down south, furnishing the cottage and generally getting things ready for their departure today. The last few days since his return had been spent at Nantie Bett's.

Marcia had come to the churchyard today to say her farewells, yet even now, at this late moment, she still wasn't convinced that they were doing the right thing, although every waking instinct told her that it was really the only thing to do. The narrow gravelled footpath led her through an avenue of giant conifers, which shadowed the path before opening out into well-kept avenues of graves.

Barty Bendall's wasn't hard to locate. The giant branches of the cedar tree hung over him like protecting wings and as Marcia approached, the thin shards of brilliant sunshine which occasionally pierced the thick overhead blanket temporarily blinded her. Shielding her eyes, she rounded the grave, so the light fell harmlessly behind her. There, directly ahead of her, the small tablet at the head of the grave identified Barty Bendall's name in chiselled marble.

BARTY BENDALL
1901–1938

Marcia arranged the flowers, then stepped away to gaze from a short distance, sad that, even now, she felt uncomfortable in his presence.

It was all over, she assured herself. And she never again would dwell on things that could still hurt. She knew that life wouldn't always behave in a logical, predictable pattern and it wouldn't always be the strongest who survived. Often the survivors were merely more flexible—moulded by the pattern of life they endured, and able to adapt. A whimsical smile shadowed Marcia's face—who could know that better than she herself?

As her eyes travelled across the cold carved name, an inexplicable emotion tormented her. She remembered how things had been in the early part of their marriage, how Barty Bendall had loved her enough to take on her children, knowing that she was still in love with their father. She remembered how he'd emptied his pockets of money in order to retrieve the wedding ring she'd pawned, so he could put it back on her finger. So many things came flooding back, haunting her until she began to question her own part in all of it. Her eyes lingered on the headstone of that poor, demented creature who had offered her love and friendship when she'd needed it most. *That* she could never forget, in spite of the more hurtful memories which still scarred her mind. The gratitude in her soft dark eyes shone warmly as she whispered: 'I pray you'll find peace, Barty.'

Of a sudden, there came a tugging at her coat, and, looking down, Marcia was not surprised to see a small tousle-headed figure. 'Come on, Mam! I'm fed up!' Young Barty didn't even glance at his father's grave.

Laughing, Marcia grasped him playfully by the shoulders. 'All right, scallywag!' she said, thinking, here is my future—my purpose, and Curt's!

And, hand in hand, the two of them hurried away to join Curt and Florence waiting by the gate.

Marcia stopped just once, to steal a backward glance at the place where Barty Bendall and her darling Polly lay peaceful. With Curt's loving arm about her shoulders, she continued to look until the aged elm trees were no longer in her sight.

CHAPTER TWENTY-FIVE

Marcia lifted the heavy iron door knocker, letting it fall with a controlled swing against the metal plate, until the strong, familiar tones of Grandma Fletcher's voice boomed out, 'It's open! Just push it.' Marcia let the children in, then she and Curt followed, securing the door lock behind them.

'Mam!' she chided, 'I've told you not to leave the door on sneck! You could be inviting any Jack or John in.'

At this Grandma Fletcher gathered up the flour-pattered pinny, wiped her hands with vigour and, in a voice of authority, retorted, 'Nay, lass, yon door's been open to anybody this last thirty years, an' folks'll allus be welcome in this 'ouse!'

'You're an old softy.'

'Aye well! Whatever would folks think if they suddenly found our door locked agin' 'em?' she wanted to know. 'Sit thisel' down lass. I've just med a brew.'

Marcia learned not to try and interfere too much with her mother's off-handed attitude towards Curt. Grandma Fletcher was a rough and ready character with firm, immovable notions on moral issues and the sanctity of marriage, and for what Curt had done all those years before, and for whatever reason, Marcia knew it would take time and patience for Curt to earn her mother's trust and respect again. She turned now to see Curt moving the already packed suitcases nearer to the door. The disarming smile he gave her dispelled any notion that her mother's deliberately hostile attitude might be antagonising him.

Grandma Fletcher bustled the bemused Florence out to the scullery. 'Go on young 'un! Pour the grown-ups a mug o' tea each!' She waited till Marcia had taken off her scarf and coat, then she asked in a quiet voice, 'Everything all right lass?' She nodded at Marcia's affirmative answer. 'I'll tek good care o' things, yer know that, eh?— the churchyard an' such.'

'I know you will, Mam, bless you.' At that point, Florence returned with the tea, and Curt came to stand behind Marcia, while Grandma Fletcher fidgeted impatiently, seemingly embarrassed. 'Where's yon Nantie Bett?' she asked sharply, 'Not coming to see yer all off? Said she were!'

'No,' Curt replied warmly, 'she changed her

413

mind at the last minute. She seemed to think she'd make a fool of herself if she waved us away from here but we've said our goodbyes.'

Of a sudden Grandma Fletcher grabbed hold of Florence, propelling her out of the room and towards the front parlour. 'Hey, there's an errand I want yer to run . . .'

'Mam!' Marcia realised they hadn't got all that much time to waste. 'We've a train to catch!' Grandma Fletcher returned with a broad smile creasing her features, and to Curt's surprise some of its sunshine actually fell upon him.

Sensing one of her Mam's crazy antics in the making, Marcia asked suspiciously, 'What are you up to, Mam? Where've you sent Florence?'

'I've sent 'er over to yon pub, for a couple o' gills.'

Marcia had noticed with some anxiety that her mother's drinking had accelerated alarmingly since Polly's death. 'Oh, Mam!' She was greatly concerned.

'Don't gi' me "Oh Mam!"' Grandma Fletcher retorted, 'There's worse things in this world than a drop o' good ale!'

'But it's only half past ten of a morning! She'll not get served!'

'Aye, well that's where thi' could be wrong 'cause I've told 'er to let 'im know as it's a celebration like—Curt's new job an' all.'

Curt's laughter filled the room as he winked at Marcia, saying, 'They don't come any craftier than your Mam, do they? And I wouldn't mind a sup of ale.'

Grandma Fletcher appeared to be pleasantly surprised by Curt's intervention on her behalf.

414

'Well, bless me!' she declared, eyeing him up and down with something akin to approval, 'there's more to this fella-me-lad than meets the eye.' With a rush, she ran to seat herself in the chair by the fire, patting Marcia's knee and with the suspicion of a tear sparkling in her eye. 'When yer gets to this new 'ouse, an' Curt starts that new job, things'll be grand.' She collected the end of her pinny to dab it at her eyes before continuing, 'An' there's no need to worry about me an' your Dad! Just wait an' see lass. Yer deserves a bit of happiness.' Flicking a podgy hand across her snivelling nose, she laughed out loud and yanked young Barty from beneath her chair, where he was pulling the strands from the coconut matting. 'Hey! Little Barty! Off to the scullery an' fill your Grannie's tea mug again, I've dipped me floury pinny in that one!'

Marcia smiled at young Barty, who quietly resumed his dethreading procedure. 'All right lad,' she told him, 'I'll get it.' When she came back out, Florence was seated next to Grandma Fletcher who must have been telling a tale or two, judging by the gales of laughter.

Now Curt threaded his way towards Marcia. Catching her tightly in his arms, he backed her gently into the scullery, where he kissed her warmly out of sight of the others. 'Oh, Marcia— just think! This time tomorrow, we'll be in our new home, man and wife.' His eyes grew cloudy as he told her fiercely, 'I'll never let anything hurt you again, *ever*!'

Marcia knew he meant every word. Strange, she mused, how she could even contemplate a life without Polly, yet she had always known. She hoped she wouldn't miss the old cotton mill town too much. Relaxing in the assuring strength of his arms, she told Curt softly, 'I love you so much, Curt. Please God we'll be happy.'

Curt pulled her tight to him. 'I'll make it my life's work,' he told her, 'I'll make up to you for all the things you've suffered.' Their lips met again, in a firm seal of their devotion.

'Hey! You two in there!' Grandma Fletcher's voice interrupted them, 'come on, we're 'avin a celebration!'

Marcia knew that her mother's laughter was superficial, that beneath the brave charade she was heartbroken over Polly. But she and Curt played along, emerging from the scullery to see Grandma Fletcher, skirts held high, doing a 'knees-up' round the table. Young Barty and Florence were in helpless hysterics at her unpredictable antics, and Grandad Fletcher had buried himself in his newspaper, moaning about 'bloody women suppin' booze!' Marcia fought to suppress the rising tears of joy and sorrow which threatened to engulf her. Curt sensed the emotion within her and, after squeezing her hand, he dragged young Barty into the centre of the room, where he joined Grandma Fletcher in her little war dance. Florence quickly followed to join in the excitement, when she witnessed young Barty being pulled into the activities. Passing Grandad Fletcher, Curt grabbed him too, and the sight of her entire family whooping and hollering round the table sent a comforting feeling through Marcia. Paddy, the terrier, yapped and protested from his safe hiding place behind the settee.

'Oh—Oh, me 'eart, me poor ol' 'eart!' Grandma

Fletcher, breathless and laughing, threw herself into the big old armchair, which groaned from the sudden surprising weight. 'I 'aven't enjoyed meself so much for years!' She watched as the others followed suit, flopping exhausted into various chairs then, gulping deeply to regain her breath, she crossed to the table, her expression suddenly serious and sad. Lifting the tea towel from the two jugs, which were brimful and frothy with ale, she instructed Florence to get cups and mugs from the sideboard. Young Barty was despatched to fetch the brown jug from the scullery.

The brown jug was filled with delicious home-made sarsaparilla, which Grandma Fletcher poured into two long narrow mugs, one only half-filled. 'Florence,' she said firmly, 'seeing as yer past a child, and not quite a woman, yer can 'ave 'alf ale and 'alf sarsaparilla.' She winked at Florence. 'Right?'

'Right,' Florence said. She liked that idea.

'Good.' Having poured out the rest of the ale, the old lady urged them all to 'fetch 'old of yer mugs.' Then, lifting her mug of ale, amid comments and laughter about the size of her share she told them all, 'A toast!'

The laughter died down as the proposition touched all their hearts and Grandma Fletcher continued, in a softer tone, 'A toast to our family, them as are moving away. An' them as can't be 'ere.' She sniffled, a loud grating sniffle, as tears ran down her face and her gaze moved round to embrace both Marcia and Curt. 'We wish yer all the luck and happiness in the world. Ye'll not be too far away as Dad an' me can't visit, but yer'll allus be in our 'earts. God bless an' tek care of all on you!' Lifting her pinny, she wiped her face hard and blew her nose noisily, then forcing an encouraging smile, she cried 'CHEERS!' before gulping down a hefty measure of the warming ale.

Marcia was glad of the excuse to raise her mug while surreptitiously wiping her own tears and it surprised her to see Grandad Fletcher doing the same. The slight embarrassment in his face as he caught Marcia looking at him caused them both to laugh out loud.

'Cheers!' they all repeated, until the ale had been supped.

'Good grief! Look at the time,' Marcia shouted, 'quarter past twelve!' She banged her mug down on the table at the realisation that they had less than an hour before their train departed. 'Quick!' she told Florence and young Barty, 'Visit the lavvy. I expect you've drunk all that sarsaparilla!'

'I'll get yer sandwiches ready, Marcia,' Grandma Fletcher said, rushing into the kitchen, 'yer should *all* be 'aving a proper meal afore yer goes!'

'Sandwiches are fine, Mam. We'll get summat else later, if we've a need to.'

The panic over, everyone gathered at the front door. Grandad Fletcher pressed Marcia's arm. 'Are you sure yer wouldn't like us to come an see yer off?' There followed a thick silence as everyone looked at each other, throats choked, hearts heavy, then suddenly everyone was grabbing first one then the other, tears unashamedly flowing.

'Tek care o' yerselves,' Grandma Fletcher urged them as Curt and Marcia led the family away with many a backward glance.

'We'll write Mam—we'll write soon,' Marcia promised.

Marcia felt plagued with remorse as the figures of her parents grew smaller and smaller. Putting a comforting arm around Florence's shoulders, she told her, 'Don't fret lass. They'll be coming to see us just as soon as we're settled in. Do you want to run and give her another hug?'

At this both children called out together, 'Yes! Yes!' as they took to their heels back to the dear old lady.

Grandma Fletcher watched as the children tore back down the street towards her. She left the old man's side and ran to meet them. As they collided into each other's arms, she could hardly speak. 'God love yer little 'earts,' she cried, overcome by emotion.

Young Barty clung to the ample girth of his Grandma, while the more restrained Florence hugged her just once, promising, 'We'll write, Grandma—an' you've to come an' stop with us. You will, won't you?'

Grandma Fletcher grabbed hold of her, hugging the two of them tight to her bosom. 'Just try an' stop me, lass!' she sobbed, amid her laughter, 'just try an' stop me!' Sniffling hard and kissing them finally, she instructed them with a trace of her old authority, 'Now think on! Tek care o' that Mam o' yourn.' A strange sorrow filled her eyes as she muttered almost to herself, 'Somehow, I've a feeling she'll need you both.'

Waving at her parents until they were out of sight, Marcia listened again to Curt's description of the cottage, as he answered the excited curious questions from the children. At last, she thought, it's all coming true!

As she walked towards the train, her children

happy and excited, and her beloved Curt by her side at last, she wondered at the underlying emotions which somehow marred what should have been an indescribably wonderful day. She thought on all she'd left behind and in a disturbing way she felt a stranger to herself—not at all the same person who had married Curt all those years before.

The rush of cool air as the train blew in blasted against her face, causing her to shiver. Quickly, Curt collected the luggage before ushering the children onto the train. Then, turning to encircle her with his strong arms, he urged, 'Come on, Marcia darling, there's a whole new life waiting out there for us.' Uninhibited by the waiting passengers, he reached down to brush his mouth against hers. 'I love you so,' he whispered, sweeping her into the train.

As they drew out of the station, Marcia dwelt on all her blessings. She had her children—even Polly who would never leave her—and she had her man. What more could any woman ask! She looked at Curt as he bustled about settling the children. Curt Ratheter! Now truly her husband. He had been her first love, and he would be her last.

CHIVERS LARGE PRINT -direct-

If you have enjoyed this Large Print book and would like to build up your own collection of Large Print books, please contact

Chivers Large Print Direct

Chivers Large Print Direct offers you a full service:

• Prompt mail order service

• Easy-to-read type

• The very best authors

• Special low prices

For further details either call Customer Services on (01225) 336552 or write to us at Chivers Large Print Direct, **FREEPOST**, Bath BA1 3ZZ

Telephone Orders: **FREEPHONE** 08081 72 74 75